WHILE RIVERS RUN

Brimming with life, and love and laughter and sport, in the open spaces. Captivating alike by its powerful depicting of character, its charming description of scenery, its lively dialogue, its buoyant human story and irresistible style.

By MAURICE WALSH

WHILE RIVERS RUN

BY

MAURICE WALSH

W. & R. CHAMBERS, LTD.
LONDON AND EDINBURGH

Latest Reprint, 1952

Printed in Great Britain
by T. and A. CONSTABLE LTD., Hopetoun Street,
Printers to the University of Edinburgh

To

TOSHON

WHO HAD RED HAIR ALSO

CHAPTER I

He was a big, straight-backed, middle-aged man in patched brown tweeds, and he carried a firm pad of muscle on his big bones, a pair of grey, wise eyes below a bush of brow, and a grizzled stub of moustache above a clean chin. He wore no waders, yet he stood mid-leg deep in a tidal pool at the very end of slack water and fished for finnock, industriously but without enthusiasm. At the back of his neck the round, polished knob of a gaff-handle peeped above his coat collar, reminding one queerly of an Italian bravo and his dagger—though there was nothing of the bravo about this man. He plied, as if it were a slip of hazel, a fourteen-foot, single-spliced rod that any expert would say came out of Castleconnel, but instead, had been lovingly spoke-shaved out of a clean spar of greenheart by the hands that now wielded it on this pleasant Moray shore, and, furthermore, it was not inferior to any rod anywhere, having its strength in the right place and its spring in the right place—and where these two places lie no two fishermen will agree.

This big man with the oldish yet smooth face was, for some reason or other, not fishing zestfully. He was practising casts, rather than casting to lure fish. The lithe tip of the rod lifted slowly to that nicely judged point where rod and line were in exact counterpoise; followed the explosive yet restrained flick of the wrist, and the long line soared backwards in a flat loop, straight-

7

ened at shoulder level, and, impelled by a second flick, returned without pause until the cast of flies hovered at the end of a dead-straight line and dropped on the water like a caress. But, as often as not, no sooner had the flies touched water than the fisherman lifted eyes and looked down the pool towards the setting sun or up the pool towards the lifting hills. It was only when an unwary finnock rose to a fly that hand and eye returned to duty, but, with such a silver-flashing half-pound of energy as the finnock, this dilatoriness merited consistent failure —and got it.

Not but that it was worth while to turn seeing eyes down the pool. It lay north by west and a point west, and looked directly into the eye of the setting sun. Below it the Leonach River ran flatly through a mile of green carse—across which white flecks of thistledown soared and dipped in little drifts of air—and joined the green of the northern sea through a wide mouth between great dunes of yellow sand. These far-stretching, tawny dunes held the sun even when the sun was behind depths of cloud, and a glimpse of them from the hills on the dullest of days gave one a sudden lift of the heart—they looked so like a patch of sunlight beyond the black woods of Doorn.

The tide was just beginning to make, and the lazy waves were breaking leisurely into white all across the bar; and beyond the bar the sea was laid down, a narrow shield of molten gold. Far beyond that shield lifted the smoky blue or dull purple of the great hills of the north—Ben Wyvis, that squat giant; far Ben More, a very ghost of a mountain; Morven, with its pap to the mouth of the sky; and behind all, a dim whale-back that might be Stroma, or Ultima Thule, or Hy-Brasil its

8

very self. The gold ball of the sun lipped the breast of Morven and lingered in that kiss, as well he might.

A wide and clean view, indeed! And yet it was not the view that drew the eyes of the fisherman. In truth he was impatient with the sun, in a hurry to subdue that splendid panorama in the toneless light of the gloaming. For he wanted to do some real fishing. Finnock, which are probably the grilse of the sea-trout, are a game and angry fish, but at this season they were a bare half-pound in weight, and angling for them with a fourteen-foot rod no more than a subterfuge. And so he looked at the sun with some impatience, and concentrated his mind's eye on the next pool upstream; for there was the quarry of his choice—salmon clean from the sea, and not yet altogether disdainful of a suitable lure.

Looking up the river, the fisherman saw, on one hand, cultivated slopes, yellowing with corn, merging upwards into brown moors that rolled smoothly over the horizon; and, on the other, a heavily wooded ridge lifting abruptly from the river until at last it won clear of trees and thrust a bald dome of head slant-wise into the blue. That slanting head gave the whole sweep of hill the effect of leaning over towards the river.

The sun went behind Morven, and the orange and red flare of his dying died too. The half-light of the gloaming was on all that land—subduing it, stilling it, brooding detachedly over it. The foam of the bar became dead white; the green of the sea took on purple shades; the long ridge of Morven stood black against the shine. A piebald oyster-catcher winged in from the shore, crying dolorously. A sandpiper flitted across the water, plaintively calling. The short hurrying wings of a mallard went hissing overhead. Thin flakes of dark-

9

brown sand began to float at the stream edges; the water began to lip over the round pebbles; the fisherman felt a cold edge creeping above his knee. The tide was coming in. And all of a sudden a small, live ripple of water shaped like a V came up over the tail of the pool against the current, and glided upstream.

"You are welcome!" greeted the fisherman, and face and eye quickened. "Look at that little fellow in the by-going"; and like a thistledown he landed his tail fly a foot in front of the nose of the ripple.

But the ripple went on evenly.

"So you will not rest in a poor man's water?" said the fisherman. "Very good, then"; and his grey eye lifted toward the next pool. For he was well aware that salmon, hasting from the sea, will never rest in tidal water when there is a fresh-water pool above it—as there was here. Down the long tail of that pool the river came in a steep run over an amber bottom, and only the steepest of spring tides, driven by a north-west wind, might succeed in wiping that run smooth. And he was well aware, too, that in that upper pool, at the proper state of wind, water, and light, a proper fly, properly cast, might lure a resting fish to take a careless nip and be sorry for it.

The fisherman slowly reeled in his long line, deftly caught the tail fly as it went by, and waded stiff-legged out of the pool. He stood on its margin, with the water adrip from the folds of his baggy knickers and oozing through convenient rents in his old brogans, and knowingly contemplated sky and river, waiting for that one short hour between day and dark, when, in dry August weather, a salmon sometimes puts aside disdain and lethargy.

Still leisurely, he squelched up by the brink of the

water over the soiled round stones that were a little slimy and treacherous with the dark *snoss* that the brackish tide left on them twice a day, climbed a mound of gravel, and looked out over the reaches of Urdog Pool. The water here, flowing over a clean bottom, had a hint of light in its amber, while the margin of rounded boulders was washed clean by spate and rain and sun, and the runnels of sand between the stones were a golden brown. Along that margin, between the water and a line of dark-leaved alders, the fisherman proceeded to the throat of the pool, and there, where the river curved sharply to the right, he halted. At once his whole attitude became purposeful.

He unloosed, with rapid deftness, the trouting cast he had been playing with, and substituted for it a fine salmon cast. Then he flicked over the leaves of an old leather fly-book and picked out his lure without hesitation—a Number 5, Limerick-bend, double-hooked "Blue Charm," tinsel-bodied, blue-hackled, gay-plumaged, and a murderer. He held it up against the sky to get the light, and so tied it on, smoothing it out caressingly, and giving a final little tug to test his knots. Now he was ready.

II

Where the water made a sibilant babble in the throat of the pool the angler waded in and commenced to fish; first, quick short casts merely to wet his fly, and then gradually lengthening ones as he moved foot by foot down the boil, until at last his fly, slanting downstream, covered the whole width of the river. Presently he hunched his shoulders in concentration, for the Blue

11

Charm was moving over a likely spot, just where the eddies straightened out into the first wide reach. He was quietly certain that his fly was moving over fish, and, since it was the right fly at the right time and in the right manner, he was equally certain that a fish would rise to it. Moreover, had he failed a hundred times in similar circumstances (and he had), he, as a true angler, would cherish that absolute certainty on the hundred and first occasion.

And then the sudden boil, the electric touch, and the unhasty strike. Not the firm strike of spring, but merely a momentary stiffening of the wrists. By Izaak! he had him. The line went out with a hiss from the unratcheted reel—unratcheted for a reason—and the fisherman set himself in the water, his shoulders back, one finger on the line, and his whole body braced. The hooked fish streaked across the pool and got the line it asked for; it slanted back and downwards and took the line willy-nilly. And there it came out of the water for the first time—a flash crescent of silver, with a black tail whipping savagely.

"Fifteen pounds, if an ounce!" whispered the fisherman.

The salmon straightened out and forged determinedly downtream, the rod holding queerly still in one set curve. Would it stop, or would it break away over the steep tail of the pool—letting the rod jerk straight, and a fragment of gut atrail in the water? The angler held all he dared, and his little finger was stung almost unbearably by the hissing line. A bare half-dozen yards from the suck of the outflow the fish stopped and turned. Now was the critical moment. An old fish, long in the pool, would be inclined towards stubbornness and a bottom stone with a cutting edge. But this was a clean-run fish and his energy barely whetted. Fight he would, and fight he did. He leaped clean out of the water in a down curve and charged up the pool in a furious zig-zag. The angler reeled in just as furiously, the point of his rod thrown well behind his shoulder. Not many yards of line had been left on the drum after that first rush, and he was anxious to regain what he could to play with.

From first to last that fight lasted all of twenty minutes, and not a single minute wasted. At the end of fifteen the fish, for the first time, followed the pull of the gut and came within a few yards of his enemy, swaying from side to side and showing glimpses of white belly; but seeing his enemy so close at hand, he went upstream in a last frenzied rush. The beginning of the end! That rush spent him, and he lay sluggish at the end of it. Holding him so, one-handed, the fisherman extracted his gaff from its hiding-place between his shoulders. The point was guarded by a cork, and this he detached with his teeth and held there. Then, with the gaff in the heel of his hand, he slowly wound in his fish—now his fish surely—manœuvring it gently downstream so that at the proper moment it floated past him, lying over on its side and spent utterly. Deftly the gaff was slipped under and driven home with an upward draw. The tail gave one splash and was out of the water—and the game was up.

"Eighteen pounds, anyway," said the fisherman, backing carefully out of the water. "A cock-fish, and clean as a new shilling."

As he sat on his heels, one big hand holding the salmon on the gravel, and the other raised for a finishing tap with the gaff handle, he stiffened in that attitude and his eyes stared along the curve of the shore in front of him. His face lost all expression and his mouth opened a little. His ears had remained open all the time, and what they had heard was the sound of voices from away round the curve—voices modulated by distance and yet with an unpleasant modulation in them.

Now this fisherman was not poaching—not really and truly poaching. He wanted a fish for a certain purpose, and he knew that Sir Hugh MacIan, or Sir Hugh's keeper, Johnny Ross, would not mind his taking a fish out of Urdog Pool in mid-August—if he could. But that was a matter between Sir Hugh, Johnny, and himself, and not to be bruited abroad amongst strangers. And, since the voices he now heard were strange voices, it was up to him to take the initiative while yet there was time. He took it with a promptitude that showed the character of the man. The veil of alders, heavily underwooded, was at his right shoulder. The rod went butt-first amongst the trees; salmon and gaff were deposited behind the trunk of one; he even took time to remove some fish-scales from the stones before he himself stepped among the branches and leant a shoulder against a twisted bole. In that fading light anyone moving on the beach might look and look again and not see him.

CHAPTER II

I

THE two men that came round the corner were not looking for anyone. They were evidently concentrated on the same mood, and that an unpleasant one. The hidden angler, though the twilight was deepening instantly, noted that they were young men by a certain litheness of carriage and set of head. One was of middle height and broad, the other a little taller and a good deal slimmer. They walked as far apart as the gravel margin permitted, and did not once look at each other. The slim man carried his hands in his pockets, and the broad one occasionally gestured with his left arm. Both were in flannels and bareheaded. Whatever quarrel—sudden it must have been—had lifted between them came to its crisis within ten yards of the concealed fisherman. The two halted and faced each other, the slim man with his back to the alders.

"A meddling young puppy—that's what you are, MacIan!" The heavily built man was the speaker.

"Keep the lid on it, Don." MacIan's retort was more provoking than pacifying.

"If I do boil over," warned the man addressed as Don, "you'll find how hot I am."

Young MacIan was silent for a moment, and then spoke in a reasoned sort of chagrin. "Oh, hell! No use you being a dog in the manger."

"I am not. Miss Carr is marrying me."

"Has she told you so?"

Apparently she had not, for the reply was forcible.

"What the devil is that to you?"

"Only this," said MacIan, and his tone was now firm and quiet: "Until Norrey Carr accepts you, I am going to admire her as much as I like, and tell her so."

"I have warned you."

"Shucks! you and your dam' warning!" exclaimed the other with sudden exasperation.

"I have warned you."

"Oh, go to blazes, Webster!"

And there it happened. Two grown men—but young —found the domain of language too limited, and thrust over the boundary into action. Webster—Don Webster in full—took a stride forward, his hands clenched at his sides. "You will drive me to it," he growled, and he gestured with his right fist. It was a gesture more admonitory than pugnacious, for it is very probable that, at the back of his mind, he did not anticipate an undignified bout of fisticuffs. If so, the other surprised him.

MacIan had promptly taken up an attitude that showed he was a useful man of his hands. And a useful man of his hands, seeing a fist half-launched, does one of two things: counters if he has time, and side-slips if he has not. Time in plenty there was here, and so a right-hand snapped into Webster's face, drawing red from a lower lip and flooding a brain with the same colour. There was no mistaking the whole-heartedness of Don Webster's next move. He launched himself, hands clutching, on the lighter man, who again tried the proper move—a side-step out of distance. But side-

stepping on rounded stones is precarious, and was here disastrous. A stone rolled, a foot slipped, hands went off guard, head came forward, and a round-arm, wholly unscientific, but thoroughly adequate wallop got home above MacIan's left ear, and after a complicated, head-bumping tumble, he found himself sitting on the stones aprop on his hands, and there was on his face the half-vacant, half-intense look of a small boy doing mental arithmetic. Don Webster towered over him.

"You are a d—d fool, Alistair MacIan," he cried, and there was disgust as well as anger in his voice—"and so am I, but now you know where you get off"; and forthwith he swung away and stumped off round the curve of the shore—and so out of sight.

That should have concluded the episode fittingly enough. But a good boxer dislikes being knocked silly at any time, and feels particularly outraged when knocked silly by an unscientific haymaker. Knocked silly, but not knocked out! Not by a long shot! Alistair MacIan scrambled to his feet and thrust forward after the man that had put him down for a mere short count and wanted to call it a completed job of work. Ill-fate had not yet done with him. Unstable ground, unstable feet, unstable head hurled him forward, in one falling, battering-ram lurch, head-first against a big boulder of smoothed quartz. The thud, on the very top of his head, had an oddly sickening sound. He flattened out, lay very still, arms abroad, and face to the cold stones.

"By Hepplewhite!" exclaimed the astonished fisherman, and came out of his hiding.

Very completely indeed were the senses knocked out of young MacIan. As the fisherman lifted him by the shoulders, his dark head drooped forward helplessly.

"A thundering clipe to give yourself, boy."

He turned the limp body gently over, and, with spatulate, knowing fingers, felt first the back of the neck and then the crown of the head. He peered at his fingers in the growing dark. "The skin is not broken, anyway," he muttered with relief, "and the bone is sound. Praises be for the stiff neck and thick head of the MacIans!"

He straightened up and ran his hand under his old tweed hat, and stood so in thought for a little while. Then he bent over the prostrate youth, gripped him at the shoulders, and, with a careful, powerful, pivoting motion, swung him on the broad cushion of his own back. In the process the legs dangled in an oddly ludicrous manner, like the legs of a marionette.

The fisherman picked a sure footing across the stones, bent below the alders, swished through a belt of whins, and came out on a smooth expanse of pasture—a field that might be green in daylight, but was now wan in the half-dark. A quarter-mile away, on the first swell of slope, a single orange-yellow light looked steadily at him, and towards this he went, smooth-strided—head down, elbows forward, breath drawing easily. His old hat slipped off, and, perforce, he had to let it lie. At the limit of the grey field he came to a wooden gate that let him through on to a cart-road twisting up the slope. Half-way up he passed the gable end of farm

18

steadings, and a dog came round the corner and barked once.

"Right, Fruachan!" said the man throatily, and the dog came to heel and sniffed at the hanging feet.

At the slope-head he entered a wicket-gate in a garden paling, and a gravel path crunched beneath his feet. Before him was a low cottage with a jutting white porch. The porch door was open, and the inner door was open too, so that the light shone on some brilliantly red geraniums on the window shelves. He scraped his feet on the bass and cleared his throat with intention.

"Got my salmon, Uncle Aelec?" cried a light young voice.

"I have that," said Uncle Aelec. His breath was coming heavily now, but he held it in and made his voice calm. "And the rightful owner of it as well," he added. "Easy now, Margaret!"

He bent below the lintel and entered the lit, good-sized kitchen-living-room. There was in it the flavour of peat, and a glow amongst white ashes on the open brick hearth.

The cry that greeted Uncle Aelec and his burden was a small one, but no young woman—and particularly no red-haired young woman—can suppress a skirl when one is due.

"There you go now!" he chided. "Shift yon cushion on the settle. Easy now, easy! He is no' murdered—nor kilt either."

Very gently he let the limp body slip on to the couch that filled most of the back wall—an old-fashioned, high-backed, horse-hair, mahogany couch, covered with a blue-and-yellow-striped Navajo blanket. The young woman slid a pillow under the limp head, while her

19

uncle straightened out the helpless limbs. The youth lay desperately still, his face clean-cut and white, his eyelashes very black, a trickle of blood at the corner of his mouth—still, remote, a little awesome.

"Who is it? Is he dead? Was—was it you ?" the questions came quickly.

"Not me, Margaret, lass. He is not dead, anyway. He was breathing in my ear right enough. If you want to know, he is young Alistair MacIan, the laird's nephew—the Yankee one." He wiped his warm brow and took two or three deep breaths.

"How still he is—and white! Oh, uncle! look at the blood on his chin."

"I wager he bit his tongue then. He gave himself the deil's own dunt. Are you up in anatomy?"

"I have to be."

"See if his neck is all right. Go on, girl! I want to be sure."

She knelt by the couch. The young man was in tennis flannels and his neck was bare and finely brown. On that brown neck her strong, small hands were very white. "It—it seems all right," she breathed.

"The stiff-necked MacIan! I needn't be afraid."

"The top of his head—what a lump!"

"Ay! It will be bigger yet."

"And another here over his ear."

"That one he deserved, I'm thinking."

"Did you do that?"

"No, no, my girl! I hadn't hand or part in it. His own cousin, Don Webster, gave him that one."

In a few brisk words he told her what had happened, while she, still on her knees, watched the calm face on the couch.

"He is badly hurt," she said at the end. "We must send for Dr Angus, uncle."

"If we have to, but let us go canny as long as we can. I wonder, now, is this a case where a drop whisky—what do you think, Margaret?"

"I don't know. Wait! I'll sponge his face and neck."

"Right, my lassie! But good whisky in moderation never harmed a body, and we'll try that as well." There he was wrong. Even the best whisky is bad for a dunted brain-pan.

She was quicker than he was. While he was at the wall-cupboard, near the fireplace, pouring the amber liquor from an old cut-glass decanter, she was in and out of the scullery at the rear with basin and sponge. He stood over her, glass in hand, pucker-faced in admiration of the deft way her hands moved about the boy's head.

And then the closed eyes opened calmly and looked into the blue eyes above. It was as if he waked out of a quiet sleep. Alistair MacIan looked steadily for a moment, and then spoke with a half-humorous certainty, "I never did like red hair," and immediately lapsed into what seemed equable slumber.

III

"Oh, the wretch!" exclaimed young Margaret. The light from the hanging lamp shone on her hair, and that hair was one shade—or maybe two—redder than red copper. It was closely shingled too, and, whether by art or nature, it curled over her ears and outlined a shapely small head on a lovely shaft of neck. Any man

21

was welcome to dislike that hair and be for ever a poor judge. Probably she knew that.

"Well, now!" said Uncle Aelec; "isn't he the quick one to bring his dislikes with him in his waking?"

"He is welcome."

"He wants a lump over his other ear, maybe. Let me try my remedy now. I like the way he opens a conversation."

The young man spluttered and came alive. "The real hooch," he muttered, with an intake of breath.

"Well you know it," said Aelec. "You talk well. Try another taste, now."

He took it readily, and Aelec let his head drift back on the cushion. Margaret had moved back, and the hurt youth turned his eyes towards her. A twinge of acute pain twisted his features, and very gingerly, and still grimacing, he brought his head to its original position. "Christmas! Who has been doing things to me?"

"A lump of a boulder mostly."

Without moving his head MacIan turned eyes on Aelec, and most of his faculties were now behind his gaze. "I don't seem to know you," he said. "Where am I?"

"Croft o' Drum. I'm Aelec Brands."

"Croft o' Drum—Aelec Brands! I know. Johnny Ross says you're the cat's whiskers."

"The bluidy Turk! What did he call me that for?"

"But how am I here?"

"Accident!" Aelec Brands was not sure if a sudden enlightenment would help. He added cautiously: "Down by the river—at Urdog Pool—you don't remember? Lying on the stones, you were."

Alistair turned his eyes to the ceiling and waited for memory to flow. Wait! Where was he? He had left Highland Drum after dinner to walk down to Buntness for a hand at poker—the short-cut by the river it was. Don Webster was with him, and Paddy Joe Long was to follow. My aunt! He had it. Don Webster—the saturnine devil. By heck! what a kick he must have in that right of his. Here he lifted a hand to the side of his head and felt the bump with cautious finger-tips. "Some sockdologer," he said aloud, and his hand crept to his aching crown piece. "Ouch! What fell on me? Did Don do that too?"

"No, then. There's where you dunted the stone."

"You found me lying?"

Aelec Brands nodded.

The lad was silent then, and slowly a frown blackened and blackened on his brow: a troubled frown, more than an angry one.

"I will never believe that," he said to his own thought.

"You have a gey lump to show for it, anyway," said Aelec Brands.

"It isn't that; but Don would never leave me lying."

"I see! Maybe you'll mind sitting on the stones with your mouth open?"

"After Don's haymaker?"

"Just so. He was glowering down at you, and you up at him, and says he, 'You're a d—d fool, MacIan, and I'm another,' and off he went round the shoulder of the pool as if his nose bled."

"Right! I get that—and then the sky fell on me?"

23

"No; but whatever was in your head—and I misdoubt it was good—you made a splurge to go after him, and went your length against a lump of stone big as the table there. Your friend—if he was that—was out of sight then."

The young man sighed with some relief. "That's better. I would hate to think the worst of Don. But whereabout the ringside were you?"

"Oh, I was looking on with my mouth open too—I bit my tongue when you dunted the stone."

Alistair MacIan grinned at that. "So did I," he said ruefully.

"Man!" said Aelec Brands admiringly, "but you're game"; and the words brought a little colour into the lad's face.

"How long ago was that?" he asked quietly.

"Half an hour, maybe a bit longer."

"Don and Paddy Joe will be waiting for me at Buntness. I think I'll make a shot at getting up." He tried it before Brands could protest, and made a poor business of it. His ill-used neck muscles protested agonisingly, the room swung and rocked before his eyes, and he barely suppressed a groan behind clenched teeth as he sank back on the couch.

The young woman at the table-side winced. "He can't leave yet, uncle," she cried.

"I'm thinking he can't leave to-night," said her uncle.

"Sorry to be a nuisance," excused young MacIan, a hand at his damp brow.

"No trouble at all," assured Aelec Brands. "You're no' beholden, Mr MacIan. I'm one of the clan, and this bit house is yours. Your Uncle Hugh and myself ken each other fine. A night's rest and you'll be as right

24

as a trivet. Later on I could send word to Highland Drum."

"I wouldn't do that—" He hesitated there.

"I ken, I ken! We can be thinking over that.—Margaret, lass, will you see to things ben the room?"

And so in a little while young Alistair MacIan was resting on a comfortable bed, with cool linen above him and below him and a down pillow beneath his head.

Aelec Brands came back to the living-room. "He'll do fine now," he told Margaret.

"When I am done with him. Take you that basin, uncle."

She had donned a dainty American apron and held a sponge in one hand, a bottle in the other, and carried a towel over a bare arm. Her uncle, without a word, took up the basin and preceded her into the bedroom. "A bit torture coming your way," he said. The eyes on the bed, turned sideways, smiled at them.

The torture was not too terrible—indeed, not more than a slight discomfort, and that equally shared. For, sensitive as an acute bump may be, it is not any more sensitive than a girl's feelings, and it takes an experienced nurse to remain equable under eyes that constantly rove. Yet, but for a certain heightening of colour, Margaret Brands gave no hint of embarrassment. She spread the towel under the dark head, sponged the sore places with slow gentleness, applied a cold compress to the crown bump, and then set out to massage the neck muscles, a touch of olive oil on silken finger-tips.

Suddenly Aelec Brands slapped his thigh and exclaimed, "A thing I forgot! I'll no' be long"; and went out into the night.

There are surely many currents that flow out of finger-tips and out of eyes, currents that curve and twist and strike deep to that central sea where sensation becomes aware—which explains why Margaret, usually so calm, felt the flush in her cheeks. She was at a disadvantage, of course. The dark eyes in the white face of Alistair MacIan had nowhere to look but at her, and that they did industriously. And she knew exactly the roving journey they made. The bed-side lamp was on a small table at her left hand and showed the exquisite fairness of her skin, but it also lit her hair to splendour, and that splendour had much of red in it. A young woman may be slightly embarrassed by eyes that rove from ear-curls to dimpled cheek, to nose not quite guiltless of powder, to lips, to firmly rounded chin, to slenderly moulded neck with a heart-catching small hollow at its base—and back again. But if these eyes notice that eyelashes might be a shade darker than they are, and that eyebrows are a shade darker than they might be, something must be done about it. And so a single drop of water oozed from a compressed sponge, gathered to a head, and fell plump on a roving dark eye. And before that physical eye could wink itself clear, she, so to speak, squeezed a further drop on the inner eye by casually remarking, "I wonder why you never did like red hair?"

He started and gave himself a sore twinge. "How in glory did you know that?"

The naïveté of the question pleased her. "Can I not see it in your eye?"

"I'll be shot if you can."

That emphatic denial pleased her too. "How could I know, then?"

He lay mind-searching, while she, putting aside the sponge, extracted the cork of the olive-oil bottle.

"My great aunt!" he exclaimed. "I seem to remember. Did I say it that way?"

"Why not?"

"You know, when a fellow comes out of a long count, he acts as if he had been drugged, and says a lot of fool stuff."

"Frank stuff, rather," she countered, and silenced him, for he was honest.

She was massaging his neck downwards with a gentle stroking motion and with an evident knowledge of the sheathing muscles. "I should prefer moulding this neck of yours," she said easily. "My trade, you know!"

"Neck moulder? Masseuse?"

"Sculptor. Well, no! Just out of my student course at Kensington."

"You don't stay here, then?"

"No; I'm for London to-morrow."

"And mighty glad too, I'll bet a hat!" He felt himself on firmer ground now.

"In a way. Father's work is in London; and mine too, of course. And yet I'll be sorry to leave uncle. He is out catching a salmon—" She caught her lip in a quick flash of teeth, but the young man did not seem to notice the implication.

"A tough job that," he said. "Johnny Ross, the keeper, says it would tak' the deil himself to land a fish this month." He got the Doric twist quite decently.

27

"My uncle must be that one," asserted Margaret. "He would get you a salmon out of a whin-bush. A holiday with him is ideal."

"Do you like staying in this hole?"

She straightened up and looked at him in very complete surprise. "This hole!" she exclaimed incredulously. "Do you not like it?"

"Slow as a church. But for Paddy Joe Long, and Don Webster, and——"

"Mr Don Webster makes it lively enough, doesn't he?"

"I should smile," he agreed quaintly, and his own smile twisted amusedly. "What have I said now?"

"That anyone should call Highland Drum a hole——"

"Sorry. Perhaps I did not meet the real people—till to-night."

She refused to rise to that. She felt strangely disappointed at this estimate of a spot so perfect, and even felt militantly disposed to confute and confound, but she also felt that this was not the time nor the place. The youth was in no fit state for castigation. He had suffered a really severe shock, and all the sensitive nerve centres were only now readjusting themselves. The recuperative forces were furiously at work, and their reaction flooded the brain with an overwhelming weariness. Under the soothing motion of Margaret's fingers his eyelids began to weigh heavily, and a delicious drowsiness drowned him in its deep sea. Gradually she eased the massage to a halt. Already the towel had been slipped from below his head, and now she moved the down-quilt up to his neck, turned low the lamp, lifted the basin noiselessly, and tiptoed to the door. There a whisper halted her.

"Thanks, Miss Red-Head."

"Good-night," she whispered back, and shut the door between them. But she was not actually sure if she had had the last word after all.

CHAPTER III

I

AELEC BRANDS had stepped outside the porch and paused, as was his custom, to examine the night, and a beautiful, clear, calm night he found it. The sky, deepest blue, was a galaxy of stars, and eastwards over the Bin of Cullen was the brightening promise of a half-moon. The sand-dunes, spreading from the river mouth, were a brown shadow, and a touch of phosphorescence showed an occasional gleam where the bar broke leisurely. The sigh of that breaking came intermittently to his ears like the sigh of a child sleeping. Beyond was the dark plain of the sea, with the far light on Tarbat Ness winking across it, and still darker, the long line of the hills outlined itself starkly against the pale glow of the north. Now and then a restless oyster-catcher gave its plaintive call as it winged its way up the river, and now and then some little spiral of air, on a ploy of its own, whispered "hu-u-s-s-h" amongst the trees far up the slope. But all these small sounds made but the faintest ripple on the abiding stillness that lay on all that land star-deep.

"A grand night," said Aelec Brands, "and more to come!" He felt a touch at his wet knee. "Right, Fruachan! Come away, then."

As he passed the gable of the croft-steadings he saw a light in the bothy window at the end of the line. "Not in bed yet, Andra?" he muttered. "Lazy enough you'll be when I rout you out the morn."

Dog at heel, he crossed the grey field, went unerringly

through the whin-belt, and came amongst the alders where his fish and tackle lay. He took the last few steps with caution, sliding his brogues through the thin grass, so as not to tread on the tip of his precious rod. Reaching his particular tree, he was already crouching, hands agrope, when Fruachan growled at his shoulder—a low-pitched whisper of a growl, not of anger, but of information. "Hst, lad! Down, now!" Aelec Brands carefully straightened amongst the branches, whilst the dog crouched flat at his heels. He bent an ear upstream, but for a time there was no sound but the sigh and gurgle of running water. He could see the curve of the shore dimly, and, beyond it, an occasional spectral line of foam flashing down the rapids, but beyond that all was black against the breast of the hill. And then he heard the clink of shoe on stone and darted his head the other way. The sound came from downstream, and that surprised him for a moment. The matter was made clear in a few minutes.

Again two men crunched and stumbled amongst the stones, and again two men halted within a few yards of him. For a second he had the insane notion that time had taken a leap backwards, and he waited with held breath for the first words of speech. He stood well above them, and, from the hips down, the two were clearly outlined against the white of the washed stones, but above that they were dim against the even dark of the pool.

"It was hereabouts, I think." The speaker was Don Webster.

"That the dirty work was done," added the second man, who bent down as if examining the stones. "Devil the fragment of him is in it, and no blood crying to high heaven either. 'Twas no gory battle, I'm thinking."

"I have a loose tooth to show for it."

"And Alistair a loose head, by all accounts."

"That one is Irish, at any rate," decided Aelec Brands. There was no mistaking the inflection and turn of speech. It was an adequate brogue too, leisurely, round, and giving every word full value.

"He must be back at Highland Drum by now," said Webster.

"Where else, seeing he is not lying his length here or teaching the Fenwick boys poker—at a price?"

"Ah! So they are on the road back from Buntness," thought Aelec. "What'll they think when they go up to the Drum and young MacIan no' there?"

Poised, he listened, a branch of alder brushing his face and one polished leaf touching his lips. Unthinkingly he caught this in his teeth, and, nibbling it, got the astringent bitterness on his tongue. He wanted to splutter, but dared not, and could only cautiously smooth the bitterness against the ball of a thumb.

"Let's hurry up and make sure." This was Don Webster.

"Easy now, my son, easy," expostulated the other. "The way you rushed me up from Buntness I hadn't time to fill a pipe."

Webster grunted impatiently, but did not urge further.

As the Irishman filled his pipe his eyes must have been roving. "Nice piece of water," he remarked. "Does the tide reach it?"

"Couldn't say."

"There might be a fish or two in the neck of it, anyway."

"Hopeless, trying for them this weather."

"Maybe so. Did you ever hear of a middling-sized,

black-headed worm on a Stewart tackle slipping round the shoulder of a shelf at the edge of dark?"

"You murdering Irishman!"

"There are worse methods—God forgive me for knowing them!"

"That same lad knows a thing or two," noted Aelec Brands. "I would like to show him a Blue Charm at work. That worm, now! I wonder! Not the Stewart tackle, though—but a good-sized Pennell—quicker, if it's the fish you're after and no' the sport."

And so another idle word remained to be accounted for, since it set the itch of speculation tickling in a Highlandman's brain.

II

A match scraped, and Aelec saw a pair of cupped hands with the light gleaming between the fingers. Above the hands he saw the beginning of a long nose, a black edging of brow, and the rim of a tweed hat.

"Shall we go on?"

"A great hurry you're in. Is it another peg you'd be giving that cousin of yours?"

"Don't rub it in, Paddy Joe. I have had enough of that."

"I doubt if he has, then, though you put him on his flat. How the devil you did it I don't know. Was he looking?"

"Good mind to show you! Are you coming on?"

"Are you afraid that Alistair is back at Highland Drum paying court to Norrey Carr?"

"I gave him his lesson there."

"You know damn well you did not. It would take

more than one wallop to make Alistair MacIan see crooked, and as long as he has a straight eye in his head he will pay court to any lady that pleases him."

Don Webster growled angrily.

"There you go, Don. A minute ago, all remorse, and now you'd cut his heart out. It is time I spoke to you about your temper."

At that the other laughed shortly. "As if you haven't been speaking to me about my temper since I first knew you."

"Time you were taking heed, then. If Norrey hears of this night's work——"

"I shan't tell, and the Yankee's vanity——"

"He would not tell anyhow; but I might."

"Some Irishmen we can trust."

"Just so. The Irishman you know, you trust—'tis the hearsay ones that are irresponsible."

"So they are, Paddy Joe."

"Irresponsibility has its advantages, then. Freedom of speech, for instance! If our criticism is tempered by wit you delight in our buffoonery, but if it happens to touch you on the raw we simply can't mean it."

"Is that all? Shall we go on now?"

"No—and be hanged to your tone! Wait till I relight this pipe. What I am wanting to say is that I am beginning to suspect that you are not good enough for Norrey Carr."

"I am prepared to admit it."

"Of course you are—from the viewpoint that no man is good enough for any woman. My point is that there are better men."

"I admit that too."

"Say Alistair MacIan? That touches you. Many a

good man makes a damn bad husband. If I thought—you know I have some influence with Norrey?"

"I do. You have influence with all of us when you like, Paddy Joe."

The admission, instead of mollifying, seemed to anger the Irishman. It also made him brief. "I wish to God," he said hotly, "you'd take a clove-hitch on yourself."

"All right! I'll try," agreed Don Webster mildly.

"Let us be going, then. But wait you. If Alistair is not back at Highland Drum——"

"We can tell Uncle Hugh he is over at Muiryside drinking Guinness at the Red Lion—as you taught him."

"An apt pupil, too. We can't tell your uncle that—it might be true. Let us over and see."

And here Aelec Brands decided that the right time had come to duck under the branches and step down on the stones. "Good-night, gentlemen," he saluted them, and waited for the startled pause.

"That you, Johnny?" The question was Don Webster's.

"No, Mr Webster. I'm Aelec Brands of the Croft o' Drum above."

"Oh yes! Aelec Brands." A pause, and then, "I suppose you heard us talking?" There was no mistaking the tone.

"I know you are looking for young Mr MacIan."

"Do you know where he is?"

"He is up at my place"; and before Don Webster got over his surprise, Aelec added, "and in bed—with a lump on his head like a duck's egg."

"Good God, Paddy Joe!"

"Kicked him, you must have," said Paddy Joe; and to Aelec, "Is he badly hurt, sir?"

35

"No' badly hurt, maybe, but with a gey good bash on the head."

"But I left him sitting on the stones just here," cried Don Webster, with perplexity and doubt in his voice.

"After giving him hell's own pile-driver," remarked the Irishman dryly.

"And I found him lying on his face just here, too," said Aelec Brands, "and the senses knocked out of him."

"But—but what happened?"

"I know that too." Aelec Brands did not like Don Webster's tone, and while he was man enough not to resent it, he was man enough to express his opinion. "If men will be talking and quarrelling," he said, "where another man might be about some bit business, they can blame whom they like and the blame winna stick. You'll be knowing fine what was heard, Mr Webster, and I'll tell you now what was seen that you did not see."

"I like his style," murmured the Irishman.

III

Pithily Aelec Brands told them what he had seen and done. "And it's in bed he'll stay for a day or two, I'm thinking," he finished.

"A damnable situation!" growled Webster. "Deeper in the mud than ever, Paddy Joe. The whole countryside will know in a day or two."

"If it does," said Aelec Brands firmly, "it is one of you two that will tell it."

"More or less you could not say," agreed the Irishman.

"We must see how he is," said Don Webster, and added, "if you don't mind, Brands?"

"Ye are welcome. If ye follow me and watch your

feet—" He turned, and then paused. He smoothed a great hand over his face from brow to chin, and it was as if he smoothed away one mood and superseded it with another. He smiled into the dark, and faced towards the Irishman. "I know Mr Webster," he said quietly, "but I don't know your name, sir. You are Irish, I'm thinking."

"And I trying to hide it! I am, Mr Brands. My name is Long—and longish—Patrick Joseph Stanislaus Long—Paddy Joe to his friends—tramps mostly."

"Thank you, Mr Long. I was wondering, now, if you mightn't be right about that worm."

"Worm? Which? Don Webster or——"

"About getting a fish out of the pool here."

"Oh yes! Did you ever try it?"

"No, then. I was thinking that a Pennell tackle would be better than a Stewart."

"More fun with a Stewart, though."

"If it's a matter of fun, there's a small fly I tied myself I could show you."

"Ah! I'm listening to you. Say, is that a dog you have there?"

"Ay, that's Fruachan. Maybe you'll know his breed when you see him in the light. Don't touch him yet, sir —he's no' acquainted. We can be going on now."

Aelec Brands made a wide curve round the tree where lay his spoil, and led them through the prickly whins.

CHAPTER IV

I

MARGARET BRANDS, sitting and musing in a basket-chair before the smouldering peats, heard the crunch of the many feet on the gravel and was quickly on her own. Her uncle looked in at her from the porch and grinned reassuringly. "More visitors, Margaret," he told her.— "Come away in, gentlemen."

The broad Anglo-Scot and the long Irishman followed him into the cosy room, and the dog, Fruachan, sat down in the doorway.

"How is the patient, Margaret?"

"Asleep."

"Good, that! Mr Webster and Mr Long—his friends from the Drum. I found them at the Urdog looking for him.—Gentlemen, my niece, Margaret Brands."

Don Webster bowed, short and stiff, and was acknowledged just as stiffly. Paddy Joe Long, his tweed hat crumpled against his hip, looked at her out of his two eyes, for she was well worth looking at. Slim and fine she was, and carried herself like a thoroughbred. The American apron over the white, flower-stencilled, short dress was housewifely becoming, and silken ankles rose shapely out of small strapped shoes. He came across to her and reached a frank hand, and his long sardonic face smiled with a queer sadness. "Margaret Brands!" he repeated whimsically. "It is a good name. I mind, once, reading of a Margaret Brandt and weeping with her."

The blue of her eyes gathered light and a smile for him. "I know," she murmured. "Her hair was 'an apple of gold in a net-work of silver.'"

"She had no luck there either—who had no luck ever. Copper is the precious metal in hair."

"Easy to see you are Irish, Mr Long," said Aelec.— "Will ye sit, gentlemen? Mr MacIan might be waking up soon, and I think he'll be the one to let us know— before that I would not care to disturb him."

These four people seated round the room estimated each other each in his or her own way. Don Webster, in a hard chair near the window, a man self-centred by years of life in the Orient, his strong tropic-tanned face and dark eyes clouded by a constitutional sombreness, was out of his element, and yet completely indifferent. He saw only a crofter and a more or less cultivated niece, and was too obsessed by recent events to be even condescending. Uncle and niece were well aware of this attitude. Possibly the niece resented it, but in a rather amused way; her life amongst artists had liberated her from the thraldom of class, and her mind was too much alive to be much affected by prejudices. The uncle mused detachedly over it, for he was one of the few wise ones who, having achieved a philosophy, seldom ignored any man, but would ignore princes, given occasion. The Irishman, Patrick Joseph Stanislaus Long, like a few— rare and few—of his nation, had no class-consciousness at all. He accepted all men as he found them, and so all men were inclined to lift him a little above their own level. He was at home anywhere, and very completely at home sitting on the high-back couch in this kitchen-living-room. He contemplated the smooth wise face of Aelec Brands with satisfaction, and the good looks of

39

Margaret with appreciation, and already had a working notion of their mentalities. And yet, behind his openness and his ease was a secret core that no man or woman might reach. His face was typically an Irish face—long, lean, strongly carved, sometimes strangely sad, sometimes whimsically sardonic, with wide close mouth and cheeks lined by taking thought. Uncle and niece liked him instinctively, and felt that little queer thread of race that nothing can ever quite break.

II

"Any objection to smoking, Miss Brands?" Long inquired of Margaret, who sat in the basket-chair near the fire. Permission given, he threw his pouch across to Aelec at the table-end. "Try mine," he invited. "You'll maybe find it light for you."

"Thanks. I like to flavour the smoke myself, and strong baccy has nothing to it but its strength."

"You are a smoker, I see."

The two filled their pipes slowly. Don Webster, after some hesitation, lit a black cheroot. Aelec, smiling at a thought of his own, looked sideways through the smoke at the Irishman. "You might be able to enlighten me on a small matter, Mr Long," he hazarded.

"Nothing but religion is the worse for being considered this way and that."

"Suppose, now, that a man called you the cat's whiskers, what would you think of him?"

"Thunder and turf! Did anyone call me that?"

"No, no, Mr Long. It wasn't about you——"

"Why, you wouldn't call a tramp going the road a name like that!"

And Aelec, looking solemnly at him, caught the gleam in the deep eye and the twitch of the lined mouth. "Man," he said, "you had me going that time."

Then the two chuckled together, and Margaret added her smile.

"Let me see, now," considered Long. "Suppose a man you knew and met often had a habit of saying, 'Come in and have a drink'——"

"He'd be a gey hard man to quarrel with."

"In fact, the cat's whiskers. A Yankeeism, I believe"; and Long's knowing expression indicated the closed door.

"Oh, it was only his way of saying what another man said"; and Aelec smiled reminiscently. "'A gran' chiel,' says the Moray man; 'the cat's whiskers,' says another; and there was me doubting a good man. But I suppose that's the way o't."

"'Tis so," said the Irishman. Then he stiffened at gaze. His eye had lighted on the dog sitting calmly in the doorway. "'Do I sleep, do I dream, or is visions about?' How did that tarrier dog get so far from home?—Here, Kerry."

The blue-grey, shaggy, broad-headed terrier took not the slightest notice. Aelec Brands flicked thumb and finger. "Go on, Fruachan. Meet your countryman."

The dog came quietly across the floor and touched a nose against the Irishman's tweed knee.

"You are welcome, Kerryman," said Long softly. "We are far from home, the both of us." He put a long hand on the broad head and ran it down the heavily muscled neck. "He has it in the right place.—See this fellow, Don—the jaw, and the steady deep eye, and that

41

curve of muscle behind the ears, and the way he plants his big pads—the greatest fighting-machine in the world: the Kerry-blue terrier."

"I would say a bull-terrier—" began Webster.

"I wish you had one——"

"Don't listen, Fruachan," urged Margaret. "You are a gentleman, and only defend yourself against unmannerly dogs."

"I wager he teaches them a thing or two besides manners," said Long.

"I warrant you," said Aelec. "I thought you'd know the breed."

"I should. I mind once owning a dog like that one—Haro was his name—and he helped to get me seven days in jail."

Out of the corner of an eye he noticed the slight start Margaret gave, and turned to her. "Upon my soul, Miss Brands," he said with whimsical solemnity, "that was the first and last time I was in jail"; and she smiled understandingly.

"You can always blame the dog," put in Don Webster.

"It would be a good story, I'm thinking," hinted Aelec.

"If I could tell it," said the Irishman, and proceeded to do so.

III

"It was over in New York—that's where I met the boy inside—and all I owned at the time was the terrier. One morning early I was giving him a piece of exercise down at the Battery—I had him in leash, too, in accordance with the regulations of that place—when along

42

comes a large policeman—cops, they call them—leading a police-dog; you know those overgrown, long-legged, slab-sided, shovel-headed, three-quarter-bred Airedales —one of them. As soon as he set eyes on Haro he yelled blue murder—the dog I mean—and nearly pulled the arm out of the policeman trying to get at him. 'Is that a fighting dog you have?' the policeman wanted to know, giving his brute a calming kick—a big Polack he was, and no Irishman. 'He is not a fighting dog,' I said mildly. 'He only kills in self-defence.' 'Here's a pup would put a strangle-hold on him in five minutes,' he challenged. 'He might,' said I, 'and again he might not.' 'There's a hundred iron men'—dollars, he meant—'behind this bozo—' 'I have no iron men,' I told him, 'and if I had I would not bet them on a dog-fight—'tis against the regulations.' My intentions were peaceable, as you can see."

Margaret chuckled, and he chuckled back.

"'Take away your sawed-off runt,' he ordered then; 'I can't hold this tiger for ever.' He might have dragged his own beast away, but I did not tell him so, having acquired wisdom at its usual price. Meantime, there was Haro sitting calmly at my feet, admiring the Statue of Liberty with a peaceful eye. 'Come on, boy avic,' said I. 'You are a gentleman, and the dog of one besides'; and away we went. It happened when my back was turned, and whether by accident or design I will not be saying. Anyhow, the Airedale slipped his leash, and the first I knew of it was Haro and myself on the ground, and he on top of us, worrying indiscriminately. Ay! he knocked us clean off our feet. I tell you I got out of the storm-centre as soon as possible, but I was still tied to the leash with a bloody hand. 'Take off your dog,' I yelled.

'Take off your own,' he yelled back. 'How can I,' I shouted with reason, 'and sixty pounds of brute on top of him?' 'Let them settle it their own way, then'; and his mouth wide as a door with laughter. That's the way it started."

"It couldn't start any other way," commended Aelec Brands.

"And then I heard a voice bellowing in my ear—it had to bellow, for the Airedale was waking the dead—'Damn your sowl! Why wouldn't you give your tarrier a chance?—le' go that leash!' 'You go to—'—your pardon, Miss Brands—a warm place I meant. 'How can I let it go and it twisted round my hand?' I thought it was the policeman, but no—a small, rough, sailor-like man with a clasp-knife in a leather belt. 'Is that the way?' said he; and he had the leash cut before I could stop him—if I wanted to. He seemed to be a knowledgeable man about dog-fights, and might be a Kerryman himself from what he knew about the Kerry-blue in action. He was hopping about the circumference of the cyclone on his hands and knees, trying to see what poor Haro was doing under the smother of the Airedale. 'Tell me,' he demands—and our heads together—'has he his hoult? Has he his hoult yet—or is the —— false to his breed?' 'He has not,' said I; 'but give him time— give the pup time.' 'Time?' said he. 'We have lashins of time, man; I'm thinking this is going to be a good fight.' It was."

"But was there no one there to stop it?" cried Margaret.

"It was in the early morning, as I said, and the folk that use the Battery Park at that hour would rather a dog-fight than breakfast—and they need the breakfast. The only man that could stop it would not, for his dog seemed

44

to be having it all its own way. Haro was underneath and on his back, and stayed there, while the big Airedale scrambled all over him, taking a bite where he could and talking for the two of them. The Kerry-blue had nothing much to say, only now and then he gave a small deep growl, not so much of anger as content. He was ten pounds lighter than the Airedale, and his natural method of warfare looked like self-destruction. He fought best from below, like all his breed. See this fellow here. A back like whalebone, a broad shaggy head manipulated by a neck that's one layer of muscle, and big flat pads like a set of boxing-gloves. The Airedale could reach no vital place, and Haro patiently sought for the grip he wanted. And in time he got it—when the other's energy began to slacken. 'Ye sowl, ye!' roared the sailor-man. 'On his back now, boy!' And so it was. The Airedale lost heart and tried to drag away, but the Kerry came with him, rolled him over, and muzzled him against the ground. 'Take off your dog,' roared the policeman. 'Take off your own,' I gave back, and, indeed, I would have stopped the fight then if I was let; but the policeman jumped in and gave Haro his number eleven on the side of the head.

"The rest of the fight I saw only out of the tail of an eye. The kick half-broke Haro's hold, and the Airedale wrenched himself loose and proceeded from that place at two miles to the dead minute, his ki-yi going out in front and the Kerry-blue coming behind, with the small sailor-man hanging on to the bit of leash and moving in standing jumps, like the devil going through Ballyhahill. That was the last I saw of my dog—or the sailor, who came out of Kerry, I suspect—a bad, dishonest place where dogs are concerned."

45

"He did not bring back your dog?" inquired Margaret.

"I doubt it.   I wasn't there to see."

"Arrested?" suggested Aelec.

"Must have been.   I was in a reduced condition at the time—and a second policeman had turned up out of nowhere in the middle of the protest I was making.   Their arguments subdued me.   I remember the police-court quite distinctly, though, and the justice saying 'Seven days in the Tombs.'   And it was so."

IV

"Many a good man goes to jail," said Aelec Brands. "I helped to put them there myself when I was a policeman in Glasgow."

"Go on, uncle!" protested Margaret.   "You were only a 'special' constable during the war."

"You see, Mr Long," explained Aelec solemnly, "I pretend I was a policeman so as to hide that my real business was a maker of antique furniture."

Again the two chuckled.

"I was wondering," said Long.   "That grandfather clock and the Welsh dresser are not *made* antiques, are they?"

"No, then.   The clock is Chippendale in his good period.   Not so sure about the dresser, but it is old."

"And your dog is an old breed, too.   You got him in Glasgow, of course?"

"From an Irishman.   There's a bit story—Ha!   Did you hear yon?"   And with, "Tell you another time," Aelec Brands was at the inner door before anyone could move.   He turned the handle quietly, and put head and shoulder inside.   "Are you waked, then, Mr MacIan?

46

Ah, that's good. . . . Here are Mr Long and Mr Webster to look in on you. . . . Hush!" And Aelec coughed.

"Ay, faith!" said the Irishman, at his shoulder. "He has a gift that way. Let me in at him."

Aelec Brands moved aside, and Long, with Don Webster following in some hesitation, entered the room. Aelec shut the door on them, walked to the smouldering fire, poked among the ashes with a long-tongs, and built up a little pyramid of red peats. "A nip coming in the night air," he remarked, "and my feet no' that dry."

"Heavens, uncle!" said Margaret, jumping up; "you'll get your death. Change your things at once. Go on, now."

She hurried to a side-hatched box below the old dresser, and picked out some small black peats. With one of these she brushed aside the ashes, and then built the others round the back of the glowing coals. Her uncle stood towering at her shoulder, his eyes affectionately on her red crown. "What do you think of our visitors, Margaret?"

"Mr Long is a pleasant man—and frank—but he has his reserves, I think."

"So! Mr Don Webster is reserved enough too."

"And makes it plain." After a pause she added musingly, "So these are Sir Hugh's nephews?"

"MacIan and Webster. Ay! You weren't expecting to meet them?"

"No. Lady Sara wanted me to, but there was no time."

"And that reminds me—you're off to-morrow, and I with a salmon for you down at the Urdog."

She did not seem to hear him, but steadily pursued

47

her own train of thought. "Not a happy situation, is it?"

"Eh? The salmon——"

"No. The two young men. A double jealousy at work—love and gear."

"Hardly that. Young Alistair is the heir, and, anyway, both have plenty of gear without considering Highland Drum—though 'tis a nice bit nest-egg, with the laird's forestry schemes beginning to hatch out. MacIan has a good-sized fortune that his father left him in the States, and Webster has made his own money—China way. 'Tis said he's settling down and building a house near London."

"With the prospect of a wife to adorn it."

"If his cousin will be minding his own business."

"Just so. Are you aware that this Miss Carr is Norrey Carr the famous actress?"

"I had heard as much. She'll have a way with her?"

"No doubt. Aelec Brands, look at your wet feet."

"Right, woman, right! Who's speirin' anyway?" He bustled into an inner room through a door near the head of the couch, and left Margaret on her knees before the fire, her graceful cropped head leaning forward, and her eyes on the licking peat-flames.

CHAPTER V

I

PADDY JOE LONG went across to the bed, whistling the
"Corkman's Retreat":

O'er hedges and ditches, he tore his old britches—
    He ran like the wind—he ran like the wind.
He tore his old britches o'er hedges and ditches,
    And she close behind—and she close behind. . . .

"A dim funereal light wherein the dying man grinds
his teeth. Let us dispel phantoms while yet he swears."
The Irishman turned up the light and started back from
the bed. "Jehosophat Columbus! Brands's brand in
pyjamas."

"'Tain't no pyjamas," protested Alistair MacIan,
grinning ruefully. "An honest-to-God nightgown, Paddy
Joe."

"None of your Yankeeisms! A nightshirt, you mean.
Wear one myself if I wasn't afraid of society." Long
placed his hand on the arm outside the bed-clothes and
ran it down to the wrist, where it gripped for a moment.
"Muscle in repose should be smoothly soft—like
yours, son, and your pulse is like a rock. An even
thing I don't kick you out of your night-attire for a
malingerer. What?"

"Go on. Haze a fellow not able to help himself. Are
you two the vanguard of Highland Drum?"

"No, boy. Brands found us looking for you down at

the river and brought us up. Outside this house no one knows."

"And need not."

"Depends on you. Needn't know how it happened, at any rate."

"I shall be all right by morning. Is that Cousin Don back of you?—Forward, Don, where I can see you. I have a crick in my neck."

Don Webster went to the bed-end and placed his hands on the wooden bar, his dark face set, and his clouded eyes on the face that was a little less white then the pad of linen on his brow. That white face smiled quizzically. "Take an eyeful of your handiwork, cousin."

"I never knew this happened, 'Stair."

"It wouldn't, if you hadn't been in such a blamed hurry—not the way it did, anyhow."

"The whole thing was d—d silly."

Alistair MacIan opened his eyes. "How do you get it that way?"

"Grown men behaving like guttersnipes."

"But if a point couldn't be settled in any other way?"

Don Webster made no reply, and Long chuckled. "In these islands," he explained, "our sense of dignity often saves the other fellow's skin—and our own. You see, young fellow, Don is not one damn bit sorry for standing you on your ear, but he is touched to the quick at his loss of dignity."

"Rot, Paddy Joe!" protested Webster.

"Should think so," agreed the American. "Where I come from we settle a point one way or another, and the licked man stays put."

"The primitiveness of a young people. Don, here, having licked you——"

50

"Licked me! Not that you could notice. He had me only groggy, and was lucky to beat it. You must try again, Don."

"That folly is done with," maintained Don Webster with emphasis, but yet a thought settled down at the back of his brain.

"Enough talk," said Long. "You have a head on you, boy, and need a rest. We'll be round in the morning and make our plans."

"Just a moment," requested Alistair. "Say, Don, does Paddy Joe know why we rough-housed it?" He asked this a little shamefacedly.

"Yes. So does Brands. He was about somewhere—poaching, I suppose."

"Will he have told the girl—Margaret, he called her?"

"Why wouldn't he?" said Paddy Joe. "He is too good a man for a sense of dignity. Son, had you sense to notice the lovely curled red hair of her?"

"Hell! I made a bad break there," admitted Alistair naïvely. "The first thing I said when I came out of the count was that I despised red hair."

"You ungrateful pup! And she has poured coals of fire on your head by giving you her room."

"Who told you?" cried Alistair, startled.

"Look round you, man. Sorry! that was a sore twinge. That bed-cover and the ruffled pillow-slips and the dressing-table yonder with its array. I can't quite locate that young beauty. What is she?"

"Sculptor. Lives in London."

"Did she tell you so much? A sculptor! I thought I caught her taking elevations of this nose of mine. Damn it for a beak!"

"I hate being a nuisance. Could you and Don horse me up to Highland Drum and smuggle me in?"

"Stay where you are, boy, and in the still watches of the night you'll maybe mull out an apology."

"I tried one already and got shot over. She is a clever kid." MacIan's hand smoothed across his brow, and his eyes closed for a moment.

"Good-night now," said Paddy Joe.—"Come away, Don." He turned the light low, and moved towards the door.

Don Webster took one pace after him and paused. "Let us forget that this happened, MacIan," he said in a low voice. "I am sorry about it."

"Right, Don! It will make no difference to me one way—or the other."

Webster still paused, as if contemplating what that meant, and then without a word followed Long out of the room.

II

"The patient is doing fine," said Paddy Joe to Aelec and Margaret at the fireside.—"I hope," turning to Margaret, "that you will not be inconvenienced, Miss Brands."

"Not she," put in Aelec. "It's for me the settle there will make a bed. Do you think he has taken any hurt, Mr Long?"

"He has a head, of course, but a night's rest should settle that."

"If it does not, we might get Dr Angus over from Muiryside."

"We might. I'll be over early in the morning, and

52

we'll see. Meantime, nothing need be said—anywhere."
His look expressed much more.

"Just as well," Aelec agreed. "A lump of stone will
take a lot of blame. There's a sandbank the other side
of Urdog Pool, and I mind falling over it myself once."

"And a hard knock you gave yourself, too.—Good-
night now, Miss Brands." Long shook hands warmly
with the two, and Don Webster, murmuring a word of
thanks, could do no less.

"I'll put your feet on top of the road," Aelec volunteered. "It's rough going hereabouts, and you'll no'
manage the short-cut this hour."

They followed him into the night, that was still serene,
and was now made faintly luminous by a half-moon low
down in the south-east. Scarcely a word passed between
them. There seemed nothing more to say, and the detached calm of the night possessed them. Where the
cart-track debouched through a wooden gate on the
main road that swept in a grey line round the first swell of
the slope, Aelec Brands bade them good-night, and with
a "See you in the morning," they left him there. He
stood, pipe aglow and slow spirals of smoke dying out a
foot from his face, and watched them fade into the half-
dark the tall Irishman moving with an easy sway of
shoulder, and the broad Anglo-Scot striding firmly.
Then, for the third time that night, he turned riverwards,
the terrier following sedately at his heels.

"I have great trouble with that fish," was his quaint
thought. "By Adam! the next chiel that interrupts
me—I'll drown him."

He was not interrupted this time. He recovered his
salmon and tackle, and won clear of alders and whins.
As he walked he lifted the salmon in his great right hand.

53

"Between eighteen and twenty pounds, Fruachan," he said. "A nice fish for August. I wager you, my brother Dod will wish he was here."

Fruachan maintained an agreeable silence, and a mood of quiet satisfaction filled his master's heart.

CHAPTER VI

I

SOME time in the night it had rained a small shower out of a mist that had crept down from the higher hills—Cairn Rua, Cairn Kitty, and big Ben MacDhui behind all—but with lift of sun a cleansing wind had come in off the sea, washing the air clear and making the woods dance in the new light as if they had no inkling of the sere time that was almost upon them. It was now a fresh young day, with a gentle breeze, and the sun was well over the crown of the moors.

But young Alistair MacIan was still abed. He had not spent a restful night. Before the house bedded down, Margaret had again ministered to him—changing the compress on his head and massaging his neck; but youth will not easily lie in one posture all night, and when, in a half-doze, he instinctively made to turn on one side or the other, the resulting twinge woke him up very definitely to the realisation of a dull but persistent headache. That headache was still with him in the morning, though his neck muscles no longer protested, if he lay reasonably still.

Aelec Brands was an early riser always, and Margaret Brands was an early riser this morning. Truth to tell, she liked to snuggle down for a last forty winks, each wink a minute, and it was very pleasant to be at last wakened by Else MacLean (wife to Andra the farm-hand), bearing a cup of hot tea with cream in it and half a lump of sugar, and a bit of crisp buttered toast as well. Then, indeed, she waked up fresh as a flower, without yawns, with clean eyes touched with blue in the whites, cheeks faintly flushed, copper hair tousled, and neck and shoulders like ivory that is very new. But this morning she was up and dressed, and had the kettle singing on the black rack over the peat fire that Aelec had already nursed out of the smoored ashes, long before the stout and slightly frowsy Else MacLean shuffled up from the bothy. And by the time that Aelec returned from the byre, where Andra was milking the three cows, she was industriously stirring the porridge. He paused to admire the way she held the spirtle, little finger lifted and wrist curving gracefully.

"Lumps in it, and we'll ken who to blame," he warned, and turned towards the door of the inner room. Her eyes followed him.

The sounds of all these morning activities came to Alistair MacIan as he lay abed, gingerly moving his head from side to side to discover if he might not make a sally at getting up. His efforts had not taken him far in that direction, but he was able to turn his face to the door when Aelec entered, and his greeting was cheerful enough.

"A long night, Mr MacIan, I'm thinking," said that man of the wise eye. "Does the head still stoun?"

"A little; but I've had heads that could beat this a mile."

"The cheerful word for it, Highland Drum," commended Aelec.

The lad was game, but one could gather as much from his face. It was now a face white almost to haggardness and with shadows under the heavy-lashed eyes; a faint line or two rayed out from the eye-corners, and a faint line was impressed at each side of the mouth, and these might be due to humour or taking thought—or just living. The material fact was that the bones of cheek and jaw stood out firmly, and that suffering would only make that face more reliant.

"Do you like porridge?" Aelec asked.

"I do. I was whaled into taking it as a boy, and, Lord! how I hated it—the flaked kind. But I do like your Scotch porridge."

"They are a good diet. An egg, now—or maybe two—and a bit finnock?"

"Only a cup of tea—another taste I have acquired—hot enough to skin a lizard."

"Good, then! A puckle pillows under your head and you'll be feeling fine. Margaret outby is having designs on you first. She used to be a V.A.D. nurse, and has no mercy on poor helpless loons."

And in a little while Margaret had dealt with him faithfully, and he was none the worse of it. There was a blue-black film of stubble on his chin this morning, so that the sponge would not run smoothly over it, and this amused them both, and so, in some subtle way, made intercourse a little easier. Life currents are always flowing in the underneath, and eyes and fingers touch many springs. After a sleepless night of images and thoughts he could now have told Margaret that her hair was not red—not really red—or at least not the red he disliked. But he was chary of reopening that subject, and in the end he told her nothing. What her thoughts were no male can imagine and be honest.

And then he had breakfast. He had cream with his small portion of porridge, which had not the least lump in it, and crisp toast with his scalding hot tea. But that poor head of his still persisted in aching, and his eyes hurt and had some difficulty in focusing.

II

Paddy Joe Long, on a bicycle ludicrously short for his length of leg, arrived while Alistair was at breakfast, and had a low-voiced consultation with Aelec outside the porch door. The result was that, instead of going in to see his friend, he again mounted the borrowed machine and went free-wheeling down the cart-road, his knees jutting outside the handle-bars.

And that is how Dr Angus from Muiryside arrived while yet the morning was young. His examination of the surprised patient was a thorough one. "There is really nothing to fear," he finally told Long, leaning over the end of the bed, "thanks to a soundly made cranium and a strong-cased medulla. A frailer man might have broken his neck."

"You put it nicely, doctor," said the relieved Paddy Joe. "An ivory Yankee dome on a stiff neck has served its only purpose. When can he get up?"

"Not before to-morrow at the earliest."

"Jiminy!" exclaimed Alistair; "I'm not as bad as all that?"

"Your neck muscles are badly wrenched, Mr MacIan, and must have rest—a little massage is all *they* require. But, worse than that, you have the slightest touch of concussion, and the brain is a tender organ. You cannot move before to-morrow, and even then you'll have intermittent headache for a week or so."

"But my host—Mr Brands——"

58

"Oh, Aelec Brands won't mind. Your uncle and he know each other. I believe Miss Brands is going home to-day?"

"Yes! to London."

"Then I'll arrange with the District Nurse, and send something across that will make you sleep to-night."

And that was that. The doctor left the room, and Long, having seen him to the door, returned and held discussion with his friend. "This thing can be hidden no longer, son," he began. "I mean the fact that you are here on your back. We can suppress the rumpus that led to it."

"Don't care a hoot," said Alistair sourly.

"We must keep Norrey Carr out of it."

MacIan's face grew thoughtful. "Why should she object to Don socking me one?"

"'Tisn't that. I will not have Norrey in this." The Irishman slapped the bar of the bed, and added quickly, "And there are your uncle and aunt."

"And Don and his dignity. Oh, very well! Choose your lie."

"You were walking down to Buntness and slipped over the bank on to the stones at the river-side. Leave the lieing to me."

"Some liar myself."

"All men are. Aelec Brands will only know that he found you lying, and his niece will be gone."

"She would not give us away."

"Who are we to judge a woman?"

"I bet she would not."

"Why wouldn't you?" said Paddy Joe smoothly. "Now I am off to Highland Drum to spin a yarn, God help me."

59

"And bring the whole bunch down."

"Ay, faith! Including Norrey Carr. You'll have a hell of a headache before night."

When Long stepped outside the porch he found that Dr Angus had not yet departed, though his car was purring and tremoring outside the garden paling. He was a tall, loosely-put-together, mouse-haired, diffident young man, and seemed loth to part with Margaret's hand. Paddy Joe lifted his disreputable tweed hat and went cycling down the cart-track. At the main road he looked back. The doctor was getting into his car, and Margaret waved a hand from the porch.

Dr Angus also looked back from the main road—and very nearly collided with the gate-post. But the porch door looked at him with a blank eye, and he bore down furiously on the accelerator.

III

A calm hour followed at Croft o' Drum. Aelec Brands, shouting for Andra and his pair of horses, went about his business; Else MacLean shuffled about hers in kitchen and in byre; and Margaret Brands went about hers too. This led her, in the course of time, to tap at the bedroom door and project a head round the edge of it. Alistair MacIan looked at her backwards over his eyebrows.

"Am I disturbing you?" she inquired.

"Not in a thousand years. Come and talk to a fellow."

"I want to do some packing."

"Going away to-day, of course. I am right sorry." He managed that well and sincerely.

"In spite of colour schemes?"

He chuckled understandingly. "It's not so red, you know—sort of coppery, isn't it?"

"Honest-to-goodness red. Sure I sha'n't disturb you?"

"I wish I could help."

"That would not be permissible in any case."

There were a couple of large suit-cases and a leather hat-box, and these she proceeded to fill from a tallboy and dressing-table of old mahogany. Most of the stuff was light and delicately coloured, and all of it had a touch of some faint perfume—or was it freshness? She moved about on light feet, bending, using her hands, pausing with finger to lip: lithe, lissome, unconcerned, and talking frankly most of the time. Some of the talk went this way.

"You are to be imprisoned for another day, I believe."

"A nuisance, ain't I?"

"Not you. You don't know my Uncle Aelec."

"Uncle Hugh wanted me to meet him as one of the two or three—or nine or ten—worth knowing in this place."

"That would not appeal to you, of course—you do not think the place worth while."

"Be fair. I only said the place was slow—no doubt your uncle finds it otherwise."

"He sure does." The Americanism was pat. "And you know he lived in a big city for thirty years and was a busy man. There was no need for him to take up crofting as a living, either. That is only an excuse, and Andra MacLean and an occasional hired man do all the work—except in the garden. Fruit—black currants mostly—is his hobby."

"And what does he do besides growing fruit?"

"Fish and shoot, for one thing—or is it two things?"

"And then?"

She held her lip at that. "It is not easy to explain to town-mouse——"

"But I am no town-mouse."

"I understood you lived mostly in New York."

"Not on your life. How old do you think I am? Knock off four years at Princeton before they threw me out on my ear, and four more knocking about. As a matter of fact, even when I am at home I spend most of the time at Wander Hill—that's the Country Club."

"Yes, I've heard of your country clubs," she reflected scornfully.

"But Wander Hill is the real thing—not an excuse for fast moving. There is a sound brand of golf, as your Duncan knows, and the polo is real crackerjack—last year we sent a four to Meadowbrook. I didn't quite make the team, but I play a hardish game of tennis. And there's the boxing——"

He caught her smile and grinned a shade ruefully.

"I guess you'll not let me forget Cousin Don's pile-driver." He very much wanted to explain how the disaster had befallen him and how lucky Don had been, but that would be blowing his own horn. He wondered, with unaccountable discomfort, if this young woman knew the origin of the quarrel—and what she thought of it. That brought Norrey Carr to his mind, and he stirred restlessly. Margaret, too, was silent at her packing, and it was the young man who resumed the conversation.

"We got away from the point," he said. "You have not yet told me what your uncle does besides fish and shoot and grow fruit and watch the hired man work."

"All that would seem to make him a busy man," she said, with a gurgle of laughter. "But you at your country club naturally require a multitude of amusements to help you survive sixteen hours of the day. There is more in life than even play and work—much more. Apart from your club, what have you seen of country life? Been much in the wilds?"

He smiled a little banteringly. "Nowhere else—much," he said easily. "I belong there."

"You surprise me!" Margaret opened her eyes. "You like the wilds, yet the Highlands bore you. Where *have* you been?"

"Heaps of places. Say the Tetons, back of the Yellowstone, or the Sierra Madre on the wild fringe of Mexico. That's the country Eugene Manlove Rhodes writes about. Know him? No! He is a sound man, and knows his men and places. Back there for me, I think. You get colour there and the lack of it, grandeur and a devastating sameness—and oh, boy! the air and the distances. Well, I ask you——"

"How is it, then, that our Highlands do not appeal to you?"

"Anticipation outran realisation, I suppose. You know, ever since I was knee-high I used to hear dad holding forth about his 'ain countree,' and I had made a mind-picture that had put it ahead of anything on land or sea. The real thing was very different—had to be—and it deflated me rather. Your moors are unique, I admit, with that grey and purple wash over them, but then your horizon comes bang on top of them. Coming up north, I was shown a patch of low hills—the Grampians—which are about the tallest thing you have in the way of mountains. And I have been on the shoulders of

63

the Andes, behind Valparaiso, fifteen thousand feet up, and a white bonnet a few thousand higher. Then your fishing! You are easily pleased. One of your top-notchers will catch a salmon in a month and make a song of it. I have run a forty-foot cutter in the narrows about Vancouver, and hauled twenty-pounders inboard when I had a mind. That's a fact, not any boasting of skill, for I'm a dud angler. Shall I go on?"

"Let us have the worst of it," said Margaret in a small voice.

"Your shooting, then! I have not yet tried for your red deer, and cannot say if it is what it is cracked up to be; but your other stuff, what I have seen of it—grouse, partridge, duck, and such—is tame, just tame. No kick to it, and not a spice of danger compared, say, to mountain lion—or even big-horn—on the Rockies, and the big grizzly of the Kodiak. Do not think that, as the cowboy says, I am shooting my neck to catch your eye. Only trying to give you contrasts as I know them."

"Of course. You have been considerate and re-strained—merely knocked us down, and rubbed our noses in the mud, and walked on us a few times. The only thing that remains is the people. Well?"

"Don't know much about the people," said Alistair MacIan warily, his eye on her. He felt that he had had a fair innings, and—well, there was a touch of red in her hair, by Jiminy!

"You have met a few," Margaret enticed him.

"A few? Well, yes. They are good people, but they seem to live a pretty dead sort of existence. Quiet and staid, you will say. There's my uncle, now. Sir Hugh Ian MacIan, Baronet! A swashbuckling sort of handle, and to look at him, mouth and jaw, you would think he could bite rod-iron. Yet he is the mildest man imaginable, and spends his time pottering about—fishing some, shooting occasionally, fussing over a village ball-team—cricket, I mean—and forever, talking about his precious trees."

"You are good at vignettes. Go on. Whom else do you know?"

"The Fenwick boys are only here on holidays, and their talk is all Navy talk; but there's Johnny Ross, the keeper. A sound man. Been through the war—East Africa and Palestine—and observed life at unusual angles. I would like to take him out West."

"And he would not go. Then there's Mr Webster."

"Yes, Don does remind me some of folk I know. Knows the East with such absolute finality—take it or leave it—the Japanese guile, and the Chinese honesty, and all that."

"I fear you do not love your cousin. And Mr Long?"

"Paddy Joe! Not a native. He cuts a good wide swathe anywhere."

"Then there's uncle."

"Met him for the first time last night, but I like what I have seen of him."

"You should see more of him. Will you run over the women now?"

"No fear! One head at a time is enough."

"I suppose," she drew him, "you would say that they do not count—that they are much the same everywhere."

He looked boldly at the back of her neck as she bent over one of the cases. "I think," he said, "that you would count anywhere."

"Trying to make amends," she thought, with a little run of laughter, and deemed it safer to leave that subject.

IV

"You have not yet told me," Alistair insisted, "what one finds absorbing in this countryside—I nearly said this neck-of-the-woods."

"You are persistent. First I had to get your viewpoint, and you certainly did not hesitate to drive it home. You make me feel quite humble, and I doubt if I can pierce you to the heart." Margaret rose from her knees and faced him, crumpling in her hands some flimsy garment that she would have been sorry to crumple had she known she was doing so.

He looked down his nose at her, and admired the light of thought in her eyes, and the way her shoulders moved within the thin silk of her dress.

"Yours is a young country," she said tentatively.

"Old as yours, is it not?" he retorted perversely, though he knew what she meant.

"Yes, yes! But most of it—all of it except parts of Mexico and Peru—and Yucatan, say—was practically an unpeopled wilderness until the beginning of last century. Raw! Any life that moved in it brutish—animal merely—and non-cultural entirely. Mind left no mark on it. A land untoned by any contact with man the thinker. A wilderness where man was either thrown back on himself and went mad, or became absorbed in the unhuman savagery of nature."

"I can't say that I ever felt——"

"You were only after sport—a sojourner. You did not live there, and the wilderness had not time to claim

66

you. Is it not true that there is more natural ruthlessness amongst your wild men than amongst——"

"Steady on! Your own Highland records show some hefty smiting."

"Y-e-s!" she agreed slowly, "with a difference. But let me stick to my point. I want to contrast your young land with this old one that has been peopled for ten thousand years—or thirty thousand. It has been closely peopled too, and has absorbed the mentality of many races. Man is no longer himself here. He belongs to the place. There is some subtle evocation—aura is better—some subtle aura of old times and old ways, old wisdoms—old wickednesses also—that affect and claim a man: that are wholly satisfying and make life intensive in spite of all external sameness."

"Something in that——"

"And let me tell you that it will get you too if you are sib, as we say—and in race you are. Anyone it has ever claimed it has surely held, as it once held a dying man ten thousand miles away." And then in a low voice she recited Stevenson's poignant lines:

Blows the wind to-day, and the sun and the rain are flying,
    Blows the wind on the moors to-day and now,
Where about the graves of the martyrs the whaups are crying,
    My heart remembers how!
Grey recumbent tombs of the dead in desert places,
    Standing stones on the vacant wine-red moor,
Hills of sheep, and the homes of the silent vanished races,
    And winds, austere and pure;
Be it granted me to behold you again in dying,
    Hills of home! and hear again the call,
Hear about the graves of the martyrs the peewees crying,
    And hear no more at all.

"I know," whispered Alistair. "It held that man beyond doubt."

67

Both were silent for a little while, and both were touched. Then Margaret shrugged her shoulders and wrinkled her nose boyishly. The garment crumpled in her hand she smoothed ruefully, and laid with a patting motion in the suit-case. "That's about all," she remarked. "Uncle will fix the straps."

"Sorry I can't do that."

"So am I. He is a terror with straps—but perhaps all men are?"

"Sure. The hole higher up is a dare to a fellow."

A motor horn hooted outside, and Margaret, with a deft toe, flicked shut the lids of the suit-cases and ran them under the dressing-table. "Your friends from Highland Drum," she said. "You'll be glad?"

"Not so very," he said, whimsically doleful. "The air is too blame murky."

"You'll see your way all right," she encouraged him. "Say little and plead a head. I must have given you one."

"Not ever," he denied.

She shook back a curl and was out of the room in one quick movement, leaving the door ajar behind her.

CHAPTER VII

I

THERE was no one in the living-room, and Margaret went through it to the door of the porch. On the gravel outside the white paling squatted a long, low, maroon touring car. Three people had already alighted from it and were talking to Aelec Brands. One was Paddy Joe Long. Another was an under-sized, wide-shouldered old man, with a white bare head and nut-cracker jaws. The third was a young woman in some white film of dress. This young woman was bare-headed too, and the first thing that Margaret noticed was that her hair was not red, but very light and very fine, and with a matt lustre on it. Her eyes went over the garden and the cottage very interestedly, and finally rested on Margaret in the porch doorway without any diminution of interest.

"She is quite frank, anyway, is the great Norrey Carr," was Margaret's thought.

Aelec Brands was holding converse with his laird. "The laddie is doing fine, Sir Hugh," he told him. "A sma' dunt on the head never hurt a MacIan."

"Maybe not, then, Aelec," said Sir Hugh MacIan in his soft Highland drawl. "Was it poaching you were, when you found him?"

"Not at that time, Laird—and even so, you might be grateful, since I might not have come on him and me honest."

"And make a kirk or a mill of that, you'll say. Well, let's in and see him."

Aelec opened the wooden gate, and the visitors came up the gravelled path, the young woman leading with Paddy Joe, and the old laird and Aelec shoulder to shoulder.

"Miss Brands, this is Miss Carr," introduced Long.

The two bowed, and Margaret the stiffer of the two. It was Norrey Carr that put forward a hand in greeting.

They made a distinct contrast in everything but the fact that both possessed good looks amounting to beauty. Margaret Brands was fresh and sparkling, crowned gloriously, thought in her blue eyes, and with a skin so clear that it barely veiled the blood that ebbed and flowed beneath it. Norrey Carr gave a curious impression of weariness—weariness, not languor. Perhaps her heavily lashed, slightly hooded grey eyes caused, or added to, that impression. Powder or none, there was a faint peach-bloom of the finest down on her skin, giving it an effect as of pearl barely touched with brown. She was slim, but with a slimness that did not show a bone in her lissome long body, and when she moved she seemed to be moved by some force supremely supple yet supremely strong. And always there was that curious touch of weariness. And through that touch of weariness, through the calmness that was a natural pose, through the remoteness that was not an affectation, emanated another quality, more profound and very much more disturbing. It was not heat, nor electricity, nor what is called voluptuousness, but some subtle physical vibration that gave a sense of warmth. It came through the coolness of her hands; it put into her pearly skin a warmth

70

that pearls never have; it enriched the grey eyes dangerously, and made every fine hair on her head alive. A
disturbing quality indeed.

Margaret Brands may not have noticed all this, or,
being a woman, she may have noticed much more, but
beyond a doubt she was aware of the light fine hair, the
perfectly kept skin and teeth, the unusual attractiveness.

"What a lovely cottage, Miss Brands. The red of
those tiles is just gorgeous." Norrey Carr's voice had a
slow, soft huskiness—the huskiness of voices trained to
carry to far reaches of auditorium.

"It is nice, isn't it?" Margaret agreed.

Norrey Carr placed her hand on the Irishman's arm.
"Is this the sort of cottage you are always talking of
building in the wilds of Kerry, Paddy Joe?" she asked
him.

"'Tis so, girl. And much the same vision in the doorway as well."

"Alas! am I losing you, Paddy Joe?" said the great
actress sadly.

"Did you ever find me, woman?" said Paddy
Joe.

"Out of my road, people," interrupted Sir Hugh.—
"Margaret, my dear, Sara is going to have your life for
neglecting her a whole fortnight, but I am grateful to
you for nursing that nephew of mine. Will you let me
see him?"

Sir Hugh could be very brusque when he liked. He
looked the part, with his lean hawk face, straight mouth,
and undershot jaw, but in truth he was the most considerate of men in a countryside that is considerate beyond
all other things. He left the others in the living-room and
shut the bedroom door behind him.

"A nice mess you have made of yourself, Alistair MacIan," cried Sir Hugh, walking straight across to the bed.

Alistair grinned at him. "Has Paddy Joe been shooting his mouth about it?" he inquired, in his sometimes deplorable slang.

"He has. He said it was lucky that you fell on your head."

Sir Hugh was beginning to like this strange American nephew of his, and he was also rather shy of him. Brusqueness was his shield. He was an old stay-at-home Highland gentleman who had not been outside his borders once in twenty years, and the incoming of this youth from a nearly incomprehensible new world affected him more than he would say or show. Alistair was heir to Highland Drum too, and Highland Drum was the apple of the old man's eye. The estate had been developed along certain lines towards a permanent scheme of forestry, and the man who was to succeed Sir Hugh in carrying on this scheme must be considered thoroughly —almost passionately—must be probed and moulded and finally thirled to an ideal. There was the fear. Uncle and nephew were still strangers to one another, looked at life from different angles, could not communicate with each other readily. All there was at this juncture was an instinctive liking, and having that, Sir Hugh had hope also.

"Been talking to Dr Angus," he told Alistair. "He insists that you lie quiet for a day or two. You'll do that. Your Aunt Sara will be down to see you in the afternoon, and she thinks that you will be quieter here than anywhere." His tone implied that the aunt's opinion was final.

"Shall I not be a nuisance to Mr. Brands?"

"To Aelec Brands! Why would you? Aelec and I would do more than that for each other, and no favour thought."

"Mr and Miss Brands have been mighty kind."

"Of course. They count—you'll find that out. A dashed nuisance, Margaret's going off to-day. I don't know what Dod Brands can be thinking, hauling her back to London in August. Ought to know better—docs too." Sir Hugh stopped suddenly and, after a short pause, said quickly, "Miss Carr's outside. See her for a minute?"

"Glad to, uncle," said Alistair evenly.

"I'll send her in to you." He placed a hand on Alistair's arm. "See you this evening," he said, brusque to the end, and pulled the door open.

Alistair noted speculatively that his uncle had made no inquiry as to how the accident had befallen.

"Will you gladden him with a look, Miss Carr?" Sir Hugh invited, not so brusquely; and she came quickly, with an undulating litheness wholly feminine. Margaret noticed as much with the least little twinge. For once, somehow, she was not content that her own quickness and litheness were boy-like.

Paddy Joe Long strolled after. "He is my friend," he said, "and I will stand by him against all women, especially this one."

III

Norrey Carr, holding Alistair's hand, leant to the bed and scrutinised him. "Not bad, Alistair?" she inquired gently. "Really all right, aren't you?"

The dry coolness of her hand tingled in him and there was a trace of colour in his cheeks. "Why, yes, Norrey,' he smiled. "You're a cure in yourself."

"He has the finest nursing, anyhow," said Long at the bed-end.

"And a very pretty nurse too," Norrey added.

"She is going away to-day," Alistair told her calmly.

"She doesn't live here, then?"

"She lives to Lunnon Town—like yourself," the Irishman told her.

"I should have seen that."

"You shouldn't," said Paddy Joe. "That girl is not a London product—too much depth below the polish. But you——"

"My dear," interrupted Norrey, smiling at him, "whatever I have below you'll be the last to find out"; and she turned to Alistair. "If your nurse is forsaking you, 'Stair, I'll take her place."

"My poor fellow!" Paddy Joe commiserated.

"Don't let him phase you, Norrey. I'll stay abed long enough with you for nurse."

"You will that," said Paddy Joe.

"Leave my patient alone, Paddy Joe—don't you see he is tired? Come on and let me consult Miss Brands about his treatment.—I must have you well, 'Stair."

She patted Alistair's hand and caught hold of Paddy Joe's sleeve. She, too, avoided the subject of the accident.

In the living-room Sir Hugh and Aelec were looking out of the wide window and talking intimately. Margaret sat on the arm of a chair, and Norrey Carr came across to her, smiling pleasantly.

"I hear you are away to London to-day, Miss Brands."

"This afternoon."

74

"I am surprised at your father," said Sir Hugh gruffly, "hauling you back to London this weather, Margaret."

"But he is not, Sir Hugh," denied Margaret quickly. "He wants me to stay."

"You should stay, then.—Make her, Aelec."

"No," said Margaret. "Dad will be home from Geneva to-morrow."

"Geneva, indeed! He might have come to the Drum."

"But it was not pleasure that took him to Geneva."

"You see, Mr Long," explained Aelec, "my brother George is a policeman, same as I was."

"Give him his due, uncle," protested Margaret, rising to the bait; "he is Superintendent at New Scotland Yard."

"He could be no less," said Paddy Joe. "Thank God, I am an honest man myself."

"An honest man yourself!" mocked Norrey Carr. "Are you honest with yourself?"

"No, girl; but I am honest with you."

"I am afraid so, Paddy Joe. Bad as you are, I could not do without you."

She said it smilingly, with a curious affectionate crinkling of the eyes, and Paddy Joe smiled his queerly sad smile back at her. At once Margaret realised that there was some fine bond of friendliness between the two, and this realisation set Norrey at a new angle.

IV

While the others were getting into the front seat of the big car, Sir Hugh stood at the garden gate with Aelec

75

Brands. "What do you think of the lad in there, Aelec?"
he asked, a certain diffident inquiry in his tone.

"Right as a trivet in a day or two," answered Aelec,
patently misunderstanding.

"Of course, of course!" snapped Sir Hugh, looking
sideways at him. "Not much of the Highland laird
about him, is there?"

"His father was a MacIan—and, anyway, he is a
Macdonald on the other side. Blood like that will tell."

"Not a bad lad, I think?"

"He wouldn't be. He has spirit."

"Too much sometimes. He does not hit it off very
well with his cousin Don—but that is not very surprising."
Without knowing it, Sir Hugh's eye turned towards the
young woman in the driving seat, and Aelec noted that.

"Yon young lady is no' a Highlander either," he
remarked casually.

"That is not considered much of a fault these days."
Sir Hugh lifted his broad shoulders. "Ah, well!—I
should like him to like the Drum. He doesn't now,
I fear."

"Give him time, laird, and give us time too. We
have him amongst us, and if the core is sound——"

"Thank you, Aelec. It is what I wanted to ask you.
I'll send you across a brace or two of grouse for his
dinner."

"I have a chicken killed for his dinner—but the
grouse'll no' be wasted."

The old laird laughed, pressed the heavy shoulder of
his friend, and hurried towards the car.

CHAPTER VIII

I

In the afternoon Margaret Brands finished her preparations for going away. Her leave-taking of the Croft o' Drum filled her with a dreichness greyer than usual—an unusual touch of lonesomeness. While the pony—a cross between a hackney and a shelt—pawed the gravel and softly butted its muzzle against Aelec Brands's broad breast, she went into the inner room to say good-bye to Alistair MacIan. "I am on the top of the road," she said lightly; "if you know what that means."

"I get the slant of it," he said. "I hope you'll have a comfortable journey."

She leant an elbow on the low newel-post of the bed, drawing her gloves through one hand, and, in her travelling costume, she looked young and fine and very gallant. The costume was of a rich and soft shade of blue, with a swinging cape showing a lining of grey silk, and it had a soldierly smartness. Her hat, helmet-like, fitted so close to her head that all her hair was hidden except a curl or two about her ears—copper-red, embracing a face very tenderly coloured, and vigorously alive. There was in her eyes a quality of thought that was altogether apart from her good looks, and that might be equally attractive or that might abash very definitely. No man with wits would care to dare lightly the level look of Margaret Brands's blue eyes. Alistair MacIan met those discerning eyes now, and they gave him a little stab of apprecia-

77

tion, just touched with embarrassment. Here was a young woman who was different, that had to be taken at her own value, that plainly weighed a man actively instead of passively. And that was why he said, "I hope you'll have a comfortable journey," instead of the "Sorry you are going" that was in his mind.

"It will be a rather weary journey," she replied, "but dad will be at the end of it."

"You don't care a whole heap about London?"

"Not a very big heap, at any rate."

"An old burg, London. Should it not have acquired that aura of old places that appeals to you?"

"It has its own—yes, but—" She laughed, and gave a little shrug. "No time to go into that now."

"I am interested, you know. If this old pumpkin of mine was a bit clearer I might find a snag for you."

"No doubt you could."

"I shall be in London soon, too—I'm rather tickled with London. Could we not meet there some time?" There was no over-boldness the way he put it.

"Father and I will be very glad to see you if you care to call," she said graciously; and added, "we live out of the way, though."

"No place in London is much out of the way."

"High Barnet is. Uncle will give you the address. Good-bye now, Mr MacIan. Your head is no worse, is it?"

"Much better, thanks."

Their hands met and grasped firmly. Hers was cool and softly strong; she was glad to note that his, while warm, was dry, for she had a curious dislike for a moist hand. She smiled brightly at him from the

78

door, and he smiled back, though he did not then feel like smiling.

II

Uncle and niece had reached as far as the incline of the railway bridge on the outskirts of the little town of Muiryside, when a telegraph-boy met them. He vaulted off his bicycle while it was still at a good speed, skidded and braked with practised ease, and cried to Aelec, "A wire for you, Mr Brands." Internally he cursed his luck, for it meant his missing a satisfying gorge of gooseberries and white currants.

Aelec had pulled up as quickly as the boy, and reached a hand for the buff envelope. Margaret said no word, but drew in a deep breath.

"Brands, Croft o' Drum! For me, right enough." The happy grin that spread over his face as he read the wire reassured Margaret. "He cut it fine," he chuckled. "By Chippendale, he did!"

"Dad, isn't it?"

"The very man. It is for you. '*Called to Prague for ten days. Writing. Stay at Croft.*' Where else would you stay?"

"It must have been delayed in transit," considered Margaret, who could not see her father so nearly making a blunder.

Aelec examined the telegram. "It was, but not at Muiryside." He turned to the boy. "All right, Charlie —except you'd like to run out for a puckle goosies— eh?"

"I'll wait till you're hame some time, Mr Brands."

"That'll no' be long. Come you out on Sunday, then."

"Ay, will I," said the lad; and his red cycle seemed as live as a cow-pony as it swung round on the road.

"Well, and what now, my lass?" spoke Aelec, holding the restless pony on a stiff rein.

Margaret lifted her eyes from the wire that she had taken from her uncle's hand and smiled. "They say it is unlucky to turn back."

"What? Would you go on to London and leave me?"

She placed her gloved hand on his knee. "Of course not. We had better turn, then."

But Aelec did not turn. Instead, he mused with half-shut eyes, "Ay, it's unlucky, they say." And then, suddenly, "Tell you what you might do, since we are so far on the road. Take the train as far as Barnagh, and run across and see Mrs King. You know she wanted you to come."

"Do you think I should?" she hesitated. "Are they still at Reroppe Lodge?"

"She is. Tom might be across at Loch Ruighi with Archie MacGillivray. You could borrow the school-mistress's bike at Barnagh station and be there in no time."

"And my luggage?"

"Take your small bag—and the salmon. Davy Thomson, the keeper, will fetch them. Tell him it was caught honest."

"Will you manage all right, uncle? There's Mr MacIan."

"Plenty to look after him—except you'd like to do it yourself."

That remark, carefully made, without emphasis, seemed to decide her. "Mind, I'll not stay long."

"You will not, then. Over to-morrow only. I'll be at the station for you the following evening. We'll need our time now."

He flicked the pony with the whip, and they went at a hand-gallop towards the station.

It might be that Aelec Brands was too proud of his niece to set her attractions over against the attractions of even a great actress in the eyes of any man.

CHAPTER IX

I

It was the afternoon after Margaret's departure for Reroppe, and Alistair MacIan was out of bed for the first time. His neck muscles were still twingeful, but the eye dizziness was no longer troublesome. He, Aelec Brands, and Paddy Joe Long sat on a sloping-backed bench on the green outside the cottage porch and soaked in the sunlight. The terrier Fruachan lay, stomach on the grass, and his great head was stretched forward on his paws. It was an afternoon of sun, warm, but not too warm, and the thinnest of hazes dimmed the far prospects. The cottage looked west by north over the yellow Doorn sands, and the down-sloping sun had just come round the corner. On the carse below them the sheep-dotted, creek-scarred level had turned a greyish green, and the tall thistles were beginning to shed their down. If the gentle drift of air lifted into an occasional heat-swirl, a puff of down lifted with it and wafted lazily across the flats towards the river. With some mystic wizardry of its own that shimmering grey-green carse, with the thistle-down floating and dipping, held the eye against the splendid wide prospect of sea and mountain.

Paddy Joe Long sat well down on the bench, homespun legs thrust out, chin on breast, tweed hat pulled down, bulldog pipe tilted up at a rakish angle, blue smoke drifting as from under a pent-house roof; and when he spoke he spoke through shut teeth. "At this moment," said he, "there is not one thing in the known world that I could put my finger on and say, 'Wrong, be japers!'"

Aelec Brands removed his pipe from his mouth and rubbed the polished bowl of it against his nose. One arm rested over his thigh, and his great brown hand hung loose. "If only my brother Dod—and Margaret too—were living here with me——"

"A discontented breed, the Gael—always. Thank you your dour Scots God that you live here yourself. It is great folly to make absence regretful instead of enjoying the pleasure of anticipation."

"You don't know Dod."

"Except that he prefers life, and it crowded."

"Does he, then? It puzzles me that a man of his parts should be so held to brick and stone. He used to be able to tie a wee hook—no bigger than my nail there—would set the salmon shouldering each other to get at it. A hen-grouse whispering *Yow-ho-ho* on a fine October morning, and an old cock answering *Cabok-cabek*, and he could show you the two tussocks of heather that hid them. A November evening with a haar in off the firth, and a wing flick-flickering at the other end of the Doorn sands, and he'd say, 'Yon's a widgeon—or a mallard drake—or a golden-eye—or a danged auld sheldrake'— as the case might be. I've seen him knock over a poacher of a scart down by the bar at two hundred yards with a rook rifle, and a solan-goose couldn't come out of a dive as far away as the Sutors yonder but he could tell you the fish in its beak. A sound man!"

"A sound man, surely," agreed Long. "It might be that it is for his daughter's sake that he holds by London."

"I don't see any man leaving London and a good

profession for a one-horse show," argued MacIan. He was sitting stiffly in his seat, but probably that was because of his neck muscles, for his knees were crossed comfortably enough, and he smoked a cigarette lazily. He was bare-headed, yet the occasional drift of air did not move a single strand of his sleek black hair. Aquiline faces are usually meagre above the eyebrows, but this youth possessed a good head, and gave an impression of mentality rather than of the mere falcon qualities of force.

"The American," remarked Paddy Joe, "is not a discontented breed. He is only restless. In the States I saw men who could not sit down in railway trains—who could not sit still in their own drawing-rooms."

"Our restlessness has carried us far."

"Not as far as Aelec Brands has gone on his own road, and he has discovered the philosophy of Plotinus for himself.—Why did you leave Glasgow, Aelec?" The Irishman had very soon reached the stage of using the familiar northern name.

"I was born hereabouts," Aelec told them, "and Glasgow was always a strange town to me. It is a grand town to work in, and has decent folks bidin' in it, but it is no' the place for a Highlandman to achieve auld age in. So I came away."

"Why wouldn't you," said Paddy Joe.

Alistair laughed, and turned to him. "What about your own restlessness, Paddy Joe? Is it not time that you holed up in some Irish bog and let the legions thunder past?"

"Ay, and long past time," the Irishman agreed simply. "There's a reason or two I have—and here's one of them coming up the road now."

They looked where he was looking, and saw Norrey Carr and Don Webster come round the end of the croft-steadings some fifty yards down the slope. The two walked close together, and the woman was as tall as the man. She moved effortlessly, and the Japanese parasol over her shoulder made smooth curves against the gold of the Doorn sands far behind her. Don Webster's powerful shoulders almost touched hers.

"I want to get that girl safely married," said Paddy Joe. "'Tisn't as easy as it looks, and be damned to it."

"You have business with her?" commented Aelec. "Yon's a fine strong chiel with her."

"He is strong enough," said Alistair.

"But slow, you would say," said Long, completing his meaning. "Did you find him that?"

"I could show you—oh, bah! He stood me on my head, at any rate, and there is no use girding at the luck. All the same——"

"Exactly. Don is so damn sure, isn't he?"

"I like the way the young lady walks," remarked Aelec.

"Why wouldn't you? All proper women walk straight-footed."

"She could move fast if she wanted to."

"On or off the stage she can. I have seen her hold down a house with a gesture."

"It was on the stage I first saw her," half-mused Alistair. "Remember that season in New York, Paddy Joe? It was then I met you, too."

"It was so, boy avic. 'Tisn't much we have learned and nothing forgotten since that day."

They were silent then, watching the approach of the two. As Don Webster pushed open the gate for her, Norrey Carr waved her parasol at them. MacIan and Aelec got to their feet as she came up the path, but the Irishman made no move at all; hands deep in pockets, feet at the stretch, hat-brim over eyes, he smoked peacefully on. Alistair, too quickly on his feet, felt a rush of dizziness that seemed surging towards the blinding-point, and, holding his breath, reached a hand back to the bench. Norrey Carr stopped before him.

"Glad to see you on your feet again, 'Stair," she said, taking his hand. "Sit down and let me talk to you." She gave his hand a small push, and he sat down readily. His dizziness had already ebbed. She sat between him and Paddy Joe.

"A cigarette, Norrey?" Alistair tendered his case.

She looked upwards under her lashes at Aelec Brands. "I smoke only when I am on holiday, Mr Brands," she excused.

"My niece Margaret smokes at her work," Aelec said, and held a match for her in the steady bowl of his hand. "I'll get a canvas chair for Mr Webster," said Aelec; "and myself will get Else MacLean to draw a cup of tea for you, Miss Carr."

"What a dear you are! You know, I was hoping for a cup of tea after that walk. How many miles is it?"

"One," said Paddy Joe, "short. Women, God forgive them, are useful sometimes. If this one had not turned up, we might have got no tea.—Half a lump of sugar for me, Aelec Brands."

86

"And a taste of cream?"

"I leave that to yourself, my stout fellow."

"Did I hear Paddy Joe's voice somewhere?" wondered Norrey Carr. She turned towards him, her knee touching his, and put a hand on his arm. "I am here, near you, Paddy Joe."

He turned a lazy head and looked at her, his face melancholy but his eyes smiling. "You are," said he, and his eyes crinkled. "Damn it, Norrey, but you are nice. You remind me of Joan of Arc.

> Joan of Arc had cropped locks like the lint,
>   And the grey eye wide-set and a moulded mouth ;
> And so won the love of leal men without stint,
>   And dried the hearts of iron men with love's drouth."

The woman's nostrils quivered, her eyes had a grey soft glisten under a web of long lashes, and the dramatic sombre huskiness came into her voice. "Joan of Arc! Alas! The fortress I beleaguer is very hard to take, Paddy Joe. No Joan of Arc am I, hearing ghostly voices. I only know that there is life—a little of it—and love too. Like a stealthy tiger I would pursue what I want, and, having it, seek my lair circumspectly and in fear, for there are many opportunities for disaster, and little time to enjoy."

"Thou stealthy tiger! What pursuest thou?"

"I know what I pursue."

"And I only know what thou pursuest not."

"That you do not know either, Paddy Joe," said Norrey Carr. She turned to Alistair, and was no longer dramatic. Small talk went back and forth between them, and the young man felt the subtle appeal of her in every nerve of him. Any young man would—or any old man either. Don Webster, the silent one, sitting

87

back in the canvas chair, knew as much, and he watched Alistair with a sullen eye. Long, in turn, watched Webster, and presently addressed him.

"This better than slaughtering grouse, Don?"

"It is all right," said Don shortly.

"You folks have certainly got a strangle-hold on the art of taking things easy," said Alistair, a touch of envy in his voice.

"It is an art that takes ten thousand years to acquire," said the Irishman, "and damn few of us have acquired it."

"That reminds me of a theory Miss Brands was propounding."

"How jealous of Miss Brands I should be if she were here," said Norrey Carr.

"How jealous Margaret Brands might be if she were here," murmured Paddy Joe, and Alistair felt his face grow warm. "Let us have the thesis, fellow."

"It amounts to this: That you are a ghost-ridden lot, without self-volition or originality; that these islands have been peopled for such a terrific stretch of time, and by such a variety of stock, that they have acquired something spiritual that infects you all. How many different races have squatted on you, Paddy Joe?"

"Hard to tell. Picts, Britons, Scots—how do I know? Fomorians, Firbolgs, Tuatha de Danaan, Milesians, Danes, Normans——"

"Don't forget the Anglo-Saxon," reminded Webster.

"Glory be! How did I forget the only honest man?"

"Rather a wild theory," argued Don. "I would say that climate is the only agency——"

"I don't know, Don," interrupted the Irishman.

88

"Some of these races had a strange persistent wisdom, garnered slowly, like fine honey. When you come to think of it, these specks of island have been peopled so thickly and so long that the substance of them must have been used over and over again, and if there is anything persistent in life, then we are surely ghost-ridden. Maybe Margaret Brands was right—that wise young woman."

"I am to become spook-ridden too," concluded Alistair, "being a likely subject and not inoculated."

"No self-respecting ghost would haunt a Yankee," said Don Webster with derision, and Alistair had difficulty in curbing the little hot devil that rose within him.

"Don, boy," said Paddy Joe pleasantly, "some day someone will stand you on your ear, and no one will be sorry but yourself."

"Hush!" reproved Norrey Carr. "Here comes the tea."

III

By this time Aelec Brands had set on the green a cane-legged, tray-topped table with its due load of tea things. "Else MacLean," he told them, "is a shy woman—clean apron and all—and she'll no' set a foot ayont the porch."

"You have willing helpers," said Long; but Norrey Carr was first to her feet.

"Will you pour the tea, Miss Carr?" invited Aelec, who had been well trained by his niece.

She did that with practised ease, and Aelec did the serving.

"A griddle scone," said Paddy Joe, "one day old, or two days old, or not more than seven days old, with a

89

scraping of butter, slightly salt, and an application of honey—clover or heather—'tis a good food.''

"But excuses even an Irishman speaking with his mouth full," said Don Webster.

"'Tis true for you," agreed Paddy Joe.

The terrier did not show any dislike for Norrey Carr. He came quietly and laid his head on her knee, and looked at her out of his deep eyes; and she placed a long fine hand on his shaggy head, and fed him bits of buttered scone. "What a darling ugly dog!" she said.

"He is a good judge, Fruachan," complimented Aelec.

"He is a fellow-countryman of my own, that fellow," Paddy Joe told her.

"My poor old boy!" said Norrey to the dog, her arm on his neck, "you could not help that, could you? And what took you wandering?"

"In Glasgow I got him," informed Aelec, "from an Irishman."

"He must have liked you well," remarked Paddy Joe.

"It was the first time I saw him, and I only saw him once after." He held the small cup and saucer cupped in his great hands, and his eyes narrowed reminiscently.

"I wouldn't say you got him dishonestly or anything like that," Alistair prompted, "but how did you prise him loose from an Irishman?"

"Give him time," said Long. "He is getting to it."

"During the war it was," said Aelec agreeably, "and I only got him in trust. The powers that were in it did not think I was swack enough for sodgerin', so they made a 'special' constable out of me—down Cowcaddens way, not far from the shop I had. Plenty of your countrymen thereabouts, Mr Long."

"I'm no credit to them," said Long.

"And they no credit to their country," added Webster.

"A rotten sense of humour you've got, Don," said Alistair a little disgustedly; and Webster frowned at Norrey Carr's understanding smile.

"It was yon time of the Sinn Fein troubles too," resumed Aelec, "and up and down the Clyde the police had their eyes on certain men—and the men had their eyes on the police. One morning early, about the time when honest men are turning over for a last blink, I was coming home from a night patrol, when I met my friend Inspector Gilmour and a squad of plain-clothes men. 'Come on, Aelec,' says he, 'and let's show you how a real policeman does his work.' And, being given to curiosity, away I went. We got our man in a garret-flat, and made our call without chappin'; but, quick as we were, he was elbow-up on the bed, and a gun covering us. 'Not a chance, laddie,' said the inspector, cool as you like. 'There are too many of us. Have sense, and save your neck this once.' The lad saw that, and became quiet like a trapped tod. 'Ye have the call on me,' said he, putting away the pistol, 'but later on in the game I might fill a hand myself.' A small black-haired man he was, with a face like milk and no smile on it—a terrible man, they said."

"Such is the stuff of heroes," said Paddy Joe. "Cuchulain himself, of the Red Branch, was a small, dark, sad man."

"Maybe that. This man was no joke either. It was in searching the room we found the dog—a bit pup he was, a black curly mite under a chair, growling his wee chest out. I hauled him out by a hind leg, and grippit him in a safe place, and when he found he couldna use his teeth he became quiet, like his master. 'That one is mine,' said he. 'I'll be holding you responsible for him from now till hell freezes.' 'Have you no one could look after him?' inquired the inspector, casual-like. 'No,' said he, prompt as that. 'I would not know God Himself in this town of Glasgow.' Which was maybe a lie, but it is no' like he'd name a friend to *us*. 'I'll take care o' him,' said I; 'he's a game wee nickum.' The lad looked me all over then, so that I would bide in his memory. 'Thank you,' said he. 'I will mind you for that. He is worth taking care of—the finest strain of the Kerry-blue terrier, and honestly come by. If I never claim him you'll not be sorry.' 'What name have you on him?' I asked him. 'Fruachan-Gorm, and that means Blue Heather.' 'Thank you for nothing, mister,' said I. '*Ish binn an beul bidheas iadtha.*' 'Wo! Wo! Wo!' said he sadly; 'and is that your race? Gael against Gael! Ochone the day!'"

"He had a cruel tongue," said Paddy Joe. "It was a hard thing to say to you."

"I'll no' forget the way he said it. Well, the mindin' he spoke about was not long delayed—the morrow's morn it was. I had no right to be there, but the force was short-handed and some of us 'specials' had volunteered for what you might call the rough-and-tumble work. It was yon morning that the Sinn Feiners attempted to rescue the suspects on the road from Duke Street. There was blood flowed, and my black-avised lad was one of the two or three that got clear. And there was me with a gun set on me, and no waver to it, when by runs himself, his handcuffs dangling. 'Leave be, Danny,' he cries. 'That man is keeping a dog for me.' And that was the last I ever saw of him. I am often wondering."

"A small dark man and unsmiling," mused the Irishman. "What name did he go by, Aelec?"

"Tearlath Bergin it was in the charge."

The Irishman nodded his head, and after a pause said quietly, " Fruachan is yours, then. The man that went by that name will not claim any dog any more."

The way he said it made Norrey Carr turn quickly and look at him. He smiled at her, and placed a finger on her forearm. "The sun is going down on the hills, girl, and you have barely enough clothes on you to be respectable. Go home, now, or you'll have one of your throats."

"All right! Take me home, then."

"I will not. I am fine where I am—and there are things I have to say that no woman should hear."

She leant to her Japanese sunshade and got to her feet, supple as a spring. "Thanks for the tea, Mr Brands—it was lovely. When is Miss Brands coming back?"

"To-morrow. You'll be always welcome to a cup of tea, Miss Carr."

"I must come round and see her." Norrey turned to Alistair. "When do you come back to us, 'Stair?"

"On my two round feet——"

"Come on, now," she invited.

He hesitated. He wanted to accept the invitation, and he was not certain whether it was because of the woman's appeal or because of a certain desire to pique his cousin Don, but he knew that the queer dizziness of head with

93

the dull ache behind it would be no safe companion on a mile of road.

"Maybe he is no' rightly fit for walking yet, Miss Carr," put in Aelec; and the silent Don Webster smoothed the frown off his face.

"Am I, then, spurned even before my old age?" declaimed Norrey. "Alistair I forgive; but if Paddy Joe Long thinks he can do as he pleases and not please me, he is mistaken. Come!"

She slipped a finger inside the Irishman's collar so that he felt her touch upon his neck, and he, displaying some remarkable trick of muscle, lifted out of his chair as if plucked by a magnet.

"Very well so," he agreed calmly, and, putting his arm within hers, and his shoulder to her shoulder, moved towards the garden gate with, "See you later, folk."

For an instant Don Webster slumped glumly in the canvas chair, as if determined to stay there, but in the same instant thought better of it. "Let her have her chaperon," he muttered, and strode after the two.

CHAPTER X

I

ALISTAIR MACIAN and Aelec Brands settled themselves down on the wide bench and watched the three depart. Now that Norrey Carr was gone, Alistair had no desire to move, and it did not strike him as peculiar that he, of the restless spirit, could while away a whole afternoon sitting on a bench and talking to a man twice his years.

The Irishman and the actress moved well together. He was taller than she was, and his long legs, moving easily from the hips, gave his shoulders a lazy swing that matched the lissome sway that carried her forward. Don Webster, firm-strided, moved a little apart. Norrey, before she turned the corner of the steadings, swung a shoulder back towards them, the other resting against Paddy Joe in leaning, confident abandon, and twirled her raised parasol. They gestured in salute.

"There would be a great friendship between these two?" mused Aelec aloud.

"Unique. Recognised everywhere. Something fine about it, too. Paddy Joe is supposed to be a free-lance journalist, but really he is unofficial manager for Norrey; and, besides that, he is something between guardian and father-confessor—one moment blunt as a kid-brother, and next acting foil to her whims like an old dad. You saw?"

"I did. She goes her own gate, that young woman."

"By and far, you might say. And yet, I have never seen her do anything important without consulting Paddy Joe. Strange, isn't it?"

"It is, then," said Aelec. He produced his old leather pouch, and, elbows on drawn-up knees, ground a brown flake of plug between the heel of one hand and the palm of the other. "Women," said he consideringly, "are kittle cattle. They have the qualities that jabble a body's thoughts the wrong road."

Alistair said nothing, but looked at him sideways with amused eyes.

"There's yon young woman now, and I by way of observing her calmly as she sat here graceful as a branch of rowan, and maybe the rowan and she are moved by the same art—all aware of itself."

"You did not accumulate your wisdom in this neck-of-the-woods," said the Princeton graduate; but Aelec did not seem to hear.

"To look at her sitting here," he went on, "swaying a bittie now and then, you would not think there was a hard bone socketed into a hard bone. Like a coaching-whip, she was."

"You are some observer."

"And why should she be stirring the blood of even an old bachelor like myself?"

"And why wouldn't she?—as Paddy Joe says."

"Ay! Paddy Joe. Does she stir him too, I'm wondering?"

"Perhaps he has a harder shell than most of us—than Don Webster, for instance; and he seems hard-cased enough."

"That man is hard-smitten, anyway."

"No doubt of that. It is quite accepted that there is

an understanding there—not a regular engagement, so far as I know."

"He takes it for granted. I was keeping an eye on him as he sat on the green there. You know, young MacIan, in this place when we meet a body we observe him, because, as you might say, we have nothing else to do; or, as we would say, it is important to know the men that might trouble us, or that might not."

"Your views on Cousin Don would be interesting."

"I was only going to point out to you the way he felt towards the lassie. His een, like two pin-points, glowered at her and already owned her. In her company anywhere he is a man set apart from his fellows. Love— what we call that—to you or me might be only an obsession; it possesses him like his blood."

"The nature of the beast, I suppose."

"He could be terribly jealous—and dangerous at that. For a draw of breath, before he got out of his chair, he was mad with the Irishman."

Alistair laughed at that. "Think of anyone being mad with Paddy Joe," he cried.

"Think o' that, now," said Aelec. "Let me tell you, boy, that as things are, Don Webster will have that young woman, and Paddy Joe and you can gang any gate ye like."

"Will you give the young woman any say in the matter?"

"You're speirin' now," said Aelec Brands. His face was wreathed in smoke as he held his hands round a match to protect the flame from the gentle drift of air moving Firthwards towards the setting sun. Alistair was tapping a cigarette on a silver case.

"Man," said Aelec, between puffs, "you should smoke a pipe. You've a grand jaw for it."

"Guess I must learn. It seems to help you fellows in your cogitations."

"It does that. Sitting here, and smoking, and admiring the bonny view——"

"The view looks all right to me without any haze of smoke. How is it that you get those great purple splashes all across the green?"

"The shallow places—ten fathom about. A hand-line out there, now, and you might catch a puckle whiting and haddock, or, if lucky, a whale of a halibut. Good eating, halibut."

"You have a practical mind, after all."

"After all! You'll be thinking that Aelec Brands is a man given to idleness, a maker of excuses for idleness to lean on?"

"I'll be glad if you correct my impression," said Alistair laughingly. "I had observed that your hired man worked, but with little zip, and that his wife, Else, puts a heap of fuss into a little work, but—perhaps this is the slack season with *you*."

"Fine I knew your thought. What I would need to warn you about is not to confound work with drudgery. I catch myself doing it often enough. See this croft o' mine and the bit garden I have here; in spring and early summer, with the work piling up a week ahead, I am often wondering if I am no' just a natural-born auld fool, like a hen on a chalkit line. That clump of black-currants, now, behind the bee-hives. They're ripe and ower ripe, and I could be getting tenpence a pound for them from Hector Macdonald of Muiry-side. That'll be the work between now and harvesting, and let us be thanking Providence for willing hands."

"Ready, Capting! You know I rather admire your philosophy."

"Take you good note of it, then. Let us work a little —as we must—and rub our minds against a few congenial ones, to keep them polished."

"You can get these minds here?"

"You can get them most places for looking. A man here and a man there, a mile or ten miles or twenty miles away—all the better for the small spice of variety. There's your uncle, now, and Tom King of Loch Ruighi, and Archie MacGillivray of Aitnoch Hill, and others you'll no' have heard of; and there's yourself too," finished the wise Aelec, and had the blood in the lad's face.

II

Aelec Brands relit his pipe, his eyes, unwinking, not on the bowl but on the darkening hills beyond the sea that was blue and green and richly purple. "You can see the width of Scotland to-night," he said. "That wraith of blue away yonder is Ben More on the other coast of Sutherland."

"Some sunset, I grant you. I never saw that suffusion of light before. What is that peak away north there with the sun reaching down on it?"

"The pap of Caithness—the Maiden Pap."

"Pretty obvious name, isn't it?"

"All Gaelic names are. That's Morven, lord of Scaraben, ahint."

"That's flat territory north of it."

"Caithness, land of brawn and brains—a dreich, tree-

99

less land with a desperate bad coast and sailor-men to dare the deil—as hardy a breed of fishermen and deep-sea men as ever tailed on a rope."

"It looks a quiet enough coast from here."

"It was never ower quiet, the same Caithness. I was reading a history of it lately—your uncle has it—by a dominie who lived about the 'fifties, and had the same way of writing as well. We must tell Paddy Joe about him. 'The men of Caithness,' says he, ' were always noted for their love of liberty, and sent three regiments of Fencibles to help in suppressing the late Irish Rebellion!' In another place he complains how the land is overrun with tinklers—MacFees, Newlands, Williamsons, and that ilk. 'They remind me,' he says, 'of the lower classes of the Irish.' And, by his own showing, he was never outside Caithness but for three days he spent in Edinbro'. I ken something of what are called the low Irish—dealt with them professionally, man to man, as you might say, in the Cowcaddens—and in habit and mentality they are a good bit removed from the tinkler clan.—Queer chiels the tinklers! Some of them are come of the best blood of the clans, outlawed sons of chiefs and princes, too proud to do a hand's turn, and so, generation after generation, going down the slope."

"What gets me," said Alistair, "is the way your traditions are localised. Take this blanket-spread of county, not any bigger than a good-sized ranch, and up at Highland Drum Uncle Hugh has a whole shelf of old books dealing with it from all angles—history, archæology, ornithology, sport, every blamed thing."

"And some interesting stuff too, mister. You should read Charles St John and Dick Lauder."

"I will. Is it really a fact that that spit of land across there has a whole history to itself?"

"Ay, then, and as good as a novel. Them Caithness men were regular Kilkenny cats; a mixed breed, Norse and Gael, and the two bloods did not mix well. You can see the line of cleavage this very day. Up about Lybster you'll find big, fair, stocky lads, and down Dunbeath way tall, lean, black devils. Anyway, the Sinclairs clouted the Keiths, and the Keiths clouted the Gunns, and the Gunns clouted all round them, and whiles the real Mackay came up over the Sutherland border and took on the lavins."

"An interesting time. Say, how many counties are in this land of Scotland?"

"Orkney and Shetland, Caithness, Sutherland, Ross and Cromarty, Inverness, Nairn—wee Nairn—Moray, Banff—all the north was once the Province of Moray; thirty—twenty-five—about that."

"And all with their own local histories?"

"Ilka ane o' them. Our records up here are mild and mannerly compared to some of the real clan country and the Borders. Foray and battle even on. I will say, though, that yont there in Caithness was made the pithiest speech-before-battle I ever heard tell of—and I'm no' forgettin' the auld Greeks either."

"Let us have it."

"A Hielan' man it was made it—Glenorchy, one of the Campbells out of Argyll. As usual the Caithness men were argy-bargying about the earldom, and Tearlath, the king down in London, would put in his spoke. 'Go ye to the devil, Hielan' Stuart,' said they, 'and mind your own business.' 'Good!' says Tearlath, that canty, humorous man. 'I'll send ye a Highlandman to teach you manners.' And he up and made Glenorchy, out of Argyll, Earl of Caithness. Glenorchy was a good man of his hands besides being a Campbell, and he was nane blate, as they say. Away north he marches, two hundred miles o'er ben and glen—savage country for marching— with a tail of a thousand Hielan' caterans—lads of Glenorchy, Glenlyon, Glenfalloch, Glendochart, Achallader, all about the shores of Loch Awe and the flanks of Ben Cruachan—the family hill—bonny country and bonny men—tall, hairy, swank lads in the philabeg and rawhide brogans, with claymore and dirk, and no' a pound o' baggage in the thousand. They lived on the country, and it never a friendly country to the Campbells: a stirk here, a sheep there, a salmon net in a pool, a gralloched deer, a puckle fowl, a quern o' meal, and the clans closed in behind, buzzin' like bees and bidin' a maybe hurried return. A last march of thirty miles and there was Wick town in sight, and Sinclair of Keiss in front of it with fifteen hundred Caithness men. 'Will ye be for it, then, you Campbell robber?' says he. 'Tomorrow will do as well,' replies the canny Glenorchy, thinking that a night's rest in the dry heather of Yarrows would be no bad thing for his tired fighting men. 'Tomorrow be it,' agrees the Sinclair, and back to Wick with his men for a night of jollity and a boasting of how the Hielan' bodachs were feart and would run the morn. But in the morning when they sallied out, sair-headed no doubt and empty about the middle, there were the Highlanders posted on the Haugh of Altimarlach, calm as the hills and fresh like a tod. It was while the Caithness men were working up for the higher ground that Glenorchy spoke to his clan—in the Gaelic of course— and this is the English of it: 'Kinsmen, we are this day in an enemy's country. He that stands this day by me I will stand by him, my son by his son, and my grandson by his grandson; and be ye remembering that, if this day goes against us, lucky will be the man that ever wins home, for far is the cry to Loch Awe and far are we from the help of Cruachan. *Saus e*—fall on.' That was all."

"And they fell on?"

"They did that. With the thought of two hundred unfriendly miles behind them, and Wick town with its spoil in plain view ahead, they went through the Sinclairs like a puff of wind through chaff and were hacking through the High Street before height of day."

"And held it?"

"For a time. A thousand men, two hundred miles from home, could not hold Caithness for ever, and it angry. They held it long enough to make a Campbell bargain and to bring home to the Sinclair that Charles Stuart could bite six hundred miles away." Aelec finished abruptly with, "The sun is about down now, and I'll go inside and build a peat round a peat"; and in his own mind he added, "There endeth the first lesson."

III

Alistair MacIan made no move to follow Aelec within doors. He sat on, one knee over the other, hands in pockets, chin tucked in, a long-ashed cigarette hanging from his lower lip, and unwinking eyes staring beyond the glory of the north-west, where the heavens were vivid with gold and orange, and the strung black hills cowered below the immensity of the sky. Presently Aelec Brands put a head round the corner of the porch and looked at him for a full half-minute before speaking. In the toneless evening light the two, thus set, took on a surprising stillness.

"Are you coming in?" Aelec at last spoke.

Alistair lifted his head slowly—the voice did not startle him—and spoke without looking round. "How long have we been sitting here?"

"A matter of two hours—or maybe three."

"Or it might be four?"

"One hour or four—small differ anyway."

"So you say and believe, Aelec Brands. It strikes me as mighty queer, all the same. We have scarcely moved all that time."

"And what for should we?'

"Why should we, indeed? That was what I was thinking, and my thoughts led into many strange byways—dangerous too, perhaps."

"No' much danger in thinking—if a man thinks."

"I am getting a slant at you fellows at last. After all, you only accommodate yourselves to the only possible existence in this place. Men do the same everywhere."

"Your way of putting it. Another might not be so bold as to say that it is we do the accommodating."

"That it is the place that moulds? I see. Back to the same old theory." Alistair pulled himself together, rose slowly to his feet, and gave his head a settling shake. "I have another thought now," he said, "and a sudden one. Guess what it is?"

Aelec Brands looked sideways at him, and replied without hesitation. "You're thinking of walking round to Highland Drum."

"A whale of a good guess! How did you get to it?"

"Are you fit enough for it?"

"Absolutely. This afternoon of sun and laze has fixed me."

"Mind you, I am sorry you are going. Whatever Paddy Joe Long says, you are not a restless man."

"Thanks for all you imply by that," murmured Alistair.

"If you maun go," Aelec said, after a pause, "I'll see you to the head o' the road."

Pacing slowly, the two set off down the slope, and, where the cart-road debouched on the highway, Aelec halted. He felt that the young man wanted to go on alone. The two clasped hands.

"Thanks for everything," said Alistair. "Miss Brands will be back to-morrow?"

"Ay, will she. I'll try and keep her a week or two yet from that London."

"I must come round and thank her. That theory she unloaded on me—I should like—there's a snag in it somewhere—I'd like to get one of us on to it."

"You'll be welcome always, of course."

"And I'll ask you—might I?—to show me some of this country that should be mine—the place and some of the men."

"Surely, surely!" Aelec paused, and then went on quickly, "Care for a day's fishing? Would you be fit?"

"Of course. I would like some real fishing. Miss Brands—how did she put it?—you could lift a fish out of a whin bush, she said."

"I have done it," said Aelec, "after hiding it there first. To-morrow, I was thinking of a day on Loch

Ruighi amongst the trout. You'd meet Archie Mac-Gillivray and, maybe, Tom King."

"I am with you. When do we start?"

"The morning train from Muiryside—eight o'clock. Ower early for a sair head?"

"No fear! I'll be there."

IV

Alistair MacIan moved along the dusty margin of the road, slow-paced, straight-footed, hands in pockets, and no one would have taken him for a hustling American of the States. But, slowly though he moved, his thoughts were very busy, and hinted at some new orientation of motive not yet realised by himself. Something like this they went:

"Do in Rome as the Romans do—trite old saw. True enough, too. Where men take things easily hurry does not seem to cut much ice—leads nowhere. When there is nothing to do, is it possible that one gets to like doing nothing? Yet, do these people do nothing? Aelec Brands and Uncle Hugh? Doing nothing ends in slovenliness—a nigger's paradise. No sign of that anywhere. That cottage is a picture—ordered garden, trained fruit trees, straight fences, every sign of busy hands. Yet there was an unbroken placidity and one strangely alive—placidity with an edge to it. Is it that a certain philosophy ensures its own inevitable mode? More, is it that a certain philosophy is inevitable for right living? Questions to be considered. Anyhow, a good rule seems to be to take life as it is lived, to try to comprehend it by following the course it takes in different places—with discretion. Awkward sometimes! A butterfly in Paris, a gunman in Chicago, in London a cockney, in Dublin—what should a fellow be in Dublin?—a rebel?—I'll ask Paddy Joe! In the Highlands a mystic—is it? Say, it would be some fun to go back to Wander Hill and preach placidity. About now the boys will be discussing the nineteenth hole—that first cocktail after a shower tastes good. The lights will be on over the card-tables, and a couple or two zigzagging a Charleston. I guess they will be playing cards, too, at Highland Drum—bridge at fivepence a hundred. Norrey Carr doesn't play much. Norrey Carr! Norrey Carr! Norrey Carr! Yes! Nothing wrong with red hair, is there? I suppose up to a certain stage one can have duality of—sensation. Um! Up to a certain stage——"

The road he was on took a wide curve round the hillock that was Croft o' Drum and into the wooded valley between the croft and the next slope. In a long mile it came round in a half-circle to the Leonach River, which it crossed by a graceful suspension bridge, and so went on to the little country town of Muiryside. A quarter of a mile short of the bridge, and within sight of the Scottish towers that upheld it, a stone-pierced gateway on the right gave access to a fine avenue of limes. Within the gateway a plain three-roomed cottage served the purpose of a lodge.

Alistair entered through the open gates and went slowly up the lifting curve of the avenue. In a few minutes he brought into view the old house of Highland Drum, grey against the bold, wooded hill behind it. It was not the usual type of Scots baronial hall, being a long, flat-fronted, three-floored building of incut whinstone, the third storey dormered and with a flat roof of lead on top. A columned portico of mellow sandstone

sheltered the wide white door, and some modern im-
prover had built on at each end an immense bow window
with sandstone copings. A flush of Virginia-creeper
partly clothed the harsh whinstone. The sedate old house
looked out over a policy of forty acres, clumped with
trees, grazed on by sheep, and dappled with the green
fairways of a nine-hole golf course. It had an aspect of
security and serenity altogether apart from its solidity—
almost a spiritual quality.

It is not necessary to follow Alistair MacIan into the
quiet old house of Highland Drum, where his Aunt Sara
went sedately about her household duties and his Uncle
Hugh talked endlessly about his trees; where Norrey
Carr, a denizen from a more restless world, held dour
Don Webster on a string, and herself remained free to
let that string go and seize another; where Paddy Joe
Long looked on with ironic eyes, knowing Don Webster
behind his mask, knowing Alistair and his duality of
mind, knowing the woman to whom he was foster-father,
foster-brother, and waiting his own time to tie a string
securely at both ends.

CHAPTER XI

I

AELEC BRANDS and Alistair MacIan got off the morning
train at Barnagh, and, lightly burdened with fishing-
baskets and tackle, faced the four-mile tramp across the
hills to Loch Ruighi. A bare quarter of a mile took
them into the timeless serenity of the moors. A pine
wood, still and darkly green, rose up between them and
the station, and before them to a far-off horizon the purple-
brown moors lifted and dipped and folded in curves that
were clean and strong and infinitely sure. The sunlight
lay on the quiet breasts of them, and a single cloud
shadow flowed and vanished like a dream. One winding white band of road lifted and dipped out of sight,
and came up again far beyond, a thin white thread.
On the margin of this road the two fishermen walked
sturdily. Alistair filled his lungs with a great breath
and remembered a verse that Margaret had quoted.
"'And winds austere and pure,'" he said.

"Ay so," Aelec agreed. "The air is like spring water."

"This is some real country," the American admitted,
"and no stint of it."

"I do believe," Aelec told him, "you could walk on
heather from here to the Mull of Kintyre, and that's
over again' Ireland. Wait, now, till you get a glimpse of
the loch."

A half-hour of steady marching took them to the head
of the last brae, and they looked down the sweep of the

moors at the shining expanse of Loch Ruighi. A gentle breeze wimpled the mirror of it, and the grey walls of The Wolf's Island stood starkly out of the shine. The two men halted and admired.

"Perfectly adequate," said Alistair quietly. "How do you keep it all to yourselves? If we had this in the State of New York it would be ringed with flivvers, and you could not see the water for blown papers."

"We have a gamekeeper that terrifies strangers, and allows only two boats on the water—Archie Mac-Gillivray's and Tom King's. That's Archie's house in that patch of green above the willows, and there's Tom King's summer cottage on the other side—up there on Cairn Rua—and no' another house within the horizon."

"Except that old building in the water."

"And it's been empty these three hundred years or more. Yon was one of the strongholds of the Wolf of Badenoch."

"And he?"

"Love-son of a king, and a royal old robber baron—middling honest as barons went that time. He did no more than burn Muiryside and a bit of Elgin."

"He had a pretty safe place to hole up in."

"You might think so. Yet his own brother—but honestly come by—blew him out of it with cannon—culverins they called them—" Here Aelec stiffened at gaze. "Can ye swear, MacIan?" he cried.

"Some."

"Look at that boat, then—comin' out behind the island. It's the old *Nancy*."

"But why must I swear?"

"Man, dear—how are we to fish the loch?"

"Is it Chippendale or Sheraton you swear by in stress of weather? Say, there's a lady in that party."

"Of course there is. That's always the way with Archie. He is too soft with the ladies. A pleasant-spoken woman can wheedle the boat out of him at any time."

"Is not the boat his own?"

"Ay, but in weather like this he might jalouse that one of us would be up for the fishing, and he should have waited till well past train time before giving the *Nancy* to some ordinar' Grantown tourist. Come away down and let's hear what he's got to say—I'll knock his auld brown head off."

Aelec left the road and led the way over the heather. The ground between the tussocks was damp and treacherous, and Alistair admired the energetic certainty with which his leader picked a secure path. The young man did not find it altogether easy to equal the immense strides hither and yon from tussock to tussock. Ten minutes of brisk going brought them to firm ground, and presently they scrambled into and across an ancient cart-track, and so came down to the margin of Ruighi. Before them stretched a perfect sickle of pale gold sand, and the clear lake water came in, wavelet after wavelet, and washed to their feet in little sibilant babblings.

"My!" cried Alistair. "That water looks tempting. I am for a plunge in it before the day is much older."

"You'll find it bite. Come on, now, and let us find Archie."

Beyond the curve of beach they came on the out-flowing burn, crossed it by a ramshackle bridge, and proceeded along a pebbly shore to where a low dry-stone pier jutted into the water below a big willow. A hundred yards above and across a patch of thin corn a grey stone cottage looked down at them through blank windows. The porch door was open, and a black dog slept on the flagstone. Aelec turned his back to the loch, placed his hand by his mouth, and hallooed shrill as a gull. "We'll see who's in it," he said; and as he spoke a big bearded man appeared in the doorway. "That's Archie's brither, Hamish."

The big man waved to them, pointed over their heads towards the distant boat, and turned back into the house. Aelec jerked round to the loch. "The auld devil is out there," he cried. "Whoever is in it must be particular friends of his. It's no' everyone Archie'd gillie for."

The *Nancy* was drifting leisurely between them and The Wolf's Island, but it was too far away to make out the occupants.

"There is a lady in the stern," Alistair noted, "and at least one of the men is fishing."

"That's good ground there—shoal water and the big fellows skirmishing up from the deep places. Wait, now, and I'll try to inveigle Archie." Aelec placed the knuckle of his little finger to his mouth, and a tearing whistle ripped the silence of the hills. It finished with the weird, running thrill of the curlew. "Archie'll ken that. Listen, now."

Like a late echo the whistle was returned off the water, someone stood up in the boat and waved a hat, the *Nancy* nosed round bow on, and the water flashed where the oars struck.

"Here they come," cried Alistair. "Is it a case of out cutlasses and board her?"

"We'll be seein'. Meantime I'll hae a smoke to myself."

Aelec sat high-kneed on a round stone and slowly charged his pipe, while Alistair balanced on the edge of the pier and watched the approaching boat. The keen clean air blew about him, and somewhere back in the lift of the moor a hill lark sang a song that was as thin and remote and apart as a voice heard in dreams. Presently the young man's eyes kindled with interest and some surprise, and he glanced quickly over his shoulder at his friend. Aelec's eyes were on vacancy as he slowly ground a flake of plug in his great hands, and Alistair turned back to the loch. In a little while he spoke calmly. "I think the lady is Miss Brands," he said.

"She is," agreed Aelec just as calmly. "I was guessin' as much this long time. That's Tom King with her— and Archie."

"Two of the men worth knowing, you say?"

"Well worth knowing."

"So is the young lady," said Alistair quietly, and Aelec smiled.

As the boat came close the youth found it difficult to take his eyes off Margaret. She was still in her blue dress and her head was bare, and the sunlight on her red hair and in her eyes was good to behold—an out-of-door girl, at home in the wilds and amongst these men.

And Margaret, though less obtrusively, returned Alistair's glance, interest for interest. It must be remembered that she saw him on his feet now for the first time, and he was not bad to look upon; a tall youngster in loose flannels, his good shoulders easily aslouch, his bare head set well on a fine bronze neck, and no weakness in his clean-cut, serious Amerindian features.

Aelec got toweringly to his feet. "Get off that boat!" he roared.

The long-bodied man in the bow—a man with a lined, lean face and very live eyes—looked up at the hills and placed a hand to a listening ear. "That sounded like the ruffian Brands," he said surprisedly.

The man at the oars, equally long and equally lean, turned a mat of brown beard over his shoulder, and his blue eyes crinkled in a smile. "We were waitin' aboot for ye, Aelec," he said.

"We guessed you'd be, uncle—and Mr MacIan too," cried Margaret in a pleased voice. "Isn't it splendid?"

"It might be," said Aelec. "We'll be seein'."

The bow of the *Nancy* grazed lightly against the pier, and Tom King balanced on his feet and stretched a long arm to Aelec. "Well met, old Turk!" he greeted. "Is this the young laird you have with you?" As Tom King grasped and held Alistair's hand his eyes had a sudden piercing force, and then smiled. "We are glad to see you up here, Mr MacIan," he said quietly. "Will you come aboard?"

"Wait," cried Aelec. "What are we doing with the crowd?"

"Get in. We'll slip across for my coble."

Alistair stepped lightly on a thwart and back to the stern, where Margaret sat; Aelec dropped into the bow with Tom King; and Archie backed the *Nancy* off shore. Margaret reached an impulsive hand to Alistair, and there was welcome in her smile as she gave him room on the wide seat, moving the points of the rods curving over the stern to her other side.

"Mighty glad to see you again, Miss Brands," he said.

Margaret looked at him carefully and spoke in a low voice. "Are you feeling all right?"

"Right as rain. This sun and air would mend a broken leg."

"That's fine."

The two sat silently and watched Archie at work. His oarsmanship did not strike Alistair as orthodox, but his short choppy strokes with a kick at the end sent the *Nancy* slapping through the ripples at a remarkable pace.

"Spell you for a turn, Mr MacGillivray," Alistair volunteered.

"No' worth while, Mr MacIan. We'll be across in no time."

"Were you by way o' fishin'?" Aelec asked behind him.

"A few trooties in the bucket under the bow there."

Aelec bent to examine a dozen beautiful, brown-speckled trout, and spoke belittlingly. "Wee, wee! 'Twas murder to lift them out of the water."

"We hae to take what comes. 'Tis maybe nae as good fishin' weather as yon day in May that you two nearly broke the record."

"We would have, too, ye auld ——, but for you." Aelec looked round Archie's shoulder and spoke to Alistair. "That was a day made specially, clouds across the sun and a brush-by of a warm shower every hour or so. Tom King and I had eight dozen on the boat by twelve o'clock, and then along comes Archie with this girl here and Mrs King, and they would have a picnic on the island, and by comes a shower of sleet in the afternoon an' no a rise in the whole loch."

"What is the record?" Alistair inquired.

"Ten dozen and fower—all honest caught," Archie told him quickly.

"Who holds it?"

"Archie, of course," said Tom King. "It was he that set the ladies on us that day."

"Eight dozen was no' bad," said Archie complacently.

"I caught three myself that day," said Margaret; "no, not three dozen—three. I hope, uncle, you're not going to be selfish."

"Me!" cried the shocked Aelec.

"You must let Archie go with Mr MacIan in the small boat and show him the good places."

"Archie is not to be trusted," put in Tom King. "Did I tell you how he nearly drowned my friend, Norman Murray, last year? No? We were up at the Corran end in my coble, I at the stern with my back turned, Archie at the oars, and Murray with his feet dangling over the bow. I was fishing carelessly, and, when a half-pounder rose to me, Archie attempted to strike with a jerk of the oars. Followed a tremendous splash up at the bow. I thought a ten-pounder cannibal had risen out of the bottom to Murray's flies, and turned, hoping to see him into it. He wasn't there. He had disappeared—he had completely and entirely vanished. 'My heavens!' I cried, 'what have you done to Murray?' Archie examined the whole circle of the horizon, he examined the crown of the sky, he looked carefully into the bottom of the boat, and said in a tone of slow and weighty speculation, 'I doot he has fallen in.'"

"It was a reasonable thesis," said Alistair, laughing. "Could your friend swim?"

"Archie gave him full time to prove that he could not.

He reached him an oar when he came up for the second time, and hauled him inboard. There was Murray, his head over the bow, spluttering and swearing, and Archie turning to me in triumph with, 'I kennt fine he was in.'"

"Maybe, now, that's a sma' ex-exaggeration," said Archie mildly. "I never drooned an honest man in the loch yet."

III

The *Nancy* touched the other shore, where a miniature dock similar to Archie's jutted out into the water. Beyond it, across the gravel, a white road curved right and left, and beyond that the ridge of Cairn Rua lifted boldly to its crown of pine. Half-way up, a squat green-porched cottage nestled on a green shelf.

Archie turned his beard over a shoulder, winked at Tom King, and somehow indicated the two young people sitting at the stern. Tom King gazed solemnly back and nodded. At once Archie swung the *Nancy* stern on to the shore and backed into harbour, Alistair fending off the bow of the small coble that blocked the entrance.

"Step ashore, MacIan," invited Tom King smoothly.— "You too, Margaret." He carefully stepped over one of the oars, lifted Alistair's cased rod, and handed it to him. His hand leant gently against the wall of the little dock, and the *Nancy* floated softly back into the loch.

"Youth is not always served," apologised Tom King. "We old fellows sacrifice it when we get the chance. There's a landing-net in the coble, and Margaret knows the good places. Meet you for lunch on the island."

Until Archie gripped water with the oars Margaret could not realise that they were being left. And then she flared up with complete spontaneity. "It's a shame! It's a shame!" she cried in high fury, balancing forward on the pier edge. "Don't let them, uncle. Don't let them. It's wrong; it's all wrong."

"Maybe it is, then," said Aelec uncomfortably to his friend.

"I know, I know," said Tom King; "but I assure you, Aelec, it will be all right."

"I'd be afraid of that bit lass mysel' an' she angry," said Archie. "I'm in a hurry now"; and he laid into the oars with a will.

"It's a shame!" cried Margaret. She stamped on the stone of the pier. "Damn!" she said, and she used the word with spirit. "I'll never forgive them." She was really distressed and embarrassed. The betrayal was somehow too obvious, implying something that should never have been implied.

"I'll forgive them, if you will," volunteered Alistair. He was not embarrassed, and he was certainly not distressed. Yet he understood Margaret's sensitiveness, and had enough sound humility to escape pique at her very evident objection to being left alone with him.

"I will not," she said; and then the thought struck her that she was being rude. "You see," she explained with a half-truth, "I was not thinking of myself."

"I hope not," said Alistair mildly. "It's up to us to make our come-back good and hard."

"Let's spoil their fishing," said Margaret vindictively. "We could take all the drifts in front of them."

"Could we?" inquired Alistair doubtfully. "As a sort of fisherman——"

"Oh, I suppose not. Let us ignore them, then. Look, isn't that a bonny hill? That's Cairn Rua."

"And that's Mr King's cottage up there?"

"Was uncle telling you? They don't live there now —except for an occasional week-end—but over at Reroppe, six miles from here. Shall we go on the loch?"

Alistair stepped gingerly into the cockle-shell, helped Margaret to the stern, and shoved off. She was still a little self-conscious at being palmed off on him—or was it he that had been palmed off on her?—and to hide it she picked up the rod and began uncasing it.

"Going to try your hand?" inquired Alistair, feathering his oars like a craftsman—feathering very particularly too, for he wanted to show that he was a craftsman. "Let me do that for you."

"I like doing this. I often do it for uncle. Keep going for the island. I see the others are going on to the Corran end—they are in flight, I think. Isn't this a beauty?"

It was a beautifully made nine-foot rod of split cane, light and supple, and with a core of strength.

"It is light," said Margaret. "Will it hold a big trout?"

"Hardy's best—a few ounces under the half-pound, and it will hold and kill anything that will take a fly. The reel and casts are in the basket there."

"Let's see your casts, then."

"Aelec—your uncle—picked some for me."

Gripping the oars between thigh and body, he leant forward and watched her turn over the damp felts of the cast-box. The black head and the red nodded close together as the little coble lifted and dipped gently over the ripples, and a breeze, cool and pleasant, blew Margaret's curls vividly about her ears.

"Grouse-and-claret, a useful fly always; Greenwell's

Glory—uncle says that it is a Loch Leven fly, but good for Ruighi too; Dunkeld—no! This is a nice cast—Saltoun, Peter Ross, with the old Butcher at the tail. Shall we try it?"

"Sure. We have a different nomenclature in America. We call that a Montreal, and that a Beaverkill. There's a Seth Green, and that teal wing is a King-of-the-water."

She threaded through the tapered line, tied on the cast skilfully, hooked the tail-fly below the reel, and reached the rod to him. "We'll change places now."

"You try first, please."

"No. I like fishing, but I don't like catching fish. Come on! You must make a great big bag. I love to be at the oars."

Alistair was very careful as they changed places. The little boat rocked and dipped, and he placed a steadying hand on her arm. He felt the cool smooth of her flesh above the elbow, and she the dry warmth of his palm. She blushed faintly as she slid out the oars.

"There's a good drift in front of the island," she told him. "Wait till I get you into position."

The oars did not struggle uncertainly in the white-knuckled grip of her firm hands, and her shoulders went back in a fine easy swing.

"You pull an oar like one man," he complimented her.

IV

Alistair flicked his cast across the ripples to straighten it out, and, as they approached the island, turned his eyes to the ruined walls of the Wolf's stronghold. The courses of small time-worn stones set in a wonderful, cement-like mortar, lifted, plumb and strong, a sheer twenty feet, and were crowned by a plume of grass. A double barbican jutted out into the water, and a big breach in the wall showed the lush grass of the inner court. Two or three old ash-trees grew in the angles of the walls.

"That's older than anything you have in the States," Margaret felt called on to say.

"Built by white hands," added Alistair. "But in New Mexico——"

"Oh, I've read of your cliff cities," she put in. "Perhaps we had better avoid controversy. Are you ready?"

She swung the coble broadside on to the ripple, steadied it there, and shipped her oars. The gentle flow of air drifted the boat steadily offshore, and Alistair began to fish. To even the oldest fisherman the first half-dozen casts of the day give the finest, most expectant thrill, and Alistair felt it now as he gradually lengthened his line. At once Margaret saw that he could throw a line and place the flies softly down where he wanted them.

She was first to see the curl and boil of the rise. "Look," she cried. "Did he touch you? Your line is too long."

"My end-dropper," he told her. "He never touched me. Let's try him again." He drew a yard of line through the rings, and laid his tail fly where the ripple had been. At once a nice half-pounder came clean out of the water and dropped on the fly. As it touched water Alistair struck, and felt that wonderfully exhilarating jar as the line checked and the lithe rod-tip bent to the pull of the hooked fish. "Got him," he cried. "He's a whale."

"Give him line," warned Margaret excitedly. "They fight like furies." She felt for the landing-net, her eyes on the taut line that moved in little odd circles.

They had a pleasant, tense two minutes with that fish before Margaret slipped the landing-net below him and brought him inboard.

"A game chap, wasn't he?" remarked Alistair, calmly complacent. "Let me handle him for you."

"Thanks. He's the pink-fleshed kind—see the gold of him. I think we are going to be lucky."

They were. They were keen, and they were on their mettle. They would show the three men that there were other pebbles on the beach; in fact, they would have nothing whatever to do with them, and would fill a basket that would simply astonish and confound. They tried the island drift twice and landed a half-dozen, and then sought fresh ground.

"The shoal between here and Archie's," Margaret suggested. "There's a chance of a big one there, and then we'll try Clunas Bay—that's off the sandy spit yonder."

"Will you not take a turn?" invited Alistair.

"Later on. You must make the bag when the rise is on. I am enjoying myself."

"So am I," admitted Alistair. "This is a day and a half."

Time slipped past and the basket filled rapidly. An hour, two hours, a part of the third went by, and the two young people, immersed in their sport, interested in each other, talking easily or in silent thought, scarcely noted the lapse of time. Then the other boat came down from the Corran end, and Aelec, hailing them across a quarter-mile of water, pointed towards the island.

"Dinner bell!" remarked Alistair.

"I suppose we are entitled to our share of lunch," said Margaret, "but I do hate taking anything from them—and I could eat heather, too."

"Why!" cried Alistair, inspired; "there's a great pile of Aunt Sara's sandwiches in that oiled wrapper, and a thermos flask of coffee. We are free agents."

"Hurrah! Let us cross to the other side—there at the pines——"

"Fine! Let me take the oars, then."

They landed on a heathery spit, where tall, straight-stemmed pines grew thinly. The road, curving with the shore, wound into sight fifty yards away and swerved off again. They sat facing each other, their backs against slender tree trunks, and the pile of sandwiches between them. Their strong young teeth bit clean half-moons in the welcome provender; they looked serious confidence at each other; they smiled happily at each other; they spoke easily when they had time.

"You know," said Margaret, "we are trespassers here."

"How come?"

"All the circle of Ruighi belongs to Tom King except this spot, and this is where the Glenellachie shootings touch the loch. The tenant is a countryman of yours and a perfect terror to poachers and trespassers."

"Wouldn't mind a pleasant adventure," said Alistair. "We could go to jail together."

"I do hope," said Margaret, after another pause, "that Tom King's conscience is troubling him—and Archie's, too."

"No need," said Alistair. "This is all of a grand day."

"Then you do find something worth while in this countryside?" Margaret queried mischievously.

"Hit me as hard as you like, but I will not deny that I am beginning to—tolerate the place."

"Your Uncle Hugh would be glad to hear even that faint praise. You just appreciate it—in the by-going, as we say. You're of the tribe of sojourners. You'll lift sail one of these days and seek variety—or some strange wilderness."

"I admit it. I have already made some tentative arrangements for a big-game trip—East Africa."

"But you have your ideal home somewhere, haven't you? New Mexico, you said."

Alistair chewed a bite slowly. "One could always change one's mind," he said at last, and gazed at the loch through the gap in his sandwich. "You live in London yourself," he added.

"Yes, but when dad retires we are coming to live at Croft o' Drum!"

Alistair masticated another bite. "You know," he proclaimed, "this country is going to see a good deal of me in the next year or two."

"Tell Sir Hugh that too."

"I'm telling you now," said Alistair.

v

Lunch was over, not one sandwich was left, and Margaret was sipping coffee out of an aluminium cup, when the beat of a motor-car reached their ears. It came into sight round the curve, going very slowly. Fifty yards from them it stopped, and an Irish yell filled naked space.

"Paddy Joe!" cried Alistair.

"And your friends from Highland Drum."

"Damn!" said Alistair, under his breath; and aloud, "They'll spoil our fishing."

"If we let them," said Margaret.

Norrey Carr, Don Webster, and Paddy Joe bundled out of the long maroon car and came across the heather among the trees. Norrey had a half-grown spaniel puppy under her arm—a brown, affectionate small beast that ever and again lifted its sad eyes and wet nose to the down-like cheek above him.

"God bless the work," greeted Paddy Joe.

"It is finished, fellow," Alistair told him.

"Cripes, if it isn't! Only crumbs left."

"One cup of coffee," said Margaret. She looked at Norrey Carr.

"Thank you, Miss Brands—if you can spare it. It is a shame to intrude on you, but the day was so fine, and I kept on envying and envying Alistair. Where's Mr Brands?"

"On the island with Tom King and Archie. We ignore them."

Norrey laid the pup down, and he immediately enveloped the crumbs.

"Puir laddie!" crooned Margaret, pulling a long ear; "I am sorry. We were greedy." And the pup attempted to lick her nose.

Thermos flask under her arm, she went down to the water by the boat to rinse out the aluminium cup. Norrey strolled after. The silent Don leant his back against a tree and lit a black cheroot. He had not been at all pleased with this sudden trip to Loch Ruighi, but now he was not dissatisfied to find his cousin and Margaret Brands in company. The appeal of the red-haired girl might turn Alistair's mind from rivalry. It might—but what appeal could be greater than the magnetic one of the great actress?

Paddy Joe looked at Alistair whimsically. "What were you by way of doing, Yankee?" he queried.

"Fish'n'."

"Caught none," suggested Don Webster.

"A few."

"The smug tone of him," said the Irishman. "Caught a dozen?"

"I smile."

"Two?"

"And then some."

"You're another," said Paddy Joe pleasantly.

Alistair gestured towards the boat, and lit a cigarette carelessly.

Paddy Joe strode down to the water. "I don't mean that you are a liar," he said over his shoulder, "but how d—d small they will be."

They couldn't hear what Paddy Joe said as he bent over the basket of lovely trout, but Margaret laughed, and there was reprimand in Norrey's "Paddy Joe!" After a space, in which some low-voiced talk went on between the three, they heard Margaret say, "Try a turn with me, Miss Carr." The Irishman laid a steadying hand on the bow of the boat, and, holding her cup carefully, Norrey Carr slipped into the stern. Margaret followed and took up the oars, and then Paddy Joe pushed the boat out into the loch.

"That's d—d silly, Paddy Joe," objected Don, straightening up.

"Safe as houses," said Alistair, sitting down against his tree. "You watch Miss Brands pull an oar."

Margaret took a quarter-mile curve off shore, and Norrey lolled in the stern and sipped her coffee. They were not silent—no two women ever are silent—or unobservant.

"I have seen a picture of Grace Darling somewhere," said Norrey, "but——"

"This is only a calm bit of Highland loch, Miss Carr."

"I must get Paddy Joe to teach me to row."

"Why Paddy Joe?" asked the frank Margaret laughingly.

"Why, indeed?" agreed Norrey, echoing her laughter. "You see, I have got into the habit of looking to him for everything. He manages all my affairs—and what a slave-driver he is!"

Her eyes roamed over the silver ripples of the loch and the brown purple-washed lift of the hills, and she drew in a long breath of the keen air. "Oh! but I am sick of London and the stage," she said, and surprised Margaret, who at once showed her trait of seeking the motive behind speech.

"I understood the lure of the—your profession was life-long."

"There are other lures." Her meaning was as clear as the great actress could make it.

"Need you hesitate, then?"

"Well, you know, I have been sadly spendthrift, and am really very poor."

"Need poverty weigh with you?"

"I suppose not," agreed Norrey. She rinsed out the cup, and trailed it overside in the water. "A woman may choose a road clear-eyed, but it is not always easy to keep to it. That is why I am saving like a miser—driven by Paddy Joe."

"I see," said Margaret, who did not see very clearly.

Norrey glanced at her. "I suppose I am a hard-headed, callous person?"

"You may be hard-headed," replied Margaret, "but you are not callous, I think. Paddy—Mr Long would not do business with a callous person, would he?"

"You have been observing him. Like him?"

"Who wouldn't? He has reserve, of course——"

"You noticed that too." Norrey looked at Margaret with a new and close interest. "He has a secret core that —that one cannot pierce." She looked down at her feet and mused, "If he has a core."

"Be sure he has."

"Thank you," said Norrey; and Margaret did not quite know why she was being thanked.

VII

Back on shore Paddy Joe went up from the lochside, chose a tree carefully, sat down, and began filling a pipe. The half-grown puppy, having found the last crumb, came and climbed on him.

"By herrings, young fella!" he said to Alistair, "you must have been working like a nailer. I never saw a nicer catch of trout." He winked at Don. "Myself now, in a similar sitivation, mightn't have spent all the time fishing."

"Shut up, Paddy Joe!" said Alistair. "You do not know Miss Brands."

128

"She has red hair, by crums."

"Oh, go to blazes!"

"Why wouldn't I?" said Paddy Joe.

"But she has red hair, you know," said Don Webster reasonably. Alistair looked at him with a cold and calculating eye. He would not be drawn, even by Don.

Paddy Joe pushed his old tweed hat on the back of his head, exposing a white brow, leant his head against the tree-trunk, and, through half-closed eyelids, watched the boat curving out into the loch. After a time he spoke half-musingly: "They are nice girls, the both of them, and they are inclined to like each other too—only for a —a certain elemental rivalry—a sort of a—of a mutual —ah!—interest in a certain——"

Don Webster interrupted him frowningly, "Don't be a blasted fool, Paddy Joe!"

Paddy Joe spoke in the slow drawl he used when nettled. "You think you have a lien on Norrey Carr, Danny—you think that she is not a free agent because you are building a big house down in Surrey, to hold her as its principal good and chattel——"

"I won't stand much of this, Paddy Joe."

"I am a free agent too," said Alistair genially, "and I could build a big house anywhere."

"If you will discuss my private affairs I will leave you to it," said Don, and he stalked off amongst the trees. He went on a line that would meet the incurve of the boat a hundred yards or so up the shore and around a point. The young spaniel, seeing him forge through the heather, found its sporting instinct alive and galloped after him, ears awag.

"The hot devil!" exclaimed Paddy Joe. "In a

minute or less he would be apt to take a swing at one of us."

"I must give up joshing him," said Alistair. "I am not interested."

"Was it that wallop that made you change your mind? No! I was thinking myself that you wouldn't be so keen on a show-down. Go on! Swear away. Isn't it queer that two men'll pitch you to blazes in the same breath, and you'll have the devil's own inclination to swat one of them."

VIII

The two friends sat on smoking contemplatively and comfortably silent. The pine tops sighed gently above them. So five minutes passed—and then things began to happen.

First came the excited and ecstatic barking of the young spaniel discovering the meaning of life.

"That pup has found its nose," said Alistair.

"On the trail of a grouse, I'll wager."

Followed a crescendo of barking, the startling "keok-kek" of an old cock, an angry shouting and then the bellowing concussion of two quick shots—and one final yelp. Not the yelp a puppy gives in fear, but the sad, hair-stirring, hoarse cry that a dog gives when hurt to the death. The two were on their feet the same instant.

"My God!" cried Paddy Joe.

"A brute at work!" cried Alistair. "This is preserved ground, and the tenant a holy terror. Come on!"

The two went at a run amongst the trees, shoulder to shoulder, and there was something very similar and equally ominous in their going. Their line took them inland on a slant, and a slight rise of ground hid what was beyond. They topped this rise and saw what was to be seen. Margaret and Norrey stood together on the far margin of the road. Near them was a tall man in the subdued garb of a keeper, game-bag on back, long crook in hand, but without a gun. Ten paces beyond, and in the heather, Don Webster stood before a big man in a plaid suit, and was being abused savagely. The big man was gesturing threateningly with a double-barrel fowling-piece. Away to one side the young spaniel was lying amongst the heather stems—and lying still. The eyes of the two runners had sought out that still body.

"Dead!" said Paddy Joe.

"Oh, the swine!" said Alistair deep in his throat.

The two girls and the keeper heard the clump of feet on the road, and turned. Norrey Carr was very pale, and there was fear and pain in her face. Margaret was pale, too, but her nostrils quivered and the flare of battle was in her eyes.

Norrey saw Paddy Joe's fighting face—the stone of his eyes, the skin-tightened cheek-bones, the grimness of his mouth, and she cried out in fear. "No, no, Paddy Joe, you mustn't!" She moved with astonishing quickness, and her hands were against his breast.

Before Paddy Joe could break free—and he would have had no hesitation in doing that as roughly as need be—Alistair threw him a word over his shoulder.

"My job! He's American!"

"All right, Norrey," said Paddy Joe quietly, and he caught and held her hands for a moment.

Alistair in that glance over his shoulder had caught the flare in Margaret's eyes, the expanded nostril, the gleam of white teeth. He went into battle.

"Notice! Blast your notice! Take yourself and your carrion off my ground." That was the big man in plaid storming down Don's protest. He was a youngish man with a discontented, weary, big-jawed face, a face, somehow, tormented by interior fires.

Alistair came up the rise from the road, moving with a peculiar rocking lightness of foot. Don Webster found himself thrust aside and felt the swish of Alistair's shoulder as he went by.

"Another darned trespasser?" said the big man belligerently.

"Yes," said Alistair. "Let me show you."

The big man threw the fowling-piece up to his breast—and got it no further. Alistair's left hand caught the barrels half-way up, and the two men swayed together and back; and then the big man loosed the grip of his right hand. "Eat some, you mug," he said, his arm already on the swing.

Whatever Alistair had in the way of boxing skill he had nothing better than his left-hand counter—an upward drive from the hip, sent home by the shoulder. The crisp smack under the jut of jaw was as definite as the smack of billiard balls. The big man gave limply at the knees, the gun was wrenched away from him, and he toppled forward against Alistair's feet.

The keeper at the roadside took a stride forward, and found Paddy Joe's arm across his breast.

"You are not in this yet, my son," said the Irishman peacefully, but the glint in his eye was not to be mistaken. The keeper undid that stride. He was not afraid. He was ashamed. He was not above shooting a dog—a poaching lurcher or a marauding sheep-dog—but a half-grown spaniel, a game pup!—A leather strap or a touch of toe in a safe place—but never cold-blooded killing like this.

"Get up, you bully!" urged Alistair, flicking the fallen man with his foot; but the big man had had enough; he didn't even hear. Alistair used his toe again.

"You're a quitter, are you? Stay put, then, and I'll make sure you kill nothing more with this gun."

He turned and strode down to the roadside where a spindly pine-trunk rose handily. He passed shamefaced Don Webster on the way. "Too blamed respectable, Don?" he said bitingly.

Crash! The stock of the piece splintered and the flexile barrels wrapped round the trunk.

"Every crime possible against the sacred rights of property," cried Paddy Joe. "Assault, battery, opprobrious terms, and malicious injury. The whole gamut, by glory!"

Alistair dropped the gun, turned to Margaret, and caught the satisfactory gleam in her eye. "We are wasting time here, Margaret Brands," he said. "Let us go catch fish."

"Certainly," said Margaret, smiling brilliantly.

"Why wouldn't you?" said Paddy Joe.

IX

Alistair pulled forcefully out into mid-loch, and the heat of battle slowly died in him. For a time Margaret said nothing. "Let me have your handkerchief, please."

Holding the oars with one hand, he reached for it, and handed it across without question.

"Draw in your oars. I am going to bandage that grazed knuckle."

133

"It's nothing," demurred Alistair, as he obeyed her; and again the black and red heads bent close as she did her work skilfully.

"I have been giving you a whole heap of practice in first aid," he said, sensing keenly her soft and firm touch.

"You mustn't make a habit of it, though."

"Was I too strenuous back there?"

"Just adequate, I would say."

"Does your—is it sheriff?—jail folk for that sort of thing?"

"Sometimes. We have a good case, though."

"Could I put the blame on you?"

"On me?"

"Yes. It was the light of battle in your eye that drove me on. And you know it was the second time to-day that there was war in your eye."

"The second time? Oh yes! When we were abandoned. You did nothing adequate that time."

"I had no cause of complaint. Still, we might do something about it."

"What can we do?"

They looked over the width and length of Loch Ruighi, but the *Nancy* was nowhere in sight.

"They'll be on the island," considered Margaret. "Probably the trout are off the rise and they are biding their time. These three will sit for hours, and talk and smoke and laze."

"We'll do a bit scouting, then," said Alistair, and brought the head of the boat round to the old castle.

Very quietly they slipped down by the western wall, and backed water as they opened out the jutting bastions. They could just see the stern of the *Nancy* where it was moored to the shore, and, listening intently, heard the lazy murmur of voices from round the shelter of the far wall.

"They are there," whispered Margaret. "What do you propose?"

"Watch me," whispered Alistair.

X

Half an hour later Archie MacGillivray saw a trout break water a few yards off shore. "They're on," he cried, rousing himself from a lazy posture against the wall corner.

"Come on, then," said Tom King, on his feet. "It is time we had a look at those youngsters. They have been avoiding us very carefully."

Archie was the first round the corner of the bastion, and his stentorian yell brought the others hurrying. "She's gone," roared Archie. "She's no' here, whatever."

She was not. She—the *Nancy*—was dipping on the ripples a hundred yards off shore. Far beyond, at the foot of the loch, the small coble was on a drift of her own, and the two occupants were fishing industriously. All over the expanse of water the trout were rising greedily to a little dun fly that Archie could match to a nicety.

"You for a boatman!" cried Tom King indignantly. "Didn't you know she'd float?"

Archie, open-mouthed, was staring at a big boulder close to the water. He walked to it, and examined it carefully. "Three-fower times I lapped it with the chain," he said with awe, "and there's the lump of stane I clapped on the bit anchor. I kent fine the place was haunted."

135

Aelec grinned. "I warned you," he said triumphantly. "We were wrong to leave the two to themselves. Didn't ye note Margaret's eye and the quiet jaw of the American lad? I warned ye—I just warned ye. That boat is anchored out there."

Tom King laughed cheerfully. "We deserved it," he cried. "We did deserve it. Aelec, my son, that young man would be an acquisition up here." He looked keenly at Aelec. "And I bet you my life we are going the right way to bring him into harbour."

"Are you so?" said Aelec sourly. "But maybe you are asking me to pay too big a price in harbour dues."

"My fine old shell-back!" said Tom King; "you'll not be consulted about the price you'll have to pay."

"I know who's goin' to pay the price of this bit ploy," said Archie, his hands at his shoe-laces.

CHAPTER XII

I

THE black-currant picking employed many hands, but did not produce corresponding results. Aelec Brands, on one knee beside his bush, did more than his share, his great hands nimble, and the rich black fruit slipping from finger to palm to basket in a steady stream. Margaret Brands too, sitting on a three-legged stool below her bush, while more dainty of touch, was scarcely less effective. But Alistair MacIan at the next bush, not used to the work, picked his fruit individually, and his eyes would keep wandering to Margaret's hands. There was something graceful yet strong about those hands that moved him—the curve of them, the set of the little finger, the way the fingers bunched round a bunch of currants. Perhaps Margaret felt this scrutiny, or it might be that the extra touch of colour in her cheeks was due to her occasional bending to a heavy-laden branch, and probably it was the hot afternoon sun that made her pat down the old panama she was wearing until it hid her eyes. As for Paddy Joe Long, he pulled currants with industry —while he pulled them—but he had so frequently to straighten his back, and light his pipe, and drive home his point, that his basket filled no more quickly than Alistair's. When not speaking or listening he hummed the verse of a song.

"Have we this sort of fruit in the States?" inquired Alistair.

Margaret looked at him in surprise. "Surely you ought to know?" she said. "You are a town-mouse after all."

"No! I only skipped the cultivated belts between town and wilderness. This is rather like the wild blueberry, only larger."

"Currants grow in the States, anyway," Aelec told him, "or did. I read somewhere of the ravages there of a disease called bigbud. We have it too, and worse besides. I am beginning to be troubled about these berries."

"Snakes! What do you aim at? They are like small grapes, and there are pails of them."

"There is the trouble. They are too good. I'll no' be surprised at a touch of reversion next year—nettleleaf, as it is called. Just a bush here and there, the best ones, going back to the wild state. 'Tis a queer thing, but it looks to me as if we have overdeveloped the blackcurrant, and old Mother Nature is taking a scunner at us for interfering in her job."

"It makes one think," said Margaret. "Progress would seem to be no more than a series of curves."

"As far as I know," said Paddy Joe, "progress or not, no one ever succeeded in making a silken purse out of a sow's ear."

"A fool proverb that," maintained Alistair.

"For a fact," agreed Aelec. "A silk purse is a useless bit finery, but a pig's ear, with a boiling of greens and a floury tattie, is better than starvation."

"That's unfair," protested Margaret. "The meaning is, of course, that no one can be a gentleman who has not the qualities innate in him."

"That's heresy, anyway," said the Irishman ironically.

138

"To produce a gentleman you must have tradition," went on Margaret on her hobby. "A gentleman must be of the people, and know the people, and draw inspiration from the past. He must know implicitly. After that come the other qualifications."

"'Tis a race of men the girl has in mind," said Long.

"A race of men will be gentle surely," said Margaret.

"Bravo, Margaret!" cried Alistair impulsively, and no one seemed to notice his use of the familiar Christian name.

"Off and on in my spare time," said Aelec, "and sometimes when I haven't time to spare, I read books of history and books about men. It could be that, having taken no course in history or politics, I am wrong, but often the thought comes to me that if I was in the front o' trouble the men that I would want at my back would be the common men."

"They would have nothing to lose," said the Irishman cynically, "and everything to gain."

"Alas!" said Margaret; "what did they ever gain that had not been stolen from them?"

"True for you," agreed Long, "but no man should need much"; and, as if to prove his point, hummed an old verse out of the Gaelic:

> If *I* had a singing brown thrush,
>   And a hound that well knew I was God,
> And a rose peeping out of a bush,
>   And shamrocks in the green green sod,
> And a little, little small house
>   And a red, red apple tree,
> I would thank the Almighty God
>   So good, and so good to me.

"All very well, Paddy Joe," doubted Alistair. "Your simple life may look good to those who have tired of the other. A matter of contrast almost entirely. Do those who are compelled to live the simple life use their minds at all, I wonder?"

"My grandfather did," said Paddy Joe.

Aelec Brands looked sideways at Alistair and smiled to himself. "What kind of man was your grandfather, Mr Long?"

"He was a small man," the Irishman began readily, "and they called him Eamon Oge Kitoch, because his name was Ned, and his father Ned, and he was left-handed. I only knew him when he was an old man, and he was small then too—and left-handed as well: a small man, walking with short strides, his shoulders swinging and his hair white as snow. But when he was young his hair was black as night and blacker, his face finely pale like a pearl, and his eyes bluer than a very blue sea—a little man who did not laugh much, but smiled now and then like the sun. That is the kind of man he was. So my grandmother told me. A woman with red hair she was—begging your pardon, Margaret Brands—though her hair was like lint when I knew her."

"The red hair is forgiven," murmured Margaret.

"And how did he use his mind?" inquired Alistair.

"It was a small doubt that troubled him always about a thing he did, and in his old age I have heard him say, 'Maybe I shouldn't have done it—it wasn't a gentlemanly thing to do.' As I told you, he married a red-haired woman——"

"In a moment of mental aberration probably," said Margaret.

"It could be. But whether it was the red hair or whether it was the lack of fortune, Eamon Oge's father gave the young couple the door, for they married without his leave and were slow in asking forgiveness. Of course he forgave them in his own time, but, before that time came, the two had to live in a mud-cabin down by the Shannon mouth above the Long Strand of Ballyeigh, where the big Atlantic rollers come rolling and the horizon is laid down like a wire between Loop Head and Kerry Head, nine straight miles apart. Don't be thinking that a mud-cabin is a degraded habitation or a degrading one. It is the last word in cosiness, as I know who have lived in one. The lime-plastered walls of sun-dried yellow clay, three feet thick, and the roof of rye thatch make for equableness, winter and summer; and inside you have the packed floor, and the open hearth with its peat fire, and the high black rafters, and the firelight dancing on the dresser of delf."

"A king's palace could offer no more, indeed," commented Aelec.

"And places like that were once the palaces of kings. Anyway, Eamon Oge Kitoch and Ellen-Honora MacCarthy—that was her name, married or single—were happier than any two birds on any bough in any spring under any sky. They had their own two selves and a roof over their heads—black and red —and a piece of bacon hanging from the collar-brace, and hens picking about the door, and a patch of garden, and a small donkey with a cross on its back saluting the sun bugle-like on fine summer mornings. And round about they had neighbours, not too near and not too far away, who were kind and witty, and had knowledge of the subtle, queer ways that thoughts run. My God! was not that a grand place?"

"No place like that ever existed but in dreams," whispered Margaret.

"And what more are you wanting, young woman that wants the sky? This year—or maybe next year—I am going back to that place, and having sated myself with foolish dreams, will start dreams afresh."

III

Paddy Joe paused there, his eyes on the ground and his long face still as a stone.

"Your grandfather remains still a gentleman," Alistair hinted.

"And he after breaking the commandment—honour thy father and thy mother. He lived a long life, though, and so must have been forgiven by some kindly Jehovah. But—to go on—that place had its little cark of care, and it was this. The only fertiliser the cottiers had for their potato patches was the seaweed, the sea-wrack, the kelp —the stuff has many names. After the big winter and spring gales the Long Strand used to be ridged with masses of torn weed, and the men gathered and piled it when they had a chance. You would think that the weed harvested out of the sea would be subject to no toll, but Sir Jarvis Allison thought otherwise. He owned all that coast and the people on it, and insisted that his domain went out to low-water. 'Any small-holder,' he proclaimed, 'that gathers seaweed above low-water mark will pay my agent five shillings a year.' It was a small rent, but the people said, 'What grows in the sea belongs to the sea and the man that gathers it.' So there was trouble. Wardens were set to watch the beach, but in spite of them the weed was taken—in the dark of the evening, or at dawn, or in high day by the daring ones. Sometimes there was blood spilt and occasionally there was jail, but never at any time was there submission. That was always the way in Ireland.

"One spring morning, after a night of wind, Eamon Oge tackled his donkey to the car and went down to the Long Strand, and his wife went too. They were not long married, and they went everywhere together, laughing and joking and having great fun by the way, and an occasional frightened kiss when no one was looking—for it was considered a terrible strange thing that a man should kiss his wife. The tide was just on the turn, little lines of creamy foam ran all along the strand, and the wrack waved and looped in the greeny-brown under-draw of the water. Ellen backed the cart against a big flat rock that lipped out of the tide, and Eamon waded straight in and began forking the weed on to the rock. He hadn't six forks gathered, and him whistling, when a cry from his wife startled him. 'Oh, Eamon, we're caught!' And Eamon looked. 'We are, by gorry!' said he. 'That's young Blair Allison and the English wife he has lately brought home.'

"The Long Strand runs for miles, clean and hard, and it is the finest place in the world for driving and racing. Blair Allison was driving—two bays tandem in a mile-high dogcart with his English wife at his side and a groom in leathers behind. She was a wife to be proud of, too—young and fine—and good-hearted, as English women are. The bays came to a prance and a halt, and Eamon Oge stepped up on the flat rock out of the cold water and leant on his four-pronged fork. The two of them looked across at each other. 'So I've caught you at it, Kitoch,' called Allison, who knew my grandfather. 'You have,' said Eamon, no smile on his face, and when there was no smile there it was a queerly sad face. Blair Allison thought for a space, while the horses pawed the sand and jerked at their bits. 'I don't want to make trouble between you and my father,' he spoke at last. 'Fork back that wrack into the sea and get off the strand.' And I ask you, now, what would a man do and two ladies present?"

"How did the two men compare?" questioned Alistair.

"As I said, Eamon was a small man—five feet six about, with good shoulders and no stomach. Blair Allison was a whole six feet, and a wild black devil, by all accounts—like all the Allisons, afraid of nothing on two feet or on four."

"A case for discretion, you might say," said Aelec, smiling.

"And I suppose his discretion troubled his conscience ever after," said Alistair, a shade derisively. "A gentleman could always crawl out of it behind the ladies."

"Not behind the red-haired Ellen-Honora," said Margaret confidently, "who knew her husband for a king.—What happened, Mr Long?"

"I'll tell you. Eamon Oge said no word at all, but shook his head sadly. The sough of the sea was all around them, and the harness creaked and the horses snorted, and Eamon never used the raised voice. But the head-shake was enough. 'Hold the horses, Murphy Mal,' said Blair to his groom; and to his wife, who had grasped his arm, 'All right, Nance, I will be quite gentle. He is a decent man's son, for all that he is a young fool.'

144

"Meantime Ellen, holding the donkey's head, says to Eamon, 'Don't be losing your temper, Eamon Oge—you know the trouble it gives and it gone from you.' 'I can't promise you that, Ellen,' said he. 'But take that fork in your hand, and if you see me losing it, hit me a clout and I'll know.'

"So Blair Allison hopped down on the strand and moved his shoulders inside his coat to loosen them. He was a grand figure of a man, and wearing the old style of driving coat—tightly fitting from broad shoulder to lean waist, and flowing loosely to mid-calf. He came round the tail of the ass's cart and, 'Forgive me, ma'am,' he says to Ellen, 'I will do your husband no harm.' At that she smiled. 'Now, Kitoch,' said he, 'there's no need for trouble. This is our ground and you know it. Pitch the weed back and get off the strand.' ''Tis a great pity, Blair Allison,' gave back Eamon quietly, 'that you should put it in them words before your wife and mine.' 'They are the only words that express what I mean.' 'You and I will make a bad match,' Eamon told him. 'I know that, but you leave me no other alternative.' 'I wish I could,' said Eamon, 'and maybe I would, if I had time to think. Look you, now, if it is a test you want, leave things as they are this time, and come round here alone to-morrow morning. I'll be alone too.' 'Tut!' says the other; 'the thing is not worth all that trouble. I'll just take you off that rock and run you across the strand.' 'Both of us will be sorry about this,' warned Eamon, 'and your wife looking on.' 'I will not,' said Blair, laughing and advancing.

"He took a good grip of Eamon by collar and *bawneen*, and drew him off the rock soft and easy. 'The rock makes a hard fall,' Eamon said to Ellen as he went by, 'and I have my temper yet. Hit me with the handle only,' and his blue eyes dancing. 'Now for a run across the strand,' said Allison, and he made to shift his hold to the back of the neck. At the same time Eamon caught him the wrestler's grip at shoulder and hip.

"'The divil blast thim horses!' said Murphy Mal, telling about it afterwards. 'The minute the coat tails began to fly, up went the leader on his hind-legs, and when he came down again it was all over.'

"It was. Blair Allison—the whole six feet of him— lay back-down in the sand, his breast under Eamon Oge's knee, and his arms spread abroad and held as if crucified against granite. There was a cry from one wife, and Eamon turned his eye to see another with a fork-handle lifted. He had Allison on his feet the same as you'd twitch a marionette. 'There he is, ma'am,' said he, 'and no harm done. Take him home with you.' And that was all."

"And the big man was satisfied?" wondered Alistair.

"He was so. You see, Eamon Oge Kitochs are exceptional. As a general rule human muscle can be compared with human muscle, and lion muscle with lion muscle, and mole muscle with mole muscle, but now and then a specimen of abnormality is evolved possessing some terrific force unrelated to muscle. Where the force has its seat I do not know. Electric, maybe! Many of the heroes of tradition were such exceptions. His neighbours said of Eamon Oge that he had wings to his heart, and Blair Allison himself said that when Eamon gripped him he felt an explosive wrench inside him as if his heart had burst."

"Was there no trouble—did the incident finish there?" inquired Margaret.

"It did. Blair Allison hadn't a mean bone in him. Indeed it was he did most to heal the breach between father and son. But the point I want to put to you is that my grandfather could never make up his mind whether he had done the gentlemanly thing."

"He was as gentle as he could be, I think," said Margaret.

"With a fork-handle to remind him," added Aelec.

"He was challenged to a show-down, and gave weight away," said Alistair, "tons of it."

"Yes! but he knew that the big man was no match for him—that is what he meant. And his wife knew, and Murphy Mal knew, and everyone knew, except Blair Allison and his wife. Would it not be the heroic thing to refrain from standing a man on his head in presence of that man's newly-wed wife?"

"Something in that, too," agreed Alistair.

"How did he reason it out himself?" asked Aelec.

"He never could reason it out, and for the reason that he could never rightly decide whether it was the fighting devil that moved him, or whether it was the queer thought that there was a foreign woman looking on— English, you understand—who might be ready enough to despise an Irishman as a coward, and despising one, might despise all, and so despise her husband."

"Whew!" Alistair MacIan whistled. "Do peasants usually deal in metaphysics?"

"Plain reason only," said Aelec. "No man worth his porridge will do a thing unless he has a choice of two reasons."

"It was the remark you made, young man of the schools, that set me going," exclaimed Paddy Joe. "'Do the proletariat ever use their minds?' said you. Intelligence, wherever it is, will use the mind to its best advantage, and, when all is said and done, I don't think much of your schools."

"And mak' a kirk or a mill o't," finished Aelec.

IV

Thereafter the talk lapsed and the berry-picking went on steadily. In their nostrils was the clean, dry aroma of the black-currant leaves. It was not a very strenuous occupation, and the afternoon sun was no more than kindly in its warmth. Occasionally a few words passed between Alistair and Margaret, working near each other, and were followed by an unstrained silence. The young man's eyes were continually attracted by her fine hands.

"You were cute to choose sculpture as a profession— you have the hands for it, you know," he remarked.

"Thank you. Sculpture is not a matter of hands—a little only."

"Not altogether, I suppose."

"It is a hard trade, for a woman especially. It demands too much restraint—as old Dick at the school used to say—the austerity that imparts soul, and the restraint that freezes action in the very moment of explosion."

"That's good."

"We talk of squareness in technique, too, but that is an ideal almost beyond reach, for it is squareness without angularity. When poor woman has been free for a thousand years, and has suffered accordingly, she may create something original—and lose much also."

"And poor man will have gained nothing," put in Long.

"No one should lose by another being free."

"And that's true, too."

"He merely confounded freedom with licence," remarked Alistair.

"There's a young lady coming up the brae now," said Aelec, "who might be free as a bird, and will maybe suffer more than she deserves between her heart and her head."

Round the end of the steadings, in the long maroon car, came Norrey Carr and Don Webster, Norrey driving.

"You may be right, wise man," said Paddy Joe, "whatever you mean."

v

The car curved in, and halted outside the palings within a few yards of the berry-pickers.

"At the end of the long day they come," chanted Paddy Joe.

"A pair of hedonists lolling in the machine," added Alistair.

"To gloat over us, spent with toil—and unrefreshed."

"Good afternoon, Miss Brands," greeted Norrey. "Are your workers willing?"

"Very—at least, when they idle they make me forget it."

"Good day to you, ma'am," said Paddy Joe. "Isn't it grand weather that's in it, thank God, and isn't it nicely your father is looking there in the car with you?"

"My apparent age is due to fear. I have noticed that none of you scoffers have the pluck to risk this lady's driving," said Don Webster. "She has just brought me down from Dulsie Bridge on two wheels at a time."

"I'll risk your driving—anywhere, Norrey," volunteered Alistair, grinning at his cousin.

"Fine, 'Stair! We'll drive off and leave them all to-morrow."

"What about a cup of tea, Miss Carr?" suggested Aelec.

"Thank you, Mr Brands, but I am on business this time.—Where are those baskets, Don?—Lady Sara sent us across for two baskets of your black-currants—for preserving, she said."

"Pick them yourselves, then," shouted Alistair and Paddy Joe with delighted unanimity.

"But the pile you have picked? One—three—six whole baskets?"

"Filling an order," Alistair explained. "These six baskets are for a gent named Hector MacDonald, poulterer, fisherer, and fruiterer—such a darn combination—of Muiryside, who pays Mr Aelec Brands, vendor, twenty-five cents per pound, of which sum we, the employees, receive two cents—one penny. Sweated labour!"

"Did not the Irishman organise a strike?" inquired Don Webster.

"The strike is now on," declared Paddy Joe, hands in pocket, "and any blackleg will be peacefully picketed where it will do him—or her—most good."

"Fine work!" cried Alistair. "Go to it, Don."

"It will be all right, Miss Carr," said Aelec, stepping to the fence and speaking as if confidentially. "Yesterday it was, Hector MacDonald says to me, 'Aelec, I've an order frae Glasgow for fower baskets of black-currants—good anes.' 'My, my!' says I, that way; 'but they're scarce this year. I'll try and make up three anyway.'

That was why I told my employees I wanted six. Still an' all, Hector will not get the six, for like enough he'd say, 'I have sale for only the fower, Aelec, but I'll tak' the two off your hands at sixpence the pound and risk makin' my ain on them.' So I had the two bit baskets ready for Lady Sara—knowing the berries had failed on her this year."

"The brasted old Highland fox!" said Paddy Joe calmly. "The only thing now is to go home in the back seat with the currants"; and he moved towards the gate.

"But won't you have some tea," invited Margaret, "and Miss Carr and Mr Webster too?"

"Sorry, Miss Brands, but we were told to hurry." Norrey looked at Alistair, but he was in some intimate contemplation of his own.

He had been considering the two attractive young women and his own reactions to them—mental and physical—and had reached nowhere. What peculiar thing had happened him in the last ten days? He was no longer bored. He could sit round and talk, or listen, or be contemplatively silent—and be almost sluggishly content. He could argue endlessly with Margaret Brands—that was the mental side, or was it? Or flirt blithely with Norrey Carr, and so bait his cousin dangerously—what side was that? He could potter round with his uncle amongst the plantations and be interested. Darn it! trees were interesting—a man's job of work there. The outside seemed to be losing its pull. Why? If Margaret Brands were not here? If Norrey Carr lifted sail, too? Or had the place some queer pull of its own? Had it? Had it? Had it? Oh, bosh! He shrugged and waked up to smile at Norrey and turn to Margaret. "Was I invited to tea, Margaret Brands?"

"Surely. The labourer is worthy of his hire."

"There'll be fresh scones," Aelec said, "and a puckle fresh eggs as well."

"I did not know about the eggs," lamented Paddy Joe. "Why was I not told about the eggs? Ah, well! Don't let him eat all the scones, Aelec, and the strike will be declared off to-morrow."

Norrey Carr smiled at Margaret, and Margaret smiled back at Norrey Carr. Hardy fighting men smile at each other before the desperate final round, but what man may read a woman's smile?

CHAPTER XIII

I

WHEN they entered the living-room they found that Else MacLean had already laid the table, and had the black iron kettle simmering on the rack over the peat flames.

"I am beginning to like the perfume of peat," commented Alistair, inhaling.

"No' a bad thing," said Aelec.

"That will be all, Else." Margaret spoke to the housekeeper. "We can manage for ourselves now"; and, turning to Alistair, "You'll need to get some of that purple stain off your fingers, and I see you have been eating the currants. Come this way."

The "back-place" was spotlessly clean, the dishes in neat piles on the shelves covered with frilled paper, the washing-board scrubbed to the bone, and the porcelain sink gleaming white.

"Turn on the cold water, while I get some hot," she told him.

She returned with the black kettle in one strong small hand and a long towel over a shoulder, poured the hot water, and dipped her little finger in to test it. "Try that. The Vim is in that corner. It is not easy to get the currant stain off."

"Your turn first," said Alistair.

The whole operation was simple, homely, quite commonplace, but with its own importance. For here, in its placid certain way, was Nature sending ripples of thought and feeling to shores that are always new and always being discovered. Only two young people ministering to each other with cold water and with hot, and drying hands on the same towel, but imagination might reach to two young people alone and doing such things intimately, and not being interrupted by any third party, as now.

"Do you like your eggs boiled three minutes or four?" came the voice of Aelec Brands.

"Say three and a half at a venture, and the blame is mine."

"Come you, then, and hold this toast to the fire. . . . Toast made at a peat fire is good toast, but the fire must be red. Keep it away from that smoky divot. I'll make the tea myself. You'll maybe have noticed, MacIan, that no woman whatever can make any tea but weak tea. My own notion is that tea should be as strong as a small donkey, and boiled as well. I'm not allowed to boil it, but strength we'll have."

"Boiled tea! Isn't he dreadful?" exclaimed Margaret.

"I am used to boiled tea," said Alistair. "A whole fishing trip on the Ottawa we boiled the water, sugar, and tea together, and the milk when we had any. Palatable, hot stuff it was."

"It is a wonder you survived."

"Tea," proclaimed Aelec, "is no' a food, nor even what you might call a beverage, but only a sort of mild tipple."

"And boiling it for two minutes," added Alistair, examining the toast for brownness, "gives it the required kick that a tipple should have."

"You'll get no boiled tea in this house," cried the

baited Margaret.—"Are you boiling these eggs five minutes, uncle?"

"Adam and Hepplewhite!" cried Aelec, coming to the business in hand.

II

The three sat at the round pedestal table, and had tea. The dog, Fruachan, sat by his master's chair, his head on his paws, and occasionally his master's hand slipped downwards a morsel that was softly taken. There was no sitting-up-and-begging for that dog.

Alistair turned suddenly to Margaret. "When do you actually return to London, Margaret?" he asked her, now using the familiar Christian name frankly.

"Next week, I suppose. I have not yet heard definitely from dad."

"I ask, because Aunt Sara has been considering a picnic up the river for Saturday, and you and Aelec are included, of course. We might combine it with some fishing."

"Man, man!" protested Aelec. "Fishing and pick-nicking shouldna be mentioned in the same breath. Moreover," he added, with a grin, "'tisn't safe to go fishing with you two. Picknicking and fishing, indeed! But still and all—when Lady Sara gives the word—we maun try it. I'll be tying twa-three Blue Charms meantime."

"That's settled, then," said Alistair. He rose to his feet, stepped to the window, and looked over the case-ment curtain. "What a gorgeous evening—clear as a diamond. Who said rain?"

"And that's the why of it," Aelec told him. "The firth is no more than two steps and a jump, and there's

Tarbat Ness Lighthouse within the throw of a stone. You'll be waked the morn by rain dingin' on your window."

"Let us take advantage of the fine evening, then. What say to a walk Highland Drum way, Margaret?"

"That would be nice," agreed Margaret readily. "What about you, uncle?"

"No' me! I'll take a turn doon the watter and see if I wouldn't coax a finnock for breakfast."

III

Aelec stood at the door of the porch and watched the two young people go down the brae—Alistair, bare-headed and in easy-fitting flannels, inches over Margaret, who was bare-headed too, and had thrown on a light dust-coat. The straight lines of it emphasised her slim fineness. Shoulders back, arms aswing, head up and turned a little sideways as she talked, she moved with the verve and directness of youth, and the evening glory shone on her as part of its own.

They walked a good steady three-miles-per-hour rate, and there was no awkward pause in their talk, nor was there any trace of sentiment. Margaret Brands, unmistakably her own sex, had a live mind, and lifted the conversation above, or at least outside, sex. The young man found this rather pleasantly unique. He was masculine and ardent enough by nature, and, in the circle of his own society, approachable and attractive females were plentiful as berries. But in that society the subjects of conversation were strictly limited either by code or inclination, and most roads of intercourse led early or late to mild flirtation—or less mild—where a kiss might be as innocent as a handshake, and a Charleston merely bizarre instead of frankly sensuous.

The dog, Fruachan, followed at their heels very sedately, but at the corner of the steadings he turned and trotted back to his master. He did not gambol on the way, or turn aside to any scent or sound, but trotted as definitely as a pony, pushed open the gate with his paw, touched his lord's knee with his muzzle, and sat upright on the flagstone of the door, dignified and content.

"Maybe you are right, *Fruachan Gorm*, Blue Heather of Kerry," spoke Aelec, looking down at him. "You wouldn't have any interest with yon two, and they wouldn't be taking much notice of you. You and I don't be noticing each other much, but we know. They two will be thinking only of themselves, and pursuing the quirky by-ways of thought and dream. You knew fine, didn't you? Well, well! Margaret is a sensible wee lass, and let young Highland Drum mind himself."

CHAPTER XIV

I

THE Leonach River flows over basalt slabs in a valley of its own making. In places this valley opens out invitingly between a chain of green knolls, wood-crowned, and giving glimpses of the great purple-washed moors rolling back to the stone-ribbed hill of Aitnoch above Loch Ruighi; and in places it narrows to a Highland glen, steep-braed, grown with birch and alder, and crowned high up by the serene sky; and here and there it closes down to a gorge of red-brown sandstone, where martins build, slender silver birches cling precariously, hart's-tongue ferns hide in every crevice, and little trickles of water slip down through green mosses. But always the river flows, smooth and strong and richly amber, in a series of long pools with a slightly ruffled run between —perfect pools for the wise salmon to rest in.

Balchrochan, the upper fishing-reach of Highland Drum, is one of the Highland glens—a full winding mile from the gorge of Farness to the narrows of Larach, where a light suspension footbridge crosses the river thirty feet above the water. It is on record that the great flood of 1829 lipped the floorboards of that bridge. Balchrochan is fifteen miles from Highland Drum, by uphill road making one immense bow on the right bank of the river. No road makes a string to that bow on the left bank—there are only the dark woods of Doorn and the mystic upland shaw of Larach na Gael.

Healthy showers in plenty had come down from the hills on Wednesday and Thursday, Friday had cleared up nicely, and now Saturday was a day and then half a day, with plenty of water in the Leonach, the wind in the right airt, and the sky not too brazen. So the picnic was "on," and the anglers assured each other that there would be at least one fish to the rod, and there were six rods. The men crowded into the big car immediately after breakfast, and Norrey Carr rushed them up to the scene of operations; and in the early afternoon the ladies were no less crowded among the lunch-baskets. "Have a nice salmon to show us!" was Norrey's last command to the men as she coaxed the long car round on the head of Balchrochan Brae.

"We will," said Sir Hugh, with the carelessness of complete certainty.

II

They started the day in great spirits. The car gone, they filled pipes, shouldered fishing-tackle, and braced backs for the drop down over the shoulder of the glen. From the very beginning of the descent Aelec Brands was craning his neck for a glimpse of the river.

"Ye ken fine ye'll nae see it this side o' the birch knowie!" said Johnny Ross.

Johnny Ross, the keeper, was a youngish man, with lean ruddy face, and eyes blue as the flower of flax, with great shoulders, tireless legs, and a fund of character that secured him his own anchorage.

"Man!" Aelec said, "I'm anxious for a look of it. There wasn't the ding o' a shower the whole night, and the land is terrible thirsty."

159

"We'll find water enough," comforted Johnny, as in duty bound.

When they got through the screen of birches and saw the river slipping strongly past, an amber glint where the sun struck, they were pleased with the size of it, and Aelec, though he noted that it had dropped more inches than he would have liked, said nothing to dispel hope.

"Noo, gentlemen," said Johnny, halting the party, "we'll no waste ony time till the ladies come!"

"The usual plan?" inquired his laird.

"Ane ahin' the ither? Ower mony rods, Sir Hugh, and a waste o' time. Ye'll tak' Mr Webster and Aelec up to the Farness Pool, and I'll doon to the Narrows wi' Mr Alistair and Mr Long. That'll gie us half the water and a cast ower the pick o' the pools comin' on time for the ladies."

"I don't mind having a small bet on our side," challenged Alistair, "and chance Paddy Joe not finding a handy rock to rest behind. Are you on, Don?"

"Dinna bet, Mr Webster!" Aelec warned hastily. "It's unlucky enough we might be without that."

And when the two parties met at midwater shortly after midday they had had neither good luck nor bad luck to report, but an even sameness of lucklessness. Such lucklessness has been the lot of good men as often as not, yet good men still fish and will go on fishing. The salmon were in the pools, too, but would rise to no lure, and many were tried. Ever and again, and playfully, they had come out of the deeps in a slanting rush; occasionally only a fin showed, and the water no more than boiled when the fish somersaulted. But as a rule they came clean out of the water in a foot-high black-

and-silver curve, and smacked the surface with white belly so that the sound resounded amongst the boulders supporting the slope.

"Any luck?"—"No luck!" "Nae luck ava!" "Damn the luck!" So went the query and the replies.

"I can't understand it," wondered Sir Hugh blankly.

"If I hadn't seen their disdainful antics I would say there was never a fish in the darn stream," said Alistair.

"In the pool below Farness," said Don Webster, "I had a touch in the first minute, and thought luck was in. I never got another."

"I had a wee rug, too, in the Ess Pool," Johnny Ross admitted. "Just a nip in the bygaun! I'm feart the spate is stale, and we a day late."

"And that's your picnic for you!" spoke up Aelec. "Ye canna combine a serious business like fishing with such rickmaticks. Yesterday was the day. No man can expect to rise a fish in stale water. 'Tis not to be expected. 'Tis again' nature. 'Twas never known to happen. You might as well——"

"Wait ye," broke in Johnny Ross. "The day is no' by, an' we'll hook a fish yet."

"Ay so!— Broon trooties among the stanes out there."

"And nice sport too," proclaimed Sir Hugh, endeavouring to be optimistic. "The ladies will enjoy it."

"Well, we had bonny weather anyway," said Aelec, resiliently cheerful. "Look at the day it is, with the sun shining and the water running, and the moors up yonder all purple, and the white clouds again' the blue——"

"And a fine lump of rock warm with the sun," amplified the Irishman, "and another behind it for a back-rest, and my pouch full of cut plug. Thank God, the afternoon is left me!—What's the time, Sir Hugh?"

"They'll be here soon," said Sir Hugh. looking at the sun. "Don, you and I will daunder down and try the Larach Narrows, while these four strong fellows quarter up the brae to meet the ladies. We'll have lunch at the flying bridge."

"One—two—three—four! I must be one of the strong fellows," said Paddy Joe, and began prising off his waders.

III

The rock-bordered pool at Larach Narrows above the footbridge is long, deep, strong-flowing, and shaped like a bent arm. At the foot of it, under the bridge, a ridge of basalt shoulders out of the water, and the split current rushes furiously by.

Sir Hugh, scrambling along over the boulders, fished the whole length of it faithfully and fruitlessly, and Don Webster fell in behind and did likewise. Having reached the bridge, the old man came back to his nephew, and hope was not yet dead in him.

"I'll give it another turn before the picnickers arrive," he said, and went up round the bend.

He had just started casting when a shout from Don reached him. He reeled in furiously, thrust his rod against the rocky bank, felt for his gaff, and stumbled hastily towards the shout. Before he turned the corner he saw the point of Don's rod curving stiffly over the current, and the line making a straight line into the breast of the river.

"He's into him!" he shouted. "Keep your point up, man! Keep it up, I tell you"; and he scrambled so recklessly that he should have broken both legs, an arm, and at least one collar-bone. But he reached Don safely, shining gaff in hand, and his eyes shining just as brightly. The salmon was butting down the current, and Don Webster, perched on a high boulder, was grinding his teeth closer and closer as it approached the fast swirl at the tail of the pool.

"Give him the butt," advised Sir Hugh tensely. "If he gets below the bridge you'll lose him."

Don gave him the butt steadily and relentlessly, and brought his head upstream.

"Bonny!" cried Sir Hugh. "We'll get him now."

It was not Don's fault that they did not. He played the fish expertly, and, aided by the heavy water, wore him down in ten minutes. Sir Hugh chose a flat rock lipping out of the current a few yards below, lay breast down on it, chin over the edge, and gestured to Don. Don manœuvred the spent fish so that it drifted back close to this rock, and Sir Hugh slowly extended the gaff. It was probably the off-throw of the current that moved the salmon away from the rock—a bare few inches out of reach. The old man thought he could reach these few small inches. His breast was over the edge, the toes of his heavy boots clinging to a ridge in the rock behind. Another inch and he had him! He made it—he made a good deal more. His toes slipped over the ridge, and he went into the river head first. Souse! Like that.

And absolutely without hesitation Don Webster went in after him. He threw the butt of the rod from him, and went straight in. He did not know whether his uncle could swim, and, had he waited to find out, his uncle would have been drowned. At most Sir Hugh would stay afloat for ten seconds—the ten seconds that might elapse before his thigh-waders filled. And Don knew before he jumped that he himself, powerful swimmer that he was, might keep his head above water a matter of half a minute before his own waders pulled him under. . . . Yet he never hesitated. There was here no question of dignity or respectability, and there was no atom of craven in Don Webster.

One thrusting shallow swoop of a dive and he was at the old man's shoulder. And then, one after the other, quick and quicker, furious, side-shouldering strokes towards the ridge that jutted out of the river under the footbridge. Thirty seconds! and the current savagely and more savagely tried to drag him away and drive him on—and already he felt his waders dragging him under . . .

IV

The four men going to meet the ladies had no more than quartered up through the birches when the blare of a motor-horn reached them. They looked up the slope, grown with rank grass, clumps of straggling broom, and patches of close-set juniper, and saw the big maroon car squatting on the brink of the drop. A woman with a film of veil floating stood up in the rear seat and looked down towards them, and Alistair threw up his hand and yelled clear and high. The veil waved in answer, and in a second or two a halloo, clear as a bell, came down to them.

"My sowl!" exclaimed Paddy Joe. "The two of you can yell like a Kerry man. That's Margaret!"

When they reached the head of the brae, panting, the three ladies were on the grassy margin of the road, and had already piled the lunch-baskets—four of them—on the running-board of the car.

"Any luck, Johnny? Plenty of fish, I hope?" This was the direct Lady Sara. She was a robust woman of late middle age, still handsome in the Scots high-cheek-boned style. In her own domain of the house she was a power, and outside it did not pretend much interest. Yet the interest was there, backed by shrewd observation.

"The water's full of them," interjected Paddy Joe quickly.

"And the catch?"

"Myself, somehow, wasn't in luck's way, but Johnny, maybe, has six or seven hidden away."

"Nae luck ava, my lady!" Johnny shook his head.

"What?" cried the surprised Margaret. "Hasn't Uncle Aelec caught some?"

Uncle Aelec shook his head and remained firmly silent.

"He has a terrible fine lot of excuses, though," said Paddy Joe.

"Not a fish amongst them!" cried Lady Sara. "Well! well! Still, I suppose, we must give them luncheon. Down at the swing-bridge as usual? There's a basket for each of you men. We'll take the rugs."

They went down the brae by a smooth-worn path that wound and twisted along the margin of a thick ten-year-old plantation of spruce. Time and again Norrey Carr exclaimed on the quiet beauty of the valley that opened out upriver—the graceful sweep of the hooded hills from the gorge of the Leonach, the purple moors rolling back to the limestone crown of Aitnoch, and the great Cairngorm, smoky blue, behind all. The austere northern sky, a washen blue, arched immensely from horizon to horizon, and a few pale clouds tinged with autumn yellow floated tenuously far up in the zenith.

"This is one of Hugh's young plantations," said Lady Sara, at Alistair's shoulder.

"Very thick, isn't it?" he remarked, looking round the corner of his lunch-basket.

"He is thinning it out this winter, and is talking of planting all this brae. Too much for him, I fear!"

"He is a hot man on forestry?" half-queried Alistair.

"*The* authority in the north," she replied confidently.

"He could teach a fellow something about it?" he inquired tentatively.

"Depends on the fellow."

"It would, of course." MacIan said no more than that, but his imagination went off on a track of its own, where it dallied with even more than trees.

v

When they got down to the footbridge at Larach Narrows and piled their loads, they looked for Sir Hugh and Don Webster, but neither was in sight. They expected to see them industriously lashing the water in the rock-margined pool above the bridge, but the two were not there, nor were they perched on the rocks below the bridge where the river narrowed and growled sternly. It was only when Alistair went out to the middle of the footway to get a longer view upstream that a shout came directly from below his feet. Immediately everyone was craning over to look.

The footbridge crosses the river in two convex swings, supported in the middle by a thirty-foot trellised standard of steel, resting on a ridge of basalt shouldering out of the rush of the river. On this ridge, holding to the foot of the trellis, crouched Sir Hugh and Don, and the wash of the current lapped their feet.

"Thunder and turf!" cried Paddy Joe. "Are they after flying?"

"Just like Hugh," said Lady Sara resignedly. "He never came home dry from a day's fishing."

The two below were certainly damp. They had lost their head-gear, their hair lay in wet strands on their glistening faces, and their sopping clothes clung to them —except their waders, which were bulging, full of river.

Aelec Brands gazed open-mouthed, first at the two marooned fishermen and then up at the heavy-flowing pool. "My lord!" he whispered to himself, "and Sir Hugh couldn't swim a yard."

"I doot they've fallen in," said Alistair, remembering Tom King's story. He spoke lightly, because he did not want the ladies to recognise that a crisis had just passed. He and the other men knew that within the last minute or two some extremely narrow risk had been taken by one or other of the two below.

"We'll hae oor work in gettin' them oot o' yon," said Johnny Ross quietly.

"Not a bit of it," said Alistair. "Watch me."

He grasped the wire side-guard of the bridge and without hesitation swung himself over, his feet searched for and found the top bar of the steel trellis, and next instant, with the light ease of a gymnast, he was swinging downwards hand over hand. Margaret Brands gasped once, and then held her breath.

With the old man safely between them, Don and Alistair slowly and very carefully climbed the trellis-

167

work. Paddy Joe and Johnny Ross lay face down on the footway, and their whole torsos projected over the edge. The mighty Aelec Brands lay across their feet and grasped a wire stay. In a minute the three climbers were hauled, one after the other, to safety.

Sir Hugh, his hands already at the straps of his waders, glanced warily at his wife, and turned to Aelec. "Man, Aelec," he cried in a voice of loud ease, "we lost him, and the rod too—he was all of twenty pounds."

"He was a ton, more like," said Aelec. "Did he pull the two of ye in after him?"

"No, no!" Sir Hugh was as brusque as ever. "Don hooked him and played him bonny. All my fault. That rock up there at the turn—I was leaning over with the gaff ready—a bit excited, I suppose. I slipped and in I went—gaff and fish and all. Don"—he looked warmly at Don—"Don jumped in and pulled me out."

"Nothing at all," said Don modestly. "I wasn't sure if Uncle Hugh could swim—no trouble to reach that ridge in the middle."

"Bravo, Don!" cried Paddy Joe, slapping his damp shoulder.

Alistair looked down at the rushing water. By Jiminy! Don was a man after all. Quick to think, quick to act, and one chance in ten of pulling it off. And both wearing heavy waders, too. One slanting dive, a lucky grip, ten furious seconds half under water, and if he had missed that ridge—two bodies rolling over and over down the gorge.

"The best ever, Don," he said.

Lady Sara had been examining her husband with shrewd eyes, and saw that he had suffered no incapacitating shock. She put her hand on his wet sleeve. "You are wetter than usual, Hugh," she said. "You are going straight home."

"Nonsense, nonsense!" protested the hardy old fellow furiously. "What's a bit damp and the best of the day before us?"

"Then you'll drive straight up to Farness, you and Don—and get a change from the minister. It's that or home."

"Oh, all right, all right, woman!—Gives these waders a pull, Johnny.—Man, Aelec, he was a grand fish."

In half an hour they were back. Sir Hugh was wearing the dominie's Sunday suit, and it was some sizes too big for him, but he was so naturally careless about appearing ludicrous that he was not in the least ludicrous. Don, however, was rather shamefaced in a cast-off suit of the parish minister's, and an old-fashioned wing collar and black tie gave him a clerical look that was incongruous and yet not unfitting.

"His Reverence Father Don," greeted Paddy Joe. "Bless me, father, for I have sinned."

He bent his head for the blessing, and neatly ducked the playful side-winder Don launched.

Alistair here banged a tin plate with a spoon. "Grub-pile!" he cried. "Come and get it."

VI

Much of disappointment vanished as the viands spread themselves on the grassy margin of the path. There were piles of sandwiches and a perfect salad, and a trifle, cold as snow; beer in great bottles, and coffee for those who preferred it, and thereafter a variety of lazy poses and the aroma of Havana and the tang of cut plug.

"It was well done, woman-of-the-house," complimented Paddy Joe. "May God increase your store!"

"And not a fish to reward us!"

"There's a bit up by the Farness," said Aelec, "that's worth another try."

"Go to it," said Alistair. "I am perfectly happy where I am."

"But we must get a fish," cried Sir Hugh.

"Johnny," Margaret reminded, "you promised to give me a lesson in catching burn trout."

"I brought a rod and knee-boots for you, Miss Margaret," Johnny said.

"I'm not going far afield," said Lady Sara. "There's a nice runnel of water coming down the hill, and we'll set the dishes to soak in it."

And so, in time, the party drifted apart to please themselves. Sir Hugh and Aelec tramped off stolidly for the Farness; Margaret and Johnny Ross went up towards the shallows where the trout lurked in the eddies behind the smooth stones; Alistair and Paddy Joe, volunteers, were helping Lady Sara to burn all the loose papers and to rinse the dishes under a tiny cascade; and Norrey Carr, followed by Don Webster, went somewhat doubtfully out to the middle of the footbridge. The floor of it, even under her light feet, see-sawed flimsily, and Don, coming behind, made it rock unpleasantly. She grasped the wire stay, and shrieked faintly.

"Go back, Don! How dreadfully shaky!"

"Perfectly safe," assured Don, taking her arm steadyingly.

Holding her breath, she peeped over the side-stay downstream. "How ruthless it looks!" she said awedly.

Down below the narrowed river, heavy and dark, shouldered against the constricting boulders and went sternly by; a thin film of vapour steamed against the lichened face of the gorge, and delicate ferns tremored and bowed in the crevices of the rocks.

"How immensely brave you must be, Don," she breathed, with a new respect.

"It was nothing," said Don.

With difficulty she tore her eyes away from the rush of waters. It put a spell on her, took her rushing smoothly forward with it, coaxed her devilishly to rush forward and down with it. "Come away," she whispered, "or I'll be throwing myself over."

"I am here to take care of you," he said. "I am ready to do that always."

"Thank you, Don."

And Don felt that he had got a fresh and firmer hold.

VII

Alistair was stirring up the last scraps into a blaze, and Paddy Joe, having finished the rinsing, lay, back to a boulder, hat over eyes, and pipe smouldering. Passing his recumbent figure, Norrey touched the sole of a shoe with a dainty toe.

"What is it now, girl?" he asked, lifting an eye from under his hat-brim.

"We are going up to see Margaret at her lesson. Are you coming?"

"Faith, I am not! Don't get your feet wet."

Don laughed, and took Norrey's arm, and the two set off round the out-curve of the brae.

"I'll be done in a split second," called Alistair after them. "I want to see how the trout bite"; and, having finished his duties, hurried away.

Paddy Joe turned an eye on Lady Sara, drying her hands on a napkin.

"All right, Mr Long," she said laughingly. "Work is finished for the time, and you may go, too."

"I am in no hurry at all," he protested, feeling for his pouch with one hand, and tapping his pipe on a shoe-toe with the other.

"I am going to sit here in the sun and finish that pull-over I promised you."

"Great! I'll watch you for a piece."

From a corner of one of the baskets she unpacked her raffia work-bag, and, settling herself comfortably on a rug against a corner of Paddy Joe's boulder, began smoothing out a soft fabric of Shetland wool.

"It is fine soft stuff," he said, reaching a long arm to feel it. "That should keep me warm all winter among the dank stones of Fleet Street."

"If you remember to wear it."

"I will so." Over the match-flame pulsing in the bowl of the pipe he watched the deft white needles click and dart. Lady Sara's face was placid as she knitted, and now and then she glanced at Paddy Joe with an equable eye, and now and again up the valley of the Leonach with an eye equally equable. Talk moved easily between them.

"You are a great knitter, Lady Sara," he complimented her. "My mother was a great knitter too."

"All mothers should be great knitters," she said evenly.

"It is a pity that good knitting does not ensure mother-hood."

"How do I know, wise woman?" and he went on quickly: "My mother always sang at her knitting, sometimes in the Gaelic and sometimes in the Beurla."

"Beurla! Is that a dialect?"

"English, it means. This way:

> While grasses grow and rivers run,
> While sea-tides flow, and the wind with sun,
>   I'll hold my heart in hand,
>   And that hand shut,
>   And welcome Love's demand
>   With a sword-cut."

"That is a pretty air. Highland, is it not?"

"Brought there before history, maybe. Here is another one:

> For Ale it has a pleasing bite,
>   And Wine a soothing smooth,
> And Usquebaugh a blinding light
>   That gleams on naked truth.
> But ale and wine and usquebaugh
>   Have lost their taste to me
> Since she to whom I'm tied by law
>   Drinks my share of the three."

"I must learn that," laughed Lady Sara. "I felt the needles keeping time to it."

"We were all great singers in our place, except my father. He could not sing a note—only, maybe, the morning of a races, but he was a very knowledgeable man, all the same. He knew all about horses—race-horses."

"One of the evils of Ireland, I believe?"

"'Tis so, ma'am—same as good whisky and pretty women. My father says The Lamb was the best horse ever looked through a bridle. A black horse, with grey points, fifteen-two; and he won the National twice. A very knowledgeable man, my father." And Paddy Joe went into a fit of musing.

VIII

"Would you not like to go up to mid-reach and try the trout-fishing?" suggested Lady Sara presently.

"There are enough at it. There is the sun here and ease with it, a wide view to draw the eye—and, best of all, a pleasant woman to talk to."

"You Irishman! Remember there are two pleasant women—and young—up the water. I wonder how Margaret is enjoying her lesson?"

"She has a good teacher in Johnny Ross."

"She has. Poor Johnny is Margaret's slave."

"Why wouldn't he? And there's more than Johnny—including a young man you have in mind. Maybe you are a bit of a snob, Lady Sara?"

"A little bit, I fear."

"And how would you contemplate your nephew marrying an actress?"

"Which nephew?"

"Either?"

Lady Sara went on with her knitting for a space, and Long contemplated her with half-shut, sardonic eyes.

"It is taken for granted that Don is engaged to Miss Carr," she said quietly. "That is how they are here. How long have you known Alistair, Mr Long?"

"Long enough to know him—lived with him, eaten with him, been drunk with him—not very drunk, Lady

Sara; just sufficiently lit up to get a good look through the windows of the mind. If you want my opinion, and that is why you ask, he is as sound as bell-metal, body and spirit—a first-rate American gentleman, and he'll be a Highland one too, give him the right twist."

"I wish we could! Hugh likes him—so do I, of course. He has gentle ways——"

"He has so," said Paddy Joe. "He has as gentle a left hand as ever you saw. He hit me with it once—in fun—and I was gentle for all of ten seconds."

"Oh, in that way! But he is really considerate, and does not talk much for an American. If we could only get him to like the old place, but—he is so fond of wandering."

"Marriage might cure him of that habit," suggested Paddy Joe.

"Depends! Marrying Miss Carr, for instance, might not."

"Marrying another young lady might, you think. I don't know, Lady Sara. All I know is that, wise though you be, you do not quite know Norrey Carr."

"Hush! Speak of angels."

Paddy Joe turned his head, to see Norrey Carr coming round the out-jut of the slope, twenty yards away. She carried her hat in her hand, the sun was shining through the matt lustre of her hair, and she moved with an undulating lissomeness that made her at home among the stones and the heather. "I knew where to find you, Paddy Joe," she cried. "Has he bored you to death, Lady Sara?"

"He has been entertaining me," said Lady Sara. "He is kind-thoughted."

"I only got a word in edgeways," Paddy Joe demurred. "Divil a word I'll get at all now! What brought you here?"

"Don't spurn me, please. All the others have forsaken me for the trout. I am only a poor orphan, and no one will take any notice of me."

"Very well so. Come and sit down and listen to Lady Sara and myself."

Lady Sara smoothed the rug, and Norrey sank down gracefully between the two. A heather hummock made a rest for her elbow, and she curled her slim ankles back under the scanty hem of her dress—scanty enough to hint at the beautiful curve of knee. "This is better," she sighed. "I need some hard training."

Lady Sara fumbled in the depths of her raffia bag and brought forth a box of chocolates.

"How good, Lady Sara!—May I have one, Paddy Joe?"

"Only two, look you," he warned. "You are getting fair mountaineous."

IX

"Do you like this place, Miss Carr?" Lady Sara suddenly questioned, absorbed in some speculation of her own.

"It is heavenly."

"Would you like to live here?" The question was no more than casual.

"In this spot?"

"Well—in this countryside."

Norrey Carr's face was turned towards Paddy Joe, and she winked at him. He stared at her solemnly.

"That depends," she replied consideringly. "I do not care for London any more, and—well! one should have an interest in the country of one's choice."

"The choice is with you, of course," said Lady Sara, no sarcasm in her tone.

"I wish it were," said Norrey Carr with a quick sincerity.

"And it is time you made it," said Paddy Joe. "You can't have me looking after you always."

"But why not, Paddy Joe, dear?"

"Well, you can't, that's all. One thing, I will not have you making two-three-ten farewell tours. You are no longer a young bit of a girsha—not young at all, and making faces at me won't make you any younger." He lifted two fingers at her. "I'll see that you do one of two things, my girl: make provision for the old age you think so far away, or——"

"Or what, Paddy Joe?"

"Choose the countryside you are going to live in."

"I am doing my very best, and a little more."

"Very well so," said Paddy Joe complacently.

Lady Sara's finger-tips touched Norrey's forearm. "You are doing very well, my dear," she said. "I wish you luck."

After that the talk grew desultory. Lady Sara knitted more slowly and with many pauses. Paddy Joe seemed to sink deeper under his hat, and was gone far on some road of his own. Norrey Carr too was sunk in some daydream that made her face wistful. Her grey eyes, weary-lidded, wandered over the wide prospect of valley, moor, and mountain, but ever came back to the face of Paddy Joe, half-hidden under his hat—the point of his lean nose, the lined mouth, the long obstinate jaw.

Once she threw back her head and whispered to Lady Sara, "He is very pig-headed."

Lady Sara nodded.

x

When the anglers, all in a bunch, returned, the three were peacefully asleep: Lady Sara with her head against the rock behind and her hands on her knitting; Norrey, head on arm across the heather hummock and a soft air moving the light hair above her ear; Paddy Joe entirely lost under his disreputable old hat.

"By Jiminy!" cried Alistair, "they have chosen the better part."

Lady Sara opened her eyes placidly and smiled; Norrey sat up and yawned frankly; Paddy Joe started up, and his hat fell off. Quickly his hand went to his mouth, that had softened strangely in his sleep, and when he drew it away the firm line was again there.

The two salmon fishers had had no luck, and were beyond the stage of making excuses. The others had two dozen sizeable trout—plump fellows with the black spots and the strong jaw of the assassin. Margaret displayed the basket with pride. "I caught three all by myself—very nearly," she boasted, and Johnny Ross smiled.

"Now for some tea," promised Lady Sara, on her feet. "Mr Long will fill the kettle, and Alistair get the Primus started."

The tea was very grateful to all, but it did not succeed in rousing Sir Hugh and Aelec out of their silence. That was soon noticed and commented on.

"Wouldn't I be a stiff-necked bonehead," Alistair said

178

to vacant space, "to keep chucking a piece of tin before the nose of a disdainful salmon when brook trout are on the rise?"

"We make no complaint," said Sir Hugh brusquely.

"Not a word," said Aelec.

"Ye could, if ye dared," said Paddy Joe.

Aelec looked down at the river and then straight across at the westering sun. Lady Sara contemplated the two old men and smiled wisely.

"I suppose," she remarked generally, "that fishing is over for the day."

"I suppose it is," agreed Sir Hugh, with reserve.

"I always said," spoke up Aelec, "and I'll say it now, that this late in the year the only time for catching a salmon is the evening." He meant "gloaming," but thought it safer to use the wider term.

"Without a doubt," Sir Hugh supported him.

"We could prove it tae," volunteered Johnny Ross.

"But, Hughie! the car has to make a double journey," argued Lady Sara, who knew exactly what Aelec meant. "You could not think of keeping Miss Carr out after dark."

"We thought nothing like that," protested Sir Hugh.

"It was never in our mind," said Aelec.

"Why wouldn't it?" said Paddy Joe.

Here Alistair came in with a wild suggestion. "Could not some of us set out ahead walking? How far is it?"

"Fifteen miles," Aelec told him, and added hopefully, "downhill."

"Some trek! Is there no short cut—the road up seemed to be swinging all the one way?"

"Ay is there," Aelec replied drily, "but it might be

179

a case of longest way round, the shortest way home.—
How far is it, Johnny, as the crow flies?"

"A matter of eight miles, aboot, across Larach na
Gael, to the back o' the Drum. No' a road for a daunder,
as ye wad say."

Alistair persisted in pursuing his idea. "Only eight
miles!" he cried. "Any wash-outs or windfalls?"

"Oh, the going is all right," Aelec told him. "There
is no road or path, ye ken, but the woods, pine mostly,
are open, and there's no undergrowth to speak of.
That's the direction—dead north; but no man has done
it that I ever heard tell of—except, maybe, Willie Raasay,
and he bides there."

"Is that a dare, Aelec Brands? I've been with fellows
who trekked twenty miles through jams and windfalls,
and came out where they aimed."

"Ay, but Larach na Gael is a chancy place—a queer
lumpy piece of territory. There is no rhyme or reason
to the lie of the land. A humplock here throwing one off
the line, a bit valley there going widershins, a brae meeting another brae at an angle, and all of a sudden a spread
of acres, big as a park, level as a board, and the Scotch
firs all round it. You'd get your feet twisted in it. Willie
Raasay—he has a bit croft there, a cow and a few yows
—Willie told me that, when he came to bide there first,
he lost his way in it the early evening of a summer's day.
He wandered about most of the evening and a good bit
of the night, and in the end sat down against a tree and
fell asleep. At three in the morning and the dawn all
around him, he waked up, and there was his own wee
house fair in front of him, and he looking in at the front
door. He was never the same man after that."

"Bats in the belfry?"

"Daft? Na! Satisfied wi' things. He says he got inside the skin of the place, and could be content no place ither. He lives alone in the middle of Larach na Gael, and mightn't see a body in a month, except the postie, or the earl's keeper, or one of us that kens him."

"I know a place like that where I come from," the Irishman confirmed. "'Tis called the Pobal Dotha, a ten-acre field, grown only with scarths of briar, and surrounded by a dry-stone wall with a single gate in the square of it. A man I know, out poaching, tried to cross it on a middling dark night—over the wall at one end and through the gate at the other—and he never could strike that gate, and in the end he couldn't find the wall either. But that place is haunted, as is well known."

"I wouldn't say Larach na Gael is haunted," said Aelec, "but it has a queer effect on a man's mind, as well as on his feet."

"You seem to know it?" said Don Webster.

"Not the width of it. Been to Willie's bothy from the other side, where there's a cart-track off the Nairn road, and round the edges of it on a roe hunt. The roes like it, and so do the capercailzie."

"Plague take the big brutes!" said Sir Hugh the forester. "Don't forget the ants, though. All through the open woods there are ant-heaps—big as a haycock—and the little beasts go about their business without a sound."

"The empire of the ants!" cried Margaret. "Remember that story by Wells!—Don't you venture, Alistair MacIan. There might be a corbie craw to sit on your 'white hause bane' and pike out your 'bonny blue e'en.'"

"Nonsense!" cried Alistair. "You folk are trying to work up an atmosphere. Look at the facts! Eight miles straight across from here, the sun setting over there, and a glow in the north for hours after. A man used to the open, and keeping his head, should come out at the other side in a matter of three hours."

"Are you for trying it?" inquired Paddy Joe.

"I would like to," said Alistair.

"I'll come with you, Alistair," cried Norrey Carr.

And here, with suspicious promptness, Lady Sara put her foot down. She would simply not permit it. It was too risky, with the night coming on. If these two silly old anglers wanted another hour's fishing, let them fish. Meantime the ladies and the young people would motor home, and Alistair could return for the two.

With that Alistair had to be content. He was considerate enough not to out-stubborn his aunt when he noted the stubborn set of her jaw. And perhaps something told him that soon enough he would experience the atmosphere of Larach na Gael.

And the two doughty fishermen caught each his salmon, and the day was complete.

CHAPTER XV

I

IT was a particularly beautiful forenoon. The rain of the previous days had washed the air clear, white cloud-islands reposed high up in the immense dome of the sky, and the September sun had the fervour of farewell in its warmth. On the lawn, outside the old house of Highland Drum, Norrey Carr lay her slim length on the hammock under the walnut trees and, with reluctance, set her mind on her new play. Her shoulders were propped on cushions, one beautiful bare arm was behind her neck, and her leather-covered typescript rested against a lifted knee. For a space she read concentratedly, then looked into vacancy, visualising the set scene, made a pencil-note on the margin of the type, and resumed her reading.

Came Alistair MacIan from the white portico of the house and strolled across the lawn. He was bare-headed, open-necked, in old flannels, with a cigarette smouldering, hands deep in his pockets, completely at ease. Norrey Carr lifted a lazy eye out of her concentration and smiled at him.

"What a glutton for work!" he said. "Am I disturbing you?"

"You are," she admitted. "But I forgive you; I am easily tempted."

"I am here to tempt you."

"I'll tell Paddy Joe as soon as he comes back. He

made me promise to do an hour's reading every morning."

"Why this rush of industry?"

"Rehearsals in a fortnight, and Crignell, our actor-manager, foaming at the mouth."

Alistair laughed. "I don't think Crignell will foam much at you. All the world knows that you hold him under your thumb."

"And I suppose that all the world knows that Crignell would like to hold me under his?"

"And what does the great Paddy Joe think?"

"He simply will not let me contemplate Crignell. Paddy Joe is very proper, and Crignell is divorced."

Again Alistair laughed. "Do you allow Paddy Joe to choose—ah—your—shall we say friends?"

"Of course. I always wait till his mind is made up. I am doing that now."

"I see. Say, Norrey, to return to the subject of temptation, it's a peach of a morning. What about that motor-run you promised me?"

Norrey was out of the hammock in one swirling, complicated, graceful motion. "While the cat's away!" she cried. "I'll be ready in one moment," and she raced towards the French window.

"As quick a fall from grace as anyone could wish," said the surprised Alistair.

As always, when Norrey Carr and Alistair MacIan were together, Don Webster was not far away. He did not trust his cousin; perhaps he did not trust the woman; and below that strong sullen front of his was an imagination that tortured him. As Norrey disappeared he came out under the portico and halted. Alistair, some impish idea in his head, walked across the gravel towards him.

"Norrey and I are going off," said Alistair.

"Off where?"

"Motoring. You had better wait and say good-bye."

The sullen fires below the surface in Don Webster glowed. "No need," he said in a curiously held voice. "I think I'll come with you."

"You can't."

"Can't I?"

"You see, we may not be back for a week — if ever."

"Yes! You ought to know better after——"

"Hush! That hatchet is buried."

"I am coming," said Don Webster quietly.

But he was not, and he did not. Norrey Carr had a mind of her own. She simply laughed at Don, and Don could overbear anything but laughter. "This is Alistair's outing," she said. "I promised him last week."

Don stood dour-faced, jealous-minded, on the gravel, and watched them go. As the car swung between the limes Alistair turned and gestured farewell, and he succeeded in putting into it such a touch of mockery and finality that Don could not then or later forget it. Jealousy is a terrible affliction. Out of nothing or out of little it will conjure up visions that torture most damnably.

Before reaching the lodge Norrey slowed down for a moment. "We have the day before us," she said. "Which road shall we take?"

"The road to the world's end, of course," gave back Alistair gaily.

"Right! I'll tell you. We'll run across and see Paddy Joe at his fishing. Where is it again?"

"Strath Conon. He'll probably cut your heart out."

"Not he—but if he did, what a surprise he'd get."

II

On the previous day Paddy Joe Long had accepted the invitation of an editor friend, and had gone for two or three days' fishing on the Conon River above Dingwall, and there the two now sought him. Norrey drove well and was in the happiest mood. So was Alistair. Talking aimlessly and intimately, but with no undercurrent, they went by the sea-road through Nairn and Inverness, and after due inquiry at Dingwall, faced the first mighty green-fronted swell of the great hills of the north, and finally ran down Paddy Joe and his friend fishing a long pool below one of the shouting cascades of the Conon.

Paddy Joe was glad to see them, and the shake of the head that greeted Norrey was accompanied by an affectionate grin. His editor friend invited Alistair to try the fishing, and the sceptical American accepted without enthusiasm. In the space of an hour he lost a four-pound grilse by being over-anxious and so over-strenuous, but succeeded in landing two hard-fighting sea-trout. He was surprised, but very pleased. Thereafter they all shared sandwiches and coffee, and in the afternoon the two set out on the return journey.

"Going back the same road?" inquired Paddy Joe.

"Not farther than Inverness," Norrey told him. "After that we'll take to the hills and get home by Grantown— if at all."

"You be careful, then," warned Paddy Joe. "I'll be

back in two days, and you'll go through your catechism, my girl."

They paused for a few minutes at Inverness for tea and then sought the moorland road by weird Culloden and the bleak lift at Tomatin, and so by devious ways amongst the moors they reached Grantown, where they rested and had dinner.

The sun was streaking long shadows through the pine-woods as they set out on the thirty miles downhill to Highland Drum. At Barnagh they left the main highway and swerved left on to the old military road that winds along the face of the moors above the windings of the Leonach River.

Alistair had never come this road before, but he had the observant eye of the outdoor man, and when they came on Balchrochan Glen from the top end, he at once recognised the lie of the country. "Look!" he cried, pointing. "Below there is where we made havoc amongst the trout two days ago, and over there's the forbidden Larach na Gael."

He chose the wrong time for calling Norrey's attention from the wheel. The brae swung in a clean curve to the left and the unfenced road swung with it—an easily negotiated swing under ordinary circumstances. But when Norrey's eye came back to her work there was an old squat little man ambling round the curve, dead in the middle of the road, with a bearded collie at his heels. The dog barked, and the little old man behaved exactly like a hen. And with that Norrey lost her head—for a moment only, but a moment was enough—and, anyhow, brake and accelerator are rather near each other, and it was the accelerator she touched. The car leaped, and Alistair, using one strong word, came into action like a sound man. He kicked Norrey's foot off the accelerator, wrenched the wheel round, and stamped on the brake. The off mudguard missed the old man by inches—the dog was already up the slope—and the car went on implacably over the lip of the descent. Luckily it went on four even wheels. It gave a slight bump as it leaped the few inches of rise from road to heather, and then slid smoothly downwards. No four-wheel brakes could hold it on that reach. It crashed through a clump of juniper, bumped through a patch of broom, and charged straight for a plantation of larch. Alistair, his right leg braced like steel, saw where a drive opened in the plantation, lifted his foot for a second and swung the car for it. He made it, and saw the long vista running down to the river. A little to the left a miniature knoll rose above the young trees, and Alistair, his mind packed in ice, rightly decided that it or destruction was the goal. Again he swung the car and felt it lurch, lift on two wheels, pause, and return. The sapling spruce crashed before them, and the front wheels took the sudden lift with a jarring check. The car slowed, tremored, stopped dead a yard from the summit, slid back and sideways into the hollow, and came to rest, gentle as a lamb. Ten seconds only, and Alistair had packed it full measure with a man's work.

"We have arrived," said he calmly. "Sorry I kicked you."

III

Norrey Carr came out of a fixed stare and her eyelids fluttered. "Oh, Alistair!" she said awedly, "are we all dead?"

"I think not," said Alistair weightily, "unless our

new friend up yonder has succumbed to heart-failure."

He turned to look up the brae and discovered that the plantation encompassed them. He could not see twenty yards.

"A sweet spot!" he chuckled. "We made it in about a split second, and it will take a day and a road engine to get us out of it."

Norrey Carr was trembling, and Alistair, noting this, patted her on the shoulder. "Cheer up, Norrey," he said. "I wonder what Paddy Joe will say." And at that Norrey gave a little hysterical chuckle.

Alistair was blessed with that hardihood that meets a crisis strong-fronted, and then hides reaction below humour—just what was required to keep Norrey Carr from going to pieces.

Meanwhile the sturdy old man had not died of heart-failure. Instead, he must have made very good time down the brae, for at this moment his head appeared round the tail of the car. His cap was off, his bald head glistened, and his blue eyes were about to jump out of their sockets. His dog was not with him, but its far-off bark of protest was not wanting.

"Oh my! Oh my!" exclaimed the old man. "Is it there ye are?"

"Good evening," said Alistair. "Have we not met before?"

"Who—me—where?" The old man was surprised.

"Perhaps we parted a little hurriedly."

"Oh dear! Oh dear!" said the old man. "But you're a grand driver. It was all my fault."

"Not at all," protested Alistair. "You were a contributory factor only."

Alistair alighted between two saplings, and helped Norrey out. Then he scrambled about in the undergrowth, followed fussily by the old man, and examined the damage. Beyond a few scratches and a bent mudguard there appeared to be none.

"She'll manœuvre on her own steam yet," he murmured; "but she'll never lift herself out of this—no room to turn. Jiminy! won't Uncle Hugh raise Cain about his trees."

"Are we stuck, Alistair?" Norrey wanted to know.

"I think so. Let us go up to the road and hold a meeting. We mustn't miss the chance of a passing motorist."

"I doot the chance o' that," said the old fellow. "This is only a by-road, ye ken."

"You met one yourself, didn't you?"

"I did that, and me wool-gatherin' doon the middle o' the road."

Norrey Carr was unusually silent, and without a word allowed Alistair to help her back up the brae. Reaching the roadside, she threw off her driving-coat, spread it on the grassy margin, and sat with her feet down the slope and her eyes staring across the wide glen at the rolling tilt of Larach na Gael. She had suffered a shock and was fighting commendably hard to get her nerve back. Alistair saw that, and gave her time. He turned aside and examined with interest the line of their sudden take-off and downhill swoop. There was little to see.

"Old earth is a dumb beast," he said. "A fellow might wonder what snapped that juniper, but no one would guess that a big car was hidden down there amongst the trees." He turned to the old man. "Could you oblige us with your local knowledge—if any—old friend?"

The little old man was moving about on restless feet

and scratching his few wisps of sandy hair. "That's it," he said. "I was just thinking if I couldn't do anything to help you. Man, it's hard—gey hard. There's a croft or twa fower mile or so doon the road. Sanny Bain has a shelt, but I doot if he has a trap. Muiryside is aboot fifteen——"

"No," denied Alistair; "it is only about eight miles across there."

"Oh, but that's Larach na Gael. Ye could never win through yon."

"So I have been told, but I guess it could be done, all the same."

"Tell you what," cried the old man suddenly. "I'll put you across it."

"But if *you* can do it——"

"Ye ken, I bide in it."

"Then you are Willie Raasay."

The old man opened his eyes. "Wha in the warl——"

"Oh, your fame is known," laughed Alistair. "But tell me, did you intend going back to Larach na Gael this evening?"

"Well, no. I was going up by to Loch Ruighi for twa days' fishin' with Archie MacGillivray."

"Some hike!" Alistair shook his head. "No!"

"No trouble at all," protested Willie Raasay. "I owe ye that much, and the road I'd tak' ye would be no' that hard."

Alistair considered, looking across at Larach na Gael, looking down the curve of the road, and finally looking down at Norrey Carr's fair head.

"No," was his final decision. "The long road for us. We'll call on your crofter friend with the pony."

From that decision Alistair would not move, and finally, and with many protests, Willie Raasay went his own road, stopping every now and then and rubbing his scanty locks, until at last he disappeared round the curve, where his dog joined him.

Alistair, staring in front of him, could not help thinking that to go five miles for a pony that had not a trap, or ten miles back to a railway station that would not have a train, would be a wicked waste of time and effort, and in the end might result in their having to spend a night together away from the Drum—ten days ago he might not have minded. While all the time, lying there in front of them, a mere two or three hours' stroll, was a straightforward bit of scrub—eight miles of it at the outside—which would mean their getting home that night with certainty, even if in the dark. Larach na Gael drew his hunter's calculating gaze. They had even challenged his ability to find his way! If Norrey were only——

But Norrey for the last few seconds had been observing his calculations with a trained eye. The accident had been sudden; the reaction correspondingly acute and brief. Already the springs of thankfulness were welling their first bubbles of gaiety at the uncanny deliverance. They were alive, both of them, sound in wind and limb. If the bubbles were a little heady, a little hectic, well— weren't they worth it? Her flesh began to tingle. She felt a mounting surge of excitement. She met Alistair's pondering look with smiling eyes. But her utterance was stage-managed to a half-humoured confidence as she said, "Alistair, I have not come too well out of this, and my sense of dignity is hurt."

"Nonsense, Norrey!"

"But it is, and I must do something to restore it. You and I will tackle Larach na Gael together."

IV

They crossed the suspension bridge, Alistair leading, and angled up the brae-face beyond. It was a stiff slope, a trifle boggy, grown with shaggy birch and black alder, and two or three times they had to pause for breath. But up brae or down Norrey Carr refused the help of Alistair's proffered hand. "I am in this for my soul's sake," she said.

"We'll take it easy, then," said Alistair. "The first mile is the worst."

She had, however, permitted him to carry her driving-coat, from one of the pockets of which protruded the tails of the brace of sea-trout that Paddy Joe's friend had pressed upon them.

"If we have to make a camp we'll not starve," remarked Alistair.

The two were not badly equipped for the venture, possessing youth, energy, an interest in each other, a curiosity for the half-mysterious, a reasonable modicum of doubt, and a determination towards success. Norrey was in a light short dress, and luckily wore strongly made driving-boots, while Alistair was in flannels and crepe-soled shoes.

When they got to the head of the first brae they found that they had not crowned the rise from the river. It ran gently inland for a good half-mile in varying dips and lifts, covered thinly with old fir-trees and with an undergrowth of bracken.

"There's the sun behind that tree, and this is north,"

Alistair considered his line. "We must make this at a slant, and take another observation later on."

"Lead on!" cried Norrey.

He took the slope at an easy pace, the tall bracken swishing against his thighs, and the girl slipped in behind him, concentrated on her work and determined to be no drag on the wheel.

"A good cover for game, this," remarked Alistair.

Almost as he spoke a cock pheasant, his plumage gone rusty, rose at his feet with a startling hysterical alarm.

Norrey gave a small scream, and Alistair threw up his hands, looked along an imaginary barrel, and clicked his tongue. "Fetch him, Towser! The next will be a tiger."

But they roused no more game. That pheasant's cry warned all the underworld, and the underworld slipped out of the way on its own quiet roads.

At last they came to the head of the rise and looked out over the upland shaw of Larach na Gael. The ground fell away at their feet in a sharp, short drop, at the base of which grew a sparse wood of pine. From their vantage-point they looked over the dark crowns of the trees across a wide expanse of what seemed all woodland—levels and slopes and billows of tree tops with the thin autumn haze softening all contours. There was nothing outstanding in all that spread, and the general tilt hid the narrow firth and the Sutherland hills beyond it.

"So that's Larach na Gael?" said Alistair quietly.

"What a lot of trees!" said Norrey awedly. "These woods may swallow us up."

"No fear," Alistair assured her. "An occasional tree looks like a forest at a distance."

194

With a glance at the sun, low down in the north-west and already an intense orange, Alistair strode over the brink of the dip, and Norrey fell in behind. At the foot of the slope they at once entered amongst the pines, where the ground was dead level, without undergrowth, and carpeted with brown needles. Presently the trees thinned out and they found themselves on the margin of a quarter-mile-wide open, grown with heather and rank grass.

"Fine!" exclaimed Alistair. "An odd open stretch like this will check our line."

At the edge of the trees, and just inside the heather, they came on their first ant-hill, a mound of pine-needles and small sticks nearly four feet in height. For some reason none of the insects were moving. Perhaps it was their Sabbath day.

"Is it really the ants' home?" wondered Norrey. "It seems deserted."

"Why, it is vibrant with the energy of the life within it. Don't touch it, Norrey. The twiddle of your little finger might spoil a month's work. Come on."

v

And they went on—for a satisfactory hour. At no time did the going present any difficulties. The slopes were easy; miniature valleys opened where they wanted them; no undergrowth troubled them; and Alistair chose his course judiciously.

"It seems easy," said Norrey diffidently.

"Don't snitch a fellow's credit," Alistair gave back. "It's not so easy as it looks. We don't see much of the sky any longer, you'll notice."

That was so. The trees, though thinly spaced, were cunningly set and grouped, and every vista was dense in foliage.

"A deceptive territory, right enough," went on Alistair. "It keeps dragging one to the left."

"I thought you were trending too much the other way."

"I am watching out. These valley channels have a deceptive trick of angling westwards, and that has to be allowed for. Still, another hour should see us over the worst of it."

At the end of that hour they reached the foot of a sharp brae. Directly in their line it was clear of trees, but fifty yards to their left a thick plantation ran down from the crest and back into the shaw—so thick that to force a way through would be extremely difficult.

Alistair halted. "We are lucky," he said. "Our way is right through the clearing, and we should get a good observation from the top. We'll have a rest up there."

Alistair reached the crown of the brae a few yards ahead and, reaching it, stopped with an abrupt check and a back throw of the hand. "Snakes!" he cried. "Where are we at?" And his voice was as startled as it could well be.

Norrey mounted cautiously to his side and followed his gaze. They looked directly into a deep dark gorge, and the river Leonach flowed sternly at the bottom of it.

Alistair was thinking rapidly and with dismay. If this was the Leonach—and it must be—then he had merely made a chord base to the arc of it—or rather an intersecting arc, for he must have curved steadily towards it. Why, they might not be more than two miles—or less—from their starting-place.

"What is it?" asked Norrey in a whisper. "The Leonach?"

"That is not the Leonach at all," he assured her whimsically, "but the mighty river Yak bounding the Land of Boul—the enchanted Land of Boul. We are due for pleasant adventures."

She smiled a little doubtfully.

"Sure!" he insisted. "The very place. Look! There is the young wood the Whip-whip-er-ling grew to build its nest in. Let us sit back here and rest."

He had landed the expedition in quite a hole, but there was no need just yet to manifest the fact too patently. He sank, cross-legged, on the ground, well back from the lip of the gorge, and drew forth his cigarette-case.

Norrey sat gratefully at his side on the dry grass. "That last pull found me out," she said. She had not yet realised how much astray they were, but yet had some doubts. "Are we not a good bit out of our course?" she asked.

"Oh, just a bit," Alistair replied carelessly. "A tack on the weather side will open port all right."

"I seem to have seen that hill over there before."

"Them's the Bad Lands of Day-before-Yesterday," Alistair reeled out, "where the sun only kisses the tops of the high hills."

That was so, too. Beyond the river gorge was a long slope of wan grey grass, with here and there a shattered Scotch fir, and beyond that lifted the heavily wooded side of a great hill. All light and life seemed drained away from the wan grass, and the scattered trees were black and still; the woods beyond were sombre green, and they too were tonelessly still—a sombre mantle draped in set folds over a dead breast. But above the woods, where the naked limestone cropped through, the light of the setting sun shone in red glory—in a sad red glory that emphasised the remote solemnity of the woods, the toneless grey of the grass, and the darkness of the gorge where the river murmured sternly but subduedly.

"I seem to remember that hill," insisted Norrey.

"Memory is playing you false. I know this land like the palm of my hand. Come on, Norrey, and I'll give you a hand down the hill."

She allowed him to slip a hand inside her elbow, and, shoulder to shoulder, the two slid down the slope and went back into the quietness of Larach na Gael.

But Alistair was no longer confident.

CHAPTER XVI

I

PADDY JOE LONG strolled up the avenue to Highland Drum in mid-afternoon, and his easily swaying shoulders kept time to the song he hummed:

> And neither mate nor maid nor queen
> Shall reign within my house,
> Lest Lust might enter in with Love
> To hold his pale carouse.
> And dreams of love and mists of lust
> Weigh heavy on the mind,
> That should be lean and limber
> And quicker than the wind.

He held a cased fishing-rod under his left arm, bore a wicker fishing-basket on his back, and swinging from his right hand was a light suit-case. Rounding the curve of the limes, he saw Don Webster coming bull-headed down the centre of the drive, his hands behind his back, his head forward, and his eyes on the ground. He was striding furiously, yet gave the curious impression that he was going nowhere, and at once Paddy Joe began to speculate, for such aimless haste was not in character. "Hullo, Topsy!" he cried. "Where're you chasing your tail?"

Don Webster halted abruptly and lifted his head, and Paddy Joe saw his face.

"How's everyone?" asked the Irishman quickly.

"I don't know," Don replied in a strangely quiet voice. "We are all right—all that's left of us."

"All that's left of you?"

"Yes. Norrey Carr and MacIan are gone away together."

Paddy Joe walked straight up to him, placed his suitcase on the ground between them, and with a little quick motion pushed his old hat to the back of his head. The white expanse of his forehead went back into his black hair, and below that white expanse his brown face had not blenched or changed. "They are gone away together," he enunciated carefully.

"In Norrey's car—two days ago."

"Two days ago, yes! Have you had word from them?"

"No. There was no need."

The Irishman paused before he put his next question, and now his face changed indeed. The colour did not drain from his face, but it drained from his eyes, leaving them glazed stone; the skin tightened across the bridge of his long nose and over his cheek-bones; and the lines at the side of his mouth deepened and hardened. His right hand, held a little away from his side, was clenched so tightly that the knuckles gleamed white, and when he spoke, though he spoke slowly and quietly, there was a brazen quality in his voice. "You mean that they have run away with each other?"

"Of course."

"What leads you to think that?"

Suddenly there was fury in Don Webster's voice and in his gesture. "Did not the cad tell me they were going away and not coming back? Did he not wave farewell from this very corner?—and there was no mistaking his meaning. I tell you, they are gone."

"What did Norrey say?"

"Norrey said nothing. She laughed at me when I suggested driving with them."

Paddy Joe leant forward and scrutinised Don Webster's face, and slowly his own face relaxed and his eyes softened. The face he scrutinised was tortured woefully from somewhere deep down, and the sullen fires in the eyes were dulled with misery. "You poor damned fool!" said Paddy Joe gently. "You have suffered a good deal, and will suffer more."

He kicked his suit-case out of the way—that new and respectable suit-case—and catching Don at the shoulder, thrust him aside with such force that he staggered to the edge of the drive. "Get out of my way," the Irishman roared. "I'd tell you to go to hell if you were not there already"; and he strode furiously towards the house.

Don Webster pulled himself together, stood staring after him for a space, and then plodded aimlessly down the avenue.

II

Paddy Joe halted for a moment under the white portico and grinned whimsically at himself, at life, at the world. "That's the way of it," he spoke aloud. "That's the way of it. A minute ago I was singing a fine song, and now I would give the world for a man it would be a pleasure to hit."

He jerked off his fishing-basket, and slammed it and his rod in a corner of the outer hall, went through a glazed door, along a drugget-covered stone passage to the right, and tapped on a white door let into the thickness of a three-foot wall.

"Come in," said Sir Hugh's voice; and Paddy Joe entered Lady Sara's boudoir-workroom—a room comfortably furnished, with a soft carpet and old-fashioned chintz-covered chairs. Lady Sara sat on one of these, and her hands were in her lap, while Sir Hugh, elbow on a round table, was reading an old leather-back book. That Lady Sara was without her knitting, and Sir Hugh away from his plantations, showed that the usual placidity of life had been grievously ruffled. Paddy Joe noted as much as he came across and leant his hands on the round table. He looked from one to the other, his old hat still on the back of his head; and they looked at him, discomfort in their glances.

"I have heard the news," said Paddy Joe, "and I see that you have been listening to Don Webster."

Sir Hugh cleared his throat as for a long speech, but all he said was, "Sorry, Mr Long."

"You'll be sorrier still," said Paddy Joe. "Norrey and Alistair went motoring two days ago—you have heard no word from them?"

"No word."

"You have made no inquiries—no search—nothing?"

"What was the use, Pad—Mr Long?" said Sir Hugh sorrowfully.

"My God!" cried Paddy Joe. "How one man's black certainty infects decent people! Some inner devil has convinced Don Webster, and Don Webster has convinced you."

"But why have we not had word from them?" cried Lady Sara. "There could not be an accident, or we must have heard."

"Is that so, indeed? Are there not places within ten —twenty—thirty miles of here where a car might lie smashed for more than two days and no one find it—or the dead under it?"

"Do you know anything?" Sir Hugh asked the question with blunt huskiness, and Lady Sara flinched.

"I don't," replied Paddy Joe. "I don't know whether Alistair MacIan and Norrey Carr lie crushed under their car at the foot of a cliff, or are sitting quiet in their seats at the bottom of a pool. I don't know whether they have both lost their memories; I don't know whether they have been spirited away by the fairies; but one thing I do know, and it is that they have not run away with each other."

"How do you know?" The question was Lady Sara's.

"Because I know Alistair MacIan, and I know Norrey Carr. You, my wise woman, in trying to understand Norrey Carr, let your Highland imagination run away with you; and you, Sir Hugh, too anxious to hold your nephew, were afraid that you had no hold on him." Paddy Joe glared at them. "In a minute or in an hour you may have the telegraph boy cycling up the drive with bitter news for you. You may open the paper in the morning and see what you'll look to see. You—but I'll say no more—to you that did not know a fine man and the finest woman in the world."

"You have said too much."

"And I'll say this. I am going out of your house now, and I'll bring back your nephew dead or alive; but dead or alive I will not bring back to this house the woman. I can take care of my own dead."

He slapped his old hat down on his forehead, and strode out of the room and out of the house.

"He was too brutal," said Sir Hugh.

"Because he was hurt too much," said Lady Sara.

CHAPTER XVII

I

AELEC BRANDS had gone for a day's fishing to Loch Ruighi, and Margaret, taking her cycle with her, went with him as far as Barnagh station, and, from there, rode across to Reroppe Lodge to spend the day with Agnes King. The evening and the moors and the westering sun were so glorious that, instead of cycling back the six miles to the station, she decided to do the twenty-odd miles to Muiryside and Croft o' Drum. The road was almost entirely downhill, at a nice gradient, and she could easily do it in two hours. "It's about the last time I'll see the moors this year," she told Agnes King, "and I must soak in enough of them to last the winter."

See her, then, sailing down the moorland road, her hat on the lamp-bracket, her shoulders back, one hand on the handle-bar and the other at her waist, and her short curls leaping backwards in the breeze she made. The level orange light made a glory of her hair, and her blue eyes shone. She rode that cycle as if it were alive, and the wheels beneath her made a loud exultant hum, that was an undernote to the song she sang so gaily:

> Sun and sky and heather woo me,
>   Shadows race and winds pursue me,
> Waters run and dreams ensue me,
>   And I lighthearted.
> Land to love and lad to lo'e me,
>   And never parted.

She had cut her daylight rather fine, took every down brae at a rush, and so came full speed round the curve of Balchrochan Glen, leaning over gracefully and entirely unafraid. Suddenly she exclaimed, and her free hand came down on the handle-bar, both brakes went on together, the tyres jarred on the gravel, and speed slackened all too abruptly. She did not actually turn a somersault—she did not even spill herself all abroad; but it was only a remarkable display of activity that brought both feet on the road clear of the cycle, which skidded, wobbled, and fell in the ditch at the moorside. "Paddy Joe! Paddy Joe! Is that yourself?" she cried.

It was the sight of Paddy Joe's long back that had caused such a sudden halt. He was sitting on the brink of the brae, looking across Balchrochan Glen. She might not have known his long grey back, but there was no mistaking the disreputable tweed hat. An old bicycle sprawled on the grass margin at his side. He turned quickly, propped himself aside on his hands, and the old, sadly pleasant smile lit up his face. "Margaret Brandt!" he cried. "Are you on the road to Rotterdam?"

"Alas, no," she cried back; "I have not yet met Gerard Eliassoen."

"Wishan, my quick one! come over here and let me talk to you. I want your advice, and I want it badly."

II

Margaret Brands, as if looking for someone, let her eyes rove down the glen and up the moor before she came to Paddy Joe's side. "Is that grass damp, Paddy Joe?" she asked.

"It is not; but sit on that." He pulled off his old hat,

slammed it flat on the grass, and Margaret, without demur, seated herself carefully on it, her feet down the slope and her dress demurely below her knees. Paddy Joe looked sideways at her. "Heard any late news from Highland Drum?" he questioned evenly.

"There is never any, is there?"

Paddy Joe turned his eyes across the glen to the setting sun and did not again look at her. "There is. Two days ago Norrey and Alistair went motoring—just the usual spin, it was thought—but they have not returned. No one knows where they are."

"Oh, Paddy Joe!"

That sudden breathless exclamation pleased Paddy Joe, and he had been listening very carefully. It showed that, though she at once pictured disaster, it was not the disaster of intrigue. That last fear sends the blood to the heart and then sullenly to the head. Margaret Brands's face flamed, and then the blood slowly ebbed and left her face with the soft pallor of milk. "You don't know, Paddy Joe?"

"No, Margaret. Don Webster insists that they have run off—eloped; and he has obsessed the old people with the same notion. What do you think yourself?"

"But there was no need," she said simply. "Alistair was not afraid of Don Webster, was he?"

"Alistair MacIan was afraid of no man."

"It might be some ploy," reasoned Margaret, keeping a firm hold on herself. "They were not very conventional people, were they? They might have met friends and gone off on a jaunt. And yet I think that Norrey would have let you know before, or before this."

"We be of one blood, you and I," said Paddy Joe.

"But what could have happened?"

"I don't know; I am not sure; but I feel that the worst has not happened. I would know that."

"You would," Margaret agreed.

"Listen, now, to me. You know I was away for two days on the Conon River. Well, Norrey and Alistair spent a good part of day-before-yesterday with me."

"They did?"

"Yes; and there was nothing in their minds then but fun. On leaving they told me that they were circling round by the moors and home by Grantown. Do you know that road?"

"I do. Not a good road in places."

"I thought so." Then he told her what had happened on his return to Highland Drum that morning. "I was too hard on the two old folk," he said, "but it made me mad to see the minds of decent people darkened by the jealous certainty of another. I flung out of the house in the devil of a temper, and wasted ten minutes looking for Don Webster. I wanted to give him what Alistair calls a sockdologer."

"You didn't find him?"

"I did not; and I'm not sure whether I am glad or sorry. Then I did the right thing. I went round to Croft o' Drum to see yourself and your uncle, and ye were not there."

"He was at Loch Ruighi."

"I heard that. I was still wrought up, though, and I swore to myself to range the road up to Grantown, and get the police there to continue the search. With that large idea still in my head I borrowed Johnny Ross's cycle and set out. When I got as far as this a strange notion came to me, and I sat down to contemplate it. That's how you found me."

"I wonder!" said Margaret, and she gazed across at the lift of Larach na Gael.

"That's it," said Paddy Joe. "There may be nothing in it; but do you remember at the picnic how he proposed to cross that place and was prevented by Lady Sara?"

"I do. Norrey offered to go with—to go too."

"The thing was put to him like a dare, and I have never seen the lad back down to a dare yet. What about it, Margaret?"

"But two whole days?"

"That was in my mind. They should have reached the crofter's house. Who is he, again?"

"Willie Raasay—but," and her voice lifted, "Mrs King told me that Willie has been at Loch Ruighi for the last two days."

"Two days!" Paddy Joe considered the many aspects of these two days.

"But where would they have parked the car?" wondered Margaret out of her own thoughts.

"Where would they, indeed?" mused Paddy Joe. He looked up the road and down the road; he looked behind and over the lifting moor; and finally, he looked down the brae to the Leonach. Slowly he put out a hand that felt blindly for Margaret's arm and pressed there hurtingly. With the other he pointed at a broken clump of junipers.

"It might not be," whispered Margaret.

He let go her arm, rose slowly to his feet, and sidled down the brae. He moved as one who is old and weary and beyond all hurry. Margaret came at his shoulder, and together they halted and looked at the smashed line through the bushes. Just beyond, where there was a ridge and a patch of bare peaty soil, there was no mistaking the track and markings of a tyre.

"Is it so, then?" said that brazen voice of Paddy Joe's. "Let us go on."

Now that they knew what they were looking for they had no trouble in following the slide of the tyres. So they came to the drive in the plantation and saw the steep vista down to the river.

"Oh, Paddy Joe!"

"Maybe what I said to Sara MacIan was right, after all. Come on, girl!" and he took her arm.

Twenty yards down they came to the smashed saplings on the right, and suddenly Paddy Joe was fiercely active. "Wait you, Margaret," he cried, and went crashing through the break.

Margaret held on to a young trunk and trembled, her mouth a little open and her eyes wide. She had not long to wait.

"All right, Margaret!" came Paddy Joe's voice in a shout. "The car is here. There was no accident. 'Tis all right, I tell you." And he kept shouting reassurances until Margaret, trembling in every limb, appeared round the tail of the car.

"There was no accident at all," cried Paddy Joe, "whatever veered them off the road. See! everything is right. Norrey's coat is gone, and so are the two trout they had. They are over in Larach na Gael—the devils!" His eyes were alive, and his voice too.

"Lost for two days! Paddy Joe, they are needing us," cried Margaret.

"They are," agreed Paddy Joe. "We two were meant to find them from the beginning."

CHAPTER XVIII

I

THEY crossed the swing-bridge and climbed the same soggy slope that Norrey and Alistair had climbed two days before. Had they looked they might have noted the breaking down of the bracken where Alistair had forged a way. And from the same vantage they gazed over the tilt of Larach na Gael. Halting at that point, Paddy Joe lifted up his voice. "Take notice," he half chanted, "we make no dare, and we would take nothing that should not be given, and hope that nothing will be taken that we would not give." He turned to Margaret. "You know," he said, "if this place is haunted, it is haunted by the dreams of the men that went before."

"And we are sib."

"Let us down into it, then, in God's name."

And the two, armoured in the right spirit, went down into Larach na Gael.

Paddy Joe was a pilot of careless confidence. He allowed the mood of the place to possess him and, perhaps, guide him. His hands were deep in his pockets, his shoulders loose, his pipe in the corner of his mouth, and his disreputable hat on the back of his head. He crooned an old song—though he crooned it through his teeth; and, when he was not singing, quaint scraps of speech came from him in a soothing monotone. He never hesitated over a choice of ways, and the way he took was always the easy one. Margaret, too, tuned herself to this mood, and for the time put aside all speculations, and what might be the beginnings of little fears. She felt ready for all emergencies, all wonders, and the light swagger of her was as characteristic as Paddy Joe's easy slouch. Somehow the venture became a sally into romance, instead of a determined tramp to attain an end.

"Do you really know your way?" Margaret put to him cheerfully.

"Fine I do. If you will be keeping your eyes open you'll be soon seeing the three hundred and sixty-five lighted windows in the palace of the king.

> O, the house that I would live in
>   Was never built by hands :
> A house upon the coast of Dream
> ' And Pagan Hinterlands :
> A low house, but a wide house,
>   And full of books and wine,
> Lean thought and airy phantasy,
>   The only loves of mine."

Time slipped smoothly by. Night came down on them, and, having not yet opened out the king's palace, they halted for a rest in an open wood of pine. They stood under a well-grown tree close by a great ant-heap, and so quiet was the night that they could hear the blood beat in their ears. Above that sound they sensed, rather than heard, the deep sustained hum from the labyrinth of the ants, and, more distinctly still, they heard the subdued hush-hush of the pine-tops above them.

"You are a good pilot, Paddy Joe," Margaret complimented.

"I am," agreed Paddy Joe. "Leg-weary yet?"

"Scarcely at all. It is perfectly lovely to drift along."

And they drifted on serenely. These two, and the two that had gone before, never forgot that walk. As Margaret had said, it was more drifting than walking, but it was the mysterious spirit of quiet that made it memorable. It is not possible in any words to picture that quietude. It was not of land or sea. It was not human. It was unearthly, yet it was not awesome—and yet it was haunted. It not only wrapped them round: it possessed them gently. It lulled them without dulling any perception. The hum of the ants, the sigh of the pines, the distant draw of air over open heather—these they heard, but these made no part of the atmosphere of quiet. That was something apart, something spiritual, something as distinctly individual as an ego. Some such spirit of quiet may be the spirit of Nirvana, the final and eternal quietude that may ensue when life has at last been subdued.

Two small incidents but emphasised the quiet of the place. As they moved across a grassy opening a silent grey shadow went above their heads, and a second or two later the long hoot of an owl startled them. Margaret gave a little cry, and grasped at Paddy Joe.

"Only an owl, girl dear," he told her, "on business. There must be ground life to attract the sad beast."

Again, as they went below a thick-topped tree, a perfect clamour of wings burst through the foliage high up, and the big black body of some bird hurtled away across the open, and crashed amongst the branches of a tree fifty yards away.

"My God . . . father!" cried Long. "The Jabberwock at last!"

"That must be a capercailzie," Margaret's voice came out of a gasp.

"The wood horse!—bolts through his jumps. He must have dashed himself to pieces over there."

"Only his method of getting out of danger. The foresters are his inveterate foe, and you should hear Sir Hugh abuse him for eating his young tree shoots."

"Why, he is as big as a turkey. He should be easily exterminated."

"Not when he startles you out of a year's growth, and then crashes from tree to tree like a catapult. I was at a roe-hunt once with Uncle Aelec, and he missed one as big as a house. The things he said!"

"I wouldn't ask you to repeat them," said Paddy Joe.

"Useful for a sculptor to know when she hits her thumb."

III

In time—and time was no longer of great importance —they came round the shoulder of a knoll, and Margaret stopped dead and cried aloud, "Look."

"My, oh my!" cried Long. "See all the windows lighted up bonny to welcome us home."

But there was only one yellow star shining at them low down across a wide level.

"It is the house of Willie Raasay," said Margaret quietly.

"And someone in it."

"Willie could not be home, could he?"

"We shall soon know."

"Paddy Joe," murmured Margaret, "I think I am tired."

"I am tired too," said Paddy Joe, "but I don't know why." Perhaps that was not all the truth.

"Let us go on," he said. "That light is within half a mile."

Paddy Joe resumed his humming, but, somehow, he now sang through his teeth as a man does to keep his courage up.

> A pleasant place for weary men
>   Shall be that house of mine,
> Where dreams shall bloom and fade and blow
>   And thoughts shall run like wine,
> Where time shall be forgotten
>   And Eternity is now,
> And man is free from Adam's curse
>   Of sweat upon his brow.

The level they moved over was of sound grass and cropped short. Once or twice the grey ghost of a sheep scurried out of their way, and coughed at them. It must have been short of half a mile, for in a very few minutes they were halted by a gate in a wooden paling, and the light that had guided them shone through a four-paned window not thirty yards away. In the path of its radiance they could discern the dark green of vegetable patches and the bright-edged filigree of small fruit-trees. The path from the gate, a brown line, ran straight to a closed door. Paddy leant over the roughly spiked gate and hailed the house loudly. "Hullo, the house! Does your dog bite?"

And immediately the dog barked once from the rear of the house—an intimation that he was there and coming. He did not bark again, but they heard his feet on the path, and presently made out the dark bulk of a huge, shaggy, stump-tailed, bearded collie. He was peaceful of intent and quite fearless in his own domain, placing his paws on the top tie-board of the gate, and lifting a nose towards Paddy Joe.

"Poor, but honest, old boy!" the Irishman made overtures. "Bite this girl here if you must have your legal nip—I'm tough, and you'd probably die." He slipped his hand forward gently on to the broad tousled head. "An old gentleman, so you are! Whom do you keep house for?"

As he spoke they stood in the light from the opened door, and a Highland voice greeted them. "Come away up—you're welcome, whoever you are.—Here, Tarleth"; and the old dog trotted away.

"It is Willie Raasay himself," whispered Margaret, and something drained out of her heart.

"Wait, now," said Paddy Joe steadyingly.

He found the sneck of the gate, and the two went up the path. The figure in the yellow radiance of the doorway—short and square—moved back into the room as they approached, and called, "Come awa' ben"; and in turn they bent below the low lintel sunk in a three-foot wall of grey stone.

CHAPTER XIX

I

THEY found themselves in a room that was surprisingly unexpected. A hanging lamp of polished brass showed it up very effectively. The floor was boarded, scrubbed almost white, and without rugs except for a single rag one, patterned as intricately as a Celtic scroll, near the hearth. The walls were lime-washed and low, and pierced back and front by deep-set small windows. The roof was wide-pitched and boarded with deal right up to the collar braces; this boarding, originally white, was now richly brown with age and peat smoke, and it shone in the lamplight where the resin had oozed. The fireplace was open and filled three-fourths of the dividing wall, and a tall man could have stood under the hewn mantel-bar; the other fourth was a shut door. A few peat coals glowed out of a sheath of white ash. At mid-floor was an oblong table covered with a deep red cloth, and against the gable was an ancient white pine dresser, unpainted and unvarnished, but almost as cleanly white as the walls, loaded with old brown delf and crowned by three mugs of copper lustre. A roughly made arm-chair of twisted wood, rush-bottomed, squatted in the far corner of the fireplace, and behind it and above it was a shelf of well-worn books. Three or four plain wooden chairs stood against the back wall, and between the window and the open door stretched a very remarkable settee—an immense old article, with straight back and ends, covered in dull tapestry, and with a beaded front bar of real rosewood. Altogether a unique room for the wilderness, and scrupulously clean, but besides and notwithstanding supremely cosy.

Willie Raasay was himself as unexpected as the room. Paddy Joe had visualised him as tall and lean and something of the mystic, but there was nothing at all of the Highland seer in his make-up. He was a little, lively, broad old man, and more than inclined to be plump, very nearly bald—but what locks he had strongly sandy —his bright eyes smiling blue out of crinkled eyelids, his round chin shaved clean, and his bare short neck showing the mark of the collar-gyve. He wore a sound suit of heather mixture. He was as merry as a cricket, and unmistakably delighted to see his visitors. He patted an open palm with a shut fist, and words were not wanting to him. "Come away ben, come away ben," he invited in a high tenor voice. "Dear, oh dear! Miss Margaret herself!"

But yet awhile all these particulars of Willie Raasay and his kitchen were not appreciated by Margaret and Paddy Joe, for no sooner had Willie Raasay spoken Margaret's name than there was a cry of "Margaret— Margaret Brands!" and Margaret, on the instant, found herself in a swirl of skirts, arms, and embraces that was Norrey Carr—Norrey Carr, bare-armed and in a long apron.

"I knew Paddy Joe would find me," she cried, half in tears and half in laughter, and Margaret in tears and laughter with her.

Paddy Joe, towering behind Margaret, swallowed once, gave Norrey a quick glance, and turned to look for Alistair—and yet, out of the flurry of Norrey's embrace,

217

it was Margaret who saw him first. Alistair, his face a little haggard and with a two days' beard, was sitting at one end of the long settee, his right leg propped on a chair in front of him, and the ankle a bundle of white bandages above a shouting pattern of carpet slipper. Then Paddy Joe began to understand. He bent and caught Alistair's hand, and Alistair met his eye fairly.

"I fell down on it, Paddy Joe," he said naïvely. "Good and hard I fell down on it. Smite me."

"Son," said Paddy Joe, "I'm after getting the hell of a lot of frights this day. This minute I could not smite anyone—but wait you."

He turned, and Norrey Carr turned to meet him. There was a certain anxiety in her eyes, but no more than anxiety, and her smile was diffident. He placed his hands on her shoulders.

"A splendid fine bit of a housewife you look, girl dear," he said. "Is my tay ready?"

"In a minute, Paddy Joe. But look, have I not the room tidy? I believe I could keep house for you in your palace of dreams."

"You do that always," said Paddy Joe. "'Tis the worst that will happen to you—in my house of dreams."

II

Margaret had gone across to Alistair and, with a frank laugh, had shaken his hand.

"You're a glutton for first aid, Alistair. What is it this time?"

"Only a sprain. All my own fault."

Alistair, too, had diffidence in his eye as he looked at Margaret, but in hers he saw only frankness, and some-

218

how he was not exactly pleased. Before he could say more she turned from him to Willie Raasay, who was actually hopping from one foot to the other.

"Dear, oh dear!" Willie cried. "I knew this morning there was a lucky day before me. But I thought you were at Reroppe, Miss Margaret?"

"But you were at Loch Ruighi, Willie?"

"So I was, and only home this half-hour. I left Aelec there, and came the short-cut ower Aitnoch Hill. My! the surprise I got, finding the young laird and Miss Carr. And me mostly the cause of it too!"

"It was no surprise to us," said Paddy Joe. "This girl here and myself are easily the greatest explorers within the four seas."

"Oh, Willie, you have not met Paddy Joe—Mr Long," Margaret introduced. "He is an Irishman," she added, as if in explanation.

"You get good people all places," said Willie, as he shook the Irishman's hand.

"Kind of you to say it, Mr Raasay," said Paddy Joe, grinning.

Followed a spate of talk and explanations until interrupted by Willie Raasay.

"I'm thinking 'tis time for a drop tea and a pan of fresh trooties," he said, while yet the talk was at its height. "A good job I brought a puckle groceries from Farness."

"'Tis a kind thought," commended Paddy Joe. "I am not hungry myself, but my fellow-pioneer could eat rod-iron."

Willie bustled about fussily, yet with purpose. The big black kettle, already filled, was at the side of the hearth, and, with a single motion, he swung it on the crook and ran the crook directly over the fire. A quick poke or two amongst the coals with a pine splinter, and the kettle was wreathed in yellow flames.

"Let me help you, Willie," volunteered Margaret.

"So must I," cried Norrey. "See my apron."

"To be sure," he accepted readily. "The cloth's in the drawer at that end and the cutlery the ither, and the ware—you see it on the dresser. We'll boil a puckle eggs and make a bit toast as well. You'll be needin' something, I'se warrant."

"You left your house well stored, Mr Raasay," said Norrey. "We did splendidly, and always put everything back in its place."

III

While the three moved about and in and out of the "back-place" Paddy Joe sat by Alistair, and the two talked.

"What gets me," said Alistair, "is how you two tumbled to the situation and ferreted out that car."

"When Margaret Brands and myself set our minds on a problem," said Paddy Joe complacently, "you can put Q.E.F. to it. I tell you, boy, that girl is no small potatoes."

"I know it." Alistair looked aside at Paddy Joe, a new and disturbing thought in his mind.

"Yes so," said Paddy Joe musingly. "That girl at a man's side, and where would be popes and princes?" He looked at Alistair and smiled. "Don Webster is in a tear of a rage—a mile high anyway," he said pleasantly.

"He would be," agreed Alistair. "But, you know, I was much more afraid of you than I am of Don."

"Only it wasn't exactly fear, was it?" said Paddy Joe understandingly.

"No—but if anything happened that ward of yours it would be." He put a hand on Paddy Joe's arm. "It was my fault," he said again. "I was too keen to show you my woodcraft, but—Jiminy! didn't I just fall down on it!"

"You got this far, didn't you?"

"Hit against it. After the first hour I was lost—absolutely—and with the night on top of us we hadn't a chance. I kept our plight from Norrey as long as I could, but I think she suspected all the time. She has got sand all right, Paddy Joe."

"Why wouldn't she?" said Paddy Joe.

"Some time in the night we struck this place, and found the door on the latch and the larder stocked. That was luck, and we had our trout in reserve. The old scout never locks his door—no need, I suppose—and always leaves food about. You know, when he goes on a hike, he scatters grain all over the place among the pine-needles for his hens, and takes his cow across to his nearest neighbours—miles away—Greystones, he calls it. We missed the milk."

"The only foolish thing ye did, son, was not to stick by the house until he returned. You knew he'd be back in two days."

"If I'd stuck till daylight I believe I could have made Highland Drum—I believe I could, Paddy Joe."

Paddy Joe laughed.

"What is it, Paddy Joe?" called Norrey, from the fireside.

"Nothing. You watch that toast—Alistair here only running to form."

"Perhaps so," half-admitted the young man. "We took a chance at the first show of dawn, and then this happened me." He pointed to his bandaged ankle.

"Why the hurry?"

"Oh well!—I knew the old people would be worrying."

"And Don?"

"I never thought of Don. I had mighty poor luck, hadn't I? Deserved it too. This is the fourth time this ankle's let me down—once in the game of my life at Harvard, once after a big bear in Kodiak—the third time you know about; but this fourth time was about the worst. Hell of an unlucky cuss!"

"You are not."

"I was in too much of a hurry, and damn that rotten stump! Even then I tried to make it, but—" He shook his head and grimaced. "I had a lovely time getting back, and wouldn't have made it but for Norrey's help. I think we lost ourselves again. It was midday before we made the house. After that I gave up. Norrey was a regular brick, and the hardest job I had was persuading her not to take a chance at getting out herself for help."

Paddy Joe nodded. "You did the right thing, son— the only thing. She'd never make it."

"What are they saying and doing at the Drum?"

But here came the call for tea, and Paddy Joe was glad of it. None of the talk up to the present had given an inkling that the Highland Drum people had sat still and thought foolishly, and Paddy Joe hoped for the best.

IV

Alistair, with a shoulder from Paddy Joe, managed to hop to the table, and the four made a sumptuous meal.

There were loch trout, boiled eggs, brown oatcakes, toast, butter slightly salt, and tea with milk that was three-parts cream. Willie, who insisted that he had had supper at Greystones, did not join them, but waited at table adeptly and kept the small talk going. "It was a gey good spirit you all showed," he said. "'Tis a queer thing, but this hoosie draws folks that are wandered. Did ye ever hear of the time I lost my ain self in it?"

"Aelec mentioned it."

"In the early part of a summer evening it was, too, and I daunderin' roun' after a puckle sheep. I didna ken the quirk of it at the time, being fresh off the sea."

"A sailor?" inquired Alastair, scarcely hiding his surprise.

"No' what you could call a sailor, maybe. For thirty years back and forth I was a steward on the Burns and Laird boats out of the Broomielaw."

"You'll know Dublin, then?" the Irishman said.

"Ay, and all the ports right round to Westport. The last time I was in Dublin the bonny Custom House was burning and the shots duntin'. I thought it the right time for me to give up the sea. No' that exactly—the last turn of the screw. Man, ye get awfu' tired of going out and back the same road, and no rest at the hinner-end. I wanted a placie where I could sit, and see things sitting year in year out."

"You've hit the placie dead centre," commented Alistair.

"Have I no'?" agreed Willie. He turned to Paddy Joe. "That picture there I bought in Dublin," he said.

"I was wondering how it got so far from home," said Paddy Joe.

There were only two pictures in the room, close together on the back wall. Paddy Joe had noticed them the moment he entered, and his eyes, wherein were surprise and speculation, kept continually straying to them. Supper over, he rose and went round the table to have a closer look. "God rest you!" he whispered, "and you so far from the land you loved."

The picture he looked at was an old tinted engraving, in a maple frame, of a young man in the white leathers and green body-coat of the Georges. He had one hand thrown forward and up, and the other in his breast, and his face was invincibly proud and desperately sad.

"I bought that," Willie explained, "at a sale on the Dublin Quays. I wouldna have bid for it, only I thought it a bittie like Robbie Burns."

"This man's name was Robert also," said Paddy Joe. "He was a sadder man than Robbie, and Robbie was a sad man too."

"Who is it?" Margaret asked.

"His name is like to be forgotten—even in Ireland. Do you know that song that begins, 'She is far from the land where her young hero sleeps'?"

"One of the great songs."

"This is that young hero, Robert Emmet, and he was hanged, drawn, and quartered in Dublin town in the year 1803. I have seen the place—before the church of St Mary's—and the wooden plugs are still in the wall where the gallows was raised. He was an Irish rebel—foolish too, I suppose—and the morning they hanged him was a fine morning. Young, and he had a sweetheart, and when the hangman with his noose asked him 'Are you ready, sir?' he whispered a desperate 'Not yet, not yet.' But he died like a man." Paddy Joe's nostrils quivered, and he threw up his hand in salute.

"Oh dear!" cried Norrey. "Don't make me sad, Paddy Joe."

"Why wouldn't I? I am sad myself. His epitaph was to be written when Ireland became a nation—that was his last wish."

"But is not Ireland now a nation?" inquired Margaret.

"It was always that, but not the nation he meant—and every Irishman knows as much." Paddy Joe turned and glanced at the other picture, a cheap print in a cheap frame of Raphael's Madonna with the Bambino and St John. "Are you a Catholic, Mr Raasay?"

"No, then. Like the Aberdeen man I ha'e given up releegion and joined the Auld Kirk. Is that a Roman Catholic picture?"

"It was painted for a pope, anyway."

"I got it from a pedlar man—a wee broad mannie, his face shaved blue and big jawbones under his ears—and the only stranger that ever came in and went out of the shaw on the Leonach side without help. He said he came from a place called Campaana in Italy, all ditches and marshes—an empty place like this, but different forby, because there was evil over it, and at night time men died in it from breathing the breath of the spirits that haunted it. It could well be. He gave me that picture when he was going away, and he stayed the big part of a week. 'It is the best I have,' he says to me—'the Mother of God looking at you over her Bambino's head; and if you look at them a long time they will smile at you.' I have noticed it often."

"You would," said Paddy Joe, turning to the table.

Alistair was lounging back comfortably; Margaret leaning elbows on table and her chin in her cupped hands; Norrey sitting very straight, and her eyes brooding on vacancy.

"What is our programme now, Paddy Joe?" Alistair queried, but he looked at Willie Raasay.

"I would be in no hurry, whatever," said that man.

"How far is it to Highland Drum?"

"Five miles the shortest road—and ten anyway by the cart-track to the Nairn road. But wait till I tell you. Ye ken it's no' often anything happens me these days, and when it does I deave all my friends wi' a' the ins and oots. Up by at Loch Ruighi there was Archie MacGillivray and Hamish and his wife, and Davy Thomson and Mr King, and to-day there was Aelec Brands. Well, Aelec, too, had to hear all about the way the car nearly rid over me, and how it went doon the brae like a shootin' star and brought up in Sir Hugh's woodie. 'An' the queer thing is,' says I to him, 'that though I never before saw the young man'—meaning you, Mr Alistair—'he knew my name, and had been warned about the short-cut across the Larach.' 'Stop,' says Aelec. 'Stop, now, and begin over again. Tell me what the car was like and the two in it.'"

"'A careless tow-head,' says you," put in Paddy Joe, "'and a rawbone Yankee.'"

"I did well enough by the gentleman, maybe, but, fegs, I missed the bit eddication to limn the lady. I did so."

Paddy Joe gestured with his hand—hopelessly.

"Aelec guessed quick as winking," went on Willie, "who ye were. 'I'll eat my brogues,' says he, 'if yon weren't Miss Carr and the young laird, but 'tis a queer thing that I never heard of it. I haven't seen anyone from the Drum for two days, of course, but, still and all, I should have heard.' That kept in his mind all day, and the last thing he said to me was, 'I'll be speirin' Sir Hugh.'"

"But will he see Sir Hugh to-night?" Margaret inquired quickly.

"He will that, Miss Margaret. Archie is sending a present of trout to Sir Hugh—he caught some good ones with a wee engine of his—and Janet had twa-three sections of heather honey for Lady Sara."

"Enough," cried Paddy Joe. "If Aelec Brands sets out to speir a thing, he'll get to the bottom of it and beyond. He'll know where the strays are holing out."

"Ay so, Mr Long. And if I ken Aelec he'll be round by the Nairn road and in the cart-track with a motor before the night is far spent."

"And with Cousin Don burning the air," added Alistair.

"Oh dear!" cried Norrey. "I think I'll hide under the couch."

"If ye would like to make sure," volunteered Willie, "it would be no trouble to trot across to Highland Drum —a bittie over an hour——"

"You might miss the car," objected Margaret, "and you have been on your feet all day."

"Give your hunch a chance," said Alistair. "Another night will not harm us."

"Just so, Mr Alistair. There's a bed for the ladies——"

"A very comfortable bed too, Mr Raasay," complimented Norrey.

"And I have no complaint against this fine old couch," said Alistair.

Margaret rose from the table. "Won't uncle be surprised to see me here?" she chuckled. "He'll be thinking I stayed at Reroppe.—Come, Norrey, and let us wash up before they arrive."

"Na, na!" cried Willie. "The puckle dishes can bide the morn. I'll just shift them to the back place."

VI

When Willie returned from the "back place" he found the four arranged on the long settle, Margaret and Norrey at the two ends, and Alistair next to Margaret. "I see you are avoiding the fireside chair," said Willie.

"We have no cause to complain," said Paddy Joe, his head over the back of the settee and his eye watching the smoke from his pipe drift against the deep brown of the ceiling.

Willie picked a hazel-wood pipe from the top of the book-shelf, and let himself down between the wide arms of the chair. The Irishman bestirred himself a moment and slid his pouch across the table.

A comfortable silence settled down amongst them—a silence that seemed to ray in through walls and roof, and that was part of the great quiet of Larach na Gael, that could not be barred out by any walls or affected by any human currents. Speech made no ripple on that quiet, and presently Margaret spoke softly to Willie. "This place is not haunted like the Campagna?"

228

"There is no evil in it, whatever."

"That much can be felt."

"A strange atmosphere of repose about it," murmured Norrey.

"Too much supper we had, maybe," said Paddy Joe, and found a subtle elbow in his ribs.

"No repose about you," he complained. "Do that again and I'll sit over by Margaret."

"Any spirit that haunts this place," half-mused Margaret "—haunt is not the word. It would be a gentle spirit, at any rate."

"I have not seen any, Miss Margaret," said Willie. "Maybe in the half-gloaming or the middle of a sunny day, and you wool-gathering, you'd be imagining grey wraiths of shadow among the trees or round the side of a humplock. But it would be all imagination, for when you blinked your ee there would only be a sheep grazing, or just naething at all."

"Or just naething at all," repeated Margaret. "But perhaps something was there that could be seen only when the mind was—well, wool-gathering."

"On the old tack!" Alistair put in. "You think the past haunts this place?"

"I know it does."

"It only appeals to me as a strayed bit of the wilderness."

"Did you always feel the same sense of ease in the wilderness?"

Alistair went into the recesses of memory for a space. "No! In the wilderness you felt—that is the real unpeopled wilderness—there was always a sense of desolation. You felt up against something—not human—and had to buckle your mind down to the thing in hand."

"You felt differently in Larach na Gael. You felt there was a haven round every corner."

"If this place is haunted by the past," Alistair went off on another tack, "I would like to know some facts about it."

Margaret looked to Willie Raasay.

"I couldna tell you," he replied. "There is nae record of the place that I ever got hold of. Larach na Gael—the 'place of the Gael' that means—and why, I couldna be sayin'! There was never a battle in it, and there's nae auld ruin or building in it of any kind—except this hoosie. I am by way of thinking sometimes it was a kind of sanctuary, the same as you'll get in the deer forests—only a sanctuary for men. A place where the clans kept a truce, and a good many of them joined lands about here—and always tulzieing at that. But it is no' the exact thing to say the place is haunted—'tis only the feel of the place, ye ken."

"Margaret has made her point," said Paddy Joe, settling himself down in the way that portended talk. "I would say myself that every place in these islands is haunted, and no place more than another place. If you live long enough in a place—or are kin to it—the spirit of the place gets hold of you. The theologians speak of a Guardian Angel, and that might be the same thing—safeguarding you when necessary and destroying you if necessary. In extreme cases an actual physical form is assumed. I remember an aunt of mine——"

"Who saw a ghost?" Alistair put in.

"She did, then. Everybody's aunt's seen a ghost, as Mr Dooley says."

"Go on, Paddy Joe," urged Norrey. "Tell us about it."

"Why wouldn't I?" said Paddy Joe. "This is the time for talk."

VII

Paddy Joe knew it was the time for talk. Enough had happened to set a small devil of unrest at work. And so he essayed with all his might to gather the minds of three of his listeners inside his own, and, aided by the mystic spirit of Larach na Gael, give them a fresh vision for a little while.

"It was a place unlike this, and yet not unlike it on the spiritual side," he began. "Moyvaunbwee it was called—the yellow-white plain—and why, I don't know, for it was only a great spread of marshland grown with green grasses and ruddy rushes, and with little pools of water everywhere—not far from the sea, near the mouth of the Smeorloch River. At the inland side of it the thin-skinned farm-land sloped back and back and back, and up and up and up, to the heathery flat top of Cahirconree—a weary slope dotted with white houses, where the cocks crowed when they had no right to crow and the dogs howled without reason.

"Down by the edge of the marsh was the household of the MacCarthys—the people I am now telling you about. That household for twenty years had consisted of the widowed mother, two tall sons, and a grown daughter, and these four lived in a world of their own— equable, subdued, self-sufficient, barely touching elbows with the scarcely less quiet world round them. Their backs were turned to the weary slope of Cahirconree, and before their eyes, all their waking hours, was the

231

wide, desolate, water-splashed, russet-green level of Moyvaunbwee Marsh. That's the sort of place it was."

"I can see it," whispered Margaret to Alistair. "Can you?"

"It weighs on me already."

"And that is a good sign," murmured Margaret.

"Twenty years, I said," went on Paddy Joe. "Ay! Twenty years drifted by before there came a break in that household, and then, in sunny May weather, the mother died; and Maire, the daughter, was left alone in the house, in the bawn, in the byre, fifteen hours out of every twenty-four. All alone!—for the men of Ireland are out-door men, and a house is only a shelter and a sleeping-place. All day long and every long day Maire did her own work and the work her mother had done by her side for twenty drifting years. For twenty years mother and daughter had lived in a communion so close, so sure, so implicit, that soul had mingled with soul in some mystic unity; saying little to each other, not needing to say anything—sedate, subdued, continent, within the inner circle of content. You can picture the unity for yourselves.

"And now Death, that bungler, had failed to complete his work, for he had only snapped the physical tie without unloosening the tie of soul. No longer in day or dark was there anyone at Maire's right hand or at her left. There was only a great silence and a loneliness greater still: a loneliness more terrible than the loneliness of the wilderness, more apart than the loneliness of cities—a spiritual want plucking at the roots of reason. Loneliness like that is the highest ordeal that God allows mortals to suffer—for a little while, only for a little while;

God is merciful as well as just, and He subdues the loneliness with melancholia and enriches it with that fervour of the imagination we call madness. You can see whither Maire was drifting.

"At first her brothers' incoming from the fields brought some relief from the tension of the long day, but in time the growing tide invaded even that solace. It was as if some dark power was gradually withdrawing her into some still world of its own. A silence grew up between her and her brothers. She no longer lifted eager eyes to them; she did not notice the troubled looks that at last they cast at her and at each other. She was slipping surely.

"For a time night brought her peace, because it brought her oblivion. She slept then, and had no dreams. It was the long day that bore her down—the long summer day declining so slowly into the long still evening that went down and down, and still down, into the toneless unhuman solitudes of the gloaming. Before her eyes always was the weary, heat-hazed expanse of marsh, where the little lines and splashes of water shimmered in the sun, or shivered in the wind, or silvered wanly in the half-light. Out there the redshank was never weary of complaining; the pillibeen flapped and cried drearily; the golden plover whistled lonely; the curlew called and called for rain. And lonelier than anything else in all the world was the long-drawn-out, faraway crow of a cock coming down from the hill-farms in the dead middle of the day. My God! the distant crow of a cock in the sunny, still day. 'Mother of God! will the night never come?' That was her cry.

"Wirra! Why did I start telling you this?"

"The solace will come at the end," said Margaret softly.

"You might not think so. Ye can see, if I have made ye see, that the strain Maire was bearing had its breaking-point. That came at last, at the end of a long July day. It had been a day of sun and haze, but now, in the evening, the air was clear like crystal, and the stillness there filled all earth and all naked space. No shore-bird cried, no dog howled, no cock crew; not even did the midges sing their thin song. In that rare air the usually blurred lines of Moyvaunbwee Marsh were drawn with a point of steel, and the blue ghosts of mountains round far Carntoul loomed ethereal but distinct. Far out in the west a gold bar of light was laid down; that was the sea—and the gold ball of the sun, not yet tinged with red, stood up above it.

"Into that abiding stillness Maire came out of the ark of the house, and went across the bawn to her milking, carrying in one hand the zinc-hooped wooden pail and in the other the three-legged stool and the looped spancel. Two or three of the cows stood head-adroop about the bawn, and these she milked, but no age-old croon helped out that milking. There was only the great silence with, lost in the middle of it, the little frothy hiss of the white lances striking into the pail. Some of the cows had moved into the cool gloom of the byre, and, finished outside, she went in there. The cows stood heads to the stalls and patiently chewed the cud. In contrast with the brightness without there was a luminous twilight within, and under that low *scraughed* roof there

234

was a stillness, an eeriness, a hint of some strange desolation satisfied with itself. One shaft of light, now tinged with orange, came through the western doorway and little motes sailed in it.

"Maire went to the end of the byre and resumed her milking, her forehead resting against the warm flank of the cow, and her hands rhythmic. That cow was the one Maire's mother had always milked, because it would not give its milk easily to any other. Maire remembered that now, and she remembered, with woeful distinctness, every turn of the old croon her mother used to sing:

> Braon bainne—ubh circe—bluir'ime—do'n sean duine
> Braon bainne—ubh circe—bluir'ime—do'n sean duine.

"She turned her sideways, as if listening to that croon, and at that instant a solitary corncrake broke into its rasping evening cry in the meadow beyond the haggard. That sudden breaking of the tense wire of stillness broke as well something in Maire's brain—some last over-taut thread that held her in time and place. She threw up her head and looked wildly about her, and a little gasping cry was wrung out of her throat: 'Mother of God! Mother of God! What will I do?' Then she dropped her head against the cow's flank, and her hands hung listlessly in abandonment.

"The orange shaft of light shone on her hair and on the side of her face, and a shadow that darkened that light made her lift eyes with a start. Framed in the western doorway, in the very path of the sun, stood a tall Woman. The orange glory made a halo all round her, and left the pale oval of her face in shadow; yet Maire knew that the Woman was looking at her, head dropping forward gently, and a tender smile on her lips and in her eyes. She was robed in flowing white, and over the white was a blue mantle.

"The tall Woman came within the doorway, and Maire drew in a long breath. She trembled through all her being, but she was not afraid. The Woman moved along the line of the cows, and, as she moved, her arm lifted and her hand went soothingly over the sleek backs —so would one do who was used to cows; so would one do who might have lain content near a cradling manger. Maire turned her face away, bowed her head, closed her eyes, and, in an ecstasy outside the domain of imagination, listened to the soft swish of that approach. It came to her, paused, and went on, but, for a single moment, she had felt the ineffable touch of fingers on her hair. Then there was nothing but the silence. Oh! but there was more than silence. There was a peace that wrapped Maire round, that was of her and in her— a gift vouchsafed to a simple peasant girl outside the command of princes—the peace that passeth all understanding.

"In time Maire lifted her head. She was alone in the byre with her cows, and the cows were quietly chewing the cud. That was all."

Paddy Joe dropped his chin on his breast and went into one of his fits of brooding.

"It was enough," murmured Margaret softly.

IX

Thereafter silence gradually claimed its own, settling down imperceptibly, smoothly, in soothing tides. For a time one or other drifted into speech and out again, and then there was no speech at all, nor any need for it. Silence, restful and unhurried, was the natural mood. Willie Raasay, cuddled deep in his chair, one foot podgily asprawl, the other in-toed under his chair, might be asleep, or in a trance, or just sheer lazy. His hazel-wood pipe was in his mouth, and one hand held it there, or, rather, it seemed as if his hand tugged against his teeth to keep his head from nodding backwards.

Norrey Carr, lounging in the couch corner, was wrapped in that atmosphere of weariness that was always hers in repose. One slim foot was snuggled under her, and an arm, resting on the couch-end, supported her leaning head on spread fingers. So sitting, she could see Paddy Joe's lean profile, and knew that he was not asleep only by the firm clasp of his jaw on his pipe-stem. Presently he took the pipe from his mouth, and the hand that held it dropped between his knees, and in a little after that Norrey knew that he had drifted into sleep by the singularly softened line of his mouth. As that sleep deepened, his head began to lift gradually to that point where it would jerk backwards and waken him, but before that juncture Norrey shifted a shoulder towards him, and slipped her arm along the top bar of the couch. His head rested above her elbow, and his shoulder touched hers. Then his head began to lean sideways uncomfortably, and his friend, slowly straightening out of her corner, moved her own flaxen head until it brought up against his, gently, yet firmly. So he slept at ease. But Norrey Carr did not sleep at all.

Margaret Brands by this time was asleep too. Her healthy young body, after hours of sun and exercise, called for sleep, and she slept despite herself. Her corner

237

of the couch cramped her, and she instinctively moved
out of it so that her shoulder touched Alistair's arm.
He sat well over her, so that her head, resting on the
back of the couch, barely reached his shoulder, and, in
a short time, that head, drifting sideways, rested thereon.
He smiled a small smile to himself, and set his mind
resolutely on keeping that prop from twitching. He
turned his head sidewards, and his eyes were very near
her lovely red crown—so near that a loose hair tickled
his cheek and made a muscle jerk. Below the line of
her brow he could see her nostrils twitch occasionally
with a humorous, small-animal-like twitch that moved
him queerly, and below that he saw the angle of her
silken jumper lie on the white of a breast that rose and
fell gently. A thin line of fire seemed to twist in and out
in the course of his blood. His roving eyes followed her
slim figure to the shapely black shoes, that were grey
at the points from switching through heather. And he
remained awake and thinking.

x

Time passed. The silence did not change. The
quietude, a quality apart from silence, overlaid all things
as, time out of mind, it had overlaid all things in Larach
na Gael. Outside and inside, in moonlight or lamplight,
in dawn or dark or noon, it charged all things—of the
body or of the mind—with its own current, possessive,
unobtrusive, placid, permanent, and allied to some
eternal certainty.

Time passed. Willie Raasay was asleep or in a trance.
Paddy Joe and Margaret slept surely. Norrey Carr and
Alistair remained awake. Alistair felt waves of drowsi-

ness sweep over him, but held off sleep resolutely, lest, sleeping, he might jerk that little tired red head off his shoulder. Norrey Carr, slumbrous though she seemed, was not wooed by sleep for a single moment. There was some mental fibre in her that would not yield to weariness. She had a crick in her neck from holding her head immovable against Paddy Joe's black pow, and her left arm, below the elbow, prickled with needles and pins. Yet she made no slightest move. Her eyes, under heavy lashes, stared unseeingly in front of her; her pearl-down face was clean of all expression; there was nothing to hint at what moved in the current of her mind—a little joy snatched secretly out of greyness, a moment all her own in years of make-believe, a small sacrifice slowly consumed to atone for a planned future — or mere friendliness. Something did move, without doubt, for, still as she was, she gave the impression of one withdrawn into some secret chamber of dreams.

The motor-car must have slipped up with more than usual silence, for only one of the five heard it come. The first intimation that the others had was the tap-tap at the door—that opened with the tap to disclose the big figure of Aelec Brands, a smile on his face.

Willie Raasay lifted his head. "I heard ye, Aelec," he said. "I have them here safe for you."

"Fine I knew it," said Aelec, "you auld spider!"

XI

The sleeping ones roused themselves characteristically. At the first tap on the door Margaret opened her eyes, realised whereon her head rested, and sat up straight with a start. Goodness! how had that happened? She turned and looked at Alistair, astonishment fighting the haze of sleep with pleasant results. His dark eyes smiled at her with confidence, and straightway her blue eyes smiled back at him.

"Thank you," said she; "And very welcome," said he; and both felt friendly and at ease.

Paddy Joe Long started awake at the first tap, but he started up before his eyes opened, and his eyes were still shut when his hand covered his mouth. When he drew that hand away the ironic line had displaced the soft one. Norrey Carr twisted her head back and forth, gingerly drew a lifeless hand off the couch back, and, with a rueful, teeth-showing grimace, began rubbing sensation back.

"Sleepy-head-softy!" she mocked Paddy Joe.

"Girl dear, the dream I had."

"I know. I made you dream."

"'Twasn't about you at all," he said gruffly.

Aelec Brands bent under the low lintel and Don Webster followed him.

"All in a row," said Aelec. "Good gracious me! Where did that girl come out of?"

Margaret laughed at his surprise. "Paddy Joe and I are the real rescue-party," she boasted. "We have been here all the evening."

Don Webster, evidently nursing his sour temper, made small effort to smooth his brow. His imagination, having already run away with him, was still out of control, and was picturing for him a rival wandering in the wilderness under the moon with a desirable maiden, and sheltering in a cottage where romance might enter at a whisper.

His mind had been torn by storms of doubt and desire, and only one idea was now clear in his mind—the need of finding out how things stood—how he stood. But, dimly, he knew that the moment he started to find out his temper would take charge, and that he would say and do things past recall—things that might lose him Norrey Carr. He could never risk that—he simply must not risk that. And yet he had to do something. He strode across to the couch and looked down at Alistair. "Well, Mr Cocksure?" he said, in that curiously held voice of his.

Alistair looked up at him, and decided at once what he must do—and that was nothing. He did not even shift his position, leg on chair, shoulders alean, hands in pockets. His eyes met Don's squarely and held them. He did not even smile. So their gaze held for seconds— and then Norrey Carr spoke.

"Here I am, Don," she said, and he turned his eyes on her. She was there beyond doubt—all of her—as she always was—beautiful, alluring, calm, with that touch of weariness that seemed to offer harbourage, none of her substance vanished, none of her appeal lessened, the same Norrey Carr that had always filled him with the terrible urge for possession, who would always have that urge no matter what happened. And, God! what might not happen?

"I am glad you are all right, Norrey," he said quietly.

"Thank you, Don," she said equably.

XII

At once the tension slackened. The others in spite of themselves had been held silent, watching the play of forces. Now Aelec leant across the table and thumped Willie Raasay's shoulder. "We're a trouble to you, Willie," he said.

"The ither wey aboot. One of my lucky days, Aelec. Now that ye are here, sit ye doon and bide a whilie."

"Thanks, Willie, but it has been a long day, and there's the motor purring away outside. You haven't met Mr Webster?"

Don and Willie greeted each other, and Paddy Joe, levering his lazy length upright, lifted shoulders and arms in a great breath. "Home was never like this," he half-yawned; "but we'll gang and prove it."

The talk lasted another five minutes, and then came the good-byes, the thanks, and the promises to return. Aelec gave Alistair his broad shoulder as a prop. Outside the door the young man whispered, "We couldn't ask the old gentleman to accept anything?"

Aelec shook his head. "It couldna be done. A present of game, maybe, or a couple of days with Johnny. Leave it now."

Long and Webster came last, and while the others went down the path the Irishman drew Don aside out of the light from the door and window. There he faced him, leaning forward, and his face close. Don Webster sensed the set of that face.

"Have you anything to say, Don?" Paddy Joe questioned, in a hard whisper.

Don Webster had nothing to say.

"If you have, say it now, where no one can hear you."

Don Webster said nothing.

"Have you anything to say against Norrey?" urged Paddy Joe almost anxiously.

"No," said Don firmly. "I have nothing to say

against my future wife; and, by God! I'll allow no one else to say anything either."

"Come away home, then," said Paddy Joe, and he swung away and strode down the path. There was a grin on his face, and a hand rubbed his hair under his hat. "Hell!" he whispered; "I never had a day like this that finished so quiet in spite of me."

But perhaps it was Larach na Gael under the low moon that possessed them with its own quietude—the quietude now of a burnt-out world. The light was a waning light that had taken a million years to wane, and would not die for yet a million years—or was it the glimmer of the beginning of things that would take a million years to grow? The moon, low above the trees, was like a wan flame seen through bars, making narrow bands of radiance and profound bands of shade. The limbs and foliage of trees stood up against that radiance without a stir, and the whole wide shaw was hushed, content, unawed, and eternal. The cluster of people about the low car spoke in whispers.

The car was a big open six-seater, and the three people in the back made a nice fit. Alistair had to sit sideways, and one arm was across the back-rest. That arm was next to Margaret. In time, because of the jolting over the rough track, it slipped down on Margaret's shoulder, and Margaret let it stay there. She did not make the slightest move towards him or away. So would a boy allow a companion to rest hand on shoulder. But then, her whole behaviour had never varied, had given no sign of any under-feeling, had been just friendly. Suddenly Alistair had an intense desire to exert a little pressure, just the least possible tentative pressure—just a hint of a desire to draw her to him. He contemplated her yielding, and his heart gave a stir. He contemplated her unmistakable withdrawal—it would be unmistakable—and frowned in the dark. He dared not do it, but the temptation bided with him.

So they went homewards to Highland Drum.

CHAPTER XX

I

It is now necessary to take a flying leap to London, that grimy web holding men and women like flies. Some of the flies think they are spiders, but in truth there are no spiders. London is like one of those dusty cobwebs seen dangling in the corners of old barns, and of no apparent use to any live spider. And yet, perhaps some sardonic spider sits outside it all and draws to London all the people that are not fit to live anywhere else, and all the people who must be taught to live somewhere else.

Margaret Brands returned to London to keep house for her father, and try her hand at moulding clay into things seen in vision. Norrey Carr returned to London to work steadily at rehearsals; Paddy Joe Long to wield a free lance about Fleet Street, and keep an eye on his friend's affairs; Don Webster to pursue his resolute courtship, and complete his new house in Surrey; and Alistair MacIan—well! Alistair returned because the ties of Highland Drum had not yet tightened, and because he suffered from duality of mind and emotion. He had been to Paris with some of his compatriots, and was now back in London for the first night of the new play, and to make the postponed arrangements for his big-game trip. And so, with these five young people in the cobweb, it is necessary to jump to London—and out of it as soon as possible.

On an October afternoon Norrey Carr, Alistair, and

Paddy Joe Long dived underground in the Strand, and came to the surface again in the stale air of King's Cross station, that strictly utilitarian terminus. Alistair, undismayed in the labyrinth, set out boldly to discover the suburban platform, took two wrong turns, and cheerfully admitted that he was lost. "Larach na Gael—with a difference," he grimaced over his shoulder.

"Not in the same breath, please," Norrey chided him.

"If you were to ask a curt communist—" suggested Paddy Joe.

"A what?"

"A railway porter."

"Hadn't the gall. Here's one—you ask him."

Curtly enough, but with practised clarity, they were directed to the steeply sloping suburban platform, to which presently came a smoke-belching monster from its hole in the earth. In the milling, cloud-wreathed press they scrambled into a carriage already half-full, and settled down, with the inured, to travel ten upward miles in exactly thirty-eight minutes. The people around them, the people that bobbed past the windows were all of a character, set in the same mould, steeled in the same indifference, devastating, heart-breaking, impervious, awesome—gregarious without being intimate, withdrawn yet huddled in herds, alive yet apparently without soul—and all grasping evening papers. The ritual grasping of these evening papers might appear to a naïve countryman as the only reason for the existence of such beings.

With effort, and stopping every few minutes, the train toiled uphill: Finsbury Park, Stroud Green, Crouch End, Highgate of the tunnels—fine old country names

246

applied to rows and rows of grimy brick, basement houses—these were left behind. After East Finchley the houses were smitten with semi-detachedness, and Totterage way the eye was caught with the green of grass and the bare bulk of trees—forlorn sad fields, somehow divorced from nature, without the intimate character of the clean grey-green winter fields of the open spaces where the grass grows in tussocks and every tussock has its tongue—between these two is a rabbit-run, yonder a covey of partridge snuggled last night, and that—that is not a tussock, but a big brown hare in its form.

At last, beyond the Great North Road, at the foot of Barnet Hill, the Suburban drew in to its terminus, and the three young people alighted. About them and above them straggled the dormitory of High Barnet, once a pleasant provincial town of butchers, bakers, cobblers, and such decent craftsmen, and now a desert of cheap villas and a mere sleeping-place. The narrow High Street, wide enough for the old coaches, was now a gut through which poured a roaring tide of cars, buses, and heavy lorries on their way to Birmingham and the North.

A short distance beyond the old coaching inn of the Green Mouse, Fitzhugh Avenue turns off Barnet Hill and slopes steeply to the sewage farm. Some little distance down, and long before that disastrous neighbourhood was heralded, the three explorers halted at a cast-iron gate leading to a semi-detached, narrow-fronted, bow-windowed, concrete-faced villa. On the cast-iron gate was an imitation bronze plate that read "San Michaelo," and above the fanlight of the recessed doorway was the number 4.

"A sound job of work!" boasted Alistair. "We made it."

"Hope Margaret got my wire," said Norrey.

"Sure to. Success always crowns our efforts."

A neat maid in cap and apron opened the door to them. Yes, Miss Brands was at home—would they please come in—who would she say?

"Friends from the North," said Alistair. "She is expecting us."

II

They found themselves in a narrow hall, where a perfect twelve-pointer head stared from the wall into vacancy, and sidled through a door on the left into a bow-windowed dining-room, furnished in dark oak and with a great bookcase of read books against the far wall.

"That girl was Highland her own self," said Paddy Joe. "Did you see the light in her eyes when you said North?" He moved towards the bookcase and looked along the shelves. "*The Demi-gods*—I must give her *Deirdre*—Powys and Liam O'Flaherty cheek by jowl— *The Man who was Thursday*—*The Duchess of Wrexe*: she would get that because of Dr Christopher, that fine Highland man—John Buchan, the poor wandering lost derivative: but she is a Scot, of course—*John Splendid*, my darling man—*Poems and Ballads*, yes! Fiona Macleod: 'Cold, cold it is under the brown sod, and cold under the grey grass'; Yeats obsessed him, but hadn't half his vision—*The Shadow Line*: a short story of fifty thousand words—Thomas Beer: American impressionist—yours, Alistair? and *West is West* also. *The Grey Coast*: one of those d—d young Scots. Thank God, I don't see Joyce."

There was a zooming patter, almost too quick for human feet, on the stairs outside, and Margaret Brands swept into the room like a clean wind—bare-headed and her red curls leaping, her neck rising out of a pale blue overall that, in spite of its coldness, was alive with the rush of life within it, her eyes sparkling, her teeth flashing, her cheeks flushed, and the transparent skin delicate as a rose. There were flecks of dried clay on her fingers. "Welcome, oh welcome!" she cried. "I've been dancing up and down since your wire came."

"You darling!" exclaimed Norrey; and the two embraced and kissed.

Paddy Joe looked at Alistair knowingly, and with a back-handed, small boy's gesture, wiped his mouth slowly. Alistair flushed, and Margaret laughed. She shook the Irishman's hand sturdily, and did likewise by Alistair—no difference in the friendliness, no difference in the hand-clasp. Alistair made the slightest effort to retain her hand for a second, but the loosening of her own firm clasp was too unmistakable. Her beauty struck him afresh and from a new angle, somehow. Back at Highland Drum she had been just a good companion, a live brain, a dashed good sport; only very occasionally did the woman in her send a thread of fire through his veins—and there was always Norrey's subtle counter-attraction. That is why he could come to London and cross to Paris, and keep this visit to High Barnet as something pleasant to look to later on. But now, and for no additional reason, some new element entered into his appreciation, and made a profound change in that compound. The colour of her, the verve, the emanation, the—oh! he had been a darned fool, anyway.

249

Margaret took possession of the party like a March breeze. "Come away up to my den—my studio, I should say. It's nicest up there. The tea things are there too." She had them out in the hall forthwith. "Janet," she called, "bring up the fresh cakes—and the scones——"

"That's a good afterthought," said Paddy Joe.

"And the honey, Janet." Margaret Brands chattered over her shoulder as she went ahead up the stairs. "This is a pokey wee house, but the attic is splendid. In there is dad's room—he doesn't keep any handcuffs in it, Paddy Joe—and next door is our drawing-room. The stair is only carpeted to this turn; respectable people don't see round the corner, and lino is good enough for the likes of us—our Scots blood! Here we are, now.— Shut the door, Alistair.—Take off your furs, Norrey; oh, anywhere! You are at home now, and please, will you do the talking?"

The attic was indeed a splendid room. It included the whole cavity of the roof, and had many angles. In front it was lit by a small semi-circular window set in a pointed arch, and at the rear was a big dormer window through which gleamed the late October sun. The walls were grey, and the floor was covered with a green cork linoleum and a few black rugs. The fireplace was set cornerwise in one of the angles, and in it a coal fire burned merrily. One end of the room, where the light from the dormer came in on the left, was devoted to the paraphernalia of Margaret's art: a thin canvas cloth was draped over something that stood on a pedestal; a great oaken tub with green hoops had a similar cloth drawn over it; a common kitchen table held an array of oddly shaped tools and a block of plaster crumbling at the edges; and fixed to the wall were a couple of wide shelves cluttered with a wonderful disarray of clay models. One full-sized modelling of an athlete's arm and shoulder had fallen sideways, and the arm was thrust out over the edge of the shelf in the startling attitude of a boxer launching an over-arm right hook. In front of the fireplace was a round table covered with an embroidered linen cloth, whereon rested a Japanese tea-set. A low ottoman, covered with a brilliant cretonne, and a few odd chairs were arranged round it, and within the fender an aluminium kettle sat on a gas-ring that was not yet lighted.

III

Norrey Carr threw her furs carelessly over the ottoman, and her lithe figure stood revealed in some costumier's perfect creation of dark blue and tan. Margaret, bending over the gas-ring, and without appearing to see, appreciated fully the picture she made.

"Do you like the flavour of China tea, Paddy Joe?" inquired Margaret.

"I do, ma'am. We need refreshment after the trouble we had. As usual, this American lost us in a wilderness called King's Cross."

"You should have come by bus—much nicer."

"I wanted to travel the secret ways of the aborigines," explained Alistair. "We'll go back by bus."

Norrey had moved over to the dormer window and her nose was at the glass. "What a lovely outlook you have here, Margaret!" she praised.—"Come and see this, Paddy Joe."

"I see nothing but the backs of houses," said Paddy Joe, walking towards her.

251

"But look down there. Aren't these grounds beautifully kept?—Whose are they, Margaret?"

"The garden of the Green Mouse round the corner—a mere public-house, but an old coaching inn once, I believe."

"Them there places do have good beer sometimes," considered Paddy Joe. "Guinness's stout as well!"

"I hear you, son," said Alistair. "Busy just now."

Norrey turned to the room and laughed at Alistair. He had wandered to the business end of the attic and had encountered the striking arm launched out from the shelf. He was in a crouch, his arms weaving and his head ducking back and forth under that threatening fist.

"Cross him, ye devil!" cried Paddy Joe. "Cross him or he'll get you! Wow! what a wallop!"

"Big boys!" laughed Norrey. "Really you have an adorable place for work, Margaret—won't you show us some of your things? Is that one under the cloth?"

"Formless as yet, and should not be looked on. After tea, I'll show you all I have. That arm threatening Alistair is mine—not my arm, but my modelling."

Alistair straightened up and examined the arm with fresh interest, running his finger down the tensed triceps. "Great!" he said. "Remember that quotation of yours—'Action frozen in the moment of explosion'? This is it."

"That was the last thing I did at the Art School—modelled from life, of course. Old Dick—that's the Head—said it wasn't bad—not so very blank bad, he said."

"I bet you! That model had a good arm.—Say,

Paddy Joe, do you remember that evening at Madison Square with Dempsey and Firpo in the ring?"

"I do so; and the cursing I gave Dempsey for nearly losing me my last twenty-five dollars."

"There's the blow frozen—an over-arm right—that sent Jack through the ropes."

"Never mind it now," said Margaret, plainly gratified. "Come up to the fire and have tea and talk."

"Will we be meeting that great dad of yours?" inquired the Irishman.

"Yes. This is one of his early days, and he should be home any minute—long before you'll have to go, at any rate."

IV

They were half through a very talkative tea when Margaret's father, tapping softly at the door, came in.

George Brands did not at all resemble his brother Aelec. He was very tall and thin, and his easily slouching shoulders were not in the least policemanly, nor was his easy-fitting lounge suit of grey worsted. He was clean-shaven, long-nosed, sandy-haired, and his very light blue eyes were not particularly keen, nor did they seem to be observant—rather were they the slightly hazed eyes of the dreamer. There are scores of men like him in all the North—tall, lean, light-eyed men, mostly with drooping moustaches, and usually famous as deer-stalkers, game shots, or poachers. Possibly their qualities are those of the great detective. A first-class poacher, for instance, must be highly intelligent, observant, daring, and subdued. George Brands was a very great detective.

"My friends of the Drum, dad," cried Margaret, on her feet.

"Welcome they are indeed," said her father, and his accent was the Highland *blas* he had brought out of Inverness forty years before—that slow, gentle draw of words that is natural to the Highlandman. No doubt he could assume varied accents, as all Highlandmen can, but his own special accent would always remain native and undiluted.

He shook hands in a manner almost shy, and took a chair by Paddy Joe.

"Have you heard lately from your Uncle Hugh, Mr MacIan?" he inquired politely, while Margaret poured his tea.

"Last week, Mr Brands. Aunt Sara does the writing, though."

"They are both well, I hope?"

"Very well. Aunt mentioned that my friend Aelec was very fit, and deadly amongst the partridges."

"Never anything wrong with Aelec. Last week it was, he sent us two brace of birds—off his own stubble, he said, and that might be. The laird is easy on him."

"It would not pay anyone to be hard on the same man," said Paddy Joe.

"You two seem to be hinting," said Margaret, with a chuckle, "that Uncle Aelec is not above poaching.— You have no room to talk, dad, if Uncle Aelec is to be credited."

"He is not, then, and that is well known."

"He is a dear, truthful man, I think," maintained Norrey. "Remember all the nice things he said to me, Paddy Joe?"

"I do not," said Paddy Joe.

"He could not say anything else, Miss Carr," said the Highlandman.

"He would not," said the Irishman. "It is well known that the Gael says the nice thing without meaning it, and the ugly thing without meaning it either."

"The usual thing among decent folk," said Alistair, always inclined to pursue Paddy Joe's thought to its lair. "A man rags only his friends."

"A bit more than that to it, son—" began Paddy Joe, and was stopped by Norrey.

"Don't get going yet, Paddy Joe. Let me speak to Mr Brands—the object of our visit.—You see, Mr Brands, to-morrow evening is the 'first night' of our new play at the Rajah, and I insisted on Crignell—he is our actor-manager—giving me a whole box for my friends— all of you. I should very much like you and Margaret to be my guests for the evening."

"How lovely!" cried Margaret impulsively.

"Margaret has accepted, anyway," smiled George Brands; "but it is a great pity for me, I'll have to be at Folkestone all to-morrow."

"You couldn't manage it, dad?"

"Not this time, Margaret.—It is very good of you, Miss Carr, but indeed I will not miss seeing the new play. I have seen most of your plays, I think. I have a pass for the Rajah—in the way of business—but I will say the nice thing as well as the true thing this time, and it is that it is not business altogether that takes me there."

"Now, Paddy Joe!"

"Very well so," agreed Paddy Joe. "That goes."

Norrey caught hold of Margaret by the arm. "Now, Margaret, this is the new programme, since Mr Brands can't come. You'll pick me up at the Rajah at six, and we'll dine early. Paddy Joe will allow me only a small plate of soup and a smaller cup of coffee. Then after the play—if we survive—we'll have supper somewhere—I must have supper. You will stay the night at my flat—I have a spare nook. You must! We'll throw the men out—on their ears—as Alistair says—and talk all night."

While Norrey was speaking Paddy Joe turned aside and looked at George Brands's profile out of a set face, and there was some inexplicable challenge in his look.

"That is a splendid treat arranged for you, Margaret," her father said. "I hope you will not inconvenience Miss Carr."

"I fear I shall, dad."

"You won't, faith!" said Paddy Joe, the tension gone from his face.

"Which ear should a fellow fall on?" wondered Alistair.

George Brands turned to Long and again smiled. "Another time I've said the nice thing and the true thing, Mr Long."

"I take off my hat to you, sir. You are a good judge and a quick one."

"Whatever do they mean?" Norrey inquired.

"Mr Brands has just paid you the highest compliment," Alistair further mystified her.

"The young devil is Highland after all," cried Paddy Joe.

"Why wouldn't he?" chuckled Margaret imitatively.

CHAPTER XXI

I

Margaret, Alistair, and Paddy Joe came to their box in good time. They had dined early with Norrey Carr and Don Webster, and then Don had gone to escort his chaperoning aunt to the theatre, while they had taken a taxi and dropped Norrey, all nerves, at the stage-door.

"Never you mind, girl dear," Paddy Joe had said, his hand on her arm; "'tis the thoroughbred has nerves."

"I wish you'd let me retire, Paddy Joe," she had said miserably.

"I will, too—New Year's Day as ever was."

The narrowish doors of all the boxes were shut, and only the faintest sigh came through from the huge auditorium. The usher found their number and threw the door open, and then the deep sustained hum struck them as with a blow—a sound more than a little awesome and not at all pleasant. Margaret hesitated a moment, and Paddy Joe patted her robed shoulder. "Mankind in the mass only, and safely leashed," he said.

The curtains were yet half-drawn, and the triangle they made was an intense haze of light. Above their heads was the subdued glow of an alabaster basin.

"Prepare to be seen, Margaret Brands," said Alistair; and to himself he added, "and you're worth seeing, by Jiminy!"

He slipped off the graceful, blue-caped, squirrel-collared wrap that hid her evening dress of black and gold—colours that admirably emphasised her colouring: the copper of her hair, and yet more the lustre of her skin. He placed a chair for her near the front of the box, and as she sat he looked down on her slim silken shoulders, the long curve of her arms, her fine hands curving from the wrists, and felt his manhood alive in him. "What a dub I am!" was his thought, but he wasn't sure why.

"Let me see the kind of crowd is in it," said Paddy Joe, behind them, and Alistair leant over Margaret and flicked the curtain aside.

It seemed as if all eyes turned on them at once. Margaret bore the ordeal calmly. She settled down into her chair, and one arm rested with easy casualness on the broad cream bar of the box. Alistair took a chair at her side and a little behind; while Paddy Joe stood leg-wide behind them, his white shirt-front bulging, his hands deep in his pockets, and a cynical humour round his mouth. "A terrible great crowd!" he said. "What came they out to see?"

'Women clothed in rich garments, mostly," said Alistair promptly.

"Who dream of the palaces of kings," added Margaret.

"It is well for them to have at least dreams," said Paddy Joe.

A first night is always an early night, and already the house was full from the ocean of the pit to the gallery, a mile up in the sky—no, not the sky, but in a dimness that looked like the roof of a cave. That towering concave cliff of faces was no more than a mottled surface through which eyes looked and looked. The dazzle of black and white, the glister of gems, the sinuousness of arms, the blare of colours were not half so intoxicating as the wandering electric shock of avid eyes.

"Is there any excuse for crowds?" wondered Paddy Joe.

"They hurt one's sense of dignity, I suppose," considered Margaret.

"Be fair," defended Alistair. "Is it not that they cold-douche one's egotism?"

"And a bad thing to do," said Paddy Joe. "The only crowd I feel at home in is the race-course crowd. It is in the open, and it has an interest that is individual, yet mutual. Crowds in cities drive one to introspection, and that leads to the absolute in disbelief. One must believe in something."

"All the great faiths came out of the open spaces," said Margaret, "and all the great doubts were hatched in cities. Cities have destroyed all the great races."

"London is far from dead, I would say," Alistair maintained.

"It is already dead as two door-nails," said Paddy Joe.

II

The orchestra was tuning up when Don Webster and his aunt arrived. She was a thin, strong-boned Lowlander, using the unmitigated Glasgow accent, and making no attempt to hide it, for, like all Glasgow people, she was as frank as the day. And anyhow, the Glasgow accent cannot be hidden, evaded, or belied; it has to be buried with the user, and, no doubt, draws itself out down the vistas of Paradise, that are possibly slightly inferior to the Clyde between Tignabruaich and Ailsa Craig. "You're from the North, Miss Brands," she said, when introduced. "The North bodies never lose their accent somehow."

"I am, in fact, a Cockney, Mrs Kerr; but I belong to the Croft o' Highland Drum."

"A bonny wee place! I mind me spending a Friday to Tuesday at Sir Hugh's.—How are your uncle and aunt, Alistair?"

"Great, aunt!" She was not really his aunt. "Let me introduce Paddy Joe—Mr Long—Mrs Kerr. He is Irish, aunt." And like a set response came the acknowledgment.

"Never mind, Mr Long, you get good people everywhere."

"So 'tis said, ma'am. I was never in Glasgow myself."

She lifted an eye to his lean, serious mask and considered him. "You know, we put up with a good deal from the Irish on the Clyde, Mr Long."

"Why wouldn't you?" said Paddy Joe; and Alistair laughed.

"Is it a fact, Paddy Joe," he inquired, "that the Scots have a prejudice against the Irish; and if so, why?"

"'Tisn't. The Scots took the wrong fork of the road once on a time, and went to bed with the English. They have been kicking each other ever since, and the Irishman says, 'The divil mend ye!' Be easy, now, and let us listen to the fine fiddling."

The orchestra was playing West Country airs, the author and the characters of the play being out of that nation. At the end of the quaint Celtic lilt of the Raggle-Taggle Gipsies the lights gradually lowered, a few bars of Richard of Taunton Dean swelled up, and the curtain rose on an apartment house dining-room, with Norrey Carr and Shaw Crignell—or rather, Mary Joyce and Dick Quinlan—partaking of six o'clock tea. That first scene tempted failure grievously. It not only brought on the two principals at the rise of the curtain, but it involved them in fully fifteen minutes of dialogue that had to create an impression that must dominate the whole play. Norrey Carr and Crignell, superbly matched, created that impression inevitably. Though their every word belied it, though the future they outlined denied it, the whole audience was made to realise that they loved each other, and would go on loving each other tragically. They made it real, and intrigued the mind to leap ahead and speculate, and so assured success, given a just development. With Norrey it might be sheer acting —some said it was not; with Crignell the whole world knew it was real. Norrey, in a light summer dress, her chin in her cupped hands, never changed her posture for minutes—a static pose held tensely to hide emotion. Crignell, a dark and sombre Cornishman, took the bit in his teeth and would go to hell his own road—and call it heaven.

The play is too well known to need outlining. It turns on a misunderstanding of two self-contained brothers who thought that each loved the other's sweetheart, and who loved each other so well that they set out to sacrifice happiness to that love.

"They'll put it across, sure enough," said Paddy Joe confidently, at the end of the first act. "Good business for little Diggery, bedam!"

"How Norrey made her effects!" cried Margaret admiringly. "She was as still as a panther, and her heart came out of her mouth to belie her words."

"It was good acting," said Don Webster quietly, but the accent was on the last word. He would have liked to be sure. All through the act he had been very still; his eyes devoured Norrey, and the subconscious atmosphere created by her and Crignell weighed him down.

"Acting, of course," agreed Margaret. "I know." Somehow Margaret felt a sudden touch of sympathy for him, and that made her elaborate. "A woman in love would scarcely make it so manifest—on the stage or off."

"Do you think so?"

"I know—as a woman."

He rose to his feet, hesitated, and went towards the back of the box. "I'll run round and tell her how well it is going," he said, over his shoulder. He glanced challengingly at his cousin as he went out, but Alistair was not looking.

III

During the interval Alistair and Paddy Joe, with a word to the ladies, slipped out for a smoke—and perhaps a drink. In the first curve of the passage they ran against two of Alistair's friends—young American men: cool, clean-shaven, with the carved American features. One was tall, dark, and serious-faced, the other chubby and dark, and both had dined well but with reasonable discretion. They were old acquaintances of Alistair's and Paddy Joe's, and were very likeable men.

"Got them!" cried the chubby man, blocking Alistair's way. "We have business with you fellows."

"Nothing doing, Sam. Playing honesty for a bluff to-night and our hobo friends barred."

"Sam is wrong," corrected the tall man. "We have

really no business with you sharks. All we want to know is, who is the stunner—that the English word, Paddy Joe? —I say, who is the stunner you have got in your box?"

"Ah!" sighed Paddy Joe. "Maybe you should tell them to go to hell, Alistair."

"Will you please proceed to that region?" requested Alistair mildly.

"We demand our diplomatic rights," said the tall man, who was in the American embassy.

"Gwan, you're only a Yank."

"My aunt! and what are you?"

"A Highlandman, of course."

"You astorantic renegade! Are you aware that you have spoiled this show for us? Even little Sam here finds his allegiance to the great Norrey slacking down like webbing after rain. There's a party of us in the stalls —you know the old crowd: the Watersons and Bebc Kondunck—and we looks up and sees a vision. Then there's you agrinning and asnooping round her shoulder; and says we, every last one of us, we'll weld that there party to our party with the hoops of a pleasant evening. This is us, the deputation."

"He says his piece well, by dam!" said Paddy Joe. "Listen, son. That young princess is the daughter of the confidant of nations—he knows all about you—and her uncle is a prince in his own right."

"She and I come from the same place in Moray," added Alistair.

"Right, all right! Be a sport, fellah, and bring her to supper."

"Sorry, Tommy! We are having supper with Norrey and her party."

"Glory!" cried the chubby man. "Bring them all along."

"Can't promise. Depends on Norrey's plans."

"You might give a fellow an introduction, though," said the tall man. "Won't he, Paddy Joe?"

"Why wouldn't he?" said Paddy Joe.

"Come along, then," agreed Alistair. "You are spoiling a drink for us."

"Nevah mind! The night is young yet. Who is she?"

"If you must know, she is a Miss Brands—Margaret Brands—a rising young sculptor, genuine to her finger-tips—and no man's fool, Tommy Rhodes."

"No need to tell us that, son."

As Alistair led towards the box he looked curiously over his shoulder at Tommy Rhodes. "I thought you were a woman-hater, Thomas," he said. "What's happened you?"

"I'll tell you later on," replied the other.

IV

Margaret looked up and smiled as Alistair opened the door. She had moved her chair to the back of the box, and she rose to her feet as they came across towards her. Mrs Kerr was placidly chewing chocolate bon-bons, and scarcely noticed the visitors. Margaret had thrown on her blue wrap negligently, and it covered one shoulder completely and left the other bare, and in the glow of the alabaster lamp above her she seemed a diaphanous mixture of fire and ivory. She had a natural boy-like sway of shoulder, and the lines of brow and jaw were more clean-cut than any boy's. As Alistair looked at her he realised wherein she differed from her sex. In a world where languor was a pose she was alive, where indifference was studied she displayed interest, where thought was stagnant her thought rippled, where women claimed independence in surrender she had no need to claim anything. And yet, combined with the mentality was the appeal of sex. For she was a woman surely: her hair, her eyes, her voice, her form proclaimed that, and with a subtle insistence. He realised that she would be doubly attractive to his compatriot, young Rhodes—and would be attracted in turn, for Rhodes could pull his weight with most women if he cared. "Blast it all!" he swore to himself.

"Two old friends, Margaret," introduced Alistair. "Mr Rhodes and Mr Lacy—Miss Brands."

Margaret bowed and smiled. The two young men did likewise, and for once found their diplomatic tongues unhandy.

"They mean well, Margaret," spoke Paddy Joe.

"Dumb guys, ain't they?" said Alistair.

This roused Rhodes. "We are here," he said, "to warn Miss Brands that we are about to complain to the management."

"So we are," confirmed Sam Lacy, taking the cue; "it's a shame the way this box has kept butting into our line of vision."

"That was me," said Paddy Joe. "They were astounded at seeing him in respectable company."

"Astounded at your luck," said Rhodes.

"Well you might be," said Paddy Joe complacently.

"Paddy Joe and I are not used to boxes," said Margaret.

The chatter went on for some minutes, and it was very apparent that the tall young American was pleased

265

with Margaret and her poise. The orchestra was beginning to slow down for the curtain before he could tear himself away—or rather be ordered away.

"Get out of here," commanded Alistair. "We don't want to miss any of this."

"Hope to meet again—soon, Miss Brands," Rhodes said, and drew Alistair into the passage with him. "You'll arrange that supper with us, young MacIan?" he said firmly.

"I can't promise, Tommy. If Norrey and Don have other plans——"

"Change 'em."

"Where at, then, you poor moth?"

"The Corners."

"We're not members."

"I am. Here's my card."

"But, The Corners—isn't it rather——"

"It is not. All the best—most respectable people go there—the élite of the others too, of course. The safest place in London. We—our party are going round immediately after the show, and I've secured a table. There's the curtain. See you then."

"Go to glory!" said Alistair. He was turning away when Rhodes twitched him by the coat lapel.

"Hey, fellow!" he said humorously. "I may have a hard row to hoe, but if you are hoeing I'll make you hoe like hell—and that goes for Paddy Joe too."

"I'll warn him," said Alistair smoothly. "I use an axe myself."

v

When the final curtain dropped there was no doubt as to the success of the play. The actors were recalled

266

time after time, and Norrey Carr, with Crignell holding her hand, received her own special ovation. The demand for the author too went on with its usual persistence until the management decided that the right time had come for him to make his reluctant appearance. He was a small, broad-shouldered, dark-haired man with the brown healthy face of the countryman, and the management had certainly no hand in the short speech he made. He smiled at his own thoughts.

"Ladies and Gentlemen," he said, in a voice loud enough but untrained to the platform, "I thank you for your reception of my play, and for your appreciation of the great acting that made it. I can assure you that the play is quite unreal from first to last, and is only an illusion of a sacrifice we should all hope to make—in imagination. That is its appeal—sordidly decided on. If it has any object beyond popularity it is that it might induce an occasional individual to put, as Stephens says, a threepenny bit in the hand of a dead man and be ashamed to take it back. If it does that, the illusion is justified, and I shall go on accepting your largesse with a conscience no clearer than it would otherwise be. Again I thank you."

The audience accepted that with applause.

"Cheeky beggar!" remarked Don Webster. "I suppose it pays."

"Truth-telling is justifiable, even if it is harsh," said Alistair.

"It is not, Alistair," denied Margaret urgently. "Don't you see how uncharitable it would be."

"A lie worth telling is worth telling," contributed Paddy Joe. "But it shouldn't be boasted about. That's where little Diggery was wrong."

"It was a nice play," said Mrs Kerr. "I liked the funny parts best."

"That's all that can be said about it, ma'am," agreed Paddy Joe. "It will run a year."

"I hope not," said Don Webster. "Shall we go round now?"

"Give the girl time, man," expostulated Paddy Joe. "We'll find a crowd, anyhow."

VI

When, finally, they got round by the proscenium they did find a crowd in Norrey's room. Already she had got rid of her stage make-up and substituted for it her own. As ever, she was a little weary and a little remote—but not the weariness unto death and not the remoteness that evades challenge. She provoked challenge, set men's pulses to the old tune, for she was simple yet complex, frank yet secretive; she promised much, yet hugged what she possessed, and, somehow, made manifest that when at last she would yield she would yield gloriously.

As soon as she saw Margaret she came straight through the press to her and tucked an arm inside hers. "Was it too bad for words, you darling?"

"Just wonderful!" cried Margaret in a rush. "You do not know how wonderful you were, Norrey Carr. I give you no credit for your intuition—but what a head you must have!"

"How dear of you!" acknowledged Norrey, and the faintest tinge of colour came to her face. She reached a hand towards her friend. "Was it all right, Paddy Joe?"

"Right as rain, fine woman," he said, giving her palm a little commending pat.

"It was great work, Norrey," Alistair complimented, and shook her hand warmly. He had been standing back and observing the two girls together, and had discovered that his mind no longer suffered that strange duality.

Here Don Webster brought forward his aunt and introduced her, and for a minute or two the talk went into commonplaces. And then Alistair noticed Crignell edging gradually through the press, and hastened to get in his request. "Will you have supper at The Corners, Norrey? You haven't another arrangement?"

"Leave it to you. Are you a member?"

"No. A couple American boys—you know Sam Lacy?"

"Why, I adore little Sam."

"He is thinking of transferring his allegiance," and Alistair nodded towards Margaret.

"Margaret, you wretch!"

"Not he," denied Margaret; "but I would like to inveigle the other—Mr Rhodes."

"Tommy is your victim already," said Alistair steadily. "Anyhow, they insist on having supper with them at The Corners. Not bound to go if—you know The Corners?"

"Best place in London," said Norrey. "Margaret will enjoy it—and Heaven keep Mr Rhodes."

Here Crignell intervened. He was arm-in-arm with Diggery, the author of the play. "What about a bit of supper, Norrey?" he proposed. "The old place—we have a nice little party."

"Sorry, Crig! Alistair has arranged for The Corners."

The queerly sullen set face of the actor never twitched a muscle. "Right! To-morrow night, then," he said easily. His eyes, intolerantly sure, rested casually on Margaret. If he expected her eyes to waver and droop before his, as most women's did, he was mistaken. Her blue eye observed him with a casually detached interest that was impersonal and critically indifferent. He looked at Norrey Carr with interrogation.

"Let me introduce Miss Brands—Mr Crignell—Mr Diggery."

"I hope Mr Diggery will keep on giving us inspiring illusions," said Margaret.

"What good will it do?" he said provokingly, with his pleasant smile.

"D— the bit, my son!" said Paddy Joe agreeably.

"Hullo, Paddy Joe!" acknowledged Crignell. "Are you in this crowd or are you coming to supper with us?"

"I'm with Alistair's crowd. You've got hold of a good thing at last, Crig, thanks to Diggery."

"I rather think so. A dashed relief too. Norrey and I sha'n't have a thing to worry us the rest of the season—and your old rag can say what it likes at that."

"I wouldn't be so cocksure, Crignell," put in Don Webster.

"Really?" said Crignell.

"Exactly," said Don.

The two men looked at each other. They were much alike, strong, reliant, self-centred, passionate withal, and they disliked each other with and without reason.

But now the crowd had attracted itself round them, and the talk broke up and gathered and broke up again.

Alistair's supper party extricated itself as soon as possible. Crignell called after Norrey as she went out: "Sorry I did not know about The Corners sooner. Bring Miss Brands to-morrow night."

Norrey did not seem to hear.

CHAPTER XXII

I

THE night club known as The Corners covered the whole top floor—the attic floor—of a nobleman's mansion in the West End. The front of that mansion faced a park, and there was a walled garden at the rear, giving on an obscure laneway. The entrance to the club was from that laneway. The noble owner of the mansion was a sleeping partner in The Corners. The live partner was unique in that he was a real Englishman, an honest inn-keeping Englishman, with all the peculiar respectabilities of his class. Besides, he had brains. He realised very clearly what London wanted and what London would be none the worse for. A place to which certain—and select—men could come and bring whomsoever they cared to bring. Absolutely no one was barred and no questions were asked—as long as he or she was brought by a member. But it was no easy matter to become a member. This selectness meant good food, good drink, good dancing, good play, and no permanent element of disorder. The club never opened before 11 P.M., and closed some time after the early milkman's round, and between these wide hours, at certain seasons, as many as five hundred people—not mean people or little people —used the rooms for their various purposes. The English innkeeper, who considered it a plain, profitable necessity, ran it squarely, without any secret sidelines, as a decent Englishman would. That is all one need know about it.

The theatre party halted at a plain door in a high wall, and Alistair touched an electric button. Perhaps ten seconds elapsed before the door opened to frame a tall, thick, young man in ordinary attire. Alistair presented Tommy Rhodes's card.

"He is in the club and expecting us," Alistair explained.

"Right, sir! Will you bring your party this way?"

They followed him down a narrow passage and into a small room furnished with a table and several chairs—and nothing else. There he left them, going out by the door through which they had entered. There was another door in the room—a heavily panelled door with a patent lock—and in less than three minutes this door clicked open and Tommy Rhodes hurried in. "Fine boy!" he cried joyously to Alistair. "You never failed me yet, old son. Glad to see you all."

Alistair did the necessary introductions, and then Rhodes ushered them through the patent-lock door into a wide and immensely long passage, lit by electric basins and without a single window. In fact, that passage was only a covered way leading by the side wall of the elegant garden to the rear of the house. It ended in a lift, and at the top of the lift was the night club.

"There are about twelve of us," said Tommy Rhodes, while they waited for the ladies' return from the cloak-room. "I have secured a big table at the far end."

"My poor Norrey must be starving," said Paddy Joe. "Here they come."

Through a curtained doorway they entered the club proper. The whole top floor of the house had been gutted clean out. Down the centre ran the dancing-floor, one hundred feet long by a quarter of that wide, and the polished smooth of it was surrounded by a strip of rich wine-red carpet wide enough to secure a passage for guests and green-coated waiters. Eight feet above the centre of the dancing stretch, and underneath what was originally a roof summer-house or ornamental turret, was a railed gallery, where a dance-band played barbaric syncopated music. The ceiling of the long room ran to a sharp angle and was decorated by long stretches of mirror that reflected the floor and the dancers at queer and dizzy angles. Between the mirrors were wall frescoes of startling colours and startling art. All round the dancing-floor were recesses of all shapes and sizes, some barely allowing space for a small table and a couple of chairs, some for a table to seat a dozen or a score, others holding several small tables, and all conveniently curtained. Probably these recesses originated the name of the club. The temperature of the place was that calculated degree that is just the fraction of a fraction sultry.

II

It was yet too early for a crowd, though a score or more couples were dancing. The period was that of the Charleston, and whether one-step, foxtrot, waltz, or tango was throbbing overhead, the Charleston rhythm was modified accordingly on the floor below.

"Our table is at the other end," Rhodes informed them, "as far away from the band as I could get it." He moved to Margaret's side and edged Alistair away.

"Dance down to it, Miss Brands?" he suggested, his hand just touching her elbow; and at once the two slipped on to the polished floor.

"The darned pup!" said Alistair to Paddy Joe. "It was on the tip of my tongue too."

"The old dog for the long road," said Paddy Joe, "and the pup for the *bohareen*. Maybe you're not old, but the wind is good."

"I will not dance with any of you," warned Norrey, "till I have had something to eat"; and Don drew back the hand he had half-extended.

Margaret was a good dancer, and the Charleston was not outside her compass. Basically the Charleston is not sinuous, and certainly not lethargic, and, amongst other things, it possesses rhythm in a high degree. It sets a little spot dancing in the brain, and that little spot sends its message to the limbs. Margaret danced with grace and verve.

"You have made the Charleston your own, Miss Brands," complimented Rhodes. "I should like another turn, but must let you know our crowd."

They drew in to the carpet as the others reached the head of the long hall, and Sam Lacy greeted them loudly from a good-sized alcove, where a long table was laid, and where he was lazily jazzing with a young compatriot, while a third, a leg over the corner of the white cloth, watched the slow swirl of cigarette smoke. "Good boy!" he shouted to Tommy. "The early bird for yours."

"And a hook in the worm, maybe," said Paddy Joe.

There were six American folk in the party. Two were dancing, and now drew in to the alcove. There were two Miss Watersons, their brother, and a Miss Kondunck. The ladies were all young, all slim, all beautifully and scantily attired, and they all had the characteristic American shingle: that convex sweep over brow and ear that suits so well the straight-grained American hair.

"Have I met you before, Mr Lacy?" wondered Norrey Carr, with mock hauteur.

"Don't you believe them, Norrey," he besought. "My allegiance is like glue."

"All right, Sam! Get me something to eat and I'll forgive you."

The waiters, who had been hovering ready, came quickly to their duty, and supper began. It was an elaborate meal, long-drawn-out, but quite informal. The music never ceased, and, between courses and during courses, if the syncopation set feet atwitch, a couple here and there slipped out for a turn down or across the floor. Norrey Carr danced very little. She was hungry and at the same time tired, and this sort of life had lost its freshness. To Margaret Brands it was entirely fresh, and she let herself go in the gay abandon of it. She sat between Alistair and Tommy Rhodes, and the latter claimed her with insistence. His lean, fine face was flushed over the cheek-bones, and when he looked at Margaret some new seriousness very nearly ousted the usual quizzicality of his glance. Occasionally he turned a contemplative eye on Alistair, but Alistair did not carry his heart on his sleeve. He was quieter than usual perhaps, and had made no move towards the dancing-floor, but there was serenity in his eye. And yet he was cursing himself good and hard.

"This girl has the devil of a pull," went his thought, "and I don't seem to have fallen for it in time. If she gets in with this crowd—well, I'll only be among others in the ruck. Is Tommy Rhodes hit at last, I wonder?— decent chap too—and if he means business, by Jiminy! he means it."

276

And so the supper went on. Presently Alistair took a
turn with Norrey, and Paddy Joe, driven by himself,
asked Mrs Kerr to dance, and was rewarded by a delight-
ful one. "All Glasgow people are great dancers, of
course," he remarked. "You and I at a single-reel
would astonish these loungers."

"We would indeed," she said, with a laugh. "Even
in Scotland the eightsome is going out."

"It is so. Sure, the last time I was down in Kerry,
ten miles from a railway station, I found them one-
stepping through the reels."

They returned to their alcove, and Mrs Kerr had some
more champagne. Margaret had had a little, but preferred a smooth Barsac. Norrey took only the lighter
wine too, but at the end had a liqueur with her coffee.

"Why not try the Yankee lassie," whispered Mrs Kerr
to Paddy Joe, and he turned his head aside and inspected
Miss Kondunck, a tall brunette with very black hair
and eyes. She must have felt his gaze, for she turned
and looked at him unsmilingly.

"I wouldn't blame you, Miss Kondunck," he said.

"What for?" she inquired promptly.

"For suspecting my intentions. I wonder what kind
of dance this Charleston is?"

"The best ever, of course."

"It wouldn't be so hard to dance, maybe, if a man
had a good partner?"

"Want to try?" She got his meaning very quickly.
"Come on, then"; and they went out amongst the
growing crowd of dancers.

"The rhythm is the thing. Let us one-step it," she suggested.

She reached him a hand and found herself in his arms. He stood well over her, his shoulders firm, and his arm velvet and steel. If she had any intention of leading him through the dance she forgot it. She felt caught up into security and ease, and abandoned herself to his poise and certainty. Paddy Joe was naturally a great dancer—a man dancer—with perfect muscle control, a sense of time, and an antic imagination. Like all great men dancers he danced from the hips down, and head and shoulders remained rigid.

"You nearly got me," his partner murmured. "You are a whale of a dancer."

"'Tis the partner I have."

"Irish, I see!" And added quickly, "I am half Irish myself, you know."

"I would never doubt it. I might know your native village even."

"St Paul."

"Is that place in Ireland?"

"No, but many Irish live there."

"Ay so! I knew a good man once in a town over against it—Minneapolis. You wouldn't know him, I'm thinking. He was a conductor in a street car—but he owns a whole fleet of buses now."

"Was he Anthony James Carmody?"

"Glory to God! You know him?"

"He wants me to marry him."

"Why wouldn't he? Did I forget to say the small world it is? And you going to marry Anthony James!"

"I didn't say that."

"Same thing."

278

"Not quite."

"You must have run away, then. I know Anthony James. The first time I met him was in a street car, he conductor and I fare. He rang the bell before I had time to sit down, and then I sat on a lady's lap—one hundred and seventy pounds of me. 'Sorry, ma'am,' says I; 'these bog-trotting Irish have no manners.' She laughed and would be pleasant, but the man she was with, a big, fine fellow too, was not pleased, and suspected me—and the woman more. He called me a name I had never heard before, but it shocked the passengers and Anthony James. 'You are bad company for a lady,' says bold Anthony to him. 'Get off my car.' The man's refusal set out to be emphatic, but before any of us could move our poor feet out of the way he was on the street. And he didn't get his fare back. 'Have you anything to say yourself, *sugan* feet?' says Anthony to me. 'Not a word,' says I; 'only, from Abbeyfeale down to Hungry Hill on the Cork side of the border the manners are pig's manners.' I knew the accent fine. 'Meg-eg, meg-eg,' says he, imitating the bleat of a goat. ' Is it from there you come? You and I will continue this discussion when I come off duty at the end of this trip.'"

"Did you fight?"

"No, no! 'Twas only our way of introducing ourselves. We became good friends. One should do the right thing by Anthony James—and that is not running away."

"Our partridge will be stone cold," she said; and they moved towards the recess. Paddy Joe noticed that her eyes, with a narrowing of speculation, rested on spruce young Waterson.

"You'll have sense now," said Paddy Joe.

"Say, Billy," she called to Waterson, "Mr Long knows Anthony James Carmody like a brother."

"Brother to a prince, and nothing else but," acknowledged the young man gallantly, but he frowned in spite of himself.

Norrey Carr, passing on Don's arm, patted Paddy Joe's shoulder. "Whom don't you know, Paddy Joe?"

"You," said Paddy Joe.

"And that is true," she agreed, "though you think you do."

IV

Norrey Carr did not get back to their alcove for nearly half an hour. Her progress was a triumphal one. The club was now crowded, and the great, the famous, the notorious knew the distinguished actress, and took pains to greet her. Don Webster did not much like this popularity. He felt that the breath of fame in her nostrils could be of no help to him in his wooing, and yet, had he really understood her, he would have known otherwise. She had reached a pass where she saw through the flimsiness of the life that surrounded her. It meant nothing; and to-night, after the long strain of rehearsals and the final strain of a first night, she wanted a refuge of quiet. And so Don Webster's solidity and certainty appealed to her. He had not enough insight to see that her softening towards him was due to the present circumstances, and, with ingrained egotism, put it down to something else.

When they got back to their table they found it empty. Paddy Joe was not in sight; Tommy Rhodes was dancing with Mrs Kerr; and Alistair with Margaret, and talking a good deal. Norrey sat down with a sigh of relief and a small yawn. "I am tired, Don. You have been a dear to-night."

"I want always to please you, Norrey," he said quietly.

"I know. Queer how this sort of thing palls?"

"Leave it—to-morrow, if you wish." She shook her head, but he persisted. "Why keep it up when you are sick of it?"

"My contract. Crignell must be considered—he has been generous."

Don cursed Crignell silently. "But this new play— if it catches on, it may break records—a year—more."

"My contract expires at New Year—with a fortnight at the Dublin Gaiety."

"Will you decide then, Norrey?"

She looked vacant-eyed across the room, her face suddenly bleak. "I will decide at Dublin," she said quietly, and added, "one way or the other—and a third choice is not mine."

"At Dublin, then," said he. "I will be there. Care to go home now—you're played out?"

"Soon. Let Margaret enjoy herself a little longer. Is she not lovely to-night?"

"I suppose so. She is a clever girl, I would say."

"More than that. That young American is hard hit. I wonder, is Alistair jealous?"

Don did not reply. Since the adventure of Larach na Gael he could not think or speak of Alistair with equanimity; and while speech was bridled, thought was unbridled and damnable.

V

Margaret and Alistair were dancing with perfect unison, and talking busily. It was Margaret who had asked him to dance. She had found him leaning across the table, smoking and talking to Mrs Kerr, slipped her hand from Tommy Rhodes's arm, and placed it on his shoulder with open friendliness. He looked up and smiled.

"I've not had a dance with you ever, Alistair," she said frankly; and next moment they were on the floor. Alistair and Margaret danced well together, with the ease that is instinctive and leaves the mind free for talk. She felt his arm with more than the casual tenseness required by the dance, and looked up at him smilingly. "I must be a butterfly, I fear," she said. "I feel my wings growing."

"This is not real sunlight, you know." He was inclined to be admonitory, and she hid her smile.

"I know. That's the distressing part."

"Remember how you lectured me at Highland Drum lest I like this sort of thing?"

"An occasional night is excusable."

"You can have all the nights you wish. Didn't Crignell invite you for to-morrow night, and I'm sure Tommy Rhodes would like to incorporate you in his circle?"

"Think so?"

"A shame the way you've broken up the poor chump! Used to be considered an impregnable sort of cuss too— one of the best, all right."

"He has asked me for what he calls a date."

"Why wouldn't he, in the words of Paddy Joe?"

"I don't think a steady round of this life would appeal to me—not this night life, at any rate."

"But there are lunches, teas, dinners, motor rides. Tommy is a persistent boy. But you are right about this night life. A futile sort of existence, isn't it?"

"Do you find it so?"

"Well, isn't it? Take a look round you and what do you see?"

"A good many handsome, well-groomed men, and a gorgeous array of women. See that queen that has just come in?"

This was a tall woman of nameless years, with black eyes, black brows, and intensely black hair. She had a splendidly erect torso, and was draped from neck to ankle in a black tasselled mantle that fell in curving diagonal folds. Her hooded eye and aquiline lemon face seemed to dominate the room.

"Do you know her?" Margaret asked.

"I don't know her," Alistair replied, after a single glance. "I know who she is, but—I don't know her crowd."

"Of course not," said Margaret, appreciating his tone.

"Yes! a good many groomed men," he half-mused; "well dressed and richly fed—tall, stout, short, cadaverous—some ugly brutes too, and all their eyes turned inwards. Smugly satisfied, aren't they?"

"Probably with reason. These are the successful ones of the earth."

"Successful? If you mean nosing along a nice comfortable groove—yes."

"Rather hard on them and on civilisation, are you not?"

"You started me on this months ago—and now I am warning you. Don't let this sort of thing get you."

"I must watch out," she said mildly. "I should be safe, however, with dad and Uncle Aelec to correct my outlook."

"And don't forget me too," he said, with a chuckle that was very boyish and self-deprecatory and attractive.

"I will not," she said, and her smile was more serious than playful; and after a short silence, "You certainly have dealt drastically with the men. Anything to say about the ladies?"

"Some spectacle! Gorgeous, you said."

Alistair, in his present mood, was inclined to be didactic about women, but he repressed the inclination and attained his object in another way. "Bebe Kondunck," he said, "—she has just been dancing with Paddy Joe—Bebe showed me a letter from my sister last week."

"You have a sister?"

"One. Married, too, and has two kiddies. The letter said three words about the kiddies, whom I wanted to hear about, and had four or five pages about dress and dances and cocktail parties, with a little scandal on the side; and how bored she was one night when some arrangements miscarried and she had to sit quietly at home." He looked down at her admiringly. "My dear girl, if you were to talk your thoughtful stuff to these women here, they would think that—that you had bats in the belfry."

"Am I so different, then?"

"You are ever so much more beautiful."

"The atmosphere of the place must be affecting you," she said laughingly.

They danced on silently for a space.

"I think Norrey is tired," said Margaret in time. "Let us take her home."

"Very good. There she is, dancing with Paddy Joe. She looks tired, too."

VI

Paddy Joe was dancing very gently with Norrey, a smooth gliding dance of perfect ease. Her long fine arm was over his shoulder, her light fine hair touched his cheek, and her eyes were weary as with dreams. Both were silent as they drifted. Presently they turned into their alcove, and Margaret and Alistair followed. Rhodes bore down on them, but Margaret, appearing not to see him, slipped along to the Irishman's side, and he immediately laid hold of her arm.

"You have been avoiding me, wench," he reprimanded.

"Same to you, Paddy Joe."

"We'll try one whirl, then"; and they moved out on the floor.

"Blast you and Paddy Joe!" said Rhodes to Alistair. "Squeeze me out, will you?"

"You warned us, old hoss," said Alistair cheerfully.

"No pre-emptive rights, are there?"

"Not yet."

"Fellow, the gloves are off."

"Mine have been off for some hours," Alistair told him mildly.

"You did not lack partners," said Paddy Joe to Margaret, as they fell into step. "I only wanted to hint to the kind heart of you that Norrey is washed out. She is high-strung, that girl——"

"I know. Alistair and I had decided it was time to take her home."

"'Tis what I'd expect from you—the two of you."

"Let us go in, then."

"Not yet; she is watching us. My, but you have a neat way of dancing!"

Margaret chuckled at her thoughts.

"Is it a joke?"

"I was just thinking of the lecture Alistair gave me."

"He's as game as a pebble, that lad."

"You should hear his righteous indignation on the pleasure-loving habits of us modern women."

"What other habits are worth cultivating—for women?"

"Dress and pleasure our sole aim, he says."

"And why not, in the name of God?"

"You have even a worse opinion of us, I fear."

"'Deed no. One must take woman as one finds her. What she wants we give her. Emancipation, for instance!"

"She took that in spite of you."

"And went on doing what she always did. You can't change women that easy. We gave her freedom, and she insists on harem-ising herself for us; and did you ever in all your days see such a lovely crowd of odalisques as there are here?"

"How are we to reform ourselves?"

"You can't. But there is a good deal in the old saw about the dog and the walnut tree."

"Late in the day for that."

"It can be done—figuratively. You may not have noticed that most of the males in this place are of a certain type."

Margaret lifted eyebrows. "A handsome, clean, well-set-up type."

"But not masculine. Sometimes I imagine that so might the eunuchs look in a sultan's harem. Ultimately the odalisques will be left with their eunuchs, and the real men will have moved out to the wilderness, each with his one woman." He looked down and smiled his twisted pleasant smile. "Sometimes," he said, "'tis the woman who takes away her man."

Margaret dropped her eyes for a moment, and then lifted them boldly. "Sometimes," she said imitatively, "the man makes a mistake and allows another to take away his one woman."

"I always said you and I are of one stock," he said evenly. "We will go in now."

VII

All this time Alistair had been sitting, one leg over the end of the table, shoulders sagging forward loosely, a smouldering cigarette in his fingers, thoughts in his eyes and dreams behind the thoughts. His gaze wandered down the long room and into the alcoves, and he faced the issue of life starkly.

"I do not belong to this bunch," he decided. "Living in crowds, they know nothing of wide horizons. These men think they are gods because they think themselves omnipotent in their own narrow spheres. Arrogant beasts! Small things fill the world for them—the best of them: paint on canvas, wood tortured, stone in towers and columns, their own hothouse thoughts in print—everything artificial. Here in this vitiated air they are most natural because—well, because the universal lure attracts them. . . . Yes! I suppose these women are responsible for this sort of thing. Gorgeous butterflies!"

Yet gorgeous was hardly the word. Their attire was too subtle to be gorgeous. It did not embellish—it merely displayed charms in the simplest, most alluring, most subtly revealing way. It was subjective instead of objective, implying insistently that woman's object is one and one only. Look at that long-limbed woman slipping along in a rhythmic wriggle, hips asway under loose silk, smooth shoulder blades outlined, lovely curves of arms thrown wide, slim breasts and slimmer flanks no longer precious like jewels—or that posed woman over there sitting aside in her chair, long arm behind the column of her neck, showing the shaven arm-pit, the exquisite line of leg revealed from narrow ankle to massive thigh—or that sinuous woman, leaning across the table, a manicured hand toying with a liqueur glass, bare-shouldered, bare-backed, the curve of her breast swelling from her exposed side, her flesh a suffused marble. . . . These, satisfied with their object, might well be satisfied.

His eyes sought the floor at his feet and he went into deeper brooding. "I do not belong here," he decided. "I belong to the open. Then why am I here? Why the thundering blazes am I here?"

Margaret, coming in from the floor on Paddy Joe's arm, passed close by him and saw his brooding face. She laid a hand on his arm and spoke softly, as if inspired:

"Blows the wind to-day, and the sun and the rain are flying,
Blows the wind on the moors to-day and now . . ."

Alistair lifted his head and looked at her, a light in his eyes. "I have not forgotten," he said:

"Where about the graves of the martyrs the whaups are crying,
My heart remembers how!"

Paddy Joe looked from one to the other and said nothing at all. Paddy Joe knew when to be silent. Margaret twitched his arm, and they went on to where Norrey chatted with Don Webster and Tommy Rhodes.

"I think I am tired, Norrey," Margaret said, putting a small yawn into her voice. "Will you take me home when you are ready?"

"I saw you and Paddy Joe putting your heads together," she accused.

"What if you did? I am taking you home."

"When you use that tone I give in.—Don, will you bring Mrs Kerr round to my flat?"

"I had better take her to her hotel."

The American protested strongly at what he considered a ridiculously early break-up of a pleasant evening. But Margaret was calmly obdurate. She would not have a last turn, she would not have a final cocktail, she would go home. She would not even promise anything for to-morrow—she was in Miss Carr's hands.

Miss Carr smiled at Mr Rhodes. "Ring me up to-morrow—or to-day, I suppose, about noon," she solaced him, "and I might have something to tell you."

And with that the hard-hit man had to be content.

CHAPTER XXIII

I

NORREY CARR had a well-equipped four-roomed flat in the select Portobello Mansions, and, at 2 A.M., the four friends crowded into the comfortable sitting-room, and found Norrey's maid nursing an old-fashioned, healthy coal fire.

"Still out of bed, Betty?" Norrey clicked her tongue in reprimand. "What did I tell you?"

"I was just going, miss. I thought you'd like some coffee." She turned to a small table whereon stood a spirit-kettle and a glass-domed percolator.

"That will be all right, Betty. I like to make coffee. Off you go, you poor dear, and don't be in a hurry waking Miss Brands and me in the morning."

"That girl would be a comfort to a man," said Paddy Joe complacently, when she had left the room.

"She is a jewel," Norrey agreed. "I think she loves you, Paddy Joe, but then you make love so flagrantly."

"Does he?" wondered Margaret. "Why do you not make love to me, Paddy Joe?"

"No need. Don't you love me already?"

"I do," said Margaret. "I love you all."

"That's the damnedest thing ever was said to me."

Like decent-minded people after a night's entertainment they were in splendid form. Even the tired Norrey had revived completely and looked round her room affectionately. "It is fine to be home," she said. "Let me get this percolator going."

"I did enjoy this night," cried Margaret, bubbling over with spirits. "Let us talk about the play."

"Have some coffee first."

"Was that night club really a wolfish place?"

"She-wolves only," said Alistair.

"All of us?"

"Every last one of you," said Paddy Joe.

"The music of that delicious band is still in my ears. Listen." She hummed a one-step, and her nimble feet moved to the rhythm of it on the carpet.

"Don't waste that," laughed Alistair, his coat already off, and the two went zigzagging about the room.

"Tireless young devils!" remarked Paddy Joe.

"Take off your coat and sit down."

"Wait till I fill this pipe. Haven't had a decent smoke this night."

He stood leg-wide and filled his pipe slowly, pressing down the tobacco with a little finger, and watching Norrey's long hands busy about the coffee-maker. "The queerest contraption I ever saw for making coffee! Don't waste that match."

"It makes good coffee, as you know."

"It does so, but what a devil of an hour for drinking coffee."

"The whisky and soda are over there, if you prefer some."

"Perhaps when I'm going. My father was very fond of coffee, but he used to drink it to keep himself awake. He went in for a debauch of coffee and Dickens at the same time. He had a great pile of tattered blue-covered volumes of *All the Year Round*, and when my mother would see him of a night haul a bundle out of their press, she used say never a word but brew him a big pot of coffee. She made it in a brown earthenware pot, same as you'd make tea, and drew it over the *greesoch*—red-hot peat embers."

"How did it taste?"

"Good. It would lift the top of your head off. My father used read half of the night, drinking cups of it and smoking like a kiln. I mind the first book I read, I read over his shoulder. It was a story by Robert Buchanan called *Matt: A Tale of a Caravan*—about a wandering artist and a Welsh maid. My father was a faster reader then I was, but he always waited at the end of the page for me. That's the kind of man he was. It was my first glimpse into romance, and never again in heaven or in hell will I get a glimpse like it. I read the book again quite recently, and it's a jolly good story, too, but then Robert Buchanan—Scot though he was—was a greater writer than he ever got credit for."

Paddy Joe slowly puffed at his pipe and looked down at Norrey Carr sitting relaxed and very beautiful in a low chair, her hands in her lap and her dreaming eyes fixed on the glass dome of the percolator, inside which vapour curled.

As if musing to herself, she murmured, "One could always make coffee in an earthenware pot." And Paddy Joe said no word, but his nostrils dilated in a long, slow intake of breath.

II

Margaret and Alistair were not dancing all this time. The temperature of the room and the soft carpet dragged at their feet.

"Too hot in here," said Alistair, and Margaret allowed herself to be manœuvred through the open door into the narrow entrance hall. Against the wall by the door was an old oaken settle without cushions. "Let's cool off," he suggested; and the two sat side by side.

Margaret fell into her favourite posture, her slim cleanly-built body straight, but a little forward, her hands resting firmly on the polished seat, with the fingers tapping out a tune, and her ankles crossed comfortably. Alistair sat leaning forward, an elbow on his knee, and felt in a vest pocket for a thin cigarette case.

"Two left. Have one?"

Margaret shook her head, and silence settled between them. The murmur of Paddy Joe's voice came drawlingly from the room inside. And then Alistair began tapping the cigarette on the silver case, and the tapping went on so long that Margaret was induced to turn her head and look at him. His eyes were on the floor, and his healthily-pale aquiline face was set in firm lines. At that moment he spoke, without looking up, quietly and almost casually. "Margaret," he said, "I think I have fallen in love."

A warm twinge leaped from somewhere and she found her heart beating at her side, and just as quickly some inner guard whispered an urgent "be calm." She was. "I suppose you are not very sure," she said, in the very tone that he had used.

He looked quickly at her and away again. "I am," he said. "I am in love with you."

That direct statement and sudden glance did stir her just a trifle, and she had to fight down an inclination to move restlessly on the settle. She did not want any movement to break the static calm. She made no reply, and, after a pause, Alistair spoke in his casual, yet careful way. "I would like to propose to you."

"Would you mind if I did not accept?"

"I would. I expected you would refuse me, however."

He realised how calm they were, and his mind cast back over their few months' acquaintanceship. From the beginning they had been frank, friendly, genial even, but never had there been a trace of sentiment. Never had he detected anything in Margaret's looks or acts or speech that might evince a deeper interest—no touch of warmth, no touch of unrest, no touch of jealousy— and once he had looked for all three. Even this tentative love-making lacked sentiment. He wanted to set the pace and could not.

"I was afraid—I knew you would turn me down," he said. "I had no reason to expect that you—that you took that sort of interest in me."

"Indeed," she said a little wickedly. "I always thought that your own interest was attracted in another direction."

That remark had leaped to the surface out of Margaret's own thoughts. She, too, had been thinking. Why had Alistair suddenly found her desirable? After leaving the North he could go on to Paris, take up the threads of his own life, and only visit her finally with Paddy Joe Long and Norrey Carr? Norrey Carr? Did he make love to Norrey too? Or was this casual sort of thing love-making? Was she herself desirable now because— well, because other men found her attractive? Very good, Master Alistair! She gathered her feet under the settle and clasped her hands behind her head.

"I know what you mean," said Alistair. She would, of course, hold his past against him—the scrap with

Don Webster, the sojourn in Larach na Gael—his whole blasted inconsequence. He placed the cigarette in his mouth, where it hung unlighted from his lower lip, thrust his hands in his pockets, and sighed profoundly. Margaret gave a small chuckle that was somehow mocking yet sympathetic.

"I am serious enough," he said glumly, "but I might have known darn well that I wouldn't find you easy."

"And you darn well won't," said Margaret to herself —but aloud she said nothing.

III

Out of the ensuing silence Alistair spoke musingly. "I suppose a fellow should make up his mind sometimes —in a worth-while issue—get his teeth in and hang on." He looked aside at her and grinned. "I did not actually propose, Margaret," he said.

"Only an idle inquiry, Alistair?"

"No, it wasn't, either. But I don't want it to spoil our friendship. That was all right between us, wasn't it?"

"Why, yes, Alistair," Margaret said generously. "You know, I think I like you better than any man I know."

"And that's something. Let our friendship go on, but I warn you that I am now one of your suitors—my only job in life for the present."

"One of my suitors?" cried Margaret. "Have I so many?"

"If you get into this night crowd you'll have a few. There is Tommy Rhodes—he is hard hit."

"Perhaps. Who else?"

"I have thought for a long time," he said, flushing a

little, "that you and Paddy Joe have a whole heap in common."

She nodded understandingly. "So we have." She looked aside at him. "Paddy Joe would be a hard man to resist if he took love-making seriously."

"He would," Alistair admitted gloomily. Then he shrugged his shoulders. "I don't care. I have my teeth in." He turned to her suddenly, "When are you going North again?" he questioned abruptly.

"Have you not heard? Dad is going abroad with the Royal party, and I'll be at the Croft early in November and for some months. Uncle Aelec promises to convert the barn loft into a studio for me."

"Fine! You can hire me for odd jobs and as a model of Faithfulness."

"Are you going back to Highland Drum, then?" Somehow she felt a little glow of pleasure.

"Straight as a racing pigeon."

"Ah!" sighed Margaret. "If you were only going back to Highland Drum for the sake of Highland Drum."

"One thing at a time. A live urge is better than a dead pull."

"And your big-game trip?"

"Forget it. At present I hold down a whole-time job."

"I think, Alistair," said Margaret quietly, "that in the end you will go on your big-game trip."

And there Alistair had a small cold pang, a sudden small sinking doubt if ever he could make this girl care. Before he could speak, Paddy Joe's voice came from the room inside. "The coffee is biled over. Stop that girl's talk and bring her here."

Alistair jumped to his feet, and suddenly he was

angry. His eyes blazed at her under his brows and his hands clenched themselves.

She shrank in spite of herself, and her heart jumped and then raced. She tried to smile, but weakly.

"I have a good mind to shake the cold reason out of you," he said angrily, "and let in a little sentiment—you—tantalising witch. You have set me a task, and the task only makes you more maddeningly attractive. Oh bah! What's the use of talking?—but, by the Lord! —oh, go away and have your coffee. And by Jiminy! you have got red hair."

Very humbly she went. If he only knew, this sudden touch of male brutality had stirred Margaret very deeply.

CHAPTER XXIV

I

It was the last day of the grouse-shooting—a clear, keen December day. The quartering sun shone diamond-like in a sky that was washen blue overhead and a translucent pearl all round the far horizon. The brown moors rolled and lifted mile on mile, and every contour was as firmly drawn as in a master's etching. Southwards, far beyond the last curve of the moors, the silver-shot purple wall of the Grampians lifted itself out of the void, ethereal but very palpable; and northwards, beyond the dark woods of Doorn and the yellow glare of the Doorn sands, spread the mountain-rimmed, steel-blue plain of the Moray Firth, with the squat shoulders of Ben Wyvis lording it over the whale-back of Eilean Dubh. There was no breeze, yet the air seemed to drift into the eye of the sun, and in drifting it had the clean, keen touch of cold water on a hot June day. It is only in the so-called "grey north" that a day so austerely brilliant may be experienced.

One morning, a week before the end of the grouse season, Davy Thomson, the head-keeper, stumped into the gun-room at Reroppe Lodge, where long Tom King was romping on the mat before the peat fire with his three-year-old son, Neil Forbes King, while his beautiful, tall wife leant an elbow on the mantelpiece and laughed at and with them.

"I'm thinking," said Davy, "we hae too many

cocks on the ground, Mr King. They are sparrin'
a'ready."

Tom King, tousle-headed, sat shamelessly on the rug,
his son between his knees, and looked up at his servant.
"You'll have a different tale by mid-March, David,"
he said, "unless Archie MacGillivray breaks a leg."

"Ay so! The shameless auld poacher!"

"Why don't you check him, then?"

Davy snorted at that. "Wha's to catch the auld tod?
Ae word frae yersel', Mr King——"

"Show me one feather from a hen grouse of his slaying,
and I'll maroon him for you on The Wolf's Island."

"He burns the feathers, I'm jalousin'."

"You know well, Davy, he never touches the hens,"
protested Agnes King.

"Mebbe so, ma'am," was Davy's doubtful admission.
"The white hares too, Mr King; they need thinning
oot—like rabbits they are."

"What do you propose—a drive?"

"A wee bit ane. Doon at Muiryside, market day,
Aelec Brands was speirin'——"

"I see, I see! Sir Hugh too, and Johnny Ross?"

"The young laird, Master Alistair, is up from London,
I'm tellt."

"And I must have Lady Sara," cried Agnes. "I long
for someone sensible to talk to."

"Aelec's niece is at the Croft enoo," hinted Davy.

"What? Margaret back again. I must have her too,
Tom. She is a lovely girl."

"Don't I know it, woman? She has the loveliest red
hair that was ever seen in day or dreams."

"You were always partial to red hair, Thomas, but
I'll risk it, especially as Lady Sara has hinted to me that

299

there is something in the wind between her nephew and Margaret Brands. I have never met the American nephew, and I must see the two together to find out."

"You mean to gloat over another victim?—Have we enough for our wee bit drive now, Davy—with Archie, of course?"

"Oo ay! he's the ane to fill the bag for us. Seven will be enough, Mr King."

"You surely do not expect to bag many grouse? They are as wild as curlew."

"There's ae wey o' doin' it that I ken," said Davy, with a grin.

"Honest, I hope?"

"Honest enough—up here," said Davy. "I'll arrange it for the tenth, Mr King."

II

And so on the tenth, two motor-cars—Alistair's new six-cylinder Studebaker and Tom King's flivver—moved out from Reroppe Lodge and slipped up the open, winding, moorland road. In the leading motor Margaret Brands sat in front with Johnny Ross, and in the back seat were Sir Hugh and Alistair MacIan, their ready guns projecting at each side of the car. Lady Sara had elected to stay comfortably at the Lodge with Agnes King, and Margaret was out with the guns at her own request.

"Keep the guns out o' sicht if ye can," advised Johnny Ross over his shoulder.

Tom King drove the flivver a few hundred yards in the rear, Aelec Brands at his side and Davy and Archie behind. "Do you dare allege," said Tom King, "that a cock-grouse, picking amongst the roadside gravel, will wait till a gun in the car gets within range?"

"Ay will he," Davy asserted confidently; "but no' on the road. He'll slip into the heather and watch with a head out of a tussock, as long as the car keeps moving. The meenit it stops, up he gets, and then's yer chance."

"If that's the case—and I want it proved—we should make a bag. Why, all the old cocks will be down on the roadside on a day like this!"

"Ay, and a puckle hens as well. I warned the young laird——"

"Who would shoot a hen, whatever?" wondered Archie.

"I dinna ken—yet; but I'll hae an eye open, I warn ye."

"Aren't they silly fowl?" said Tom King.

"They are not educated to cars," said Aelec. "Each year they forget, and each year learn, that a man on his two feet means danger. You wouldn't have a bird within two hundred yards of the road if as much as a shepherd——"

"I'll put two pellets where they'd be hard to get at in ony dawm shepherd that comes doon this road the day," said Davy with emphasis.

"So ye should," agreed Aelec. "Who taught you this poacher's trick, David?"

"Wha but Archie MacGillivray?"

"It was a cousin of mine over in the Cawdor Moors learned it to me," said Archie, his blue eyes crinkling over his fine mat of brown beard. "He was a crofter, the same as yourself, Aelec—all thae crofters are given to poaching."

"Sir Hugh has hinted as much in my hearing," remarked Tom King suavely.

"And in mine too," said Aelec.

"This cousin of mine was a poacher, whatever," said Archie; "but he used a horse and cart for the job, and the shelt kenn't the business same as if he was a Christian. Man, he would slow down and come to the halt as smooth as an eel. I never missed a—but what am I saying?"

"The truth for aince, ye auld scunner," said Davy.

"Thae motor-cars are a bit jerky kind for good shooting, I'm thinking," said Archie.

"We shall soon know," said Tom King. "See! They are slowing down."

III

At no time did the Studebaker exceed a five-mile crawl, and the old flivver had now and then to roar on a loosened clutch to maintain its distance. Alistair, his neck craned so that he could look over the wind-screen, suddenly stiffened. "On the road—two hundred yards about," he whispered to his uncle.

"I see him," said Sir Hugh quietly, running his left hand down the barrels. "He is into my side."

Johnny Ross, of the experienced eye, had been on the look-out also. "On your side, Mr Alistair," he warned out of the corner of his mouth. "Nearer here—inside the bent post."

Alistair's quick eye at once picked out the lifted head in the heather.

"I see it too," whispered Margaret excitedly. "Is it a cock, Johnny?"

"Look at the head on him," said Johnny. "I'll stop as quiet as I can, Mr Alistair, an' ye'll hae tae be quick. I'm nae up to this slow driving."

Alistair held his gun with tight muscles, and noted that a little pleasant throb of excitement went through him. The old cock's head remained as still as a bit of stick thrust into a clump. The car slowed down and stopped exactly in front, a grouse seemed to explode from the heather, and Alistair's gun banged on the instant. But the car had stopped with just the slightest jerk, and Alistair felt that jerk as he touched the trigger. The grouse soared into the moor on spread wings, and a stentorian bellow came from the car behind. It belonged to Davy Thomson. "Dom it, man! She was a hen."

Beyond doubt the bird missed by Alistair was a hen. Johnny Ross explained quickly. "The auld cock is still there. He's been in the wars afore. He dodged down and thinks he's deceivin' us. Slip out and you'll get him."

Alistair fumbled open the door, and did not even take time to reload the empty barrel. The road was fenced from the moor by a few sagging strands of wire strung on posts that leaned at every angle, and Alistair in two strides had an active leg over the top wire. As he was in that unbalanced posture the wary old cock whirred up with an alarming "Keok-kek," and Alistair, in a hurry, threw up his gun and fired. He knew, even as he pressed trigger, that he was behind his bird. Instead of going straight ahead the veteran had slanted off at a sharp angle, and Alistair in his unstable position could not pull the sight on him. The kick of the gun threw him off his precarious poise, and he lurched backwards. The angle of his knee caught the wire, the wire sagged easily, and Alistair was on his back on the grassy margin of the road, his legs to the sky, the gun above his head, and apt American phrases impinging the crisp air. Margaret's shameless peal of laughter rang out, and Alistair paused to call her a darned vixen. Johnny Ross smiled, but admiringly, for he noted how the young man, at the risk of his head, had held the fowling-piece out of harm's way.

As Alistair kicked his feet free from the wire, a gun banged heavily from the flivver behind, and he jerked his head up in time to see the old cock he had missed check, crumple, and fall like a stone. The old bird had not been wise enough, after all. He had slanted in the wrong direction, and though he was moving at a furious pace, he was not more than sixty yards out abreast of the second car—a reasonably safe distance at the angle and the speed, not reckoning with Archie MacGillivray.

"Try for him, Archie," shouted Davy, and Archie threw up the long barrels of his gun in one smooth motion, and pulled trigger in the very act.

"*He's* no hen, anyway," he said calmly, his leg already over the side of the car.

Alistair gathered himself up and strode back to his seat, and a perfectly unabashed grin met Margaret's ragging.

"My poor Alistair!" she mocked. "That is what is called wiping your eye."

"It was the back of my head got the wipe," said Alistair.

"Never mind her," comforted his uncle. "You'll soon get your eye in. We all know you can shoot."

"Ye hae to be quick," said Johnny, "but you were ower quick. Wait ye, and the laird will show us.—

Your bird is still there, Sir Hugh—just at the turn yonder."

The car jerked, slid forward, slowed down, and jerked still again, and Sir Hugh's bird came down with a clump forty yards out.

"Bravo, old sportsman!" cried Alistair admiringly. "Give me another chance, so I can put my tongue out at someone."

"Plenty of chances atween here and Ard na Sidhe," Johnny promised.

IV

Plenty of chances there were, and Alistair acquitted himself nobly, but he forgot to put out his tongue. The game was an absorbing one, and even Margaret, though she shrank a little at the thud of the shots and sometimes murmured "poor thing," was pleasantly absorbed—too absorbed yet to admire the glorious sun-lit spread of moors all round them. Sun-lit, indeed, the moors were, and yet the sunlight did no more than touch their surface. Below it, and despite it, they were changeless and serene, unrelated to sun or sky, remote from humanity, resting in that uncaring immobility that knows the certainty of dominion.

The road, a pleasant brown mixture of sand and gravel, wound gently upwards for three miles, and then dropped into a small valley at the foot of Ard na Sidhe—the Fairy's Hill. In the bottom of the valley a stream ran under a high-cocked bridge, and on the near side of this the cars drew in on the grass and halted. Beyond the stream a wire fence came in in a rigid line over the contour of the moors, and ran directly up the shoulder of the hill and over its crown.

"This is the Reroppe boundary," Johnny explained; "and yon's the earl's ground."

The whole party bundled out of the cars, and clustered round Davy laying out the bag on the grass.

"Mak' siccar there's no' a hen among them," advised Archie.

"Twelve and a half brace," said Davy, straightening his back over the line of dark-plumaged bodies, "and no' a hen among them. Thank ye, gentlemen. A bonny bag for a bit jaunt."

"It was a shame to slay the lovely things," murmured the repentant Margaret, looking down at the row.

"A shame that uncle and I should have all the sport," said Alistair apologetically.

"Only your share, MacIan," explained Tom King. "Plenty of cocks left."

"Ower mony," said Davy. "You'll see them back to the road by afternoon, and Aelec and Johnny to pick them off."

"Dinna mind me," said Archie. "I wouldn't maybe know a hen from a cock."

"I suspeck as much," agreed his friend Davy.

v

"Well, and what's the programme now, Davy?" inquired Tom King.

"Whatever you say yoursel', Mr King"; and Davy cocked a suggestive eye at his employer.

"Of course, of course!" He swung his light game-bag to the front, and, from the depths of it, extracted a great wicker-covered flask with a silver drinking-cup screwed over the nozzle. "There's good water in the burn, and, as Neil Quin says, whisky slightly polluted with water is good for man and beast.—Can we offer you anything, Margaret, my dear?"

"I am neither man nor beast. Go and wash the taste of slaughter out of your mouths."

Now that the excitement was over, Margaret felt sorry for the slain grouse. While the men refreshed themselves with whisky and laughter at the burn-side, she gazed sadly at the stark line, and presently bent down and ran a gloved finger over the sleek white-ridged breast of an old cock. "Poor thing!" she murmured. "Curiosity is always dangerous, and it killed you. Oh dear! Oh dear! I'll never go shooting again."

"Agnes is like that too," said Tom King at her shoulder. "She will not go out with the guns any more. Had enough of it?"

"Only a little sudden squeamishness!" Margaret smiled up at him over her shoulder.

"You could make yourself cosy in the car here until the hill beat is over. We go back to Reroppe then."

"But I want to look down at Loch Ruighi from up there."

"Of course! You mustn't miss that view. And it might be that, if you use your gentle wiles, the man you'll be with will forget his blood lust."

"Whom do you think I could tempt?" she inquired innocently, straightening up.

"Any of us, you rogue — any man this side of senility. Still, you might try your hand on youth for once."

Here the others returned from the burn, Davy last and clearing his throat with appreciation.

"'Tis a good dram would make Davy cough," said Archie, smoothing his splendid brown beard.

"Now, Mr King," said Davy briskly, "I want three to drive—me and Johnny——"

"And me," added Tom King, lifting a hand against the protests of Aelec and Archie.

"Vera good, sir! Archie, you'll place the guns. Sir Hugh at the first rocks—a good puckle hares come round that flank—Mr MacIan at the limestone showder, Aelec at the cairn, and yoursel' this side of the earl's wire on the ither showder—this side, mind you. We'll hae nae poachin'."

"I would maybe fire at a wounded beastie the wrong side o't."

"An' no' that muckle wounded either. Gie's five minutes, and then climb awa'."

VI

The three set out briskly down the road, crossed the fence, and spread out round the base of Ard na Sidhe, old Davy taking the short inside line, and the athletic Johnny the long outside swing, with Tom King between. In five minutes the others, the men each carrying a game-bag, faced the hill-shoulder. Alistair held two wires apart for Margaret to slip through, himself vaulted lightly over, and brought up the rear close behind her shoulder. "Give you a hand in the steep bits," he volunteered.

"No fear! I could race you to the top."

"I believe you could," he said admiringly.

He fell back a few paces to admire the verve of her going. She wore a plain, close-fitting little hat over her

308

copper hair, and her head was thrown well back. A knee-length coat of rough tweed hid the fine lines of her, but the doe-skin spats she wore could not hide the thoroughbred slimness of her ankles. She picked her way behind Sir Hugh over the first few hundred yards of marshy, grass-matted ground, and she moved with the activity of a boy, her arms aswing from the shoulders and her shoulders with a little dare-devil swagger all her own.

"The best ever," said the young man to himself.

Archie led the way in canny zigzags up the first steep slope. A quarter of a mile of this and the slope flattened to a wide shelf where limestone cropped through the heather and many huge boulders were scattered atilt. Here Archie waited. "Your stance, Sir Hugh! They'll come at you round the knowie yonder. Watch out for an old grouse, too."

"Right, Archie! the spot I was looking for." He puffed out a long breath and wiped a red brow.

"I think I should stay here too," said Margaret, but a little doubtfully. She turned to examine the prospect. "Oh, but I can't see the loch from here. I must see the loch."

"You'll see it from the next stance, Miss Margaret," Archie told her, and added, "You get the best view from there"—which was an honest lie, for there was a splendid view from the summit cairn. Margaret was not aware of that, and accepted Archie's statement.

The party went on and faced the next ridge. This was steep, but short, and they did it in one burst. The triangular flat at the head of it came to quite a sharp angle at the spot where Archie halted them, and a great, flat, weather-worn boss of limestone stood breast-high out of the heather.

309

"This is the place ahint here, Mr MacIan," informed Archie. "The beasties will come in over the shoulder, and, if you keep still, they'll go lolloping by ye. You'll no miss mony.—There's the loch now, Miss Margaret.— Come on, Aelec!" And they went on.

"How lovely!" cried Margaret. "This is the place for me."

VII

Far down the long, lazy-flowing brown slopes Loch Ruighi spread its mirror under the low northern sun. The ruined walls of the castle on The Wolf's Island stood grey against the sheen, and were faithfully reflected in the still water. Beyond the loch the ribbed hill of Cairn Rua lifted in bold steps to the dark pine-wood crowning its summit, and on its first ridge nestled a squat green-porched cottage. Far beyond, the blue and silver ridge of the Grampians ran across the horizon. Margaret's eye roamed far and wide over that splendid panorama.

"See that wisp of smoke going straight up?" She pointed to the near side of the loch. "There, amongst the willows? That's Archie's house."

"I know. And that's Tom King's famous summer residence on the other side."

"On Cairn Rua? Yes. That is where he met his wife—before he acquired Reroppe from Lady Mary Clunas."

"Was there not some romance? Your uncle hinted as much to me."

"I think so, but the parties concerned will say little. Is not Agnes King very beautiful?"

"No doubt."

"Of course she is. Hers is the real classic beauty. Not much red hair amongst the Greeks?"

"And they perished. Any race running to red hair will not perish easily." He grimaced at her and added, "But red hair is sometimes unkind, ain't it?"

"I suppose it is. Let's see if your white victims are appearing."

She turned to the limestone slab and peeped over, her chin just level with the top. Alistair carefully rested his gun in a niche and placed his arms on the boulder. The mere drift of air there was touched their faces keenly. In front of them the acre-wide stretch widened out and curved out of sight over the down slope of the hill a few hundred yards away. It was sparsely grown with stiff-stemmed heather; here and there the basic limestone pushed through the thin skin, and here and there patches of peat made little brown islands. As they gazed a faint yet clear halloo drifted up to them.

"That's Tom King rousing up the hares," Margaret noted. "They'll come from over there."

"Are they honest-to-goodness white?"

"Like big white cats with, sometimes, a touch of grey or brown on the outer hairs."

"In August, during the grouse drives, I saw some hares, but they were bluish."

"The same—they turn white in winter. See, there is one!"

Over the lip of the slope a white beast loped easily.

"'A big white cat' hits the bull's eye," Alistair agreed. "Rather like our snow-shoe rabbit, but longer in the leg. That chap is in no hurry."

The hare took a few lazy lopes, stopped, turned sideways, sat up, and flicked a listening ear. Again came the distant halloo, and the victim loped forward and again halted.

"Keep those tactics right along, bo," adjured Alistair in his occasional slang, "and you are dead meat."

"How could anyone plan to hurt the timid unsuspecting creature!"

"How could anyone, indeed?" he agreed. Yet his hand rested on the barrels of his fowling-piece.

They remained so still that the hare came on without appearing to notice them, and in a minute or two was within long range. There, fifty yards out, it made its final halt. They could see its great eyes, and noted the timorous way it sat aside, head back and ears trembling. By then a second and a third hare had appeared over the far slope.

At last the sitting hare decided definitely to move from that vicinity, and at a steady, easy, haunch-lifting lope went by the limestone boulder, not ten yards from the watchers. Suddenly Alistair gave an alarming bark, and at once the easy lope shot to electric energy. Head back and ears flat, the astonished beast reached madly for the shoulder of the slope, and Margaret was compelled to laugh. Her laugh changed to a cry of dismay. For the sportsman's instinct, never far below the surface, leaped alive, and Alistair snatched his gun level. His thumb touched the safety-catch, his forefinger the trigger, and the hare turned a clean somersault, rolled, kicked, twitched and lay still, in plain view, on the exact brow of the slope. Another yard and it would have been out of sight.

"O-o-h! How could you?" Margaret was honestly grieved.

"Sorry," said Alistair. "It came over me sudden-like." He jerked out the empty cartridge, slipped in another, and clicked the breech shut.

"Sorry! And you getting ready for the next! Kill away, then."

She moved away from him to the end of the boulder, gathered her skirts, and sat down amongst the dry heather stems, her back to the stone. Carefully she drew the rough coat over her knees, looking tremendously detached, and hiding passably well a certain calculation in the eye. Alistair laid his gun against the rock. "Right, you tyrant!" he said. "No more slaughter." He paused and added reflectively, "A fellow's humanity could be nicely rewarded by a certain red-haired individual—not to be named."

"And your last victim in plain sight?"

"Damn that hare!" he muttered. He walked across to it, trundled it out of sight down the slope, and came back. "He is not there—he was never there—forget it," he besought.

He, too, sat in the heather, back to the boulder, a couple of yards from Margaret, who smiled when he was not looking. The fowling-piece leant between them, and Alistair moved it to his other side. "No drawn swords," he said.

VIII

"It is glorious up here," Margaret resumed conversation. "Who would take this for winter in the north?"

"Be equally salubrious, then," Alistair suggested.

The drift of air no longer reached them, and the sun at its winter zenith had a distinct warmth. Their eyes strayed wide over moor and loch and mountain, but their minds stayed at home and wrestled with an ancient problem. The shouts of the beaters were heard only remotely and bore no import; soon a shot and then another and then many sounded loud or faint from above or below, but these too were unheeded; and the white hares drifted past, hesitatingly or with purpose, and were not startled by even a handclap.

Margaret, very equable and long accustomed to cloak her feelings, examined, head atilt, Alistair's profile. It was a good profile, with sensitive mouth, and just now it was set in seriousness, reflecting some inner cogitation not altogether satisfactory. In truth he was only giving Margaret a chance to forget her humane indignation before reopening an old subject. In time he turned a speculative eye on her and caught her smile—a smile that was friendly yet mocking.

"Heard from Tommy Rhodes lately?" he inquired.

"Yesterday. Mr Rhodes is a good correspondent."

"He would be. I find him that too. He has written me twice in a week. I suppose I'll have to take his hint—broad enough, at any rate." He waited for Margaret's curiosity, but it did not evince itself, so he went on: "He would like to spend Christmas in the country—he that was always a town-bird!"

"That would be nice."

"For whom?"

"For him—for all of us. He should enjoy Christmas and the New Year at the Drum. We hold a brief season—but quite a season. The Farmers, the Golfers, the Territorials give very good dances at the Muiryside Institute, and there are any number of roe-hunts and hare-drives."

"I suppose I'll end by inviting him."

"He's your friend—but you are not compelled, are you?"

"Not that you could notice. There might be some advantage in getting him up, though. I could get Archie MacGillivray to put a charge of shot in him—or Johnny Ross—Johnny certainly would."

"Is this the Highland or the American savage?"

"Male only."

"Not much male brutality about you, Alistair."

Perhaps there was the faintest touch of taunt there. Alistair felt at a loss for a reply, and to cover his silence fumbled in the side pocket of his shooting-jacket and brought forth a serviceable-looking briar and a not-too-new leather pouch.

"You are becoming quite a pipe-smoker," Margaret remarked.

"Thanks to your uncle. One needs to acquire calm when dealing with red hair." He did not give her time for a retort before he added half-musingly, half-questioningly, "I suppose Tommy has already proposed?"

"Mr Rhodes? Why should he?" she put evasively.

"I couldn't say, but I have."

"When?"

"Two minutes ago."

"Did you? Not a very suitable time or place! The shouts and shooting of savage men all around us, in the middle of a Highland moor, on a cold December day."

"And where else would a Highland maid have love made to her?"

"You manage the apt come-back when you like. I am sorry I cannot reward you."

"That is the fourth time you have rejected me."

"Rejection! Was it that, Alistair?"

"What was it, then?"

"I don't know." She stirred restlessly in the heather, and was now wholly serious. "All this talk of love is so cool, so detached!—Love is not like that—it cannot be. You simply cannot be in love, and I'll not overestimate the reasoned liking I have for you. I suspect myself, and I suspect you no less. Seeing you every day—knowing that I may see you any day—why, it is only the liking of propinquity, the attraction of red hair. That's not love as I imagine it. You do not really love me, Alistair!"

"How am I to prove it?" he asked patiently.

Margaret did not answer for a full half-minute. The delicate blood flushed her cheeks, and some surge of emotion went through her. That surge might be sorrow for hurting him, but it looked uncommonly like disgust—a sheer chagrin towards some unnamed stupidity. Then the blood ebbed and left her unusually pale, and her voice was toneless when she replied. "You'll have to go away, I fear. Perhaps that is the test required of you—and of me, too."

"Bah!" cried Alistair. "Enough said. I know you don't care."

He jumped to his feet and thrust the unlighted pipe back into his pocket, and Margaret turned away and got to her feet a little wearily, without any of her usual resilient grace. His mind was in a commotion of futile fragments of reason, protest, argument, and fury. Everything was so hopelessly askew, and he felt in his innermost core that everything should be so splendidly right.

"You make me wild," he cried almost rudely. "Reason—reason—reason—mind—distrust—this test and that! I have a jolly good mind, Margaret Brands, to give you a jolly good shaking." He took a stride towards her, and his hands were out to grasp her shoulders. She shrank and quivered—but her eyes were hidden. Unluckily, were they hidden.

"Bird over!" shouted a stentorian voice, and there was Davy Thomson out on the level, and a brace of grouse coming down on them at a furious speed. Alistair's anger immediately swung on the unfortunate birds. He snatched at his gun and swung it forward, left arm well out. He saw along the barrels the black speck hurtling towards him on a lifting curve, thrust his stiff left arm forward, and fired. The bird fell with a clump ten yards behind him.

"There's brutality for you, now," he snapped.

"Love is like that too," said Margaret. Her tone implied something so subtly provoking that he swung towards her. She was leaning on the boulder, watching Davy Thomson stump towards them.

"That was a gey guid shot, Mr MacIan," he called. "I'se warrant no' mony hares got by ye."

"Snakes!" exclaimed Alistair; "our goose is cooked." And the ludicrous dismay of his tone drew a chuckle from Margaret.

IX

Davy ambled round the boulder, his thick shoulders leaning against the weight of his plump game-bag, and approached the dead grouse. He stood looking down at it, and did not take time to choose his words. "Weel, I'm domned! If it isna a hen!"

Margaret's hand went to her mouth, and Alistair displayed his character in the emergency. He was still full of baffled anger, and one hen or ten did not seem

317

to matter, yet he managed to put contrition in his voice. "Sorry, Davy! I must have picked the wrong bird."

"You did that," agreed Davy. He bent and lifted the body, and took his cue finely. "Ah weel, it was a fine shot, onywey. Ae hen back or fore is no matter." He grinned at them over his shoulder. "Dinna say a word, and we'll tak' a rise oot o' Archie. I'll slip it on til him." He looked all round him in the heather. "And noo, whaur's a' the hares?"

"There's one over the brow there," Alistair told him with desperate calm. "That's all I shot."

"Eh?"

"I think they must all have gone over the shoulder to Sir Hugh," explained Margaret.

Davy looked from one to the other in an astonishment that gradually vanished. "Like enough," he agreed. "Thae beasties tak' queer anterins." He strode to the brow of the slope and stood over the dead hare. "That one is here, onywey." Then he lifted his head and winked at Loch Ruighi, and came back to them, his face smooth, and the hare's forelegs trailing in the heather. "I have five in this bag that I walked up," he told them. "They'll keep up oor score. Lat's doon to the laird—the ithers'll follow. Hielan' Drum micht hae an extra few."

They found Sir Hugh sitting on a stone, his slain all around him—ten hares and a brace and a half of grouse. In a little while the others came in together, and, as ever, Archie displayed the best bag—a dozen hares and two brace of grouse. Aelec, whose prowess Archie respected, had one less of each. Johnny Ross had four hares, and Tom King a bare two.

Then they had their joke with Archie, and Archie rose to it, and—

"Now for Reroppe," said Tom King.

"What about a take ayont the road?" suggested Archie.

"Heather too long. We'll have a quick bite at the Lodge, and before it gets too late try a beat over Tomlachlan. There's a nice covey in the turnips, and a good few pheasants, and a woodcock or two, at Leonach side."

That was the programme that was followed, and little need be said about it.

x

All that afternoon Alistair was very silent, and even a little grim. He shot with a cool deadliness that was unusual, and his companions, concentrated on the splendid sport, did not notice his gloom, though they commended his prowess. At dinner that evening, however, the quick eye of Agnes King noted his absorbed reserve, and shrewdly traced it to its source. She noticed that Alistair never once looked at Margaret, and that Margaret was ever glancing at Alistair with an eye that was at once gentle and impish and hopeful. "These two are in love," was Agnes King's decision, "and the little rogue has been teasing him. He feels baited. If he gets really angry she is in for a surprise, and deserves it. But they are nice young people and will find their way."

Going home, downhill, in the big car, the cosy pack in the roomy rear seat were full of talk and reminiscence, but the two in front never spoke a word. Margaret

319

snuggled into her corner, and night hid her dreaming eyes, while Alistair, his two strong hands grasping the wheel high up, stared straight ahead in the path of the lights. He spoke for the first time in the half-circle of gravel before the portico of Highland Drum.

"Stay where you are," he said to Margaret; and, "Get in, Aelec. I'll drive you round."

"No need at all."

"Get in! You'll never manage that bundle of hares"; and Aelec made no further protest.

Alistair drove them up to the palings outside the cottage garden, and waited till both had alighted, and till the blue terrier had greeted his gods and sniffed round the game. Then he slipped across the seat and leant over the door under the hood. The diffused light from the cottage window showed his serious face. "I'll say good-bye for two weeks," he said. "I'm off to London in the morning."

"A sudden call?" said Aelec, after a short pause. Margaret said no word, but her heart beat into her throat in a single bound.

"Yankee restlessness only. I have suddenly decided to put through that big-game trip."

"Lucky you, then!"

"Will you come?"

"I doubt it could hardly be managed."

"Why not? I can make all the arrangements. I would like better than anything to have you."

"You mean that?"

"Of course."

"By Chippendale! I'm with you."

"Uncle!" cried Margaret.

"Never mind her," cried Alistair rudely. "It is time

we men ruled the roost. Shake on that." He thrust his hand out, and Aelec's met his firmly. "So long, Margaret"; and he noted that her pressed hand did not respond to his clasp. "I'll be back for Christmas—with Tommy Rhodes probably—but first I might run across to Dublin to say good-bye to Paddy Joe and Norrey. Jiminy! I wonder, could we tempt Paddy Joe?"

"Try him," said Aelec. "No lion could stand up to the three of us."

"Ye are very brave," derided Margaret. "Give my love to Norrey."

"A lot you know about love," said Alistair bitterly.

"Mr Rhodes and I will show you," retorted Margaret wickedly, and marched up the path.

"Oh, ho!" said Aelec to himself. "I'm no' in East Africa yet."

CHAPTER XXV

I

ALISTAIR spent ten days in London, and was extremely busy all that time. Even then, ten days were little enough for his arrangements, and, but for the experts in big-game equipment that certain firms employ, he would have been compelled to leave many loose ends. With these experts he discussed such things as Winchesters, Springfields, big and little bores, steel-tipped bullets, rounds of ammunition, the merits of shorts, riding-breeches—even plus-fours—and camp equipment without end. Finally he got things in train, and left one grizzled expert in charge to make final arrangements.

"When you are ready," said this man, an old hunter himself, "give me particulars of your party, and fix your date. I'll ship your things and see to the bookings. As you know, Norton of Nairobi will do the rest; put you through the customs, fix your headquarters, hire a *safari*, engage a white hunter—the most important bit —get you a game permit, and wangle a district for you. Lions, as you say, with a chance of roan and kudu— you'll take your chance with rhinos—have to! a buffalo head if you're in luck. Elephants are tricky, and I'd leave them alone unless you stay a year. That will be all right, then."

Alistair saw a good deal of his compatriot Rhodes during the ten days, but both avoided the subject next their hearts till three days before Christmas.

"This London is a dead hole," said Alistair then. "Why in tarnation do folk crowd together in towns? I'm off to Ireland to-morrow."

"Oh!" was all the expression Rhodes gave to his disappointment.

"Sorry to lose me? No! Well, I'm only running across to see Paddy Joe Long. Should get back to Highland Drum on Christmas Eve at latest. Will you join me there? I've spoken to Uncle Hugh."

"Thanks, 'Stair," accepted the other brightly; "that will be fine."

"I suppose I'm a darned fool to ask you."

"And I a shameless pup to accept."

"Sorry, Tommy. You know what I mean? Glad to give you a fair show."

"I know. I wouldn't accept otherwise."

"You may as well know, too, that I have proposed— more than once."

"So have I." Tommy would have liked to add, "Any luck?" but did not.

"Indifferent, are you?" half-quizzed Alistair, sensing his curiosity. "Well, if you want to know, I haven't cut much ice. She likes me—that's all. She has queer ideas."

"Miss Brands! Fine ideals, I'd say. You are lucky— she won't admit even liking me."

"But she does, Tommy, and that's why I'm peeved. Here you will be, making hay, and I treed by a rhino—probably married when I get back. Blast it all!"

"No quarter given or received," said Tommy Rhodes.

"I get you. Oh, I'll stand you on your ear, son—if I can."

"Same to you, fellow. Come and have a cocktail on it."

II

Next morning Alistair caught the Irish mail at Euston, and spent six tiresome hours crossing the flat, fat, frequently murky heart of England and the sterile, breaker-washed coast of North Wales. At Holyhead he went aboard the white-topped *Hibernia*, and after some three hours of rolling and pitching in a wicked cross sea, drew in to the clean, green basin of Dun Laoghaire, calm within its granite walls and sheltered below the wooded slope that ran gently back to the queerly foreign cone of the Sugar Loaf. He stepped from the boat, through the customs barrier, and into a waiting train that set him down within half an hour at Westland Row in the heart of Dublin. There, instead of the nearly extinct jaunting-car, he took a taxi, and by 6 P.M. was making inquiries of an attendant in the dusty, dim-lighted passage inside the stage door of the Gaiety, round the corner at the top end of Grafton Street.

The attendant was cautiously circumspect. Miss Carr was not in the theatre—wouldn't be till nearly eight—hadn't her address—knew nothing about a Mr Long or a Mr Webster—couldn't say if Mr Crignell was available—the manager might know—who would he say?—Mr MacIan—his card, please—yes, Mr Alistair MacIan!—he would see. He closed an inner door after him, and in two minutes was back with Crignell himself. Crignell was quite glad to see Alistair.

"Hullo, MacIan!" he cried welcomingly. "The clans gathering as usual?"

324

"You do hedge yourself in," laughed Alistair. "I had lost hope of getting hold of any of you."

"Have to be careful, laddie. Actors are kittle cattle, and inquiries are not always happy ones. You're all right, of course."

"Thanks. Where does Paddy Joe hang out?"

"Couldn't tell you. Staying with some cronies—Ballsbridge way. He's just back from Kerry, boasting high and wide of a four-roomed bungalow he has acquired at a place called Ballybunion—hell of a name, isn't it? Going to hole up there and write another novel—and a play for me. He might, too. I'm at the Shelbourne—Stephen's Green—just across there—two minutes' walk. Norrey is there too—and that friend of yours, Don Webster."

"He would be. Come along and have dinner with me."

"Sorry, old chap. Putting an understudy through her paces—flu has hit us—I'll get a bite later across the road at Mother Mason's." Crignell looked at his watch. "Yes, you'll probably find your crowd at the Shelbourne. They went to the races somewhere, and should be back. So long, then! Come behind after the show." He turned to go, stopped, and called Alistair back from the door. "By the way, MacIan," he inquired quickly, "have you any pull with Norrey?"

"Not particularly," said Alistair defensively. "Paddy Joe is your man."

"Paddy Joe won't take sides—I've sounded him. You see," Crignell went on to explain, "Norrey's contract with me expires next week, and she will not say one way or the other as to renewal. A friendly word—it means a lot to me——"

"No doubt," agreed Alistair quietly. "Did you speak to Webster?"

"Oh, damn Webster!"

"I don't mind. He is my cousin, but I won't take sides either."

III

Alistair went back to the waiting taxi and drove across to the Shelbourne. His friends had not returned. He engaged a room and postponed dinner for half an hour, but at the end of that time, his healthy young body calling out for sustenance, he dined alone in the great columned and almost empty dining-room. Ever and anon he glanced at the door, but no one came.

"Probably having dinner somewhere," he considered, "and may go from there to the theatre."

He looked at his watch, found he had nearly an hour to spare, and decided for coffee, liqueur, and a smoke in the lounge. In that comfortable room he stretched himself out in a deep-armed easy-chair, lit a cigar, and looked through an evening paper. The cigar was a good one, the evening paper was dull, even for Ireland, the green Chartreuse had a certain soothing effect. He had not slept well the previous night, the day's journey had been wearisome, and a fifteen minutes' snooze would do him a world of good. The cigar butt in the ash-tray at his side sent up little fat spirals of smoke and slowly died; the paper slipped from his knees to the floor; the room was warm—the thick carpet dulled all sound. Alistair slept on.

He was waked at last by a hand on his shoulder. Yes, that was Paddy Joe. But where was he? Highland Drum—London—Dublin? Of course!

"I thought I knew the long legs of you," said Paddy Joe, reaching for his hand. "Man dear, you're welcome; but where did you come out of?"

"London." Alistair was on his feet and shaking his head clear. "You are divilish hard to find in your own bailiwick, Paddy Joe. I've been waiting here for you since about seven."

"Jabers! I have been in the front lounge the last two hours."

"What? Say, it can't be that late?" It was on the stroke of ten. "Snakes! I did have some sleep. Norrey —she been here too?"

"No. At the Gaiety beyond—Don as well. We had a gay day, I'll warrant you. The races—by motor—and a couple of winners to square us. Then Norrey thought she'd like to circle round by the Wicklow Mountains, and we made the circle a taste too wide. We had high tea at a place called Enniskerry, and just made the Gaiety in time—Crignell cursing as usual."

"Shall we go round?"

"For the last act? Not worth while—Norrey's dressing-room is only two by four. Let's go up to her sitting-room—she has a private one. We'll turn Bett out to flirt with the lift-man, and surprise Norrey and Don when they come in."

Ordering a drink, they went up to the second floor, and found Norrey's suite at the quiet end of a long passage. Betty, the maid, jumped up from an arm-chair in front of the fire. She smiled at Paddy Joe.

"I'll relieve watch, Bett girl," said he. "The lift-man is waiting, but if you make love to him I'll throw the pair of ye down the well."

Presently a waiter brought a tray with whisky and soda, and the two friends sat atalk at either side of the fire, a small table between.

"Did anyone tell you about the big house I'm after buying?" began Paddy Joe, with boyish glee.

"Crignell mentioned it when I saw him at the theatre. Whale of a mansion, I believe?"

"All of four rooms, my boy—a villa, they call it, and I'll name it Moyvaunbwee. At Ballybunion—the sweetest spot in the ring of Ireland, looking across at America out of Shannon Mouth. I'll be looking down on the Ladies' Strand under the cliffs—with the Little Cave and the Grand Cave, the Lady's Rock, the Nine Daughters' Hole, and the Castle Green over beyond. The ladies bathe there in summer in elegant costumes, though I mind when I was young they wore long chemises. And in winter the great rollers come coursing in and lift to the black cliffs with a white mane—a white mane lifting like the soar of a bird, and dropping back gentle as snow. A great place!"

"Did you steal a Liberty Bond—or what?"

"A Liberty Bond? Oh yes! A yarn it was—full length. You knew I was working at it. The publishers say they are pleased with it, and offer two hundred in advance of royalties, and a whack out of the American edition—if lucky. Things are coming my way at long last, and maybe I'll try Crignell with a play—that lad Diggery gave me an idea."

"Good for you," cried Alistair, and then he grinned. "But what are you going to do with poor Norrey?"

"I'll get Norrey off my hands before the week is out," he said calmly. "I'm going to marry her off on Don Webster."

Alistair threw up his arms and laughed before he reached for his glass. "You are a caution, Paddy Joe. I never could get back of the paternal, big-brother relationship between you and Norrey."

"Simple enough. We understood each other. I believe I am the only one that ever understood that girl. A devil of a spendthrift she was, but she trusted me, and listened to the abuse I gave her. I bet you I made old Crignell toe the line to her contract, and now she has something behind her hand—won't need it, though, after all."

"Not with Don. Is Don your final choice? There is Crignell, you know."

"Wouldn't let her look at Crignell," said Paddy Joe positively; and Alistair lifted an eyebrow.

"A more suitable match, I would say—affinity of interests and all that—decent chap, too, I found him—isn't he?"

"He is so. But he is a divorced man."

"Not his fault, was it? Have you these old-time prejudices?"

"I have, then. Crignell was never on my waiting-list for Norrey." In turn he grinned at Alistair. "Once, not so long ago, I was inclined to cross out Don's name and put your own at the top of the sheet."

"And at the time I wouldn't have minded," admitted Alistair.

"Red hair is responsible for much," said Paddy Joe. "When did you last see your— How is that fine girl, Margaret?"

"Unapproachable as ever—when I last saw her—ten days ago at the Drum." And he added with casual calmness, "She gave me my marching orders."

"Thunder!" exclaimed Paddy Joe, with real dismay in his voice. "Not as bad as that, Alistair lad?"

"Well, not exactly." Alistair paused and went on. "I may as well tell you."

Briefly he told how matters stood, and Paddy Joe, eyes on the fire, listened still-faced. "And so you are off among the lions," he half-mused at the end, and looked up. "But you'll come back to Highland Drum?"

"Oh, I'll come back, I suppose," said Alistair. "I'll be damned well hauled back in spite of myself. That's how I feel. And meantime Tommy Rhodes will have an eight months' innings—and he can hit, too. Rotten, isn't it?"

"Oh well," drawled Paddy Joe, as if to himself, "if you come back—" and he went off into abstraction. Alistair snorted. He was about to broach the subject of the Irishman joining the big-game party, when the door opened to admit Don Webster—alone.

v

Don's black brows gathered when he saw his cousin. Alistair smiled and was the first to speak, and, for no reason at all, a touch of the old taunt was in his smile and in his words. "Here I am, Don."

"So I see," said Don unwelcomingly. "You do keep popping up."

He did not mind at the moment how churlish he might be, and indeed he might scarcely be blamed. He

330

had spent a week on tenterhooks, and at this moment felt the hurt acutely.

"Where's Norrey?" Paddy Joe asked.

"Downstairs. Having a snack and a talk with Crignell—business, she says. She will be up in a minute."

"Business is it? Maybe I should be there." Paddy Joe put his hands on his chair arms as if about to rise, and then sank back. "It will be all right, Don," he said, with meaning.

"Will it?" doubted Don. And doubt was his trouble. Norrey Carr had not yet given him his answer. With an obduracy that no longer had anything playful in it she refused to decide his fate until first she had settled with Crignell. Settled what? Her contract apparently—but there was that other thing too, and Crignell had the power to sway her—and the will. Paddy Joe, indeed, might have more influence, and was against Crignell—but Paddy Joe was not omnipotent. And now here was his fleering American cousin. Every time he saw that cousin his mind leaped back to Larach na Gael. Blast him! He would like to smash him. He walked to the centre of the room, his hand smoothing across his chin and his eyes intolerant. "Why did you run away from Highland Drum this festive season—thrown out?" he inquired.

The tone and the look nettled Alistair, and impulsively he sought to nettle in turn. "Oh, I just ran over to see the adorable Norrey," he answered lightly. "Any objection?"

He succeeded even beyond expectation—so far beyond that Don sought in the dark places for the ugliest retort. "Tired of your red-headed wench?" There was no mistaking the double meaning he put in that.

Alistair's face whitened, and his blue eyes had a hard glisten. His voice in reply was low-pitched and slow, but it had in it a grate. "Be careful how you speak of that lady."

"I'll speak as I wish."

"You will not." With a great effort Alistair controlled himself. "You need not be afraid, Webster. I am not here to pester Miss Carr."

"I would break your damned neck if you tried."

"As you nearly did, once before"; and Alistair lifted himself out of his chair.

Paddy Joe said no word and made no move. No doubt he could have stopped the trouble at this point, and perhaps he should have done so. But there was something so indignantly hurt in Alistair's face, some sense of the inviolate besmirched, that he was held moveless and voiceless. He leant back in his chair and waited his time. Alistair made a gesture towards the door.

"If I want to, cousin," he challenged, in that queerly careful voice, "I will propose to Norrey Carr as soon as she enters that door."

"I'll cure you of that notion," said Don savagely.

Whom the gods destroy they first make mad. If Don Webster had known how near he was to success with Norrey he would simply have laughed at Alistair. But some sardonic Providence, having led him to the door of success, got the man himself to crash that door shut.

As once before, he strode at Alistair arm aswing, and Alistair, that trained man of his hands, now in a different humour, strode to meet him—not on loose stones this time. Webster's powerful arm was still on the back swing for a devastating blow, when Alistair launched his counter—a clean, upward, left-hand drive from the hip, piston-like, perfectly timed, with all he had behind it. With the crisp click of colliding billiard balls it connected with the angle of the jaw, and Don Webster fell as if pole-axed. He stayed down.

"Get up, you hound, and take what's coming to you!" There was a hot satisfaction in Alistair's tone now, the first symptom of a live rage.

"Divil the up," said Paddy Joe coolly, from his chair. "Lucky for him the carpet was thick."

Don Webster turned over on his side and lifted his body on his hands, his dark head hanging and a tinge of red oozing through the skin at the angle of the jaw.

"Eight—nine—out!" counted Paddy Joe. "'Twas the roof fell on him."

The sardonic Providence made no mistake. At that instant the door opened and Norrey Carr came in.

CHAPTER XXVI

I

Norrey saw Don Webster on the floor, and she saw Alistair's attitude. That was enough. All colour left her face, that had been washed clean of make-up, and the faintest touch of fine powder showed grey against the sudden pallor of that skin. But indeed she had been more than usually pale as she entered the room, and her eyes had been very weary—the face and eyes of a woman who had at last decided some fated or fatal question, and who had not yet had time to recover her resiliency. "What is it?" she cried quickly, standing dead-still inside the door.

No one answered her, and she turned her wide-open eyes on Don Webster. He twisted to his knees, found the back of a chair, and so reached his feet. Thus supported, he stood swayingly and looked around him dazedly. There was no mistaking the graze on the angle of the jaw.

"What is it?" Norrey cried again, throwing a hand towards the Irishman, who was now on his feet, with his hands, as usual, deep in his pockets. "Why don't you tell me, Paddy Joe?"

"Nothing to tell," said Paddy Joe.

"They have been fighting?"

"You could hardly call it that," said Paddy Joe discriminatingly.

Alistair pulled himself together and his hands unclenched. He covered his smashed knuckles with his right palm, and his face twitched and relaxed. "Sorry, Norrey! All my fault!" he apologised. "It was nothing at all."

"What did they fight about, Paddy Joe?"

"Divil the thing."

"All a misunderstanding," said Alistair.

"It was not," said Don Webster dully. "We fought about you."

Had he fully recovered his senses he would surely have been more circumspect and allowed Paddy Joe and Alistair to work out the tangle by some consummate lying. Anyone but a dazed man could see that the two were searching furiously for a base on which to erect that essential falsehood.

"Fought about me!" cried Norrey, in surprise. "Fought about me?" She no longer looked at Webster, but fixed her gaze with searching perplexity upon Alistair. "There was no need for you to fight about me, Alistair?" she half-queried.

"No, no!" Alistair was compelled to tell her. "It was a misunderstanding—I would fight on your side of course, but Don is mistaken——"

"I am not," said Don sullenly. "You will have to come to a decision in this room, Norrey Carr."

"Oh damn!" cried Alistair, in desperation. "It was only a silly rag started by me."

Norrey was still considering Alistair, and now she smiled tiredly. "I understand," she said, and at once swung on the man holding the chair-back. "No question of choosing, Don," she said steadily. "But I will give you your answer now." She turned and threw the door open. "Good-bye, Don."

That was all she said, but she said it with such dramatic force that it was all she had need to say. Don Webster pulled himself together, and Alistair watched him like a cat. There was no necessity. He walked steadily out of the room without a word, and the door closed behind him. Still holding the door knob, Norrey turned and spoke to Alistair, a chiding note in her voice. "It was foolish of you to bait him, Alistair—I wish I could blame you a little more."

She must have been supporting herself by the door handle, for when she let it go to cross the room her shoulders swayed from side to side, and, as she hurried, she gave the curious impression of one balancing over a plank. Thus, and before either man could assist her, she reached the small table in front of the fire, and laid her hands on it. Very quickly Alistair placed a chair behind her knees, and she sank down.

"Thanks, Alistair. I am all right. Sit down"; and she added almost casually, "I see you have had a drink."

She moved aside the tray, leant her elbows on the table, and turned her eyes on Paddy Joe—wide-open, strangely still eyes, dark at the surface, yet somehow glowing with a light deep down. Paddy Joe was not looking at her. His eyes seemed to be focused on the edge of the table, and, with the finger and thumb of one hand, he was smoothing down the graven lines at the side of his firm mouth. Still, he noticed the move Alistair was making, and lifted his head quickly. Alistair grinned shamefacedly from the door, formed the words "Your job" with his lips, and was gone. Paddy Joe opened his mouth and——

"Let him go," said Norrey Carr.

"The devil sweep him!" cursed Paddy Joe warmly, throwing himself back in his chair and at last meeting her eyes.

II

Norrey's smooth forearms lay along the table and her long hands were twined finger in finger. "I have burned my boats now, Paddy Joe." There was the very smallest shake in her voice.

"Not at all, girl dear."

"Every last one of them. I have rejected Don Webster; Alistair is on his own road; and not ten minutes ago I declined to renew my contract with Crignell."

"Crignell will be happy if you reconsider that."

"But I can't—I dare not—it means so much more, Paddy Joe"; and she added with a simple confidence, "unless you would like to marry me to Crignell. Would you, Paddy Joe?"

"No," said Paddy Joe, "not ever."

"And what then?" She contemplated him, her eyes unwinking and her face expressionless—and then she smiled—a wan and pitiful smile. "I do wish I had courage, Paddy Joe."

"The finest thing you possess, girl."

"But no! I do wish I had courage—now. Oh! but I am afraid—and courage might mean so much!" She laid her fair head down on her outstretched arms, and her fur wrap slipped from shoulder to floor. She had not broken down—she was not anywhere near breaking down—and, though her whole body trembled,

the tremble was not one of prostration but rather of some sudden, blinding contemplation of an ineffable possibility—long dreamed and only dreamed. She spoke as if to herself in the low, faintly husky, unmodulated tone of intense feeling—all on one note that stirred the pulses like rub of drum. And Paddy Joe's head swayed oddly from side to side and his clamped jaws kept his mouth from twitching.

"I have known you for five years now, Paddy Joe, and yet I do not know you at all. Other men that I have met I could read—perhaps because I did not want to—but you, whom I wanted to know and know and know, I have not known ever. I wasn't too proud—I was afraid. Friendship—there was always that. Brotherliness — there was that too — and no more! Trust — it never failed between us — in the issues that mattered. Everything but the one thing, and that always remained a mystery. But it was always there—on my side. . . . Oh, Paddy Joe, I am afraid——"

Her relaxed hand was on the table edge, and Paddy Joe placed his strong brown hand over it. Her fingers closed firmly on the tips of his. "I knew my own heart always," she whispered. "What will you do with me now?"

"My dear," said Paddy Joe, and he bent forward, lifted her hand and kissed it with a very great gentleness. At that she sat up like a released spring, her eyes shining in a face dead white. She caught his hand in both of hers and drew it to her, and he leant forward with it. She pressed his hand almost fiercely against her breast and held it there, and all the iron went out of Paddy Joe's face.

338

"Norrey—Norrey!" he said huskily. "From the beginning you were my jewel that I hid away in my heart."

He rose to his feet, and she rose to meet him. And few women that ever lived wept as she wept.

CHAPTER XXVII

I

On the following evening Alistair said good-bye to Paddy Joe on the boat-deck of the *Puma* at the North Wall. The two men leant on the railing and looked down on the dark turgid flood of the Liffey pouring seaward with the tide. All up the Quays to the Custom House the lights wavered on the water, and Dublin beyond reflected its glare in the sky. A keen breeze out of the south-east blew in their faces, and Paddy Joe lifted his coat-collar above his ears.

"A quick run you'll have, the mate says," Paddy Joe remarked, "with a nice dip fore and aft. You'll be at Highland Drum this time to-morrow evening."

"With news to tell. Aelec and I had calculated on inveigling you out to be et by a lion—not too late to cut and run yet."

"Very well so," agreed Paddy Joe. "Jump off and buy me a ticket."

"Your running days are over, fellow."

"Time for them. I suppose your own mind is made up?"

"As regards East Africa—it is.'

"You'll be back?"

"Barring accidents. Nothing else to do, is there?"

"A lot—but I take your point. Do you know, young fellow, I'm beginning to sort of wonder if you are much good at making love."

"No better than some, you old snail."

"I was thinking the same. Tell me, now, as one man to another, did you ever kind of make the beginning of a motion that might give the inkling of the remote intention to snatch a kiss?"

"Hell's bells! I daren't with that girl, Paddy Joe."

"Myself, if a bit girl told me she liked me better than most meantime, would be apt to investigate the liking up to the kissing-point, anyway."

"Old stick - in - the - mud!" Alistair derided. "You open your mouth mighty wide, don't you?"

"True for you. The best hurler is always in the ditch."

Here the warning bell rang out, and the two friends grasped hands.

"Sure as shooting I'll be down to see you and Norrey at—where is it?—Ballybunion next fall. I want to see a little more of this Ireland of yours."

"To be sure," said Paddy Joe heartily, his foot on the first step of the ladder. "You haven't been in Ireland at all yet—this is only Dublin." He went down a tread and turned—"Give her one, son, and take the consequences."

"Go to blazes!" said Alistair.

"Why wouldn't I?" agreed Paddy Joe.

II

With a great churning of screws the *Puma* slanted her nose off the quay wall, and glided out to mid-stream. The Bull lanterns gleamed steadily in front, and, beyond them and above, the light on Howth Head beckoned confidently. Soon Dublin, below its rounded hills, was only a glow low down in the sky, and soon Ireland was only a dark shade on the horizon, with an occasional light winking. The breeze had the true tang of the sea, and the waves of the bay, with a quartering lift, sent the stout little boat alurch on the first long leg of her course.

Alistair was a good sailor, and slept soundly in his top bunk until a steward waked him with, "Seven-thirty, sir! Greenock in an hour! Breakfast any time!"

Alistair turned over on his elbow, rubbed the film of moisture off the thick glass of the port-hole, and looked out at the hills of Ayr, grey in the dawn. Bare and rugged hills they were; stern too, and a little forbidding; and the scattered houses along the grey-green slopes were built of cold grey stone. Scotland always hides behind that strong and stern front, seeming to say, "Come and find me, and let me find you." And who finds her finds warmth and trust behind that aloof front. Ireland, on the other hand, greets one with something of mystery. She does not break boldly on the vision; the distant hills are softly outlined, and lead the eye to far vistas of hazy green, where undefined dots may be hovels or mansions. Her mystery lures one, and the lured comes to love or to hate.

Alistair, to escape the slow river passage up the Clyde to the Broomielaw, disembarked at Greenock, found that he was late for his connecting train, and luckily picked up a motor-bus that set him within reach of Buchanan Street station with some minutes to spare. His train left at 10 A.M., and he settled down in his corner for the long trek across the slant of Scotland; the rolling slopes of the Lowlands, marred by slag mounds and the unsightly contrivances of an industrial civilisation; the clean lift of the birch-grown ridges into the highlands of Perth, and after that the wilderness—great stretches of brown heather, immense sides of hills, steep screes of stones, brawling burns running clear, a winding stretch of empty road, the darkling gleam of long arms of loch, dazzling ridges of snow, and, above all, the great white shoulders of the Grampians—and then the dark hills of pine, the rolling moors above Loch Ruighi, and the final brake-grinding slide downhill to Muiryside, with the pale northern sea below the strung hills of Sutherland, that were dead black against a savage red sunset.

He had sent a wire from Glasgow, and Sir Hugh and Johnny Ross met him with the Studebaker.

"Fine to have you back for Christmas, lad," greeted Sir Hugh; and there was no doubt he meant it.

"Glad to be back too, Nunks," said Alistair. "Tommy Rhodes arrived?"

"Not yet. There is some correspondence for you—probably a letter from him."

There was. Rhodes was leaving London that evening and would arrive next morning. "Uhm," thought Alistair. "I suppose he'll have to take his chance with the rest of us."

III

It was not till well through dinner that the subject of the big-game trip was raised. The dinner was a cosy homely one for the two old people and their nephew. His presence completed the table, and life was somehow more rounded for the two old folks than it had ever been. It would have been perfect but for the small fear that this youth, who had found their hearts, was not to be thirled to their way of living and their ideals; and that is why they were chary of raising the subject of his departure.

343

First of all Alistair had to tell them about Paddy Joe and Norrey Carr. He expected surprise, and was himself surprised at the matter-of-fact way his news was received.

"Anyone could see it coming last summer," said Lady Sara calmly.

"I did not. Did you, uncle?"

"Not till Sara pointed it out. Long was not a man one could easily fathom—and Don loomed large all the time. Of course, I made no attempt to fathom the young woman; forty years has taught me that much, Sally."

"No mystery about it," said Lady Sara. "They were both straightforward people—slaves to an idea only. Why, you could see them reasoning things out for themselves even to the extent of speech sometimes. The man, having reached a decision, was very hard to change, and the woman had implicit trust in the man—to the extent of blind obedience. What caused the change, Alistair?"

"By Jiminy! I think I did," said Alistair, and hesitated.

"You did well, then," said Lady Sara quickly. "These two were meant for each other."

"What a keen observer you must be, aunt!—Are you afraid of her, uncle?"

"I spend all my time hiding my fear," said Sir Hugh; and the old people smiled.

Here Alistair began to wonder if this wise aunt had deduced how he felt towards Margaret Brands. If she could get behind the unique defences of Paddy Joe Long, his own could offer no difficulty. But he had set up no defences. Anyone could see his admiration and where it led. What did his aunt think about it? Was

344

his case regarded as a pitiable infatuation, or a deplorable lapse, or something to be encouraged? These two old people were aristocrats. There was no such aristocracy in the States. There he himself, while careless of the fact, was of a circle of society that considered itself select with a selectness requiring perpetual guard, since it had no wall of custom to shield it. Here the real aristocracy was really older than history; it was natural to the soil; it acquired a sense of caste more impregnable than any artificial constitution. Would these two accept Margaret? —if she accepted him—if! He frowned, and looked across at his aunt, and she met his frown with a smile. "We are always hoping that you will make this your home, Alistair," she said. "Strong new blood is required to keep this house alive."

So apposite were her words to his thoughts that he did not notice how abruptly they had been introduced. "Yet I am off to Africa," he said, as if she must know why.

"Quite settled that you are going?" queried Sir Hugh.

"Quite."

"A long trip?"

"Eight months—about."

"When you return " Sir Hugh hesitated.

"I'll come right back here," said Alistair firmly.

"I am glad to hear that," said his uncle, and tackled the subject resolutely. "I am getting a bit old, lad, and the cares of the estate are beginning to weigh—where once they carried me on wings. You know my hobby?"

"Trees."

"Yes, forestry. I have told you something about it."

"Not enough by tons. It strikes me as a man's job."

"It is that. I have given forty-odd years to it, and am still learning. Still, I flatter myself that I do know something of the science—as it affects conifers, at any rate. That knowledge is yours for the asking, Alistair."

"You'd find me a perfect dub, uncle."

"You are an out-of-door man, and that is the kind of man forestry demands. There is no hurry, of course. I have still a hundred acres to get in—larch mostly—before sap-flow, and the real work of thinning out begins only next autumn—you might be back in time."

"If I thought I could help——"

"You would soon do that if the work appealed to you—and it is in your blood." And here Sir Hugh, mounted securely on his hobby, rode it to a two-handed finish. He extolled the cult of trees—its thrall, its variety, its permanency, its great sweep, its benefits individually and nationally—the certain serene quality in it that marked a man—the periods of rush that strung a man's character, the periods of ease where a man imbibed calmness—the side issues of game and vermin—everything that strengthened the lure of one of the really great professions. "It is surely a man's job," he finished, "and his son's job, and his grandson's too. You stand in the place of a son to me, Alistair, and if you care you can carry on the tradition and hand it down. Consider it in your own time."

Alistair was deeply touched. He thrust a hand out and grasped his uncle's. "No need to consider it further," he said with enthusiastic firmness. "I have considered it already. I know I belong out-of-doors, and I will make forestry my job. When I return from East Africa—and I don't want to go—you will take me as your apprentice. I'll go at it from the ground up, Uncle Hugh."

"From the ground up, lad—it is the only way."
There was a shake in Sir Hugh's voice, and a dew in
Lady Sara's eyes.

IV

It was Lady Sara who suggested Alistair's going round
to Croft o' Drum. Perhaps she noticed her nephew's
restlessness after dinner and ascribed it to its true cause.
"Tired, Alistair?" she inquired.

"Not a bit."

"I was just thinking that Aelec and Margaret would
be pleased to hear your news. You could run round in
the car."

"I need to stretch my legs. Care for a walk, uncle?"

"He has been on his feet all day shooting game
presents," said Lady Sara quickly. "You'll get into
your slippers, Hughie."

"At once. I bet the news of Long's downfall will
surprise Aelec."

"Not at all," denied Lady Sara. "Aelec and I talked
about the situation—quite a long time ago—and he
agreed with me."

"What other could he do, woman? Hadn't I to agree
too?—Does the old Trojan really intend to go after big
game with you, Alistair?"

"Can't draw out of it."

"I am surprised at Margaret permitting it," remarked
Lady Sara.

"Tut!" exclaimed Alistair. "She has enough of her
own way. . . . I'll be back for coffee"; and he strode
out of the room.

Sir Hugh winked at his wife.

CHAPTER XXVIII

I

ALISTAIR went at a great pace round by the road to the Croft o' Drum, and the farther he went the angrier he got. The fineness of the winter night made no appeal to him—the moon, nearly full, sailing in a sea of palest green among dark islands, silver-edged; the keen clean breeze sighing amongst the heavy pine boughs; the brown loom of the far-stretching sand-dunes, and the faintly phosphorescent gleam of the white horses leaping across the bar at Leonach mouth. He was centred in his own particular problem, and worried it, terrier-like.

Why should he go to East Africa—driven? And yet —darn it!—it was too late to revolt now. Why the— —why the—why the thundering blazes should a slip of a girl have such power over grown men? For weeks and weeks she had kept instilling into his mind the lure of Highland Drum, and here she was packing him off to savage Africa—to find out if he was in love—or she —or she! Could she care a finger-snap? Could she care enough not to yield to Tommy Rhodes's siege?—he packed some powerful guns, Tommy. And there was poor old Uncle Hugh needing him, and he ready to meet that need. How splendid it would be to settle down to work worth while! Splendid indeed!—the season's work and the season's study—and a place of his own— his own woman! And then, in the quiet season, they might run across to the States. How proud he would be to show her to his friends. She would cut a swathe, by Jiminy! But now!—And, darn it, they could do the big-game trip too—the three of them. White did it with his wife; and Margaret was fit as a fiddle, and see how she enjoyed *The Land of Footprints.* . . .

Suchwise ran his thoughts. Suddenly he stopped dead and smacked a fist into his palm. "I'm damned if I'll go off like that," he cried, "and I'll tell her so, too."

And he walked on furiously.

II

From where Aelec's cart-road turned in off the highway Alistair looked up towards the cottage, and the orange glow of the living-room window beckoned him. As he turned the corner of the steadings a dog growled in front of him, and immediately after came the chuff of recognition.

"Oh ho, Kerry boy! That you?" he called, and found the terrier's head at his knee. Alistair rubbed his hand up the broad forehead and down the powerful neck. "You know me for one of the clan, at any rate. Come on, then."

The dog led him to the garden gate, and there turned and trotted back into the half-dark.

"Aelec is off on some stunt," Alistair considered. "I hope Margaret is in."

He turned up the path and found the porch door open. He stepped within, and tapped at the inner door.

"Come in," cried a voice, and that voice Margaret's. How it stirred him!

He opened the door, and stepped into the soft glow

of the hanging lamp, and Margaret, alone in the room, rose to her feet at the fireside. "Why, Alistair!" she cried in a little breathless voice, and a sudden light leaped and went out in her eyes.

Alistair halted within the shut door and glowered at her. Glowered is the word. His brows were down in a black bar over eyes that gleamed, his mouth was grim, and his chin thrust out. My heavens! but she was beautiful and desirable, quivering with life and colour—a straight clean slip of a girl, vibrating her appeal through every fibre of him. His implacable face frightened her.

"What is it?" she said tremulously. "Bad news?"

"No; the best of news." He actually shouted at her. "Where's your uncle?"

"Muiryside—arranging some roe-hunt," she answered meekly.

"I want to tell him that Paddy Joe Long and Norrey Carr are getting married next week."

"How splendid! Oh! how splendid!" cried Margaret, clasping her hands. "You did frighten me. Come and sit down, and give me all the news about it."

The vixen was trying to evade the issue. He would show her. He took a stride towards her, and that great new voice proclaimed, "I will—when I have given you the rest of my news."

"The rest of your news?"

"Exactly. I am not going to East Africa."

She opened her eyes wide, and actually smiled. "Why, Alistair?" she wondered. "Have you not been?"

The faintest touch of raillery only added to his fury, but it also gave him his cue. "Of course I've been—eight solid months. And I shot lions and catawampuses and—jabberwocks. And I have a jolly good mind to shoot you too."

Here he actually dashed his hat on the floor, and in two strides was close to her. She shrank from him, but the chair cramped her movements. If she could only reach the other side of the table, and get control of her fluttering heart, she might yet escape—what? He towered over her most compellingly, and she made one last and gallant attempt.

"You must have been there," she said with a rush, "and come back a savage."

"So! Savage for you! Do you still care for me—just so much?"

She could only nod to that.

"Then I am going to find out how much that is." His two firm hands came down on her shoulders, and not gently. She wilted under them—her knees gave way—she would have fallen, but—but his arms were around her, crushing and ecstatic. Somehow their lips came together.

In ten seconds—or in thirty—he whispered in her ear, "Is this real love or isn't it."

Margaret's sense of humour would not be subdued. "I wouldn't know, darling," she said, "but it must at least be a very good imitation."

Her red lovely head was pressed close to his breast, and he lifted her chin. "I'll show you," he said.

III

In a minute—or in ten—Aelec Brands's big shoes scraped on the bass outside the door. Margaret tried to free herself, but Alistair kept an arm firmly round her.

"He may as well know this way as another," he said calmly; and Margaret, feeling that autocratic arm, could do no more than drop a shy head.

"Ye found sense at last," said the quiet voice of Aelec Brands inside the door. "Good-bye, Africa!"

"No," cried Alistair, "we will finish up there—the three of us." He threw a hand out to Aelec, and Aelec came, and the two hands met with a strong clasp. And a broad and trusty hand was gently laid on Margaret's hair.

"In that case," said Aelec, a little quizzically, but a little uncertainly too, "ye might as well get married to-morrow."

"Oh, Uncle Aelec!" cried Margaret, in dismay.

"Why not?" cried Alistair.

"Dad must be back first."

"What a terrible time to wait!"

"We could cable him," said Margaret.